THE LIFE AND TIMES OF
SGT. JOSEPH THOMAS "TOM" BIWAY, USMC

THE LIFE AND TIMES OF SGT. JOSEPH THOMAS "TOM" BIWAY, USMC

D.J. COTTEN

ARPress
45 Dan Road Suite 36
Canton MA 02021

Hotline: 1(800) 220-7660
Fax: 1(855) 752-6001

Ordering Information:
Quantity sales. Special discounts are available on quantity purchases by corporations, associations, and others. For details, contact the publisher at the address above.

Printed in the United States of America.

ISBN-13:   Paperback   979-8-89389-761-6
           eBook   979-8-89389-762-3

Library of Congress Control Number: 2024922141

CONTENTS

PROLOGUE

There are some people in the world who only care for themselves and seek to achieve gratification, no matter who gets hurt in the process. This is what makes one a sociopath. The question here is why such people feel this way. Most of us find it hard to understand them and they feel likewise about us who have feelings for others and experience regret over some of the things we do, especially when it causes harm to others. The following is the story about one such man although fully dedicated to the Marine Corps and the government in Washington D.C.

This is really a story of two men, one an unscrupulous Marine and the other, an upright Chicago policeman who became increasingly disillusioned with the department and eventually coerced to join the Marines. Once in the Marine Corps, the policeman was placed under the command of the former. Not long afterwards, the two developed a mutual loathing for one another culminating in the murder of one and a court martial for the other.

PART I

SERGEANT BIWAY

CHAPTER 1

The Battle for Heartbreak Ridge

It was a warm and sunny day in central Korea, where a group of US Marines were fighting the Chinese in order to regain control of Pyong Liu Ridge. That was on a Monday, April 13, 1953. The Chinese had the Marines pinned down most of that morning, but one Marine, by the name of Sergeant Tom Biway, thirty-four, leaped up out of his foxhole and rushed to the machine gun nest manned by the Chinese.

Everyone was stunned to see this. He first threw in a hand grenade upon approaching the nest, killing most of the Chinese and wounding all but one. As Biway pointed his rifle at the one soldier still standing and prepared to shoot, the gun suddenly jammed, whereupon Biway threw the gun down, leaped upon the Chinese soldier with his bare hands, and began to twist his neck until it broke. The other Marines leaped out of their foxholes too and took over the Chinese position. All but one admired the courage of this one sergeant. This day truly belonged to Sergeant Biway. Later that day, Major Fred Murdock, fifty- three, met with Biway and bestowed the Bronze Star upon him for action above and beyond the call of duty. At the end of that week, Biway's platoon was relieved upon reaching the top of that ridge, and another platoon took its place. The one who didn't harbor this admiration for Biway was Sergeant Kenneth Frisner, twenty-seven, who commanded the other unit in Biway's platoon. The day following Biway's feat, he and Frisner began to argue. Frisner simply said to Biway, "Yesterday, I saw you in action and how you murdered that Chinese soldier. He was fully prepared to give himself up, but you had to kill him, didn't you? We could have just as easily taken him prisoner. There is one big difference between us, Biway. We Marines kill because we have to, but you love it, don't you?" Biway simply replied, "That I do! Besides, the only good gook is a dead one." Frisner then walked away in disgust.

Sergeant Biway was thirty-four, six feet, two inches tall, weighed 194 pounds, had rather huge ears, a high forehead, thin lips, shifty almond-shaped eyes, a pointed chin, and a birthmark below his right eye. He was married, with two children, and lived in his home in San Ysidro, near San Diego, California. He had already spent almost eighteen years in the First Marine Corps.

Sergeant Frisner, on the other hand, was twenty-seven, five feet, seven inches tall, weighed 165 pounds, blond, was still single, and lived in Minot, North Dakota. He did have a girlfriend by the name of Ms. Nicole Mitchell, twenty-eight.

In fact, for the last four months, the ridge had been a seesaw fight between the Chinese and North Koreans on one side and the UN forces on the other. It was only on March 31, 1953, when the Chinese successfully pushed a US Army platoon off that ridge and took it back for the umpteenth time. This time, General Matthew Ridgeway called on the First Marines to retake it. Pyong Liu Ridge was situated in east central Korea just above the 38th parallel. This ridge was eventually known to the US military as Heartbreak Ridge.

After some three years of heavy fighting, over four million men, women, and children died just to achieve the status quo.

Now the question arises: Could the Korean conflict itself have been avoided altogether?

The answer is yes, but that would have meant allowing the Russians to occupy the whole of the Korean Peninsula in 1945, which would have left Korea united under the Communist regime of Kim II- sung in 1948.

By dividing Korea at the 38th parallel with the Russians in the North and the Americans in the South, the US and Russia inadvertently created a powder keg in the Far East similar to that of the Balkan Peninsula in 1914 when the Europeans referred to it as the Powder Keg of Europe. WWI originated there on July 28, 1914, as the result of the assassination of Grand Duke Franz Ferdinand of Austria (1863–1914) and his wife in the city of Sarajevo by a Bosnian who sympathized with Serbia. In 1948, the southern half of Korea held its first election, resulting in the presidency of Syngman Rhee (1875–1965), who thereafter proceeded to set up a Neo-Fascist state in Seoul. Three weeks later, the North Koreans held their election, resulting in the presidency of Kim II-sung (1912–1994), who proceeded to set up a Communist republic in the North in the city of Pyongyang.

In November of that same year in the countryside in the South, a group of South Korean peasants revolted against the Neo-Fascist government of Syngman Rhee, demanding agrarian reforms, but Rhee simply used his military to put the revolt down and largely ignored the peasants' demands. This served to encourage the North Koreans, who contemplated invading the South as early as 1949, but decided to hold off another year. China was still in the middle of a long and bloody civil war, and the Russians had yet to come up with the atom bomb. That autumn, things changed.

The civil war in China largely ended with the defeated Nationalists vacating the mainland, and the Russians successfully tested their first nuclear device. Finally on June 25, 1950, the North Koreans made their move by invading the South. As a result, President Truman successfully got the UN to intervene due to the Russian boycott, and all the UN forces were placed under the command of General Douglas McArthur (1880–1964). At first, the North Koreans were quite successful, but on September 15, after the successful landing of American troops at Inchon, the tide was reversed, and the UN forces were well on their way to taking over the North, thus uniting it with the South as they were fast approaching the Yalu River, which served as the border between Korea and China. However, the Chinese never forgot that it was exactly from there that the Japanese first invaded and took over Manchuria in 1932, then invaded China itself in 1937, thus spawning the eight-year-long SinoJapanese War, in which some eight to twelve million Chinese people perished. The Chinese debated on whether to intervene in Korea in order to save North Korea and help it take over the South or simply remain neutral. They finally decided on the former, and on November 24, the first contingency of Chinese troops crossed the Yalu River. As one US officer put it, "It's a whole new war." As a result, General McArthur wanted first to go to Taiwan and set up a second front with the Nationalists there to launch an amphibious invasion of the mainland of China, and if that didn't work, use the atom bomb in order to force the Chinese into unconditional surrender. However, as much as President Truman (1884–1972) liked McArthur's plans, he couldn't let McArthur have his way. Here it must be said that President Truman saw things the way they were, not the way he wanted them to be. By giving in to General McArthur, Truman feared that the Korean conflict could mushroom into WWIII, since he feared the Russian leader Joseph Stalin (1879–1953). As a consequence of this, Truman had to fire McArthur, and Truman himself was vilified by the American public, which in turn ruined any chance he had of being reelected in 1952. So much for the history of that war.

Early in 1951, Sergeant Biway, who had not served in Korea yet, began to despise President Truman for what he did to General McArthur, as did most Americans. Biway considered Truman's policy to be a blatant act of cowardice. In May 1952, Biway was notified that he and his platoon were about to ship out to serve in Korea, which deeply delighted him since although he was in the Marine Corps, he never left the United States up to that point except for a tour in the Philippines. He was relegated to being a drill instructor at Camp Pendleton, California, throughout WWII. He and his platoon shipped out on the thirtieth after kissing his wife, Aggie, thirty; his four-year-old daughter, Catherine; and two-year-old son, Lenny, goodbye. He had been there for almost a year when Heartbreak Ridge was finally retaken. A week later, the North Koreans managed to surround the ridge in spite of all the artillery and air strikes using napalm they had to endure. The Marines in the platoon which tried to hold the ridge lost more than half their men. After four days, they finally gave up, and the fight for Heartbreak Ridge was over. After suffering dreadful losses in the fall of 1950, with most of the troops either captured or killed, the North Koreans did manage to replenish over 80 percent of their military strength by this time.

When on liberty, Biway always complained to his companions over the lack of Hispanic prostitutes in Korea, thus making him settle for Korean ones, which he referred to as gook meat. When it came to seeking out prostitutes, Biway always made it a point to hire one who was Hispanic. As Biway put it, "They're my favorite fun." In the meantime, the regiment Biway was assigned to moved farther west in order to find an easier terrain for a long-awaited breakthrough, which never came. Finally on July 27, 1953, the UN, China, and North Korea did reach a truce, thus ending the conflict. For Biway, this was a huge disappointment. He kept hoping against hope that somehow President Eisenhower would send more troops to Korea in order to take over North Korea and invade China itself, especially since Joseph Stalin died on March 5, 1953. In fact, he considered this truce to be another act of cowardice, and his resentment of President Dwight Eisenhower (1890–1969) became almost as great it was for Truman.

In the meantime, Chinese Chairman Mao Tze Tung (1893–1976) lost his oldest son early in the Korean War, which was a great heartache to him. As for the South Korean president Syngman Rhee, he continued to rule that country for the next seven years until 1960, when his government became so rife with corruption that the people rose up in outrage, leading to his resignation and subsequent self- exile. He settled in Honolulu, Hawaii, where he died five years later at the age of ninety.

With his many medals and having killed twenty-one men to his credit, three of them with his bare hands on which he later prided himself, Biway headed back to the United States and Camp Pendleton, near his family in San Ysidro. He left South Korea that September, spent a month in Japan, and arrived home before being given a two-month furlough at Camp Pendleton on Saturday, October 24.

CHAPTER 2

The Homecoming

On Saturday, October 24, 1953, at 1:00 p.m., Sergeant Biway drove the military jeep awarded to him by the Marine Corps from Camp Pendleton to his house in San Ysidro and knocked on the door, whereupon his wife, Aggie, thirty-two, answered. It was a sunny, warm fall day in Southern California. Aggie appeared to be a little pale upon seeing him. Biway was then greeted by his six-year-old daughter, Kitty, whom Biway and Aggie named Catherine. Then Biway asked to see his three-year-old son, Lenny. Aggie was somewhat less than glad to see her husband, dreading to tell him what happened to Lenny, and it showed. Biway said, "What's wrong, Aggie? You look as though you've seen a ghost or something. Besides, I'm anxious to see my three-year-old boy, Lenny." Aggie at this point could hardly speak but had to tell Biway. Aggie said, "Tom, I don't know how to tell you this, but we lost Lenny last June. He was somehow stricken with infantile paralysis and died as a result. Maybe it's better that he did die instead of having to go through life as a cripple. I'm so sorry, Tom, forgive me. I just never had the heart to write and tell you since you were in the middle of that inferno called Korea." Biway's jaw dropped upon receiving the news. He really doted on Lenny and was really aggrieved at his loss. This was the first time in Biway's life he truly grieved over anyone. In fact, Biway was so consumed over the loss of Lenny he didn't even notice the absence of his pet English bulldog, Quince. Later on, he asked Kitty where Quince was, and she replied, "Dad, Quince was run over two months ago by some drunk. I'm sorry." Anticipating this occasion, Aggie had two quart-sized bottles of vodka stored in the kitchen cabinet. As expected, Biway started drinking and finished that day in a drunken stupor. In the meantime, Aggie took Kitty to the neighbors next door and told Kitty she would have to spend the night there, not wanting her to see her father in such a drunken state. This was definitely a very unhappy homecoming, in light of his disappointment over our failing to achieve a military victory in Korea similar to that in WWII.

The next day, having somewhat sobered up, Biway decided to leave his home and went to a nearby hotel to rent a room, not wanting Aggie and Kitty to see him in such a drunken state as he continued to grieve over Lenny. He drove by the cemetery to see Lenny's gravestone. The epitaph read, "Leonard Wendell Biway, 1950–1953. Beloved Son of Thomas and Agnes Biway. Rest in Peace." He then returned to the hotel where he was staying and started to drink heavily again as he did for the following two weeks. After that, he returned home and started to lead a normal life. He returned to duty at Camp Pendleton after his furlough ended. The following year, Aggie became pregnant again. On March 24, 1955, Aggie gave birth to a baby boy, whom she named Paul after her father in Grand Rapids, Michigan. This made Biway happy as he once again had a son. Unfortunately, the baby came down with the flu and died two days later. Biway was once again distraught, and instead of getting drunk, he simply started to spend more time in the Marine Corps, to which he was greatly devoted. He and Aggie saw less and less of one another as time went on.

Out of sheer loneliness, Aggie started to look around for business opportunities as that was her major in college in Ann Arbor, Michigan.

One day, Aggie picked up a newspaper and read the Business Opportunities section. She sifted through three different ads, one being a tavern in Marysville for someone who wanted to buy half interest in it. She called the number in the add in order to further inquire about it as she was interested in moving to Northern California away from all the crime and overcrowded neighborhoods as well as the stifling heat in Southern California.

The tavern was owned by a certain William "Bill" Decker of Marysville, a fifty-two-year-old successful businessman and real estate agent and a divorcee. He and Aggie first met on May 5, 1958, in San Diego while he was looking to buy some property near the Mexican border. In fact, he had been married twice, as was Aggie, who lost her first husband, Lenny Rheem, on Okinawa in 1945.

Bill Decker was born William Howard Decker on June 2, 1905, along with his twin brother, Warren Herbert to Reverend Noah Decker, thirty-three, and his wife, Esther, thirty, in San Bernardino, California. Noah Decker was a Baptist Minister, and Esther, a housewife. A year later, Warren succumbed to a severe case of asthma and died as a result. When Bill was four, his parents moved to Monterey, Mexico, where Noah worked as a missionary in the nearby villages. Here Bill thrived, but that was to be short-lived. In 1910, a revolution broke out against Mexican president Porfirio Diaz (1830–1915), who thereupon had to flee to France and the situation in Mexico became rather unstable. Finally in 1915, the family returned to California and settled in Yuba City, where his father was appointed to preach in a church. When Bill was about eleven, his father bought him a mare, whom Bill often took swimming with him. He loved that animal. Here Bill grew up, finished high school, and went on to the University of Southern California, where he graduated in 1927 with a bachelor's degree in business. That same year he married his high school sweetheart, Ida Ferguson, also twenty-two. They never had any children. He returned to Yuba City, where he later prospered in real estate and sold insurance as well. In 1929, he joined the California National Guard, where he served two years. When he got out, the country was languishing in a severe depression, but he continued to make money. At the same time, his wife, Ida, became increasingly ill as she was battling ovarian cancer.

She finally succumbed in 1943. This left Decker devastated. Late in 1949, he met Geneva "Genie" Forsythe, a thirty-seven-year-old divorcee from Eureka. She had a sixteen-year-old son from her first marriage, whom she called Corkey, with whom she and her parents lived in Ukiah. She and Bill started dating and later decided to get married. The marriage took place in June 1950 in Ukiah. Bill was forty- five years old then and Genie, thirty-eight. Thereafter they decided to move to Marysville, where Decker just acquired a tavern and renamed it Bill's Place. The business there was quite lucrative, and Bill and Genie lived quite well. On March 3, 1952, Genie gave birth to a little girl, whom they named Barbara. Decker doted greatly on his newborn daughter.

Unfortunately, Bill had a proclivity to drink excessively although he was not nor ever had been a true alcoholic. This led to the many arguments he and Genie were to have. Finally by the middle of 1954, Genie decided she had enough, so she sued Bill for a divorce. The divorce was finalized in March 1955, and she won full custody of Barbara, denying Bill his parental rights to ever see her. Needless to say that Bill was devastated. Thereafter Bill decided to swear off drinking, but it was too late as far as Genie was concerned. They never reconciled.

Bill Decker was about five feet, eight inches tall, weighed around 198 pounds, had salt-and-pepper hair, usually wore a Panama hat, and had a love for Swisher cigars. When he and Aggie Biway first met, he was fifty-two and she, thirty-six. After pondering it over, Aggie decided to buy half interest in the tavern he owned, and the deal was concluded on July 1, 1958. They changed the name of the tavern from Bill's Place to Bill and Aggie's.

At first, the relationship between Aggie and Bill Decker was purely on a business basis. Later on, they found they liked one another and started to go together. By September, Aggie decided to ask Biway for a divorce. Biway simply responded by not contesting the divorce since he spent most of his time at the Marine base when he was not out looking for or consorting with some Hispanic prostitute. In fact, after the death of his infant son, Paul, he would visit a brothel rather than come home to Aggie and Kitty while on liberty. This made Biway feel a little guilty as he felt he was slowly abandoning them and felt that Aggie deserved better than that.

On Friday, October 17, Biway went on a ten-day furlough and decided to drive north to Marysville to see how Aggie and Kitty were making out and meet Mr. Decker. He arrived at Aggie's apartment on Sunday morning around 11:30 a.m. and was greeted by her and Kitty, who by now was eleven. Both were glad to see him. Around 5:00 p.m., Bill Decker came over for supper as he usually did on Sundays and met Biway. The two hit it off right away. Moreover, the two learned they had a mutual love for Swisher cigars and Jack Daniels bourbon. The following Saturday, Biway and Decker drove north to Lake Oroville on a fishing trip and caught several bass. Kitty was already in the sixth grade in school and was doing quite well in her studies. While he was there, he noticed the pristine countryside around Marysville and what a great place it would be to raise a child. At the end of that week, Biway, now satisfied that Aggie and Kitty were quite happy, left and returned to Camp Pendleton. One day in the following month, he noticed on the bulletin board that a replacement was needed for Master Sergeant Dan Flannigan, fifty-four, who was approaching the mandatory retirement age of fifty-five at the

Umayoshi Marine base in Japan. After pondering it for about two days, Biway decided to apply for that position, which he subsequently received a week later, the reason being its proximity to Korea. On Friday, December 19, Biway finally arrived at the base a week after Sergeant Flannigan retired on his fifty-fifth birthday on December 12.

CHAPTER 3

Biway's Background

Sergeant Tom Biway was born Joseph Thomas Biway on December 25, 1918, in Utica, New York, the second of five children born to Joseph Thomas and Margaret Phoebe Biway. The other four children were Theresa Catherine, born on August 31, 1916; Susanna Odette, born on July 6, 1921; Irene Mable, born on September 5, 1923, but died two months later, on November 20, from a severe case of asthma; and finally, Richard Patrick on March 7, 1925, whom his parents called Rick.

Biway's father, Joseph, was five feet, ten inches tall and weighed around 180 pounds. He had straight black hair that he kept brushed back and a crooked nose. He was born in Utica on April 4, 1882, to Thomas and Evelyn Biway. Joseph grew up there, where he quit high school and hired on at a local butcher shop as an apprentice in 1897, when he was fifteen. Joseph's father, Thomas, worked as carpenter, and his mother, Evelyn, a housewife. By 1904, Joseph became a professional butcher and, in 1906, decided to move to New York City in order to make his fortune, so to speak. In 1908, he married a certain Ms. Sandra Krauss, but that marriage didn't last as she decided to go back to her former boyfriend, David Jannick. They divorced two years later. Finally in 1913, he met a certain Margaret McDougall. She was born on January 2, 1886, in Boston, Massachusetts, but moved with her family to New York City two years later. Her father, Francis, was a policeman in both Boston and New York City. Margaret was five feet, five inches tall and weighed around 150 pounds. She had medium- length light-brown hair and was rather attractive.

In those days, being a policeman in America was not the honorable profession as it is considered to be today. The pay was low, the hours were long, and they were thought rather little of by the general public. In fact, most policemen where either Irish or of Irish descent. In fact, during the

Great Potato Blight (1845–1849), many people in Ireland suffered greatly, and over 1.8 million of them perished as a result. Another 1.5 million migrated to the United States, while some 250,000 others migrated to either Canada or South Africa. Here, the Irish were very poorly received and badly treated. During the Civil War (1861–1865), many were drafted, and since they didn't have the resources to hire anyone to go in their place, as many Americans did, the Irish felt that they were being discriminated against, and there were many street demonstrations and riots in New York City, Philadelphia, and Boston as a result.

All four of Margaret's grandparents were born in Ireland, which was under British rule and had been so since 1587, and as the blight set in, the British did nothing to help, except for the English nobility who lived off the fat of the land. In fact, many Irish were so poor they had to go barefoot. All of Margaret's grandparents were forced to emigrate here in order to avoid starvation. To this day, the animosity between England and Ireland has never ceased. As Margaret's father had to work as a policeman, she along with both her brothers grew up in abject poverty. She finally left home in 1904 and worked at several menial jobs with low pay. On September 27, 1911, Margaret's father, who was fifty-nine at the time, suffered a debilitating stroke that left him in a near vegetative state. She refused to let the authorities place him in a nursing home, knowing the brutal conditions he would have to undergo there. So Margaret and her mother decided to care for him at home, and Margaret moved back in. Mary, Margaret's mother, who was fifty-six at the time, was glad to have her assistance.

Margaret's mother was born Mary Jane O'Connor in Boston on May 3, 1855, to John and Alice O'Connor. Like Mary's husband, Francis (1852–1915), John too had to take up the job of being a policeman in Boston. Margaret's father was born Francis Patrick McDougall in Boston on January 30, 1852, to Edward and Mary McDougall, the oldest of five children.

In the spring of 1914 one day after work, Margaret went into the butcher shop, as usual, where Joseph Biway was working in order to buy meat to prepare for supper and feed her father, Francis, who was still in a near vegetative state. He made very little progress in his recovery, but she and her mother faithfully stood by and took good care of him. She slowly noticed Joseph and he her. They slowly developed a friendship and started to date whenever Margaret could get away. Both her brothers, Jim, twenty-five, and Patrick, twenty- three, although married, helped out whenever they could. They were a tightly knit family. As they were out on their first date, Margaret explained to Joseph her situation, and he fully understood. In spite of this, they decided to marry and did so on June 12, 1915. Two months later when Margaret's father passed away at the age of sixty-three, Mary told her that it was better that way instead of his continuing to suffer in the state he was in. A month later, Joseph decided he had enough of the hustle and bustle of New York City and decided to return to his native Utica, taking Margaret and her mother, Mary, with him. Both agreed with his plan. They bought a small house on Utica's near east side. Joseph went to work at a local Kroger's Supermarket, which was newly built at the time, and the pay there was very good.

On August 31, 1916, Joseph and Margaret had their first child, a daughter whom they named Theresa Catherine. She had dark hair like her father and grew up to be rather slender. Next came Joseph Thomas. Jr. and then Susanna Odette on July 6, 1921. She had light- brown hair like her mother, and in contrast to Theresa, she turned out to be rather chubby with her baby fat. Thereafter came Irene Mable on September 5, 1923, who like her father was an asthma sufferer and finally succumbed on November 20, two months later. She too had rather dark hair. And finally came Richard Patrick on March 7, 1925. He resembled his father, which was to cause Biway to call him Punk later on. The reason will be explained later.

In May 1921 just before Susanna was born, Joseph bought a house on Sturgis Street since he already had two children and a third one on the way. The family loved it, and it was spacious.

While Joseph was in New York City, his parents, Thomas and Evelyn, bought a farm some fifteen miles north of Utica, where they along with his brother Daniel were to live and farm. The family, being of German origin, had the name of Doppelgang, under which they resettled in the colony of New York during the 1750s from some petty kingdom in Central Germany since Germany itself didn't yet exist as a nation. In 1851, they took the name of Biway since it had the same meaning as their original one.

Thomas, Biway's grandfather (1852–1930), was the first in the family to be born under the new name. Thomas married Evelyn Ziegler

(1850–1918) in 1879 and had two sons, Joseph (1882–1971) and Daniel (1886–1961). Later on, Joseph would bring his kids to the farm so they could go horseback riding, swimming, and work in the garden as well as feed the chickens. Thus, the kids enjoyed going there every summer. They called Joseph's brother who lived there Uncle Dan. He never married.

On a sunny summer day in 1924 when Biway was five, his grandmother, Mary, noticed him doing something strange while playing on the ground in the backyard. He was catching carpenter ants and pulling off their feelers in order to watch them groping to find their way. She also noticed a short time later when Biway would seek out and catch camel crickets and punch their eyes out with a needle.

Finally Mary said to her daughter, "Margaret, Junior"—that's what they called Biway in those days since he and his father had the same name—"is doing something strange in the yard. He is torturing crickets by punching their eyes out."

Margaret said to Biway, "Why are you doing that, Junior?" Biway simply replied, "I like doing it, Mom. It's fun."

As Biway got older, some neighbors noticed that some cats and even a dog came up missing in the neighborhood. Whether or not Biway could have been responsible for some of these cases remains unknown.

Next door to them lived the Mclaughlin family: James, the father; Penelope, the mother; with their three children, John, the eldest; Dennis, who was only slightly older than Biway and Wanda, who was Susanna's age. While Susanna and Wanda got along well, played together, and shared their dolls, with Dennis and Biway, it was a different story. Finally one day Dennis saw Biway slapping his cat around rather hard and yelled, "Cut it out, that's my cat!"

Biway replied, "Are you gonna make me?"

Dennis then said "Yes, I am" and picked up an empty Coke bottle and started hitting Biway on the head with it. Biway managed to grab the bottle from him, threw it on the ground, and wrestled him until he got a stranglehold around his neck. Dennis finally gave up the fight. Biway was proud of himself after that. That was his first real fight, and he won. Thereafter, Dennis made it a point to avoid Biway.

That following year, Biway was enrolled in the first grade at St. Paul of Tarsus Catholic Elementary School, where his older sister Theresa was already in the fourth grade. Biway had always been rather large for his age, and since he won his fight with Dennis Mclaughlin, the other kids didn't pick on him. He and the nuns and monks got along fairly well at first, but that was to change sometime later.

When Biway was in the third grade, he noticed the other kids talking about the Great War (in those days as WWI was called) and the exploits of their fathers during that war. One day one of them asked Biway, "What did your father do in the war?" Biway didn't quite know how to answer since his father never talked about the war.

That night after school, Biway asked his father, "What did you do during the Great War, Daddy?" Joseph replied, "I worked at my job as a butcher as I'm doing now. I did register for the draft in 1917 and was called two months later. However, I was rejected due to my asthma, so I couldn't get into the Army." Upon hearing this explanation from his father, Biway's heart began to sink like a rock. He felt deeply disappointed. He'd been hoping that his father did something for him to be proud of. That night in bed, Biway began to cry like a baby out of the sheer shame he felt over it. Moreover, Biway never truly believed his father's explanation and eventually considered him to be a coward. That was in May 1928, when Biway was nine.

Shortly after that, Biway began to engage in mischievous activities, such as throwing rocks at the streetlamp in front of his house; stealing apples and peaches from his neighbors' trees; running up to peoples' houses, ringing doorbells, and disappearing before the person inside could answer; and throwing empty soda bottles on the street pavement, where cars would run over the broken glass.

As time went on, Biway became increasingly blatant in his activities. He began throwing rocks through peoples' windows and pulling up newly planted flowers and shrubs when nobody was around to see it and even stole mail out of peoples' mailboxes. He eventually recruited a gang of other boys to go along with him. Three blocks over lived a seventy-year-old man by the name of Paul Farber with his wife and nineteen-year-old daughter, Dolores, who had a job as a substitute teacher since he was no longer able to work and support himself. Some nights Biway and his friends would come around to his house, yelling obscenities at him and to make fun of him. The old man did notify the Utica Police but to no avail, so the harassment went on. For some boys, this kind of activity was quite normal, so when Biway's parents were informed by his irate neighbors, they simply didn't worry too much. They just considered it as "letting off steam" and had the attitude "boys will be boys."

However, there was to be an incident that was to change Biway's life and attitude forever. In early September 1929, Biway, who was ten by then and just started the fifth grade at St. Paul of Tarsus Elementary Catholic School, had a girl in his class by the name of Diane De Wolfe, also ten. She was very outgoing and fun to be with. She and Biway were very friendly toward one another. She was only slightly shorter than Biway and was of average build for a ten-year-old girl. She had shoulder-length black hair, rosy cheeks, brown eyes, and was extremely pretty. At first, Biway treated her like any other girl he happened to like, but one night in late September, Biway had a strange dream. In it, he dreamed he was getting married, with Diane as his bride. He woke up the next morning feeling rather strange. He felt that he suddenly fell in love with Diane but couldn't shake that feeling later, no matter how hard he tried. In fact, whenever he got near her, his heart would automatically start to race, and he would break out in a cold sweat but did manage to conceal his feelings from her, but not for long. *This is definitely the girl I'm going to marry one day,* Biway thought to himself.

On Thursday, October 3, he approached Diane in order to get her alone with him. Diane asked Biway why he wanted to be alone with her. Before he could answer, two nuns suddenly showed up and called for classes to resume. That was around 10:00 a.m. after the first recess. Biway, however, didn't give up.

Diane De Wolfe was the fourth child born to Adam and Naomi De Wolfe, the others being Carla, born on October 7, 1897; Daniel, on March 24, 1900; William, on August 26, 1910; and finally Diane, on August 23, 1919. Carla was already married and had two children. Daniel was twenty-nine, still single, and living at home. While William was in college at the Universitat in Jena, Germany, in 1929. Adam De Wolfe and Naomi Phelps were married in April 1896 when he was twenty-nine and she, nineteen. By 1929, he was sixty-two and a successful architect, and she was fifty-two and a housewife. He belonged to the firm known as Brubaker, De Wolfe and Simmons, Architects. They were devout Catholics. Mr. De Wolfe even drew up plans for what was to become Kroger's Supermarket, where Joseph Biway Sr., Biway's father, worked as a butcher.

On Tuesday, October 8, during the morning recess at school, Biway again caught Diane in the hallway walking toward him, and as she did, he noticed an empty antechamber on the side of the hallway. It had a bookshelf, a table in the middle with two or three chairs where nuns and monks often conferred with their students in private. Upon noticing that the antechamber was empty, Biway suddenly grabbed Diane, dragged her inside, threw his arms around her, pushed his lips up to hers, and started kissing her rather violently. Diane tried to push Biway back, saying, "Please, Tom." (Since he learned that his father didn't serve in the military during WWI, he insisted to both his family and friends to quit calling him Junior and start calling him Tom instead.) "Stop it, I beg you." And she began to beg and cry frantically. Biway said to her, "Haven't you ever been to the picture shows, Diane? Men and women do this all the time, or haven't you noticed? Please, Diane, don't be such a crybaby and let me kiss you and let's make love." But Diane kept crying and hysterically begging Biway to stop.

Suddenly, one of the nuns by the name of Sister Mary Arnold rushed in to see what the commotion was about. She told Biway and Diane to separate themselves, turned to Biway, and said, "What did you do to this young lady, and why is she crying so hard?"

Biway replied, "Nothing really, Sister. I was only pretending, just like they do in the movies."

Sister Mary Arnold angrily replied, "Well, this a school and not a movie theatre." Then she slapped him four or five times across the face as hard as she could, and he wet his pants. Now in total shock, with his ears ringing and his pants wet with urine, he looked to his left and saw Diane sitting in a chair, still crying. Furthermore, he felt totally humiliated since Sister Mary Arnold slapped him in front of Diane. Biway was subsequently taken to Brother Gerald's office and Diane to that of the Mother Superior. Both Margaret Biway and Naomi De Wolfe were called to come to the school.

Sister Mary Arnold was born Joan Louise Rafferty on April 7, 1884, in Salem, New Jersey, to Philip and Julie Rafferty. She was the seventh of their eight children. At an early age, she decided she wanted to become a nun since she was quite religious. In 1921, when she was thirty-seven, she became the eighth-grade English teacher at St. Paul of Tarsus Elementary School and held that position ever since. Even at forty-five in a nun's habit and wearing glasses, she was still quite attractive. Biway eventually learned to despise her with a heated passion as to be seen later.

After receiving the call from St. Paul's and since Joseph usually took the family car to work, Margaret said to her mother, Mary, "Mom, I need you to drive me to St. Paul's in your 1914 Hudson. Tom's in trouble. They said he attacked a girl this morning." Mary agreed and drove Margaret to St. Paul's.

In the meantime, Naomi De Wolfe, upon receiving the phone call from St. Paul's concerning her daughter, called her husband, Adam, at work and told him to come home, pick her up, and drive her to St. Paul's in order to find out what happened to Diane.

While awaiting the arrival of his mother and grandmother, a monk known as Brother Joseph walked into Brother Gerald's office and said to Biway, "Come with me," and Biway did. Brother Joseph said, "In here," signaling the same antechamber where Sister Mary Arnold slapped him so hard earlier.

Once inside the antechamber, Brother Joseph pulled open one of the table drawers and took out a barber strap usually used to sharpen razors, then sat down and told Biway to drop his pants and lie on his stomach across his knees. Biway, with his eyes still red and swollen with tears, complied, and as he did, Brother Joseph hit him with the strap eight or nine times. As painful as it was, at least it wasn't done in front of Diane, as was the slapping he got from Sister Mary Arnold earlier.

Brother Joseph was born in 1886 under the name Pierre-Joseph Thouquet in Thetford Mines, Quebec, Canada, the oldest of five children born to Emile-Paul and Julie-Anne Thouquet. One day in January 1895, when he was almost nine, he fell through the ice in a nearby pond as he was ice skating. The people who were there pulled him out, but no one was sure whether he'd live or not. His frantic parents prayed hard, and Pierre pulled through. Since then, he decided to become a monk, if not a priest. He graduated from St. Louis Seminary in Asbestos in 1911 as Brother Joseph. Since he was as fluent in English as he was in French, the Father Superior asked him if he would be interested in teaching math lessons in New York since that was his major. Brother Joseph said yes and was sent first to St. Francis High School in New York City and later transferred to St. Paul of Tarsus Elementary School in Utica 1919. Ten years later at forty-three, he was five feet, eleven inches tall, rather slender, bald on the top of his head, with black hair on the sides, and wore horn- rimmed glasses.

From that day onward, Biway's hatred for priests and nuns grew into a near obsession, since he felt that his punishments were totally undeserved. Around noon as Biway awaited the arrival of his mother and grandmother, Adam De Wolfe and his wife, Naomi, walked in to confront the Mother Superior in her office over what happened to Diane. Adam had gray hair, wore thin rimmed glasses, and was very indignant as one could see in his face, which was red with anger. Once in her office, he saw Diane, who, by that time, became calm and no longer shaken up, sitting in a chair and then said to the Mother Superior, "Who attacked my child and where is the creep who did it now?"

The Mother Superior replied, "I am not allowed to give you that information as that is the policy of this school, but I assure you that the lad in question will be most severely disciplined."

Mr. De Wolfe said, "I assure you that my little girl will never see the inside of this school again with creeps who do this kind of thing running around." Then he turned to Diane and said, "Come on, honey, let's get you out of here." Later on their way out, Adam asked Diane, "Can you point out the creep who did it to you?"

She replied, "Yes, there he is in Brother Gerald's office, the one with the birthmark below his right eye." Mr. De Wolfe looked at Biway with a burning glow of anger in his eyes as if he wanted to kill him on the spot and stepped in to confront Brother Gerald. As the confrontation was in progress, Biway's mother and grandmother arrived, went into the office and announced themselves. They asked Brother Gerald what Biway did to get himself into trouble. Brother Gerald told them Biway kissed a girl by the name of Diane De Wolfe and these are her parents. Mr. De Wolfe asked Margaret, "Where is your husband? I want to talk to him about a lawsuit I may bring upon both you and this school." Margaret replied, "He'll be home around 6:30 pm as usual, Mr. De Wolfe. Our address is 1830 Sturgis Street." That night, Adam De Wolfe came to Biway's house as expected in order to confront Joseph Biway over what his son did to his girl, Diane.

That night, before Adam De Wolfe went over to the Biway house to confront Joseph Biway, Diane asked him, "Can I go back to St. Paul's tomorrow, Dad? Tom didn't really hurt me that much, and besides, all my friends go there."

Adam replied, "In light of what this Tom did to you this morning, Diane, I cannot allow it."

As the afternoon progressed, Adam became increasingly calm and collected, so by the time he confronted Joseph Biway that night, he simply said to Joseph, "I wish to talk to you about your son Tom. Are you aware of what he did to my little girl this morning?"

Joseph replied, "Yes, I am, and I'm extremely sorry. I myself have two daughters going to St. Paul's, Theresa, who is in the eighth grade, and Susanna, who is in the third, so I know how you must feel, Mr. De Wolfe."

Adam simply replied, "I'll let it go this time, but you must impress upon your son the gravity of the situation. Goodbye, Mr. Biway."

For added punishment, Biway was suspended from St. Paul's for the next two weeks. He resumed classes on Monday, October 21. Biway became more and more rebellious as his resentment of the nuns and priests slowly festered over time. In the meantime, he stayed away from the girls as he didn't want to be hit with Brother Joseph's barber strap or slapped by any of the nuns again. He would often make obscene gestures at the nuns and priests when they weren't looking and started writing on the bathroom walls concerning several of the monks and a nun who taught there, especially Brother Joseph and Sister Mary Arnold. Brother Joseph knew it was Biway who wrote such obscenities about him on the walls but could never prove it. In time, Biway and Brother Joseph loathed one another mutually.

Finally on Wednesday, October 21, 1931, things came to a head. One of Biway's classmates by the name of George Muhaw peeked into the bathroom stall where Biway was and noticed him writing on the wall. He then went to Brother Edward's (Brother Edward, forty- seven, replaced Brother Gerald a year earlier due to Brother Gerald's failing health) office and told him what he saw. Fifteen minutes later, Brother Edward went to the seventh-grade classroom where Biway was and called him into his office. When they both sat down, Brother Edward asked Biway, "Have you been writing on the bathroom walls? I want a straight answer, yes or no."

Biway simply said, "So what? A lot of guys write on bathroom walls. Do you plan to pin this on me?"

"No, but I want you to stop," Brother Edward replied.

Biway then said in an arrogant manner, "Are you going to make me?"

Brother Edward became indignant and said, "You need to change your attitude toward us. In fact, someone reported that you gave Sister Theresa Raymond the finger when she had her back turned to you the other day. If you don't change, we may have to expel you one of these days."

Biway simply replied, "Who the hell cares, and how would you like to go to hell yourself?" Then Biway started cursing him with every filthy name imaginable. Brother Edward said, "In that case, you're expelled as of now. I'll call your mother to come and pick you up as soon as possible."

Around 2:00 p.m., Margaret showed up in the family car, a green 1925 Hudson, and took Biway home.

When they got there, Margaret said, "Tom, why are you so belligerent toward the priests and nuns? They just want you to be good. Next Monday I'll take you to Franklin Pierce Middle School to enroll you there." Biway simply replied, "That'll be fine."

On Monday, October 26, 1931, Margaret took Biway to Franklin Pierce Middle School to enroll him. Biway found the school pleasanter, and there were no monks or nuns. However, within the week, a known bully by the name of Buddy Androszech (pronounced "androshek") started to push Biway around. During the following week as Androszech placed a ruler on his left shoulder, he went up to Biway and said, "Knock this off my shoulder!" Biway decided he had had enough, knocked the ruler off Androszech's shoulder, turned around, and started to beat Androszech up. Thereupon Androszech said, "I quit. I had enough. Please don't hit me anymore."

Biway replied, "Okay, Punk, but be careful over who you pick on next time." Thereafter Biway and Buddy Androszech became very good friends.

Buddy Androszech was very slender, Biway's height, had blond hair and blue eyes. He was born George Bruno Androszech on November 14, 1918, in New York City to Jerzy and Wanda Androszech, the youngest of their four children. Both Jerzy and Wanda emigrated from Poland during the 1890s to escape the hardship of living under Russian rule. Poland suffered almost as much under Russian rule as the Irish did under the English. They were married in 1900 when he was twenty-two and she, twenty. Unlike his older siblings, who were successful, Buddy turned out to be rebellious, and at the tender age of six, he started to associate with unruly kids and engage in criminal activities such as pickpocketing and shoplifting in stores. He was caught several times and finally sent to the State Training School for Boys at Warwick, New York. That was in 1927, and while Buddy was serving there for the third time, his father, Jerzy, was hired by two distant cousins by the names of Felix Gelinski and Stanislas Dombrowski, who opened a manufacturing plant in Utica known as Gelinski & Dombrowski Foundry Inc. Mr. Androszeck hired on, prospered, and then bought a house two blocks over from where the Biways lived. In the fall of 1928, when Buddy was released, his parents, being Polish and therefore strong Catholics, took Buddy to St. Paul's in order to enroll him there. After reading Buddy's criminal record, Brother Gerald curtly told the Androszechs, "Your son has a rather long criminal record, and that will prevent us from accepting him here. I'm sorry, folks." Then the Androszechs took Buddy to John Tyler Elementary School to enroll him there. Shortly thereafter, Buddy started to bully other children and try to extort lunch money from them. Somehow he managed to get away with it.

Biway and Buddy were soon joined by Chuck Henderson and Joe Hartwell, and they became quite a foursome. Since he learned that his father didn't serve in WWI, Biway felt he no longer had a role model except for Richard Dix, Walter Huston, and Tom Mix, but they were only Hollywood actors. However, he soon found one by the name of Eddie Duggan, who attended Rutherford B. Hayes Senior High School and was seventeen when Biway enrolled at Franklin Pierce. Although Biway and Duggan never met, Duggan at seventeen already had a notorious reputation for his criminal activities. Before Duggan could finish high school, he was arrested by the Utica Police for the umpteenth time. He was again sent to Warwick but transferred to Attica when he turned eighteen in July 1932.

As at St. Paul's, Biway again engaged in such activities as writing on the bathroom walls and extorting other students for their lunch money.

He even began to flirt with some of the girls, especially the prettiest ones. He didn't get into any trouble over this but was careful not make the same move as he did with Diane at St. Paul's.

After Duggan was arrested in April 1932 when he was still seventeen for grand theft auto and sent to Warwick, for Biway, another role model surged by the name of Jackie Brown, who himself was a part of Duggan's gang. He was rather vicious, and with his friends at night, he would ride around the city, insult, curse, and threaten pedestrians from whichever car he was riding in. He was expelled umpteen times from both Franklin Pierce Middle School and Rutherford B. Hayes Senior High School for extorting, bullying, and insulting other students by the time he was fifteen. Like Duggan, he was sent to Warwick several times for such offenses as theft, assault and battery, vandalism and burglary.

Jackie Brown was born Daniel John Brown on December 9, 1916, in Utica to Toby and Julia Brown, the second of their two children, the other child being Madeleine Brown, born on November 5, 1913. It was a family of modest income. In 1917, Toby, who was then thirty-three, was drafted by the US Army, trained at Fort Riley, Kansas, and sent to France early in 1918. On September 12, he was mortally wounded as he and his outfit were advancing on a German position in northern France. Julia Brown married eight months later to a certain Warren Tuttle, who was forty-two and a machinist at Harlow Beauty Products Inc. That was in May 1919, just before Jackie and Madeleine were stricken with Spanish influenza. Jackie survived it but not Madeleine. On April 3, 1920, Julia gave birth to twin girls, both of whom died the same day, and this was a further blow to her. Warren, her husband, on the other hand, simply didn't care. Moreover, Warren turned out to be a self-centered egomaniac with little concern for others. After losing her twin girls, Julia became more and more like her husband and ignored her son, Jackie, more and more as time went on. This made Jackie feel somehow rejected, and this would account for much of his viciousness later on.

Jackie was rather short, had short dark-brown hair, and sometimes wore glasses. Biway was hoping somehow to join Jackie Brown's circle of friends with his own, but they wouldn't accept them, considering how young they were. That was in September 1932, when Biway and his friends were only thirteen and Brown, fifteen.

Biway now felt that since he couldn't join up with Brown, he could at least emulate him, and he along with his friends did. Like Brown, Biway and his friends started to engage in vandalism, shoplifting, and harassing elderly people wherever they happened to be at night. They even started making passes at adult women who were in their thirties and forties and making obscene phone calls. Somehow, Biway and his friends managed to get away with these activities.

It was at this time that Biway began to notice that his brother, Rick, looked quite a bit like their father, Joseph, so Biway began to call Rick "Punk." One day in November 1932, Biway grabbed a stray alley cat and called Rick into the garage, saying, "Come along with me, Punk. I want to show you something," and Rick did what he was told. When they went into the family garage, Biway picked up a ball peen hammer and started to bludgeon the cat until its head was bashed in.

Rick said, "Tom, why did you do that? That cat was harmless." Biway replied, "Punk, I could just as easily do the same thing to you if you don't do what I tell you to."

One day, on Saturday, November 12, 1932, Biway called his younger brother, Rick, saying, "Punk, I want you to came along with me." Rick asked him why, and Biway replied, "I want you to do something for me."

Rick asked, "What?"

Biway said, "I'll show you once we're alone."

Rick, being only seven at the time, had no idea of what Biway wanted, so he innocently complied, and then both got on their bicycles and rode south to where Biway wanted to get Rick alone with him. That was an open secluded field near the railroad tracks just out of town. Finally when Biway told Rick what he had in mind, Rick became hysterical and tearfully begged Biway, "Please, Tom, I don't want to." Biway became angry and said, "When are you going to be a man and not such a punk? Me and my friends do this all the time. It won't hurt you, I swear." Not given a choice, Rick tearfully complied and did what Biway told him to. Out of sheer fear of his older brother, who threatened him never to say a word to anyone over this, and the shame of what he made him do, Rick made it a point never to tell anyone. Biway said, "Remember, Punk, what I did to that alley cat the other day I can just as easily do to you."

Two weeks later, Biway told Rick to come along with him to his friend Buddy Androszech's house. Buddy's parents were out shopping, so he, Biway, and Rick were alone in the house. Biway said to Rick, "Hey, Punk. I want you to do the same thing to me you did two weeks ago and to my friend Buddy here." Again Rick begged Biway but to no avail. After he finished with Biway, he was coerced to perform on Buddy Androszech. A week later, Biway along with Buddy Androszech, Chuck Henderson, and Joe Hartwell managed to get Rick in the garage alone with them. Again Rick was compelled to perform oral sex on both Biway and Buddy Androszech. Upon watching the scene unfold, Chuck Henderson became increasingly disgusted and finally said to Biway after he was offered his turn at Rick, "Count me out! Have you no decency in you, Tom? I cannot and will never do such a filthy thing to a seven-year-old child, especially if he was my kid brother. I'm leaving." Thereupon Joe Hartwell said, "The same goes for me too."

At school, Rick became increasingly withdrawn and depressed. Sister Margaret Phillip asked Rick one day, "Lately I noticed a big change in you. Do you care to tell me about what's happening? One can plainly see how distraught you appear to be."

Rick simply replied, "It's nothing really, Sister. I'll snap out of it, I promise."

Finally the Mother Superior called Margaret Biway and said, "I want to have a word with you about your son Rick. He seems to be very upset about something, but he refuses to tell any of us what it is."

Margaret replied, "Yes, Mother Superior, I too noticed it. I asked him several times, but he won't say a word to me either."

Fortunately for Rick, this abuse was to be short-lived. In December 1932 after being housed there for eight months, a girl by the name of Judy Shaan was released from the NYPI Ward at Cornell University in Ithaca, New York, where wayward children were housed and evaluated by a team of psychiatrists in order to see why they behaved the way they did. Shortly after her release, she was enrolled at Franklin Pierce Middle School and was in Biway's class. She and Biway hit it off almost right away.

Judy Shaan was born on February 16, 1919, in Utica to Andrew and Barbara Shaan, the second of two children. Her older brother, Jeremy, was born on January 13, 1917.

Judy Shaan was slender, almost as tall as Biway, and had brown eyes and shoulder-length dark-brown hair. Within a week after she started classes in the eighth grade, she and Biway began to flirt, and there was nothing to be feared this time as in the case of Diane De Wolfe three years earlier as Judy proved to be quite receptive toward him. Biway even told his friend Buddy to stop bothering his brother, Rick, and Buddy did. He too found a girlfriend by the name of Sally Perkins at that time. She was thirteen, blond, with blue eyes, and rather petite for a thirteen-year-old.

On Saturday, December 17, 1932, Judy invited Biway to her house in order to have sex with him. Judy's parents, along with her brother, Jeremy, were out doing Christmas shopping after visiting her aunt Pam Mondbauer, Barbara Shaan's sister, thus leaving Judy alone in the house, because Judy told them she felt sick. At 2:00 p.m., Biway came over, and Judy led him into the bedroom. She then asked Biway, "Is this the first time for you, Tom?"

Biway replied, "I'm afraid it is, Judy. You see, I'm only thirteen years old."

Judy said, "Well, so am I, but I've been doing this for the last eight or nine months when I was in Ithaca. Some of the boys there are really hot, I tell you."

Biway did quite well with Judy considering it was his first time but would by no means be his last.

Before Judy Shaan was sent to Ithaca, she spent seven months in the State Training School for Girls in Gloversville, New York. It was built in 1879 for girls who were deemed to be incorrigible. After several run-ins with the Utica Police, Judy was finally arrested, and the Oneida County judge decided to send Judy there for shock therapy. This only made Judy turn out to be even more wayward. For several years, rumors started to come out about how some of the male guards at that reformatory were abusing some of the girls and coercing them into having sex with them. Finally late in 1939, the school was closed down due to these rumors and overcrowding. The girls were then transferred to a new facility at Binghamton.

The relationship between Biway and Judy lasted for some six months, until Judy was once again arrested by the Utica Police on Saturday night, June 10, 1933, for breaking into a dress shop with three other girls. All four girls were subsequently sent to Gloversville.

About a month earlier, Biway and Judy invited Rick over to Judy's house because one of Judy's friends' French bulldog had a litter of pups. Biway knew just how fond Rick was especially of bulldogs and would never pass up the chance of getting hold of one. However, Judy had a cousin by the name of Sherman Mondbauer who himself was in Ithaca along with her after having been sent to Warwick twice.

Sherman was Pam Mondbauer's son and Judy's cousin. He was born on April 3, 1925, almost four weeks after Rick was. Sherman was rather heavy with baby fat, and his round face did make him appear to be rather gentle. He had short black hair and blue eyes. He had an older brother by the name of James, who was eight years his senior. Sherman's father, Walter, who was thirty-seven at that time, left Utica in order to find employment elsewhere since this country was in the middle of a severe depression. He finally found a job in Amsterdam, New York, as an electrician since that was his trade. Sherman was tickled pink one Saturday night in Ithaca when his father showed up and took him out. They were very close.

It was on Saturday, May 20, 1933, when Biway along with Rick arrived at Judy Shaan's house. Judy introduced Rick to her cousin Sherman and then showed him the pup, which was a French bulldog. She asked Rick, "How would you like to take this pup home with you?"

Rick replied, "Would I ever?"

Then Judy said to Rick, "Before you can, I want you and my cousin Sherman to play a game."

Rick then asked, "What kind of game is it?"

Judy simply replied, "It'll be rather dirty." Rick then surmised what it was.

Judy turned to Sherman and said, "Are you ready, Sherman?" and Sherman replied, "Am I ever!" Then Sherman started pulling his pants down, exposing himself to Biway, Judy, and Rick. Judy then made a comment to Sherman about his penis in admiration. Rick again begged Judy and Biway, saying, "Please, I'd rather not," but to no avail.

Biway then said to Rick, "Come on, Punk, take it like a man." Since he wanted that pup so much, he reluctantly complied and let Sherman first kiss him on the lips like a girl and then sodomize him. Biway and Judy watched them the whole time. After two hours, Biway said to Judy, "Please, Judy, let Punk have the pup. After all, he earned it."

Judy then said, "Rick, this pup is yours."

Meanwhile, Sherman kept on bragging about what a great time he and Rick were having.

After they left around 4:00 p.m., Rick tearfully said to Biway, "Please, Tom, don't drag me over there anymore. I don't like what Sherman did to me, and I never want to see him again." Biway simply replied, "Okay, Punk, have it your way."

Rick then said, "Thank you, Tom." Rick now felt that this kind of abuse was finally over with. Besides, he was happy to be able to take his new pup home, which he later named Frenchy.

On a Saturday afternoon about a month later, Sherman showed up at Rick's house and knocked on the back door. Margaret opened it and asked, "Who are you looking for, young man?"

Sherman replied, "I'm Rick's friend, Sherman Mondbauer. I want very much to see him if he's here."

Margaret replied, "Yes, he's out front playing with his new dog, Frenchy. I'll call him." Margaret went out front and said, "Rick, there's a boy here to see you. He's inside."

Rick hurriedly came in, but when he saw that it was none other than Sherman himself, his heart almost stopped out of sheer terror. Rick then turned to both his mother and grandmother, Mary, tearfully yelling, "Get that monster out of this house right now! I cannot stand the sight of him. He has no right to be here!" Thereafter Rick picked up his new pet, rushed upstairs to his bedroom, hid in the corner, and cried. Margaret turned to Sherman and said, "I think it will be better if you'd leave right away. I honestly don't know what got into Rick, but Mary and I will try to find out later." Thereafter Sherman reluctantly left. It would be two days before Rick would come out of his bedroom. He even refused to tell his father, Joseph, why he stayed there so long. He finally told Joseph, "I'll be all right, Dad. That monster who was here Saturday is truly a terrible person. In fact, he was in Warwick twice. I just don't to have anything to do with him whatsoever." Rick wouldn't elaborate any further, so Joseph and Margaret just let it go. It wouldn't be very long before Sherman once again got in trouble with the Utica Police and was eventually sent back to Warwick. This news made Rick feel enormously relieved.

Before Judy Shaan's arrest that June, Biway had already met her friend Judy Edmonds. Like Judy Shaan, she also had many run-ins with the police and spent time in both Gloversville and Ithaca.

Judy Edmonds was rather large for her age, as Biway was. She had medium shoulder-length brown hair and, at fifteen, weighed around 162 pounds. Just before Judy Shaan's arrest, Judy Edmonds's then boyfriend, Jackie Brown, was arrested for assault and battery. Biway noticed Judy's rather buxom figure, and since his own girlfriend was incarcerated, Biway approached her one day and said, "I heard your boyfriend got busted."

Judy replied, "Yes, he did, if that's any of your business."

Biway then said, "There's no need to get nasty, Judy. I just want to be friendly."

Judy said, "Sorry, Tom. I've just been so upset since they took Jackie away."

Biway replied, "That's okay, Judy. I felt the same way when they took Judy away too. Let's go on a date."

Judy said, "I will, but remember, I'm still in love with Jackie."

Judy Edmonds was born on July 16, 1918, the youngest of three children born to Tad and Martha Edmonds. In 1917, Tad was drafted into the US Army and subsequently sent to France early in 1918. Unfortunately, Tad was killed on June 12, 1918, in the German spring- summer offensive, just a little over a month before Judy was born. He was thirty-four at the time. Upon receiving this news, Martha Edmonds became so distraught that she sent Judy's brothers, Fred, eight, and Jim, six, to live with her brother in the neighboring community of Herkimer. However, when Judy was born, Martha decided to keep her. She remarried in 1920 to a banker by the name of John Snyder. In 1923, they had a son by the name of Elliot and, in 1925, a daughter by the name of Mabel. Thereafter Judy was largely ignored. Beginning at nine, Judy started bullying other girls in school, not come home until after midnight, and stealing from the poor boxes in a Catholic Church. She was finally arrested in March 1928 for shoplifting dolls from the local Kresge Five & Dime store. She was sent to Gloversville for a period of six months. That was not to be her last time.

Judy herself bragged that during her second internment at Gloversville, she had sex for the first time with a male guard by the name of Bob

Whitley, beginning in September 1930 when she was twelve and he, twenty-six.

Officer Whitley, at that time, was married, with two small children at home. However, no one was ever able to prove either way whether it was true or not. Since then, Judy never tried to hide her passion for sex, and this was the reason they finally sent her to Ithaca to evaluate her. She first met Jackie Brown in December 1931 when she was thirteen and he just turned fifteen on the ninth. After three months, Jackie was dropped by his girlfriend because he refused to quit having sex with Judy Edmonds. It was an on-again, off-again relationship between him and Judy.

Since Jackie Brown drew a six-month sentence for disturbing the peace and battery on an old man, Biway and Judy continued to see one another and have sex. Biway found Judy Edmonds more sexually attractive than Judy Shaan had been, and he wanted to continue their relationship. However, that December, Jackie Brown was released, having served his six-month sentence, and he and Judy Edmonds got back together. Biway said to himself, "All good things must come to an end."

In May 1934, a close friend of Judy Edmonds by the name of Joyce Buckey, fourteen, was released from Ithaca and enrolled at Franklin Pierce Middle School. She was in the eighth grade and Biway in the ninth.

In the fall of 1934 and since Biway became a sophomore, he was transferred to Rutherford B. Hayes High School.

Joyce Buckley was of average height and weight for a girl her age, with black hair, which she wore in a ponytail, and Biway was attracted to her.

Joyce Buckley was born on February 9, 1920, in Utica to Steven and Phyllis Buckley, the youngest of their two children. The other child was her brother, Michael, born on July 2, 1917. After Steven returned from the war, he changed. He was rather traumatized by the bloodbath he witnessed there. Furthermore, as he and his fellow soldiers were advancing on a German position, they were suddenly exposed to mustard gas, in which Buckley never fully recovered. His lungs deteriorated to such a condition to which he finally succumbed in November 1936 at the age forty-eight, Phyllis remarried four years later to Quinton Farley, fifty-three.

In November 1928, Joyce and her brother, Michael, decided to experiment with sex. At that time, she was eight and he, eleven.

Phyllis was too busy taking care of Steven to pay much attention, and as a result, the kids were largely left on their own. As time went on, Joyce became increasingly receptive to other boys, and one day at school, she and a boy by the name of Larry Holmes were caught in the act by one of the teachers, having sex in the school basement. This was not to be her last time. Finally in June 1931 when she was eleven, she was again caught having sex, this time with a boy by the name of Johnnie Clawson, who was a year younger than she was. As a result, the Oneida County judge decided to send Joyce to Ithaca to be evaluated. She was released seven months later. Soon after, she began consorting with girls like Judy Shaan and started engaging in more serious criminal activities. After spending some five months in Gloversville, she was again sent to Ithaca, where she again was released in May 1934 when she was fourteen.

Although Biway was transferred to Rutherford B. Hayes High School since he was in the tenth grade and Joyce in the ninth and still at Franklin Pierce, they continued to see one another.

The day when Biway started his classes at Rutherford B. Hayes, he suddenly saw Diane De Wolfe in two of them, English and world history, and was stunned. When Diane saw him, she blushed. Two days later when they met in the hallway, Biway shyly said to Diane, "Long time no see."

Diane replied, "Tom, I don't know what to say except I'm sorry for the trouble I got you into and watching that nun slap you the way she did. I was only ten then and quite frightened."

Biway simply replied, "Forget it, Diane. That was a long time ago." Diane was fifteen and looked even prettier than she was when Biway last saw her five years earlier. The next day, she and Biway met again and had a short conversation, in which Biway asked her, "Do you have a steady boyfriend now?"

Diane replied, "Yes, I do. His name is Kenneth Trombley. Do you remember him from St. Paul's?"

Biway replied, "Yes, I do."

Then Diane asked Biway, "Do you have a girlfriend now?"

Biway replied, "Yes, I do, and her name is Joyce Buckley. She is now going to Franklin Pierce Middle School, where I went last year."

As for Diane De Wolfe, she graduated Rutherford B. Hayes in June 1937 and went on to George Crenshaw Business College in Buffalo, New

York, where she graduated in 1939 with an associate degree in business. Soon after, she went to work as a secretary for Bledsoe, Posey, and Posey, Attorneys at Law. It was here where she met Tom Posey's nephew, Jake Snyder. They started going together, and on June 14, 1941, they married. Two months later, Jake enlisted in the US Navy in order to avoid being drafted into the Army. After Jake was sent to a naval base near Seattle, Washington, Diane followed him there so she could be near him. It was sheer luck that Jake was not at Pearl Harbor on December 7, 1941, as he was scheduled to be sent there a week later. In the meantime, Diane became pregnant and decided to return to Utica to be with her parents. The baby was born on April 19, 1942, and Diane named him Jake Jr. Unfortunately for Diane, Jake Sr. was killed in action in the South Pacific four months later. Needless to say, Diane felt devastated. Six years later in 1948, Diane met a wealthy farmer and businessman by the name of George Mitchell. He was forty-eight and a lifelong bachelor, although he had several girlfriends. He had a farm near Cooperstown, where Diane along with her six-year-old son moved in on August 1948 after her marriage to him. Diane and George had three more children, John, born on April 23, 1950; Joseph, on August 8, 1954; and finally, a daughter whom they named Naomi after Diane's mother, on June 12, 1961.

On August 23, 1975, on Diane's fifty-sixth birthday, George suffered a severe stroke, leaving him in a vegetative state. He finally died three years later on August 12, 1978, with Diane by his side, at the age of seventy-eight.

Finally on October 28, 1983, Diane married for the third time. Her husband was Warren Steedman, fifty-five, some nine years younger than she was. He was the third shift supervisor at Naylor Plastics Inc. in neighboring Oneonta. Even at sixty-four, Diane was still very attractive, and men noticed her as she went out doing her business in public. All four of her children were successful in their endeavors as they went out on their own. Finally on July 9, 2004, Diane suffered a stroke that morning in her kitchen, was rushed to St. Michael's Mercy

Hospital in Oneonta, and died just before 5:00 p.m., with her husband, Warren, at her side. She was just a month and a half shy of her eighty-fifth birthday. Two days later, her husband, Warren, shot himself in the head in order to end the overwhelming grief he felt. He was buried next to Diane.

In the meantime, during the fall of 1934, Biway and Joyce continued to go steady, and Chuck Henderson, one of Biway's friends, turned sixteen on August 30, thus enabling him to get his driver's license. Henderson's father, Joe, decided to give Chuck the old family car, a black 1922 Plymouth. Thereafter, Chuck, Joe Hartwell, Buddy Androszech, and Biway would ride around in it in order to harass and insult pedestrians just as Jackie Brown and his friends did. By emulating Jackie Brown, Biway felt more and more like a man.

On Thanksgiving Day, Thursday, November 22, 1934, Herbert "Herb" Hennessey, sixty-four, decided to go over to his brother Sam's house to spend the day with him, his wife, Betty, and their three grown children. Since neither Herb nor Sam had a car, one of Herb's neighbors by the name of Doc Irwin, who along with his wife, Sandra, who had to work that day, offered Herb a ride over since his brother's house was not that far out of their way.

Herbert Hennessey, who was sixty-four at that time, never married, was five feet, seven inches tall and weighed around 155 pounds. He had thinning gray hair with a bald spot on top of his head.

When Doc Irwin, thirty-four, arrived at Sam Hennessey's house, he said to Herb, "Wait out here at the corner of Myrtle and Farley Street. We'll come around sometime between five thirty and six thirty, depending on when we get our work done at Quinnie's barbecue." Herb then went to his brother's house, knocked, and was received. He had Thanksgiving dinner and enjoyed himself greatly. However, when he looked at the clock on the wall and noticed that it was already five thirty, he said to Sam, "It's five thirty, and my expected ride is due to come anytime. I guess I'd better get out there." After saying their goodbyes, Herb stepped outside and walked to the corner of Myrtle and Farley Street. As Herb was waiting at the corner, suddenly a pink 1928 Dodge with a white top pulled up with four juveniles inside. The driver was Curtis McNabb, seventeen, whose grandmother, who owned the car, gave him permission to drive it. The other three were Paul Vincent, Ed Snodgrass, and of course, Jackie Brown, all also seventeen. Paul then asked Herb, "Do you want a ride, Pop? We have plenty of time to take you to wherever you wish to go. We're just trying to be nice."

Herb replied, "Thank you, but I already have people coming here to pick me up, but thanks anyway."

Then Jackie started yelling "—you, you—!" and they drove off.

A girl by the name of Elsie Thompson, twenty-one, who heard what Jackie yelled out, stepped out of the house on the corner where she lived and asked Herb, "What was all that yelling and cursing about?"

Herb replied, "Oh, that's nothing," but he couldn't keep his eyes dry. To him it was like being slapped in the face unexpectedly.

About ten or fifteen minutes later, the boys in the Dodge returned and noticed Herb still waiting for his ride. It was around five forty-five and dark outside. It was a fairly mild night for November. Jackie asked his friends, "Do you have the brass knuckles handy?" and Curtis replied, "Yes, but they're in the trunk." Then Jackie said, "What are we waiting for?" This time Curtis parked the car, all four boys got out, surrounded Herb, and put on their brass knuckles. All four took turns at slugging Herb, and once he was knocked to the ground, Jackie kicked him in the head as hard as he could. All of a sudden, the neighbors began to turn on their porch lights one by one in order to see what was going on outside. Most were shocked at what they saw. Paul Vincent said to the others, "Let's get the hell out of here," and all four scurried to their car as fast as they could. Even Sam came out and said, "Oh my god, they beat up my brother! What the hell did he ever do to them?"

Fortunately, one of the neighbors managed to get close enough to McNabb's car in order to write down the number of the license plate to be turned over to the Utica Police later. In the meantime, an ambulance pulled up and put Herb on a gurney since he fell into unconsciousness as a result of the kick in the head he got from Jackie Brown. He was taken to St. Luke's Mercy Hospital. Unfortunately, he never regained consciousness and died shortly before 5:00 a.m., just four days short of his sixty-fifth birthday.

Around 10:00 p.m. using the license number given to them by one of Sam Hennessey's neighbors, the Utica Police did find McNabb's car and stopped it, ordering all four boys to get out. They were immediately taken into custody and charged with aggravated battery.

That Saturday morning since Herb Hennessey died from his injuries, the Utica Police upgraded the charges to second-degree murder. Upon being interrogated, Curtis McNabb, Paul Vincent, and Ed Snodgrass all admitted to beating up Herb Hennessey with their brass knuckles but all quickly pointed out that it was Jackie Brown who kicked Hennessey in the head as violently as he could. When he was being interrogated, Jackie Brown admitted to kicking Hennessey in the head and started cursing his friends for giving him up. All four were later taken to the Oneida County Detention Center in Rome to await trial.

Since it was ascertained that Hennessey died from being kicked in the head rather than being beaten with brass knuckles, only Jackie Brown was charged with second-degree murder, while the other three with aggravated battery. Jackie Brown's trial date was set for December 10, the day following his eighteenth birthday.

Jacky Brown decided to plea-bargain since he had absolutely no chance of being acquitted by a jury. Three days later upon his sentencing, the judge asked Jackie, "Have you anything to say to this court before sentence is imposed?" Jackie just said, "No." The judge replied, "You go back a long way with your criminal activities, ever since you were ten. Each time you were arrested, you seemed to have gotten worse. By doing what you did to Mr. Hennessey on November 22, last, you proved just what a low opinion you have of the rights and the lives of others. Therefore, I'm going to give you the maximum, but since you were still seventeen when you attacked Mr. Hennessey, I cannot impose the death penalty, but I do hereby sentence you to a period of not less than eight years nor more than twenty-five years to the maximum security prison at Ossining, New York, on the Hudson River. Court is adjourned." The other three were first sent to Warwick and eventually sent to Attica after turning eighteen.

Upon hearing this news, Biway and his friends were stunned. But Biway, in his incessant quest to rival Jackie Brown, decided to go out and do the same thing. At first, his friends were squeamish to this idea, but Biway eventually managed to convince them to go along. In early December, as Biway, Buddy Androszech, and Joe Hartwell were riding around in Chuck Henderson's 1922 Plymouth along Second Street, they noticed an old man coming out of O'Malley's Pub and noticed that he did so every night around 10:30 p.m. At that time of the night as usual, the streets in that part of town were poorly lit and generally deserted, so on the night of December 11, they followed the old man as he just left the pub.

The old man's name was Dermott McFadden, seventy-nine, and the oldest of James and Sarah McFadden's seven children. James and Sarah McFadden too came to America from Ireland to escape starvation caused by the Great Potato Blight (1845–1849) in 1848. James was drafted during the Civil War (1861–1865) but returned very traumatized from witnessing some of the atrocities perpetrated by his fellow Union soldiers on Southern white families in Mississippi and Alabama. After marrying Ann McCarthy in 1883, Dermott decided to move to Utica at her behest and lived there ever since. They had two children, a boy and a girl. His wife died in 1928, and his son was killed in France during WWI. He only had one surviving child, and that was his daughter, Mary, forty-seven, with whom he lived along with her husband, Charles McNichols, fifty-four. Their three children were grown and lived with their spouses.

After they followed McFadden for some distance, Chuck parked his car, and all four began arming themselves with brass knuckles, as Jackie Brown's gang did. Then they got out the car and surrounded McFadden. McFadden asked them, "What do you want? I only have $12 on me, but here's my watch if you want it, but let me go home, please." Buddy Androszech suddenly hit McFadden in the face with his brass knuckles over his fist, and then the others started doing the same. After McFadden fell to the sidewalk with his face already bloodied, Buddy Androszech kicked him in the mouth, knocking loose four of his front teeth and breaking his jaw. Chuck Henderson yelled, "Buddy, stop. You'll kill him. Do you remember what happened to

Jackie Brown?" Then Joe Hartwell said, "There are people coming. Let's get the hell out of here now!" All four scurried back to Henderson's car and drove off. The people who arrived on the scene were too far away to get a good description of McFadden's assailants or the car they drove off in, and McFadden himself didn't know any of them. McFadden asked those people to call an ambulance to take him to St. Luke's Mercy Hospital to be treated for his injuries. The police later questioned McFadden, but he couldn't tell them anything, and they in turn notified McFadden's daughter, Mary, who had become frantic over her father not coming home as usual.

Later that night, Biway and his friends said to one another, "Let's lie low for a good while," and all four agreed to do so.

The next day, Biway bought a newspaper and read a headline in the crime section stating, "Old Man Beaten by Four Unknown Assailants Tuesday Night." Biway, who before his sixteenth birthday almost committed his first murder, felt somewhat relieved.

In the meantime, Buddy Androszech, who always had an eye out for girls, noticed that a few houses down the street from where he lived, lived the Tarleton family, Daniel, fifty-nine; Diana, fifty-one; Jerome, fifteen; and Hazel, nine. Their two other children, Douglas, twenty-eight, and Donna, thirty-one, were married and living with their spouses. Hazel, who was nine, was of average height and weight for a girl her age, had blond hair that she wore in a ponytail, blue eyes, and rosy cheeks, and Buddy was strongly attracted to her. He would watch her and her friends walk to the corner every morning and afternoon to and from the school bus stop. Moreover, he developed a habit of sneaking up to peoples' houses and peeking through the windows when no one was around to see it. This was what he did to the Tarletons. Hazel was born on May 27, 1925, two days after her father's fiftieth birthday, and her mother was forty-two at that time. Both doted on Hazel, and Jerome worshipped her.

On Wednesday, December 26, the day after Christmas, Buddy noticed the Tarletons going out around noon, but Hazel was not with them. Instead, since she had a stomach ache, she decided to take some baking soda and went to bed until she felt better.

In the meantime, Buddy snuck into the Tarletons' backyard, where the family dog, a small Collie, barked, but Buddy learned to ignore it and looked into her bedroom window, saw her lying down, and then went to the back door, which he found unlocked, whereupon he let himself in and tiptoed into Hazel's bedroom.

Upon seeing him, Hazel, who was stunned by his unexpected presence, frantically asked, "What do you want?"

Buddy replied, "First, I want you to put your hair up in a ponytail. You look better that way." She complied, and then Buddy said, "Now open up your nightgown and pull down your undies."

Hazel became even more frantic and said, "Please don't make me, I beg you."

Buddy replied, "Look, girl, I'm not going to hurt you. Just pull down your underpants and lie down." Hazel, now terrified, tearfully gave in, and Buddy began performing oral sex on her as she cried as hard as she could.

Next door to the Tarletons' lived an elderly couple by the name of Roy and Tammy Hicks. He was sixty-eight and a retiree from the US Army, where he served for forty-two years until he retired in 1929, and she was the same age as he. They married in 1887, the same year he joined the Army. In July 1889, they had a son whom they named Philip who, by 1934, was living in Philadelphia, Pennsylvania, with his wife and three children. Roy, who was working in his backyard, heard Hazel crying frantically and went over to investigate what was going on. He looked into the bedroom window and was totally shocked at what he saw. It was Buddy Androszech raping Hazel for the second time after performing oral sex on her. Upon hearing the back door open, Buddy quickly got off Hazel, pulled up his pants as fast as he could, and made a dash out the front door. Roy immediately called the Utica Police to report the rape. The police arrived some fifteen minutes later followed by an ambulance, which took Hazel to the nearby hospital in order to be examined and treated for the rape. The police questioned Roy, asking him, "Do you know who attacked this young lady?"

Roy answered, "No, but I know where he lives. I can point him out to you if and when I see him."

Roy then led two police officers to where Buddy Androszech lived and knocked on the door. Wanda answered, saying, "What's going on?"

One of the officers replied, "Do you have a boy living here with blond hair?"

Wanda said, "Yes, that's my son, Buddy."

Next they heard the back door slam and a blond-headed boy running out as fast as he could. Roy said, "That's him, the guy who raped that little girl!" Upon hearing this, Wanda almost collapsed from cardiac arrest. She was totally stunned that her son was capable of such a thing, but then again, she acknowledged that he did bad things in the past.

Around four thirty, the Tarletons returned home and found a police officer standing at the front door. Mr. Tarleton asked, "Did something happen to Hazel and is she all right?"

The officer answered, "Yes, something did happen to her, and she is now at St. Luke's being treated."

Mr. Tarleton then asked, "What happened to her?"

The officer replied, "Sir, your daughter was sexually assaulted this afternoon, and we're now looking for the guy who did it."

"Do you know who it is?" asked Mr. Tarleton.

The officer simply replied, "I'm afraid I'm not at liberty to say, but if you go down to headquarters, the detectives will fill you in."

Thereafter, Mr. Tarleton drove Diana and Jerome to St. Luke's and then himself to police headquarters to find out whether his daughter's assailant had been picked up or not.

In the meantime, an elderly man spotted Buddy hiding in his garage, whereupon he notified the Utica Police. They walked up to the garage and said, "Buddy, we know you're in there. Either come out peacefully or we'll drag you out. Either way, you're coming with us to headquarters."

After Buddy came out of that garage, the police put handcuffs on him and put him in the squad car, while Buddy himself cried like a baby, realizing the gravity of the situation he was in. When Buddy was led into the police station, both Roy Hicks and Daniel Tarleton were there. Roy recognized Buddy on the spot as Hazel's rapist and said to the desk sergeant, "That's him." The police then led Buddy into the interrogation room and said, "First, we want you to drop your drawers," and Buddy timidly asked, "What for?"

"Never mind, just do it," said the detective.

Buddy complied, and when he did, they saw that his underpants were caked in blood as well as the blood one could see on his trousers. The detective said, "How do you explain this? We're going to have to confiscate your pants and underpants for evidence. Right now, I'd sure hate to be in your place!"

Buddy simply kept on crying like a baby while he was being booked. In the meantime, Mr. Tarleton said to Roy, "I can't thank you enough for what you did for us."

Roy replied, "That's quite all right. That's what neighbors do."

As he looked at Buddy with a glowing hate in his eyes, Daniel Tarleton began to show his outrage, and the desk sergeant who noticed it said, "We all know how you must feel, Mr. Tarleton. I myself have a seven-year-old daughter at home."

Thereafter Mr. Tarleton drove to St. Luke's and joined Jerome and Diana. He asked Diana, "How is she, and is she severely injured?" Diana replied, "She's now undergoing surgery in order to stop her profuse bleeding. They say she may never be able to have any children. By the way, Dan, did they find the filthy creep who did this?"

Daniel replied, "Thank God they did, Diana!"

In the meantime, Jerome didn't say anything but continued to pace up and down in the hallway, still trying to subdue his outrage over what Androszech did to his sister. Later, one of the doctors who assisted in Hazel's surgery went to the Tarletons and said, "Your daughter is out of danger now, and the good news is, she will probably be able to have children in the future, but she's going to need a lot of good therapy and rape counseling in the meantime." The Tarletons felt somewhat relieved, but they knew it would be years before they could put this horrific event behind them. Thereafter, the Tarletons went home for the night, and Hazel was released from the hospital a week and a half later.

The next day, Biway heard the news of the attack over the radio and surmised that his friend Buddy was behind it. He was right. Buddy told him time and again how much he wanted to have sex with that girl. Biway at one point asked him, "Isn't she a little young for that?"

Buddy simply replied, "What difference does that make? After all, she does look good with her blue eyes and her blond hair in a ponytail."

Biway grumbled, "That stupid jerk. Leave it to him to screw up every time. Doesn't he know we're all supposed to be lying low after what we did to that old man? Evidently not!" Then Biway started to worry if Buddy would spill the beans over the attack on that old man in order to get a lighter jail sentence. Fortunately for Biway, it never occurred to Buddy to do so.

The same day, Buddy was transferred to the Oneida County Detention Center to await his trial. At his hearing, his parents showed up but said nothing as the judge read off the changes against their son. Buddy's counselor pleaded no contest. The judge said, "Be back in this courtroom at 10:00 a.m. on Wednesday, January 16. I'll hand down my sentence then."

On Wednesday the sixteenth at 10:00 a.m., Buddy along with his counselor showed up to await his sentence.

When Buddy Androszech along with his counselor appeared before Judge Dan Donnelly, the judge asked Buddy, "Have you anything to say for yourself?"

Buddy simply replied, "No, I don't."

Then the judge asked Buddy, "Have you any remorse over what you did to that little girl?"

Buddy simply said, "Sorry, Your Honor, I don't feel any."

Then the judge said, "I've seen a lot of lowly people come before me, and you're obviously one of the lowliest. Therefore I'm going to sentence you to Warwick until your eighteenth birthday, which you thereafter will be transferred to Attica until you reach the age of twenty-one." Buddy was released from Attica on his twenty-first birthday on November 14, 1939, but instead of returning to Utica, decided to go to Toledo, Ohio, where his older brother lived, and move in with him since the people in Utica still remembered what happened to Hazel Tarleton and who did it.

In the meantime, the relationship between Biway and Joyce Buckley started to cool. As Biway suspected, Joyce was seeing Johnnie Clawson, one of the boys she was caught having sex with some four years earlier. She was nearly fifteen at this time, and he, nearly fourteen. In February 1935, a couple by the name of Tad and Dorothy Hawkins moved into the house next door to the Biways. Tad was fifty and Dorothy, forty-six. They had three children, Kevin, born on November 1, 1913; Virginia, on September 24, 1916; and Madeleine, on October 3, 1918. Seven months later, Madeleine contracted Spanish influenza and died as a result. Only Kevin turned out to be able to lead a normal life. Even in her early childhood, Virginia began to show signs of instability. She would suddenly start to cry uncontrollably and throw fits for apparently no reason. As she reached puberty, her symptoms grew even worse. Finally in March 1928 when she was eleven, her parents agreed with the Oneida County Psychiatriatric Association to send her to Ithaca to be evaluated. She would show signs of improvement and then relapse and again seem to improve. Finally early in 1935 when she was eighteen, she was released from the mental institution for children in Buffalo and came home to enroll in Rutherford B. Hayes High School just one grade ahead of Biway. It wasn't long before Terry, Biway's older sister, and Virginia became friends although the two went to different high schools.

Virginia Hawkins was a rather large girl with a buxom build, like that of Judy Edmonds, had short black hair, and greatly resembled her mother, although her mother was smaller than she was. As Biway and Joyce Buckley slowly ended their relationship, his relationship with Virginia began to blossom.

Unlike Biway's other girlfriends, Virginia never had any run-ins with the law nor ever associated herself with unsavory friends. Since Biway turned sixteen on Christmas Day, he was able to get his driver's license and drive his father's new yellow four-door 1933 Dodge whenever his father permitted him to do so. On Friday nights when his father didn't need the car, Biway would take Virginia out, and they'd make love but unfortunately, this new relationship was not to last.

During the last two weeks in May, Virginia felt her former depression slowly returning, and day after day, it became even worse.

After she was released that January, she was hoping she was cured once and for all, but now she was beginning to realize that was not the case. She had already tried to commit suicide on four different occasions, however unsuccessfully.

This time she resolutely decided that she was not going to go through this again, so on Wednesday, May 29, she had already formulated her plans for the upcoming Friday night.

Around 5:00 p.m. on Friday, May 31, Virginia Hawkins set her plan in motion. As Tad and Dorothy went out as usual on Fridays, Virginia told them she was expecting Biway to come over between 6:00 and 6:30 p.m. for their usual date. However, after her parents left, she locked both the front and back doors and turned off all the lights in the house. Next she went down to the basement and removed the leash from Doughboy's neck. Doughboy was a twelve-year-old German shepherd who belonged to the Hawkins family. Mr. Hawkins would spend much of his time in the basement, making wine, as that was his hobby, with Doughboy at his side. After she removed the leash, she put the chain to which it was attached over a beam, got up on a stool, placed the leash tightly around her neck, locked it, and kicked the stool out from under her. Her neck didn't break, but she spent the next twenty-one minutes dying an agonizingly slow death, suffocating while hanging in the air.

At about ten minutes after 6:00 p.m., Biway came over and, seeing that the front door was locked, began knocking, but no one answered. Biway thought to himself, *Strange, did she forget we had a Friday night date? This is definitely not like her.* In the meantime, he heard Doughboy barking from the basement. He knocked over and over again for the next twenty to twenty-five minutes. Thereafter he went home and asked his sister Terry, "Have you seen Virginia? Evidently she's not at home."

Terry said, "I have no idea, Tom. She didn't say a word to me."

Mary McDougall, Biway's grandmother, said, "Tom, since you seemed to be upset, let me give you a shot of my Jack Daniels bourbon."

Biway replied, "Thanks a million, Grandma. That's just what I need." This was not the first time Mary gave Biway a little liquor. She'd been doing it ever since Prohibition was lifted in 1933. Sometimes Biway would share it with his friends when they were out running around, as on the night they attacked Mr. McFadden. Also Biway, for the first time, lit one cigarette after another. He picked this habit up from his best friend Buddy Androszech. Since it was illegal for teenagers to purchase cigarettes, Buddy would somehow steal them and share them with Biway. In order to protect Biway from getting arrested, Mary would just simply give Biway a pack of Camel cigarettes as well as the liquor, which she would pour into an empty fruit jar.

Shortly after 9:30 p.m., Biway noticed the Hawkins pull up next door in their green 1930 Studebaker. Biway then rushed over and asked Mr. Hawkins, "Did Virginia go out with you tonight? She's obviously not at home."

Tad replied, "No, she didn't. Didn't you and her have a date?" Biway said, "At least I thought we did."

The Hawkins then unlocked the front door, went in, and turned on all the lights. As Mr. Hawkins heard Doughboy barking, he opened the basement door, saw Doughboy wandering around free, and went down along with Dorothy. Dorothy then yelled out, "Oh my god, she finally did it!" They then called an ambulance to have Virginia's body taken to the county mortuary in nearby Rome and subsequently have her buried.

As distraught as they were, they were not surprised over this. Virginia had already tried committing suicide on four different occasions, three times by poisoning herself and once by jumping into the Erie Canal only to be fished out by two tugboat workers.

After getting a little drunk upon learning that Virginia killed herself that night, Biway got up the next morning feeling sick and swore he'd never take another drink again. Later that day as he started feeling better, he said to himself, "Easy come, easy go. There are other girls at school and elsewhere," so his feeling of loss over Virginia slowly gave way to indifference.

It was at this time he began to notice his sister Susanna and what a plump figure she had. Like Judy Shaan's cousin Sherman Mondbauer, Susanna never lost her baby fat. In fact, she did look somewhat like Sherman. She was five feet, five inches tall and weighed around 150 pounds. She had light-brown hair, and with her baby fat, she had a very genteel look on her face. The boys at school all seemed to like her, and she them. In fact, she took a liking to one boy in particular, whose name was Charlie Wilson, who was her age.

On Sunday, July 14, eight days after Susanna's fourteenth birthday, Biway told his father, "Today I feel like going horseback riding. Do you need the Dodge for any reason, Pop? If not, I'd like to take Suzy here with me."

Joseph replied, "Yes, Tom, you can take the Dodge and go to Uncle Dan's place if you want."

Biway replied, "Thanks, Pop," turned to Susanna and said, "Are you ready?"

Susanna replied, "Yes, I am. Can Rick come along too?"

Biway replied, "No, he cannot, that punk will just spoil it for us." Susanna didn't quite understand, but she and Biway hopped into the yellow Dodge and headed north to their uncle Dan's farm. Before they left, Mary as usual gave her grandson some bourbon in an empty fruit jar, which he later showed Susanna after arriving at their uncle's farm. They arrived around 1:00 p.m., had a snack, and Dan led the two horses to them for them to ride. After about an hour, they reached the northwest corner of the farm, which was heavily wooded and secluded, and stopped. Then Biway said to Susanna, "I'm tired, Suzy. How about it if we took a break, tied the horses up, and got under some shade?"

Susanna replied, "That's a very good idea, Tom. I'm tired too."

They tied the horses to two small trees and went under a Catalpa tree for shade. Once they sat down, Biway pulled the fruit jar out of his pocket and said to Susanna, "I have a little hooch here. Do you want some?"

Susanna replied, "Yes, I'll have a little, very little."

Then Biway started to ask Susanna, "Do you have any boyfriends at school yet?"

Susanna replied, "No, I don't yet, but there is this one boy named Charlie Wilson. He's quite cute."

Then Biway got real personal with Susanna, asking her if she would like to have sex with this Charlie Wilson.

Susanna told Biway, "I'm only fourteen, and as far as having sex is concerned, I'd rather wait until I get married."

Biway replied, "Oh my god, Suzy, don't you know we're now living in the 1930s? Kids do this all the time nowadays, and I already had four girlfriends with whom I had sex with. Isn't it about time you had a little too, Suzy?"

Susanna replied, "No, Tom, I don't want to, if that's what you have in mind. Is that the reason you asked me to come here, so you can get me alone with you?"

Biway replied, "Yes, Suzy, it is. Just be a nice little girl and do what I tell you. I won't hurt you, I swear. Please, Suzy, don't be like our punk brother, Rick. Besides, I still have my set of brass knuckles, and it would really hurt if I were to hit you with them on." Susanna, seeing that her brother wouldn't give her any choice, began to tearfully comply to what he told her to do. She slowly stripped herself and let Biway crawl on top of her and penetrate her. Biway then asked Susanna, "By the way, Suzy, when did you have your last period?"

Susanna replied, "About three weeks ago."

Biway said, "Well, that's good." While doing it, Biway felt like a lion devouring his prey and savoring every moment of it. Having sex with Susanna was just as much if not more fun than with his other four girlfriends.

After Biway raped Susanna for the third time, he said to her, "See, Suzy, it didn't hurt, just like I said it wouldn't. By the way, would you care to take another shot of this hooch here?"

Susanna replied, "Yes, Tom, I would." After each took their turns at finishing the hooch, both got up, got dressed, untied the horses, and remounted. When they got back to their uncle's house, Susanna kept her head turned away from their uncle so he wouldn't see her eyes, which were still red and swollen with tears. They said their goodbyes to their uncle, left around four thirty, and arrived home some forty-five minutes later.

When Joseph came into the living room after working in the garden out back, Susanna suddenly ran to him with tears in her eyes and frantically said to him, "Dad, Tom raped me today at Uncle Dan's. He really did and threatened me not to tell anyone about it."

Joseph at first looked at Susanna in disbelief and called Margaret out of the kitchen, saying, "Did you hear what Susanna just told me?" Then he turned to Biway and said, "Tom, is this true?"

Before Biway could reply, Rick, who heard what Susanna said from the front yard where he was playing with his friends, rushed in, ran to Susanna, and said to her, "Suzy, Tom hurt me too."

Margaret, still stunned, said to Rick, "When did he do it, and where was it, Rick?"

Rick replied, "That was a long time ago, when I was in the second grade at St. Paul's. First, Tom got a hold of this alley cat and took a ball-peen hammer out to bash its head in in front of me. He said he'd do the same to me if I didn't do what he told me to. The first time, it was just Tom making me perform oral sex on him. Sometime later, he did the same thing but with this creep Buddy with him. I had to perform on both of them that time, and there was the third time when Tom brought his two other friends with him. That time I only had to perform on him and Buddy, while his two other friends refused to partake."

Margaret said to Joseph, "Buddy, isn't that the creep who raped that nine-year-old girl six months ago?" Thereafter Margaret said, "Rick, why didn't you tell this to any of us before? In fact, the Mother Superior called me from your school to ask me why you were behaving the way you were at that time. I couldn't tell her anything, but now I know why you were so unhappy." Then she looked at Biway in disbelief but said nothing. Then Mary, who heard the conversation from the back porch, stepped into to the living room, but she too said nothing. She was already eighty years old and never heard of such a thing. She too was stunned.

Joseph turned to his wife and said, "Margaret, call the police and then an ambulance in order to take Suzy to St. Luke's to be examined." Then he turned to Biway and said, "Tom, we're going to have to have you incarcerated just as that creepy friend of yours was six months ago." Within fifteen minutes, the Utica Police arrived followed by an ambulance for Susanna. As the police were escorting Biway out the front door and toward the squad car, he turned to Joseph and said, "At least, Pop, I'm not yellow like you are." Joseph surmised that it was because of his failure to serve in WWI. Rick, who heard what Biway said to his father, said, "Dad, I don't think you're yellow."

After Biway was taken to the Municipal Detention Center, Susanna was taken to St. Luke's and examined.

The next day, Biway was taken to the Oneida County Detention Center to be arraigned in juvenile court. At 1:00 p.m., Biway was taken before Judge Dan Donnelly, the same one who judged Buddy Androszech six months earlier. He was accompanied by his counselor, Joe Tindle, who represented him.

Judge Donnelly was fifty-five, wore glasses, had gray hair, and was rather homely. He lived alone without anyone knowing why, but he was very conscientious and cared for people.

When Biway appeared before him, he asked, "Have you anything to say on your behalf, young man?"

Biway simply replied, "No, I don't."

The judge said, "I understand you raped your sister yesterday at your uncle's farm. Is it true?"

Biway just said, "Yes, Your Honor."

Judge Donnelly replied, "Since you admitted to what you did to your sister and this is your first offense, I'm going to give you a three-way choice: Go to Warwick until you're eighteen, join the Army, or join the Navy. I'll give you time to think it over, but no later than Thursday."

Biway said to his counselor, "Tell the judge I don't need any time to ponder it. I already made up my mind." The counselor told the judge, who asked Biway, and Biway replied, "I'll join the Navy, Your Honor."

However when Biway was brought to the Naval Recruiting Center, the naval recruiting officer told the deputy who escorted him to the station that the Navy was booked, but the Marine Corps had several vacancies.

Biway then said to the deputy, "Well, let's go to the Marine Recruiting Center," and the deputy complied. The recruiting officer there told the deputy, "Bring this young man here on Friday, July 26 around 9:00 a.m. so he can report for his physical and mental exams, and the deputy agreed that if Biway passed his exams, the Oneida County Sheriff's Department would release him from custody so he could join the Marine Corps.

As it turned out, Biway passed both his physical and psychological exams quite handily, and after being released from custody, Biway was taken to the Marine Recruiting Depot on Parris Island just off the coast of South Carolina for his eight-week basic training.

At first, it was tough, and Biway was only allowed one cigarette a day, but he slowly adapted.

CHAPTER 4

The Few, the Proud, the Marines!

Biway arrived at the Marine Recruiting Center on Parris Island in South Carolina on Monday, July 29 and was taken to the barbershop to have his head shaven, issued his uniform, and joined in the 6:00 p.m. inspection. Here the training was rigorous. He had to get up at 6:00 a.m., eat a small breakfast at 7:00 and start training at 8:00 a.m. sharp. It was very grueling, and by the end of the day, Biway was exhausted. As the weeks went on, he began to thrive, and after six weeks, he knew he was going to make it through.

For the first time in his life, Biway began to feel happy. At least he was in the Marine Corps, which he considered a cut above the US Army, which rejected his father in 1917. He felt for the first time he had a purpose in life instead of running around with the unsavory young people he befriended in Utica, who were only headed for a life of misery. In short, he felt he made the team as part of the military elite.

On Friday, September 23, his boot training concluded, and he was transferred to the First Marine base at Camp Pendleton in Southern California. Here he learned the martial arts such as karate and judo in order to subdue any opponent he may happen to encounter. Later during the Korean War, he used those skills quite efficiently and, as some observed, with a certain kind of sinister pleasure.

At first, he found his superior, Master Sergeant Fred Hobbs, to be rather harsh and demanding, but after two weeks, the two began to develop a close friendship.

Sergeant Hobbs was forty-nine years old with salt-and-pepper hair. He was five feet, ten inches tall and weighed close to two hundred pounds. He had a wife, Bonnie, and six children back in Ft. Smith, Arkansas. He joined the Marine Corps in 1907 at the age of twenty- one. He was planning to retire in 1937, when he accomplished his thirty years of service in the Corps.

On Saturday night, October 12, when both Sergeant Hobbs and Biway were on a twenty-four-hour liberty pass, Sergeant Hobbs told Biway, "I know a place up the road where a lot of prostitutes hang out and there is plenty to drink. Let me take you there. They have white, black, and Hispanic broads. All you have to do is take your pick. Personally, I like the black ones myself."

This was totally new for Biway. Once he and Hobbs stepped into the tavern where the prostitutes were lounging, Hobbs immediately picked out a black one, and while looking around, a Hispanic woman who was tending bar caught Biway's eye. He then asked one of the prostitutes who was lounging at a table at the time, "That broad tending bar, does she sell herself too?"

The woman said, "Yes, she does, but she's rather expensive."

Biway decided to ask the woman who was tending bar directly, "Ma'am, I'd like to do business with you. How much will I need to pay you with?"

The woman, being from Honduras, didn't quite understand as she hadn't fully learned English, turned to the man assisting her at the bar, asking, "?Que me pregunta este joven?"

The man simply replied in Spanish, "He said he wants to do business with you and to know how much it will cost him."

Then the woman said, "Tell him it'll cost him $50 for half a night." Biway went through his pockets but only managed to come up with $38.54. He then turned to Sergeant Hobbs and said, "Sergeant, I need $12 more. Can you help me out?" and Hobbs replied, "Yes, I can."

After Hobbs came up with $12 and handed it to Biway, Biway paid the woman, and the two went up to one of the rooms to have sex. Biway was enjoying himself as they were having sex, and the woman felt very flattered at the idea of such a young Marine recruit, and a white one at that, would pay her more for sex, since the younger prostitutes only charged around $20 for doing the same thing.

The woman's name was Oneida Castro. She was thirty-five years old but never married. She was five feet, six inches tall and weighed around 170 pounds. She had pitch-black hair, a round face, and when she wore her pants as she usually did, her buxom figure showed, and that was what caught Biway's eye.

Oneida was born in 1900 in the small village of Zaragoza, Honduras, the second of three children born to Diego and Anna Castro. The family lived in grinding poverty. When Oneida was eleven, she decided to prostitute herself rather than see her family starve, especially her five-year-old brother, Rogelio. Her older sister, Marlene, was fortunate enough to marry a landowner who lived in California in order to escape the misery. In 1921, Marlene sent Oneida enough money so that she and Rogelio could come to California and start living a decent life. Rogelio moved in with Marlene and her husband, but Oneida first got a job tending bar and then reverted back to prostitution in 1929, after the sudden and unexpected death of her then fiancé, Jose Flores, from pancreatic cancer. It took Oneida a long time to get over this loss. In the meantime, Oneida with her good figure and personality made a good living.

The next time she and Biway were having sex, Biway said, "I'd like to teach you English so you can communicate better with us white people." In fact, Oneida was slowly becoming more proficient in English as she and Biway were sleeping together. For Biway, this relationship was entirely physical, and while being greatly flattered, Oneida didn't harbor any romantic feelings toward Biway either.

In the meantime, another one of Oneida's clients by the name of David Sandoval was slowly falling in love with her, and she started feeling the same way about him. One night, David proposed to her, and to his surprise, she accepted. They set their wedding date to Saturday, June 20, 1936. That was in March.

David Sandoval was born near Sacramento, California, in 1884, the third son of a wealthy Hispanic rancher who cultivated cattle and grew grapes as the family tradition. He was almost six feet tall but rather thin and had gray hair and a mustache. David's oldest brother died in 1897, shortly after his father did, and David and his surviving brother divided the ranch between themselves. David first married in 1906, but his wife died in 1919 from Spanish influenza along with his young son, Emilio, nine. In 1933 when Prohibition ended, David began frequenting taverns, where there were prostitutes and plenty to drink.

Shortly after their engagement, Oneida told her clientele that she was no longer in the business. Many were indeed disappointed upon hearing this, especially Biway. From then on, he just had to do business with the younger girls.

Oneida and David Sandoval were married on Saturday, June 20, as planned. Oneida was thirty-six and David, fifty-two. The wedding was a gala event with Oneida's sister, Marlene Martinez, who was forty-six, along with her husband as well as her brother, Rogelio, thirty, married, with two children attending. All of David's friends and relatives attended also.

Two years later in March 1938, Oneida gave birth to a set of twins, a boy named Guillermo and a girl named Alejandra. However, in May 1940, David suffered a massive heart attack and had to be taken to Santa Catalina Hospital, where he almost died. Both Oneida's brother and sister came over in order to help out any way they could.

Fortunately, David recovered, and in July 1942, they had a third child, a boy named Andres. He strongly resembled his mother. Thereafter the family led a happy life.

A year later in June 1937, Master Sergeant Fred Hobbs, after completing his thirty years of military service, announced he was retiring. For Biway, this was a huge loss. After learning that his own father didn't serve in WWI when he was nine and before he met Sergeant Hobbs, Biway never really had a true role model to look up to. There were Hollywood actors such as Walter Huston and Richard Dix and hoodlums like Eddie Duggan and Jackie Brown, but these didn't satisfy Biway. What Biway truly needed was a father figure, and Sergeant Hobbs fit the bill. All Biway could do thereafter was to emulate him as much as possible. Sergeant Hobbs's replacement was a sergeant by the name of Paul Weaver, thirty-seven, but he and Biway never developed the same rapport.

When on liberty, Biway usually went to a nearby tavern or brothel to consort with Hispanic prostitutes, but on the base, a young female lieutenant by the name of Ms. Kim Gilmore, twenty-three, caught his eye. She was five feet, seven inches tall, weighed around 145 pounds, had reddish light brown hair, green eyes, and was quite attractive.

One Saturday morning after breakfast, Biway saw Kim standing in the hallway conversing with one of her friends. When they finished and as her friend walked away, Biway went up to her and asked, "Are you free tonight? If so, maybe we can go out and drink beer and have a good time."

Kim said nothing but slapped Biway as hard as she could and then said, "Does that answer your question, creep?" Biway just walked away with tears in his eyes and wondered, "What's wrong with some of these broads anyway?" That was on December 4, 1937. Six months later in June 1938, Biway was transferred to a Marine base near Manila in the Philippines.

This was the first time Biway was ever outside of the United States. He felt a little uneasy at first but soon got over it. The only thing Biway disliked about the Philippines was the lack of Hispanic prostitutes. It was also here in January 1939 that Biway was promoted to the rank of corporal, and he liked it. In January 1940, he was transferred back to Camp Pendleton in California. Here Biway could again consort with Hispanic prostitutes and he was well pleased.

One day in August 1941, Lieutenant Fred Webber, forty, called Corporal Biway into his office to announce to him that he was being promoted to the rank of sergeant. Biway was taken aback. He was only twenty-two, and no other Marine he knew of had ever achieved such a rank at such a tender age. Lieutenant Webber said to Biway, "For the last six years since you joined the Marine Corps, your record has been totally impeccable as you carried out each and every order without any questions or complaints. Moreover, you know how to inspire fear and give orders. Now I will assign you to becoming one of our drill instructors, that is, training and drumming raw recruits into becoming real Marines. Staff Sergeant Harlan Fortson will show you how to do it. Good luck with your new assignment, Sergeant Biway. Dismissed."

To Biway's chagrin, he was to hold that assignment for the next nine years, thus depriving him of any fighting in the Pacific throughout WWII, but orders were orders, and someone had to train these men. In the meantime, Biway developed a close friendship with a follow DI by the name of Sergeant John Ballard, forty-four. Ballard got his assignment in 1943 after returning from Camp Lejeune in North Carolina. It was there where he spent most of his career and where he met his wife, Nancy. They married in April 1928 when he was twenty- nine and she, twenty-one. On February 2, 1929, Nancy gave birth to a son, whom they named John Jr.

Unfortunately, the baby had Spinal Bifida from which it died six weeks later. One April 13, 1930, Nancy gave birth to their second son and named him Douglas. Fortunately, Douglas turned out to be quite healthy with no medical issues.

In February 1944, Sergeant Ballard was suddenly being reassigned to duty in the South Pacific, and this left Biway feeling another sense of loss.

In August 1944, a group of fresh recruits arrived at Camp Pendleton to be trained by Biway. Among these was a young man by the name of Leonard Rheem, twenty-one, and married, with whom Biway was to become a very close friend.

Leonard "Lenny" Rheem was born in Grand Rapids, Michigan, on December 31, 1922, the only son Leonard Rheem Sr. and his wife, Matilda, or Tilly, had together. Matilda had three other children from a previous marriage, but her husband was killed in France during WWI. Thereafter she moved from Escanaba on Michigan's Upper Peninsula to Grand Rapids, where her two brothers lived. One of them worked for the Rheem family, which was in the business of building appliances such as heaters and stoves.

It was through her brother that Matilda met Leonard Rheem, and the two were married on October 1, 1921. He was forty-three and she, thirty-one. They had a happy marriage, and Matilda's three older children adjusted nicely and were well taken care of. Leonard Jr., or Lenny, had a normal childhood, and as he grew up, he decided he wanted to fix heaters and appliances instead of just making them. After he graduated from East Side High School in 1941, he enrolled at Quentin Freeman School of Technology in Kalamazoo where he graduated two years later.

When on liberty together, Biway and Lenny would double date with Lenny and his wife, Aggie, and Biway and his "girlfriend," Sofia Diaz. Sofia was a Hispanic prostitute hired by Biway to pose as his girlfriend in order to impress Lenny and Aggie. Sofia was twenty-four, five feet, four inches tall, weighed around 130 pounds, had pitch-black hair and tawny skin. With the brown mold beneath her nose, she appeared to be rather homely. This went on until February 1945, when Lenny was ordered to ship out for combat duty.

As the battle for Okinawa commenced on April 20, Lenny and his outfit were sent in. The battle for northern Okinawa ended rather quickly, but on May 21, the battle for the southern half of the island began as ordered by the Japanese general Ushijima. On Monday, May 28, the squad Lenny was in decided to clear out a cave where some Japanese soldiers were holed up. Thinking that the defenders inside were already dead, Lenny's squad rushed in only to find the Japanese waiting for them. One of them threw a hand grenade into the middle of Lenny's squad, killing three, including Lenny himself, crippling two others, and leaving a sixth man permanently blind.

Eight days later on June 5, two Marines went to Aggie's apartment to notify her that Lenny was killed in action a week earlier on Okinawa. Both Aggie and Biway felt a great sense of loss, Aggie, her husband, and Biway, a close friend.

Aggie Rheem was born Christine Agnes Murphy on July 9, 1921, in Grand Rapids, Michigan, the first of Paul and Catherine Murphy's three children. The other two were Paul Jr., born on October 4, 1923, and Charles, born on April 9, 1925. As a child, Aggie didn't like her first name, so she asked everyone to call her by her middle name, which was Agnes, which was later shortened to Aggie. Aggie's father, Paul, and Leonard Rheem became close friends as they often did business together. It was in Leonard Sr.'s house that Aggie and Lenny first met, and during her last year of high school, they dated. After graduating in 1939, Aggie went on to the University of Michigan in Ann Arbor with a major in business. Lenny graduated 1941 and went to Quentin Freeman Technical School, where he graduated in 1943 with an associate degree in mechanics. After he returned to Grand Rapids, Lenny and Aggie resumed their relationship. Finally on October 16, 1943, they married.

In May 1944, Lenny was notified that he was being drafted, so he decided to enlist in the Marine Corps. In August 1944, he arrived at Camp Pendleton to start his basic training. It wasn't long after that he and Biway became close friends. However, the first time they went out together on liberty, Biway offered to introduce him to some choice prostitutes, but Lenny curtly replied, "Count me out. I have a great wife, and I will not two-time her." Biway understood and desisted. Two weeks later, Aggie showed up in the couple's 1934 Ford and rented a nearby apartment so she and Lenny could be together.

Aggie, with her very dark brown hair and rosy cheeks, did remind Biway somewhat of Diane De Wolfe. After Lenny shipped out that February, Biway and Aggie continued to see one another, but Biway always treated her with respect. Up to that point, with the exception of Diane De Wolfe, Biway's relations with other women were largely, if not entirely physical, but with Aggie, he felt differently.

Two days after she learned of Lenny's death, Aggie called her parents in Grand Rapids, Michigan, to tell them the news. Paul said they already knew since Leonard Sr. and wife, Tilly, were notified too. Paul asked Aggie to return to Grand Rapids, where he and his brother had a real estate business and offered her a full-time job as a Realtor trainee. Aggie agreed and told Biway the next day when they were out together, saying, "Tom, I no longer have any reason to stay here since Lenny's death. Yesterday, I talked to my father, and he wants me to return to Grand Rapids. I hope you don't mind."

Biway replied, "Of course not, but I really want to remain in touch with you."

Aggie replied, "Yes, Tom, as soon as I get settled in Grand Rapids, I'll write you and give you both my address and phone number once I get an apartment of my own."

Biway replied, "That'll be great."

On Sunday, June 10, Aggie collected all her personal belongings, got into her 1934 Ford, and started the grueling seven-day drive to Grand Rapids. At first, Biway wasn't sure if he would hear from her again, but on Monday, July 2, he did receive a letter from Aggie, saying, "Tom, everything here in Grand Rapids is working as well as planned. I'm learning to be a real estate agent, and I just rented my first apartment. It's quite nice. I hope that one day you'll be able to come up here and see what a nice city this really is. Yours truly, Aggie." Biway was once again excited at hearing from her. From then on, they corresponded on a regular basis.

On September 2, 1945, WWII officially ended with the Japanese signing a treaty with the UN agreeing to unconditional surrender. That same day, Biway was granted a twenty-eight-day furlough. The next day he packed his belongings, got into his black 1940 Ford Tudor Club Coupe, and began the grueling seven-day drive to Grand Rapids. He arrived there on Sunday afternoon, the ninth, and booked into a hotel. The next day after reading a map of the city, he located Murphy Brothers, Realtors, drove over there, and went in. He asked the man he saw, "Is there a certain Aggie Rheem working here?"

The man replied, "Yes, that's my niece. She's in the back office if you wish to talk to her."

That was Jerry Murphy, Paul's brother and partner. Biway went into the back office, and Aggie looked up and said, "Tom, what a surprise. Was the long drive up here very difficult?"

Biway replied, "Not really, but I'm not used to driving such long distances at a time. I'm staying at the Lieberman Hotel downtown. I just got in yesterday." Then Aggie said, "Tom, first I want to introduce you to my father, Paul, and my uncle Jerry." Both Paul and Jerry were quite cordial, as was Biway. Later that night, Biway and Aggie went out on a date. Biway said, "Aggie, I'm on a twenty-eight-day furlough. That means I'll have to start heading back on the twenty-third. I'm beginning to see why you love this town." On the twenty-third, Biway collected his belongings and began the grueling seven-day drive back to Camp Pendleton.

Between that time and Christmas, Biway and Aggie kept on corresponding although two other men did ask Aggie out for a date. Biway passed over his Thanksgiving furlough in order to extend his Christmas one. On December 14, he was granted another twenty- eight-day furlough and reached Grand Rapids on Thursday the twenty-first. Since Aggie invited him to meet her parents and they fully agreed to accept him, Biway went directly there where he was warmly received by the whole family.

On Thursday, December 27, two days after Christmas, when Aggie and Biway were dining at the Lombardy Inn in downtown Grand Rapids, Aggie said to Biway, "All the time we've been together, Tom, I noticed that you never mentioned your family or where you came from except that it was Utica, New York. You don't have to tell me anything about them or Utica if you'd rather not. I'm just curious."

Biway replied, "Aggie, I will tell you now. When I was seven, one Saturday night, I along with my parents, my two sisters, Terry and Suzy, and baby brother, Rick, were in a terrible automobile accident. Our car was struck by some drunken driver. Only Rick and I survived that accident. The drunk who hit us died too. That happened in 1926.

"Like I said before, I was seven, but Rick was barely a year old. Our grandmother, Mary, who was a widow at seventy-one and in frail health, turned us over to the St. Paul of Tarsus Orphanage. There my brother and I were treated horrifically by the priests, nuns, and monks. If we showed the slightest sign of disobedience or nonconformity, either one of the nuns would slap us hard, or in some cases, a monk would beat us with a barber strap. Worse than that, we were sometimes locked up in what they would call the Quiet Room and sometimes for days on end with nothing to eat. At times, the monks would abuse us sexually, and even one nun, by the name of Sister Mary Arnold, would get me alone and expose herself to me as well as other boys. Eventually my baby brother, Rick, died from this maltreatment, but I survived, and when I was sixteen, Brother Edward, who headed that terrible place, finally gave me permission to join the Marines, and that's what I've been doing ever since."

Aggie was awestricken upon hearing what Biway just told her. Finally she said, "Tom, I cannot believe that any of the Catholic clergy would behave in such a brutal matter. Sorry, Tom, I do find this a bit incredible."

Biway replied, "Yes, Aggie, that's the way they want you to feel. This is one well-kept secret, and the church has deep pockets in case either the police or any journalist developed any suspicions of what truly happened at least at that one orphanage. Moreover, Aggie, I do not wish to talk about it any further, and the abuse I had to undergo there will stay with me as long as I live, and to this day, my hatred for the priests and nuns has never abated."

Aggie then said to Biway, "Sorry, Tom. I never had any notion of what you went through. If your story is true, these people really need to be brought to justice."

Biway replied, "Yes, Aggie, but the problem is, how can anyone prove it?"

However, Biway lied about everything. The truth is, is that after his joining the Marine Corps, Susanna and Rick both got good counseling from two top flight psychologists, and even more fortunately, they had one another to lean on, and both eventually recovered both physically and emotionally. On the other hand, Hazel Tarleton, who was raped by Buddy Androszech, was far less fortunate. Although she recovered physically and was able to have children, she never recovered either emotionally or mentally and became very withdrawn and unsociable. Finally in September 1941, when she was sixteen, she and two other girls got together and decided to run off only never to be heard from again.

Although Biway wrote home on four or five different occasions shortly after joining the Marine Corps, he never got any response either from his parents or grandmother, Mary. However, his older sister, Terry, who was inclined to write him was told by her mother ("I absolutely forbid it!") and Terry didn't write him either.

Ironically, although Aggie found Biway's story somewhat incredible at first, once it sank in that it could well have taken place, and as she eventually put credence in it, her feelings for him grew even stronger.

Finally in August 1946, Biway decided to propose to Aggie, and Aggie readily said yes. The wedding took place on September 7, 1946, at St. Benedict's Church in Grand Rapids, Michigan. It was a gala event. Although Aggie's parents, friends, and relatives as well as Leonard and Tilly Rheem were present, Biway's friends were not.

As the memory of Biway's family, friends, and Utica itself slowly faded from his mind through the years and now was not only a member of the Marine Corps but also had a loving wife, he became extremely happy. He was now twenty-seven and she, twenty-five.

When his furlough ended two weeks after the wedding, Aggie sold her 1934 Ford, collected her belongings, and rode with Biway back to Camp Pendleton, the two sometimes taking turns driving Biway's 1940 Ford Club Coupe.

Soon after, they bought a small house in nearby San Ysidro and moved in. Soon Aggie became pregnant with their first child, and on August 18, 1947, Aggie gave birth to a girl, and they named her Catherine, in honor of her mother, Catherine Murphy, and gave her the middle name of Matilda, in honor of Lenny's mother. She turned out to be a healthy girl who resembled both her mother and father.

On April 22, 1950, Aggie gave birth to their second child, a boy whom they named Leonard in honor of Aggie's first husband, who was mortally wounded in Okinawa. Biway was happy and doted on his two children. For a present, one of Aggie's brothers gave them a bulldog pup whom Biway named Quince. However, in July 1950, shortly after the outbreak of the

Korean War, Biway went to his superior, Lieutenant Randolph Duffy and said, "Request for transfer, sir."

Lieutenant Duffy replied, "Why is that?"

Biway replied, "There's now a war in Korea, and I strongly wish to serve there, sir."

Then Duffy asked, "What about your wife and two kids?"

"They'll be all right, sir. As you see, all throughout the last war, I never saw any action, but I want to do my part now," Biway replied.

Finally Duffy said, "Request granted. Dismissed." Biway replied, "Thank you, sir."

CHAPTER 5

The Nancy Ballard Affair

In April 1947, a group of new recruits arrived at Camp Pendleton who were to be trained by Biway himself. Among these was Douglas Ballard, who just turned seventeen, the son of the late sergeant John Ballard and his wife, Nancy. Since Douglas was so adamant about joining the Marine Corps, Nancy signed the necessary papers, and Doug enlisted before finishing high school.

Although Biway knew Nancy for more than four years, he always noticed what a nice figure she had; although with her glasses and mousy graying brown hair, she considered herself to be something of a plain Jane, but that July after Doug was transferred to another base near Seattle, Washington, the temptation for Biway grew ever greater. For Biway, seeing Doug's mother, Nancy, was like a great itch he couldn't scratch. On Wednesday, July 16, the day before Nancy's forty-first birthday, Biway showed up at the office on the base where she worked and asked her, "Are you free tonight, Nancy?"

After two seconds of hesitation, Nancy replied, "As a matter of fact, I am, Tom."

Then Biway said, "Well, that settles it. I'll see you at five o'clock sharp."

Nancy was taken aback by the sudden attention she received from such a young man. At 5:00 p.m., Biway showed up, and the two went to a nearby tavern to have beer and dance. Although Biway strongly wanted to have sex with her, he was careful to treat Nancy nicely, and when he took her home around 10:00 p.m., he suddenly kissed her on the lips and then apologized, saying, "I'm sorry, Nancy, please forgive me. I just got carried away. It won't happen again, I assure you."

Nancy replied, "That's all right, Tom. I had just as great a time as you did tonight. In fact, I'd like to go out with you again, but I know you're happily married, and we shouldn't be doing this."

In fact, Biway loved his wife, Aggie, very much, and his relationship with her was total bliss, but as for Nancy, his feelings toward her were totally physical, but he couldn't help himself. When he was with Nancy, his willpower would give way to his carnal desires, but then again, Biway never put any checks on those. The following Saturday night, Biway and Nancy went out for the second time, but when he took her home, she invited him in, and the two had a nightcap together. Suddenly Biway asked her outright, "Can we have sex?"

Nancy, who was not surprised, said, "Yes, Tom. I haven't had any sex since my husband went overseas and subsequently killed in the Philippines." Then both went to bed. Ever since Biway consorted with Oneida Sandoval back in the 1930s, he never enjoyed having sex as much as he did that night. Both knew this was wrong, but neither could help themselves. Biway, because he was happily married to Aggie, and Nancy, because she didn't want to embarrass her son, Doug. Both were careful to cover this up as it went on for several months thereafter.

Nancy Ballard was born Nancy Peterson on July 17, 1906, in Walnut Cove, North Carolina, the third child of John and Dorothy Peterson. The others were John Jr., born on June 4, 1902, but died some eight weeks later from cerebral palsy; Delilah, born on November 18, 1903; then Nancy; George on September 3, 1910; and finally, Mary Louise on August 12, 1914. Nancy had a very normal childhood. Her father, John, was born in Norway in 1871 under the name of Johann Peterson but later anglicized his name to John Peterson after immigrating along with his older brother, Viktor, to the United States in 1892.

Nancy's father, John, was six feet, one inch tall and weighed close to 215 pounds. He had black hair and was rather homely, and Nancy and her brother George strongly resembled him. Nancy's mother, Dorothy, on the other hand, was quite petite, five feet, four inches tall and weighed around 128 pounds with blond hair and black eyebrows. The two were married in 1900 when he was twenty-eight and she, twenty.

Nancy graduated from Walnut Cove High School in 1924 and went on to George Graham Business College in nearby Danville, Virginia, along with her childhood friend Quinn Murdock. Both graduated from there in 1926 and went to work at Camp Lejeune as stenographers for the Marine Corps. In July 1927, Quinn married her high school sweetheart and returned to Walnut Cove, but Nancy stayed on. In the meantime, she met a certain corporal by the name of John Ballard, whom she started dating. The two were married in April 1928 and had two children, John, who died in 1929 shortly after his birth, and Douglas, born a year later. In 1932, John was reassigned to duty in the Philippines, and Nancy along with two-year-old Doug followed him there.

After six months, John said to Nancy, "I do not wish to have our son raised in this jungle where there are all kinds of tropical diseases and where almost nobody speaks English. Therefore I want you and Doug to go back to North Carolina, where he can be raised properly."

Nancy replied, "John, I guess you're right. I was thinking of myself and my strong desire to be near you. I'll take Doug and myself back on the next ship to California." In 1936, John Ballard returned to Camp Lejeune and was promoted to the rank of sergeant a month later. In the summer of 1943, as he was reassigned to Camp Pendleton, Nancy and Doug followed him there, where Nancy was hired as a stenographer in an office on the base. Even after John was killed in action in October 1944, Nancy kept her job and continued to raise Doug there since she considered Southern California a great place to raise a child.

The affair between Nancy and Biway went on for months on end, but both were careful and successfully covered it up. Sometimes the two would drive as far away as places like Joshua Tree, Victorville, Apple Valley, Mexicali, and San Bernardino, where neither of them were known.

Finally in May 1948, things came to a head. One day Nancy went to work and noticed she had a case of nausea, and it continued for the next two days. She decided to see a doctor on the base, and he had the nurse administer a rabbit test on her on Wednesday, May 19. The results came back five days later, and the test proved positive. The nurse told Nancy she was going to have a baby, but Nancy was convinced that since the birth of Doug, she could have no more children. Then Nancy thought, "Oh my god, what am I going to tell Tom? I'll have to tell him, and what about my boy, Doug? He'll be totally embarrassed."

The next day, she called Biway, saying, "Tom, there's something I have to tell you, but I can't do it over the phone. Can you come over tonight?"

Biway replied, "I suppose so, but what's so urgent? I'll be there around five thirty."

During the months when the affair continued, Nancy fell more and more in love with Biway, but that feeling was not reciprocated. Had Biway not been so happily married to Aggie and doted on his newborn daughter, that may have turned out differently. In fact, Nancy may well have been the woman for Biway had it not been for Aggie.

When Biway arrived at Nancy's apartment as promised, Nancy tearfully said to him, "Tom, I'm going to have a baby, and I need to tell you now."

Upon hearing this, Biway's face turned almost purple with rage. He started fuming and slapped Nancy across the face as hard as he could and then said in an outburst, "You lied to me, you— ! You told me you couldn't have any more children after Doug was born. Why did you do it?"

Nancy replied, "Tom, this was a total surprise to me too. I was totally convinced I could not have any more children. I really didn't plan this, it just happened. Please, Tom, forgive me." Nancy was sincere.

Biway replied, "I'd better get out of here before I really hurt you. I never want to see your ugly face or hear from you again!"

Thereafter he went to a local saloon and started drinking heavily, trying to drown the rage he felt. He returned home later and told his wife, Aggie, "I'm sorry for being this drunk but this bozo in my outfit made me so mad I could hardly control myself." Thereafter he went to bed and passed out.

As for Nancy, she too drank heavily after Biway left, went to bed, and passed out. The next day she called her sister Mary Louise in San Jose, who lived with her husband, Reverend Lonnie Humbolt, and their two sons. Mary said, "I want you to get all your things together and come up here as soon as you can. Lonnie and I will see you through this, I promise. Did you call Mom and Dad yet?"

Nancy replied, "No, but I will later. I already told my two friends at work, and they'll come over after work around five thirty. to be with me. I should be in San Jose by either Sunday or Monday. I'll see you then."

By Saturday, May 29 around 10:30 a.m., Nancy packed her belongings, got into her green 1942 Ford Club Coupe, and headed north on US

Highway 101 toward San Jose. The drive was grueling, especially passing through Los Angeles. By about 5:30 p.m. and not wanting to drive any farther, Nancy checked into a local motel just west of Santa Barbara. After eating a rather large meal, she went to a local liquor store, purchased a quart-size bottle of vodka, and retired to her motel. She drank rather heavily that night and drank two more highballs before checking out around 8:00 a.m. the next morning. An hour later as she was driving through the small town of Gaviota, a ten- year-old boy who was delivering Sunday morning papers to his clients decided to ride his bike across the highway in front of her. Unfortunately, she was driving at a rather high rate of speed, and with her judgment already alcohol impaired, she slammed into the paperboy's bike, first slamming his head on the hood of her car and then throwing him to the right. She stopped as fast as she could, but upon seeing the paperboy lying there, she suddenly became filled with sheer panic and drove off as fast as she could. She thought to herself, *Oh my god, what have I done? I just can't take jail right now. If I stayed, the police will smell vodka on my breath and arrest me. I just hope and pray that someone else finds this boy and gets him the help he needs. Surely to God, he'll be all right.*

Fortunately for Nancy, it never occurred to her to turn the car radio on, so she never knew that the paperboy was found around forty-five minutes later and rushed to Mt. Carmel Mercy Hospital in Santa Barbara, where he died shortly after 1:00 p.m. that afternoon from a fractured skull and broken neck.

The paperboy's name was John Phillips, ten, the youngest son of Michael and Lydia Ann Phillips. He was found by a farmer just coming into town on his way to church, and he called an ambulance right away. Unfortunately for the boy, it was too late. He had a fractured skull, and his neck was broken, so he couldn't breathe.

About an hour and a half later, as Nancy, who was slowly sobering up, pulled off on a side road to examine the damage to her car. The right side of the hood had a gash in it, and the right headlight was cracked. There was also blood and hair on the car belonging to the paperboy. Nancy then unpacked one of her suitcases, took out a red sweater, and urinated on it in order to wash the blood and hair from the damaged part of her car. Thereafter she threw the sweater into a nearby creek and continued her drive north toward San Jose.

She reached San Jose a little after 6:00 p.m. and her sister's house around 7:00 p.m. Mary Louise and her husband, Lonnie, were glad to see her. The next day she called her parents in North Carolina and told them about her pregnancy. Both were sympathetic toward her.

As for Biway, he was apprehensive that somehow either Nancy or one of her friends would contact Aggie and tell her about the affair, but as the weeks passed, Biway began to breathe easier. He no longer had to feel guilty over two-timing Aggie.

In the meantime, that October when Doug was on furlough, he found out his mother was pregnant and wanted to know who the father was, so he drove to San Jose to consult with her. When he got there, he angrily asked his mother, "Who's the father of your baby, Mom, and how could you let this happen? Don't you know what a disgrace to our family this is? At least, Mom, tell me who the baby's father is."

Nancy replied, "It's Corporal Ted Larson. Somehow he got around me, and before I knew it, we were having sex. I well knew how wrong this was, but he was quite persuasive, so I finally gave in. I'm sorry, Doug, for letting you down."

Nancy lied to her son. Actually, the true Corporal Ted Larson was killed in the Philippines in October 1944 along with his superior and her late husband, Sergeant John Ballard. He was twenty-six, married, with two children and lived in Chicago.

After the confrontation with his mother, Doug decided to write only to his aunt Mary, and he asked her, "Is it true what Mom said about Ted Larson?"

Mary replied, "Yes, Doug, it is."

On January 16, 1949, Nancy had her baby. It turned out to be a six- pound, seven-ounce girl whom Nancy named Quinn in honor of her childhood friend in North Carolina. Her friend Quinn died on March 25, 1946, at the age of thirty-nine after a long bout with stomach cancer. She left behind her husband, Rex Whitley, along with her two children, Robert, seventeen, and Judy, fifteen. Nancy and Quinn Whitley had been close friends since they were both five years old.

To cover up the fact that baby Quinn was born out of wedlock, Mary and Lonnie told their friends that Nancy's husband died shortly after she conceived her.

In the meantime, Doug slowly began to regret treating his mother so harshly and finally told his aunt Mary about it in a letter. In January 1950 shortly before he was to ship out to the Umayoshi Marine Base in Japan, Mary wrote him. Along with the letter, she sent him a picture of Quinn taken on her first birthday. He was taken aback by just how much Quinn not only looked like their mother but him as well. She had very light-brown hair like he did and had a rather large brown mold right under her nose on the left side. Thereafter he gradually began to take pride in the fact that he had a baby sister.

After Doug arrived in Japan early in 1950, he decided to reconcile with his mother, Nancy, and told her in a letter that the situation in Korea appeared to be getting more volatile with each passing day. He was right. On June 25, 1950, the Korean War erupted, and Doug himself was to partake in the amphibious landing at Inchon on September 15. After the successful landing, Doug and his outfit were to push farther inland. As the war progressed, Doug became increasingly sick by the brutality of the war and especially the needless killing of women and children. In time, he wondered, *Just why are we here killing all these people and just how much of a threat can they possibly pose to the US?* He was becoming increasingly disillusioned by the war and the Marine Corps itself, and moreover, he hated his immediate superior, Sergeant Lloyd Rodgers, fifty-four. Sergeant Rodgers was five feet five inches, rather stocky, had gray hair, wore thick glasses, and had a hair-trigger temper. He would not hesitate to either beat or kick one of his underlings on the spot, and he already did it to Doug twice.

Finally Doug wrote to his mother, saying, "Mom, I've only been in Korea for the last month and a half, and I find this place excruciatingly horrific. Every day now I see men, women, and children being slaughtered like pigs in a pen and even babies cut to ribbons and thrown on the side of the road. Right now things are looking up as North Korea appears to be on the verge of collapse since they cannot stop us from reaching the Yalu River. Hopefully, this miserable war will be over by Christmas. Even if it's not, I will not serve another four years in the Marine Corps as my term of enlistment expires next April. I'm hoping to come home soon and meet my baby sister, Quinn. Love, your son, Doug."

On November 24, the situation in Korea suddenly changed with the Chinese entry into the conflict in order to halt the UN advance toward the Yalu and help North Korea unite itself with the South.

As the Chinese were rapidly advancing southward, it was by sheer luck that Doug and his outfit were evacuated in the nick of time. Other Marine units were less fortunate as most of the them wound up either dead or as prisoners of war in North Korea.

Finally in April 1951, Doug told Captain Charles Doesberg that he was not going to renew his enlistment in the Marine Corps. Captain Doesberg said to Doug, "Don't you know that we're in the middle of a war here and we need men like you to help us defend our country? Have you lost your mind?"

Doug curtly replied, "No, sir. Quite the contrary, I came to my senses, and I want out as soon as possible, and that's all there is to it, sir."

Doesberg replied, "Have it your way, Ballard, and good luck to you. Dismissed."

In May 1951 after being discharged from the Marine Corps, Doug arrived at the apartment in San Jose where his mother along with his two-year-old half sister, Quinn, lived. Nancy was tickled to see him once more and share her apartment with him. Since arriving in San Jose three years earlier, Nancy got a job first as a file clerk and eventually became a legal secretary at the law firm known as Barclay, Stevens, and Stevens, Attorneys at Law. Shortly after moving in with his mother and baby half-sister, Doug applied to join the California

Highway Patrol (CHP). However, since he didn't finish high school, his application was rejected. He then got a job at Viking Press Inc. and eventually became a forklift operator, but he still longed to join the CHP, so since he worked nights, he took a GED course in a local school and finally got his high school equivalent degree, and with that, the CHP accepted him in October 1952.

After Nancy got her job at Barclay, Stevens, and Stevens, she met Nate Barclay, who was the head lawyer at the firm and a lifelong bachelor who was already in his fifties. He and Nancy began dating and finally got married on April 25, 1953. The wedding took place at St. Michael's Lutheran Church with Lionel Humbolt, Nancy's brother- in-law, officiating. Nate was fifty-two and Nancy, forty-six. He also adopted Quinn and gave her his last name. Both were quite happy thereafter.

In the meantime after the outbreak of the Korean War in June 1950, Biway requested and received a transfer to a combat unit. However, it would be another year before he went overseas. In October 1951, he arrived at the Umayoshi Marine Base, where Doug Ballard was assigned earlier. He felt that he finally arrived and was anxious to join the war to prove his military skills. In May 1952, Biway and his unit were notified that they were to ship out to Korea on the thirtieth. Two weeks earlier, Aggie along with their two children, Catherine (Kitty), four, and Lenny, two, came to Japan to visit Biway before he shipped out. Biway was accorded a week's liberty so he and his wife and kids could be together. That night in the hotel where they were staying, Aggie said, "Tom, I'm frightened. I want you to come back safe and sound and be with me and the children."

Biway replied, "Don't worry, Aggie, I will, but first I need to serve my country and deal a blow to this menace they call Communism. Besides, other women are going through the same thing as you are."

After that week, Aggie and the children returned to San Ysidro, and Biway along with his outfit arrived in Korea on the thirtieth. Although Biway was enthusiastic and even euphoric, the rest of his outfit was rather apprehensive and didn't really wish to be there.

In July while trying to take Pork Chop Hill back from the Chinese, Biway suddenly jumped up and almost single-handedly shot three of the Chinese defenders dead before jumping back into his foxhole, and later that day, he was awarded his first medal. Now he was fast becoming a war hero, and that made him even more euphoric. He appeared to his fellow Marines to be somewhat indestructible since it seemed that no matter how much the Chinese fired on him, he was never hit.

As Biway enthusiastically fought the war and as the months went on, he was performing acts of heroism, collecting more and more medals for his efforts, and wrote Aggie to brag about it. It was on April 13, 1953, at Heartbreak Ridge that Biway received the Bronze Star as the crowning point of his career. To his credit, he was commended for killing twenty-one men, three of them with his bare hands, and that made him proud.

However, later on July 27, the Korean Truce was announced and went into effect. This deeply disappointed Biway as he was hoping for a military victory similar to the one in WWII. He felt that his heroic efforts went to waste, and sooner or later, either the North Koreans or the Chinese would break the truce, or so he hoped.

After he returned to Camp Pendleton in October and later learned of the loss of his son, Lenny, he became even more unhappy, and after the birth and death of his and Aggie's third child, Paul, in March 1955, Biway devoted himself almost entirely to the Marine Corps, and when he did go on liberty, he usually went to a local brothel to consort with some Hispanic prostitute rather than go home to Aggie and Kitty. In the meantime, Aggie, who felt the same losses Biway did, began looking for business opportunities and finally met Bill Decker. Aggie filed for divorce, and Biway didn't contest it, feeling that Aggie would be better off with someone else. After the divorce was granted on April 1, 1959, Aggie and Bill made plans for their wedding, which was to take place in Marysville, California, on June 12, 1959, with Biway himself being invited.

In November 1958, shortly before the divorce, Biway applied for and received a command position at the Umayoshi Marine base in Japan, where he served before.

CHAPTER 6

The Courts Martial of PFC Hermann C. Mettler, USMC

As he was approaching his fifty-fifth birthday on December 12, 1958, which was the mandatory retirement age for all Marine NCOs, Sergeant Dan Flannigan held inspection in order to say goodbye to the men under his command. They were sad to see him go, but that was the policy of the Marine Corps. That day, Second Lieutenant Preston Fuchs assumed command pending the arrival of Sergeant Biway. Biway arrived at the base on Friday, December 19 and around 6:00 p.m. (or 1800 hours military time). Biway called his first inspection. The troops lined up, and Biway inspected each and every one of them. He came upon a blond soldier who was six feet tall and very slim. Biway stopped to ask him, "Hey, you, what's your name?" and the soldier replied, "Sutton, sir. Private Dan Sutton, sir" and Biway went on. Next, he stopped and said to another soldier, "Hey, you, what's your name?" and the soldier replied, "Mettler, sir. Private First Class Hermann Mettler, sir.'. Then Biway said to him, "What's that I smell on your breath?" and the soldier replied, "I had a little snort a while ago, and it won't happen again, sir." Biway yelled out to Mettler, "Fall out and do twenty-five laps around the field!" and said to the others, "Has anyone else here been drinking?" After he finished inspecting the troops, he turned to them and said, "From now on, I want this platoon to be the fittest and the best one here in Japan, and the barracks and the windows are to be cleaned, and I mean, white- glove clean, and I will tolerate no one getting drunk here especially while on duty. Am I understood?" The men all said in unison, "Yes, sir, you are, sir!"

Some of the men already started grumbling, and one said, "I don't think I'm going to like this new dude. He seems not to give an inch, like everyone has to be perfect."

Another said, "It appears that this Biway or Hiway fellow would sooner throw you in jail as look at you."

On his way as he was being transported to the base from his ship, he noticed a bunch of young Japanese women hanging around outside the base and turned to the corporal driving the truck he was in to ask him, "Just what are those broads doing there? Are they prostitutes or what?"

The corporal replied, "Yes, sir, they are."

Then Biway said, "My only regret is that there are no Hispanic ones among them."

The driver, out of sheer curiosity, asked, "Why did you say that, sir?"

Biway replied, "That's simple. Since the Hispanic ones are my favorite fun. You ought to come to Southern California, there is a whole slew of them there."

About two weeks later, Biway approached Private Sutton and said, "Young man, how well do you know this Private Mettler? You and he seem to be quite chummy."

Sutton replied, "Yes, we are, sir. I've known him almost ever since I've been here, sir."

Private Dan Sutton was twenty-two at that time and had been in the Marine Corps since 1956, after his high school graduation in St. Louis, Missouri. He lived with his parents and had a girlfriend by the name of Nancy Ward, whom he met and dated in high school.

On Christmas Day 1958, during which the Marines were enjoying their Christmas dinner, Biway sitting at a table next to the one Mettler was at, overheard Mettler bragging about his seven-month-old son, Quentin, and showed the men who were dining with him a picture of the child. As Biway was overhearing the conversation, his eyes suddenly became filled with tears as this reminded him of the painful loss of his own two sons. Suddenly Biway got up, went out to the PX, bought a quart-sized bottle of vodka and a box of Swisher cigars and retired to his quarters for the night. In time, his desire to do Pfc. Mettler in became a near obsession.

One day two weeks later, Biway approached Private Sutton and asked him, "Are you a career Marine?"

Sutton replied, "No, I'm not, sir. I'm just here to fulfill my military obligations, which will be over by the middle of next year, sir." Then Biway said, "Dan, I have a new assignment for you. I want you to continue being chummy with this Mettler dude and report to me when, where, or how much drinking he does at any one time. The very last thing I want is to have some worthless, habitual drunk in this squad, Dan.

"Would it be all right if I called you Dan from now on? I want you to call me Tom if that's all right with you."

Sutton replied, "Yes, Tom, I'd like that very much, but why are you so determined to punish Private First Class Mettler? He is a good man and follows orders just like the rest of us. The only fault he has is that he sometimes gets a little carried away when he drinks."

In fact, Sutton was right. Private First Class Mettler had always been a capable Marine without any serious health or mental problems.

Private First Class Hermann Mettler was born Hermann Clyde Mettler on July 24, 1915, on a farm near Mt. Vernon, Indiana, the second of three children born to Hermann Sr. and Julia Mettler. His sister, Ines, was born on November 12, 1913, and his brother, William, on September 4, 1917, just before Hermann Sr. was drafted into the US Army in order to fight in France during WWI.

While he was in the Army, Hermann Sr. learned how to both operate and fix radios, and after he returned home, he started looking for work in that field and was finally hired by his cousin in Chester, Illinois. In 1921, he sold the family farm and moved there with his family. After 1934, when Hermann Jr. graduated from Chester High School, he decided to go to St. Louis up the river to find a job. After two years of fruitlessly looking for work, he returned to Chester. In 1938, he again went to St. Louis and wound up working at the International Shoe Factory. In July 1940, Mettler was notified he was being drafted, so he enlisted in the Marine Corps instead on August 1.

Fearing that the national economy would once again fall into another depression, Mettler decided to remain in the Marine Corps until he was to retire on August 1, 1960, at the end of his twenty-year career.

During WWII, he served in the Pacific and managed to escape being either wounded seriously or captured. While serving in the Philippines, he befriended two other Marines, Corporal Tom Posey, thirty-three, and

Private First Class Mark Foster, thirty. Mark Foster was from Salina, Kansas, and still single. He lived with his parents and younger siblings, including his sister Dorothy, who was twenty-one, in 1946 when Mark introduced her to his close friend Hermann shortly after the war.

After Mark Foster introduced his sister, Dorothy, to Mettler, the two started dating almost right away. Mettler was five feet, eleven inches tall, weighed around 215 pounds, had rather kinky black hair, and at thirty, he developed a bald spot on the back of his head, but Dorothy still found him attractive, and he had a rather gentle look on his face. In fact, the men in his squad often referred to him as the Gentle Giant.

The two were married on September 6, 1947, in Salina. He was thirty-two and she, twenty-two. At Mettler's insistence, Dorothy agreed to move to Chester, Illinois, where his parents and younger brother lived. His sister, Ines, had since married and moved to California. In the meantime, Dorothy became homesick not only for her family but for Kansas as well. Finally in 1951, the two agreed to buy a small house in Ft. Scott, Kansas, and settle there. The surrounding countryside was beautiful, and it was a very good place to raise a family. When Dorothy moved into her new home in Ft. Scott, she and Mettler already had two children, a boy, Steven, two, and a girl, Tilly, one. This was where Mettler planned to spend the rest of his life upon retiring from the Marine Corps, but unfortunately, Biway had other plans for him.

One night, Biway came to Sutton and said, "Dan, Corporal Alain Fouchet, my negro corporal, is leaving the Marine Corps at the end of January. I'd very much like to have you as his replacement and promote you to that rank. Do you accept?" Sutton replied.

"I'll need time to think it over. However, it does sound good to me." Two nights later, Biway said to Sutton as he was getting ready to retire to his quarters for the night, "Dan, I have something I wish to show you," and beckoned Sutton to come over to the Motor Pool lounge. He showed Sutton a two-door white 1954 Ford Fairlane, and Sutton said, "Tom, that is one handsome piece of machinery. I'd like to own one just like that someday."

Biway replied, "Dan, it's mine. I just bought it today for $500," and asked Sutton to inspect it, and Sutton did. Sutton finally said, "Tom, you made a very good deal."

A week later, Sutton came to Biway and said, "Tom, if you still want, I'll accept your offer and take the promotion."

Biway replied, "Great. As of February 1, 1959, you will be promoted to the rank of corporal. But in the meantime, Dan, did you find out any more about Mettler's excessive drinking?"

Sutton replied, "No, Tom, but I'll get on it right away."

A month later on the night of March 11, just outside the Motor Pool lounge, Biway saw Mettler, who was purportedly on duty, fast asleep by the left front wheel of one of the Marine trucks which had been parked there, and called it to Sutton's attention, saying, "Dan, I told you that this Mettler dude would sooner or later get drunk and mess up. It's high time we did something about it."

Sutton replied, "Tom, please don't be so harsh. Mettler only has another year and a half in the Corps left to serve, and then he'll be out for good. Please, Tom, try to overlook it, at least this time."

Biway replied, "Yes, Dan, this time. I'll let it ride, but this is definitely the last time."

The next day, Sutton went to Mettler and said, "Hermann, as you know, Sergeant Biway's out to get you, and he saw you sleeping at the wheel of one of the trucks. He told me to keep track of your drinking and report back to him." Mettler replied, "All right, Dan, I'll be more careful next time."

However, Biway not trusting Sutton fully would watch Mettler throw empty bottles of bourbon into the trash bins around the base, and Biway would use a pair of gloves to retrieve those bottles one by one. Finally after collecting six or seven of them, he went to his immediate superior, Second Lieutenant Preston Fuchs, and said, "Request to have these bottles taken to the naval forensics lab to be examined for fingerprints, sir. I have a habitual drunk in my squad, and I want him discharged as soon as possible."

Second Lieutenant Fuchs replied, "Request granted, sir."

On Tuesday, March 24, two Marine MPs came to Mettler and informed him that he was being court-martialed. Mettler was taken aback and asked them why, but they simply put him in handcuffs and led him from his quarters. As he was being led away, he saw Sutton going into Biway's office. Sutton looked back at Mettler and saw a very hurt look on his face. Evidently, Mettler thought that Sutton and Biway were in cahoots. After he entered Biway's office, Sutton said to him, "Why are they arresting Mettler? He cleaned up his drinking rather nicely."

Biway simply replied, "Did he really? I don't think so." Sutton then said, "You had to do it, Biway, didn't you!" Biway replied, "Yes, I did, and now get out of here!"

Later that day, Mettler was taken before the Marine Disciplinary Board, and they informed him he was being charged with conduct unbecoming a Marine, drinking while on duty and dereliction of same. Mettler pleaded guilty but was hoping that the board would be lenient due to his long military record and simply fine him, but he was wrong. Biway recommended to the board that Mettler be given a dishonorable discharge as an example to the other men under his command. Captain Robert Cowan, fifty, who headed the board, said, "Having heard both sides of this issue, you will have our decision on Tuesday the thirty-first, a week from today at 0900 hours. Hearing adjourned. In the meantime, Private First Class Mettler is to be confined to quarters."

At 9:00 a.m. on March 31 with Mettler, Sutton, and Biway sitting before the board, Captain Cowan announced his decision, saying, "Our decision is this. Due to the strongly worded recommendation of Sergeant Biway and Prosecutor Lieutenant Kilbourn, Private First Class Hermann Mettler is now dishonorably discharged from the Marine Corps with all honors and pay forfeited." Both Mettler and Sutton were totally stunned by this decision, but Biway smirked as he was delighted he got his way.

As Mettler gathered his belongings, the other Marines noticed how stunned Mettler was, and all knew it meant only one thing and that was Mettler's dishonorable discharge and wondered how Biway could have been so heartless. In time, the men in Biway's unit all universally despised him for what he did to Mettler.

A week later, Hermann Mettler returned to his family in Ft. Scott, Kansas, a broken man. He was no longer a Marine and with his dishonorable discharge, he was unable to find employment. By this time, he and Dorothy had four children, Steven, nine; Matilda, eight; Sharon, seven; and Quentin, who was not quite a year old.

Eventually Hermann and Dorothy had to sell their home in Ft. Scott and move in with Dorothy's parents in Salina. Eventually Mettler got a dishwasher job in a restaurant in nearby Abilene.

That Saturday night following Mettler's discharge, Biway said to Sutton, "Come on, Dan, let's go out and have some fun with those—." Sutton simply replied, "Is that an order, Biway?" Biway said, "No, Dan, it isn't."

On Friday, April 3, Captain Guy Maddox, forty, came to Biway and awarded him a silver medal, commending him for the discipline he instilled in his troops and getting rid of Private First Class Mettler.

On Sunday morning, April 12, Biway noticed there was a letter in his mailbox without an envelope. He took it out and read it. It said, "Biway, your days as commander of this squad are numbered. One night while you're sleeping, one of us will sneak into your quarters and put a bullet in the back of your miserable head. If not, while out on the open field, one of our bullets will find its way either to your head or back through your spine. One of these days you will die if you don't go to Captain Guy Maddox and request a transfer, and you better do it soon too." The letter was printed in capital letters and unsigned.

At 10:00 a.m., Biway called inspection and said to the men, "I have a letter here which I will read to all of you." Biway proceeded to read the letter aloud so all the men could hear what it said. After he finished, Biway yelled out, "Which one of you wrote this letter, and I want to know now, not tomorrow. Come on, speak up! If any of you know who wrote it, tell me even if you have to do so in my quarters in private." None of the men answered. They just stood there in total silence. Finally Biway said, "Unless I hear from any of you by 0900 hours tomorrow, this whole platoon goes into lockdown for the next thirty days. Dismissed."

As to be expected by 9:00 a.m. the next day, the whole platoon went into lockdown for the next thirty days, and by May 13, at the end of those thirty days, no one except for the writer himself knew who wrote Biway that letter. A week later on Wednesday, May 20, one of the men found a baby turtle crawling by the side of a road, picked it up, and showed it to two of the other men with him. Biway walked up to them to find out what was going on. One of them said, "We have a baby turtle here and we want to take it to the woods and turn it loose so it wouldn't get run over, sir."

Biway replied, "Just give the damn thing to me and I'll take care of it." Once he got hold of it, he slammed it as hard as he could against the pavement and then crushed it with his foot. All three men looked at Biway without saying anything, but Biway knew by the look in their eyes just how passionately they hated him.

Now seeing how much the men under his command hated him and looking forward to the upcoming wedding of his ex-wife, Aggie, Biway went to his superior, Second Lieutenant Preston Fuchs, and said, "Request permission to see Captain Guy Maddox, sir." Fuchs replied, "Permission granted," and Biway went to report to Captain Maddox, saying, "Request to go on furlough in order to attend my ex-wife's wedding next month and a transfer back to Camp Pendleton, sir." Maddox replied, "Permission granted for both your furlough and your transfer back to California. You will report to Camp Pendleton on July 1, next. You earned it, Biway. Dismissed and good luck."

On Monday, May 25, Second Lieutenant Fuchs called inspection and said, "Sergeant Biway is returning to Camp Pendleton, and I am now in charge here." Later as the men saw Biway gather his belongings, put them in his car, and drive off, some of them made obscene gestures at him as he was leaving Camp Umayoshi for the nearby dock in order to have his car shipped back with him. On Monday, June 1, Biway was replaced by Corporal Jack Lay, twenty- five, since Corporal Sutton refused that promotion. The mood among the men under Biway's command was almost festive since they were all glad to see him go.

On June 2, Biway disembarked in San Francisco and drove straight north to Marysville in order to attend Aggie's wedding and see his daughter Kitty once again. She was eleven and ready for the seventh grade in school. As usual, he was welcomed with open arms and invited to stay at Bill Decker's house until the wedding was to take place.

The wedding took place on Friday, June 12, as planned at St. Aloysius Catholic Church since Bill Decker decided to convert to Catholicism for Aggie's sake. It was a gala affair.

On July 1, Biway reported to Camp Pendleton for his new command. Remembering Camp Umayoshi, he realized just how far the men could be pushed, so he became more mellow toward the men under his new command but firm. There he remained until September 1963 when he was reassigned to the Marine Academy at Quantico, Virginia, for the purpose of training basics to future Marine officers.

In the meantime in Marysville on January 3, 1961, Aggie gave birth to a baby boy, and they named it Bruce, followed a year and a half later on July 21, 1962 by the birth of a second son, whom they named Robert. Both Bill and Aggie were elated, and Kitty was proud to have two baby brothers in the family. Bruce resembled Aggie, while Robert strongly resembled Bill.

After he was reassigned to Quantico, Biway was happy except for one thing, the lack of Hispanic prostitutes. In the meantime, he and Aggie would correspond on a regular basis.

In Pursuit of Ms. Carla Meyer

On a Saturday morning, July 11, 1964, while Biway was on a forty-eight-hour liberty from the base, he was staying at the Alexandria Hilton in Alexandria, Virginia, lounging by the swimming pool and around 11:00 a.m., he noticed a young girl coming out of the pool clad in a pink bikini showing her near perfect body, and he also noticed her voluptuous lips. At that time, bikinis were coming into style, and more and more women began to wear them in public. Later that day, he saw the same girl having lunch with two of her friends in the hotel cafeteria. Finally Biway approached the hotel clerk and asked, "Sir, who is that young lady, the one with the dark-brown hair?"

The clerk replied, "Oh, that's Ms. Carla Meyer, the niece of the Austrian consul, Erich Meyer. Erich and his wife invited her here to spend the summer with them. However, she hardly knows how to speak English, and this is the first time in her life she was anywhere outside of Europe. She is now studying to become a high school history teacher."

Biway said, "Thank you, sir. You've been a great help."

From then on, every time he went on liberty, Biway would return to the hotel and watch to see if Carla was there. She was usually there with her friends, and once Biway even followed her to her uncle Erich's house in the suburbs.

Finally one Friday night after arriving at the Alexandria Hilton, he decided to approach Carla directly and offer to buy her a drink. Carla, not quite understanding Biway's question, turned to one of her friends and asked her in German, "Was wunscht er?"

The friend said, "Dieser Mensch wunscht Ihnen um kennen zu lehrnen."

Carla replied, "Musse ich da tun?"

The friend said, "Es wurde besser sein."

Accompanied by her friends, Carla accepted Biway's offer, and they drank together.

A week later when Biway was again on liberty, he approached Carla and said they should drink alone together. Carla didn't quite know what to say at that point.

Carla Meyer was born on July 31, 1944, in the small Austrian village of Uhlrichsdorf, just east of Vienna, the youngest of five children born to Detlev and Louise Meyer. Unfortunately for Carla, her father, Detlev, was killed in Ukraine while fighting the Russians some two months before she was born. Detlev's younger brother, Erich, took the family under his wing, and since he was a diplomat by profession, they were well taken care of. Since then, Louise remarried.

In 1955, when Carla was ten, she decided she wanted to become a nun and teach school so her mother and stepfather, Adolf Messerschmidt, enrolled her in a convent in Vienna. Carla turned out to be a very good student. However in 1961, when she was seventeen, she suddenly fell in love with a man twice her age. He was friendly toward her and asked her to go out with him. However, the man was already married, with three children.

Since Carla was in love with him, she turned to the Mother Superior and said in German, "I cannot take my final vows as a nun since my inner feelings won't permit me to. Although I know how wrong this is, I cannot help being in love with this man, Mother. Therefore, I must leave here and enroll in a regular university."

"Yes, my child. Go and do what your heart desires, and may God be with you always and bless you," replied the Mother Superior. In 1963, Carla left the convent and enrolled a year later at the University of Vienna for her 1964 fall classes. That summer at the invitation of her uncle Erich and his wife, Carla decided to spend two months in Virginia with her two close friends who knew how to speak English rather fluently.

The more Carla saw of Biway, the less she liked him, but she was afraid of offending him, not knowing what he might be capable of when angered. Every time they went out, she was very careful not to offend him, but she became increasingly nauseated by being in his presence. She also became increasingly apprehensive that one night Biway may sexually assault her.

On the other hand, Biway was falling more and more in love with her as the days went by. He told her how much he wanted to teach her to speak English fluently and hopefully to one day marry her. For him, this could be his second Aggie, and she could bear him one of two sons and maybe a daughter as well. He was becoming increasingly euphoric over this prospect.

Things finally came to a head by the end of August. Carla broke down and told her uncle that she could no longer stand to be anywhere near Biway, and she was thoroughly disgusted by his aggressive behavior toward her. Her uncle Erich said in German, "Carla, I can go to the Marine base and get in to see Biway's immediate superior and explain how this man is making your life a living nightmare. Is this what you wish me to do?"

Carla replied, "First, I'll write his superior a letter pleading my case, since I know who he is. He is Lieutenant James Sims, thirty-nine, and he seems to be a nice, fair-minded man."

Erich replied, "When you finish writing that letter, I will take it with me to the lieutenant next Monday and show it to him."

That same night, Friday, August 28, Biway went to the hotel to meet with Carla, but she was nowhere to be seen. He even asked the other hotel guests, but they were of no help. Finally Biway hopped into his Ford and drove to Erich's house to see if Carla was there. Carla looked outside, recognized Biway's car, and said to her uncle, "I have to go upstairs and hide. I should have known he'd show up here sooner or later."

Biway knocked at the front door, and Erich answered, "Who are you looking for?"

Biway replied, "Carla, of course."

Then Erich said, "She's not here. She must be out with her new friends from Washington."

Biway left empty-handed and spent the rest of the weekend at the hotel without seeing any sign of Carla.

The following Sunday morning, August 30, Carla collected all her belongings, said goodbye to Erich and his wife, and had her friends pick her up and drive her to John Foster Dulles International Airport, where she first caught a flight to Montreal, Quebec, and from there to Frankfort, Germany, and finally her connecting flight to Vienna.

Around 9:00 a.m. that Monday morning, Erich Meyer showed up at the Quantico Marine base and asked to see Lieutenant James Sims. The Marine guard called in to Lieutenant Sims's office, and the lieutenant said, "Permission granted." Erich knocked and entered, and Lieutenant Sims asked, "What can I do for you, sir?"

Erich answered, "It's about my niece Carla Meyer. Although she went back to Austria yesterday, she asked me to come here and complain to you about one of the men under your command. She told me that this Sergeant Tom Biway had been literally making her life a living nightmare over the past three or four weeks. He has been following and increasingly behaving more aggressively toward her. She wanted to stop this but didn't know how. Maybe you can help. It would be a gigantic favor to all of us if you could. Besides, I have a letter here she wrote to you for that purpose, but since her English is quite limited, she wrote it in German. Do you wish for me to translate it, sir?"

Lieutenant Sims replied, "No, sir. That won't be necessary. Thank you for bringing this affair to my attention." After Erich left, Lieutenant Sims said to his corporal, "I'll want to see Sergeant Biway here right away and also summon Lieutenant Barbara Schuyler here as well."

The corporal replied "Aye, aye, sir" and went out to summon both of them.

Lieutenant Schuyler was twenty-nine and married. Both she and her husband joined the Marine Corps in 1953 right after their graduation from high school in Easton, Pennsylvania. Due to the German national economy, which was ruined by the 1919 Treaty of Versailles, Barbara's parents migrated from there to the United States in search of employment in 1921. They had five children, with Barbara being the fourth. The reason she was being summoned into Lieutenant Sims's office was that she knew how to read German fluently.

Sergeant Biway arrived some five minutes after Barbara did. When he stepped in, Lieutenant Sims asked him, "Can you read German?"

Biway replied, "No, sir, I can't." Then Lt. Sims handed the letter to Barbara, who took it and began to read it and translated what it said into English.

This is a part of what Carla said in the letter: "Bitte, hilfen mich. Ich finde diesen Mensch Biway ganzlich unausstehlich. Kurzlich scheitet es mir das er uberall mich folgt. Manchmal schietet es mir das dieser Ungeheuer mich vergewaltigen geht. Voll und ganz abscheue ich ihn . . . und so weiter."

As Biway listened to what Barbara was reading in English from that letter, Biway's jaw dropped, and it seemed like he was suddenly being struck by a bolt of lightning in his stomach. He never imagined how Carla felt inside about him and what he was slowly learning made him truly sick. He was in love with her, and she detested him at the same time. It made no sense to him at first, but as the minutes went by, it started sinking in. In the end, Biway said, "Will that be all, sir?" and Sims replied, "Yes, Biway. Dismissed."

After Biway left Lieutenant Sims's office, he said to Corporal Kevin McQueen, twenty-three, who was under his command, "For the next three days, you'll be in charge here. I'm going to be quite sick." Then Biway went to the PX and bought two quart-sized bottles of vodka and two boxes of Swisher cigars and retired to his quarters.

After Biway retired to his quarters around ten thirty that morning, he sat in a chair and tried his best not to cry but couldn't keep the tears out of his eyes. He kept thinking about all the plans he made for Carla and himself and their future children. Now all that was blown out of the water. It was as though someone had split open his chest and tore out his heart. How could she detest him like that, especially since he treated her with such respect and kindness, very much unlike he did to his sister, Susanna, his girlfriends, and especially Nancy Ballard? At least they didn't think he was so bad, but why Carla? he wondered. Around noon, he turned on the radio and began to drink, trying to wash away the pain he felt inside. He finally passed out around 4:30 p.m. or a little after. He came to around ten thirty that night and started drinking all over again, but he couldn't get Carla with her long brown hair, especially when she had it tied in a bun, her voluptuous lips, green eyes, and near-perfect figure out of his head.

On Thursday, September 3, after three days of incessant drinking and smoking, he showed up for inspection still half drunk and disheveled, but Corporal Kevin McQueen asked him, "Are you sure you're up to this, sir?"

Biway replied, "No, I'm not. Take over, please." Biway returned to his quarters but stopped drinking. He eventually recovered from this, but inside, the pain lingered on. He once again started to consort with Hispanic prostitutes when or wherever he could find one.

In March 1965, Biway's spirits rose even higher as President Johnson was slowly dragging this country into the Vietnam War. Now he saw his chances of achieving more feats on the battlefield and winning more medals plus a military victory for the United States to be even greater, unlike in Korea. To Biway's chagrin, it would be two more years before he was to leave Quantico for Camp Lejeune, North Carolina. That was in June 1967.

As for Carla Meyer after, she returned to Vienna, she entered her first year of college, graduated in 1969 with a master's degree in European history and sociology and went on to teach in a high school on the south side of Vienna. After she first arrived in Vienna, she still had misgivings that Biway would somehow suddenly show up at either her college or the apartment she was living in in order to force himself on her, although she took heart in the fact that Austria itself was a neutral country with the absence of foreign troops. As the months gave way to years, and there was never any sign of Biway anywhere, she gradually felt she could once again lead a normal life, and she finally married a fellow Austrian by the name of Axel Buhlen, who was twenty-seven, eight years her junior, in 1979, and they had two children, a boy, Deter, born in 1981, and a girl, Jutta, in 1986.

CHAPTER 8

The Suspension

On Saturday, April 22, 1967, Biway was notified of his impending transfer to Camp Lejeune in North Carolina. Upon hearing this, he became elated. The transfer took place on June 5, and Biway arrived at Camp Lejeune six days later.

On Monday, July 31, a group of raw recruits arrived at the base and were placed under Biway's command. The next day after the recruits had their heads shaved, issued their uniforms, and were ordered to fall in for their first inspection, Biway began haranguing them. One of the recruits, a twenty-one-yearold negro by the name of Stanley Foster, began to talk back to Biway and started using profanity to show his utter contempt for any kind of order, especially those orchestrated by whites. Biway stopped and slapped him as hard as he could and did so several times over again. Another recruit, a nineteen- year-old blonde by the name of Andrew Lathrop, began making obscene gestures at Biway. Biway, who saw it out the corner of his eye, said to Lathrop, "Did I see you give me the finger, or did my eyes play tricks on me?"

Lathrop replied, "No, you didn't, sir."

Biway said, "Who do you think you're fooling, Punk? I saw you, and you know it, so stop lying to me." At that point, Lathrop said, "How would you like to go to hell?" Upon hearing this reply, Biway lost control of himself, grabbed Lathrop, picked him up, and threw him to the ground as hard as he could. As Lathrop lay there, groaning in excruciating pain, Biway continued to holler for Lathrop to get up, but Lathrop could not and continued to lie there and groan. Finally another recruit, also a blonde and twenty years old by the name of Fred Walters, said to Biway, "Can't you see that this man is really hurt, sir? Have you no decency in you, sir?"

Biway yelled back, "Shut your mouth, you, or do you want to be next?"

Finally Second Lieutenant Steven Taylor, twenty, Biway's immediate superior, walked up to Biway and asked, "Just what's going on here, and why is this man groaning in such pain?"

Biway replied, "This punk here refuses to get up and will not follow my orders. We need to make an example out of him and prove to these other punks here that insubordination does not pay, sir." Taylor bent down and examined Lathrop and soon learned that he had a broken back. He immediately summoned the medics over and to bring a stretcher with them in order to transport Lathrop to the dispensary for treatment. There Lathrop got the grim prognosis. He was never to walk again.

In the meantime, Taylor turned to Biway and said, "Can't you tell when someone has been critically injured?" Then Taylor turned to the other men and said, "I'm now in charge here. I'm relieving Biway of his command and plan to court-martial him right away." Then he said to Biway, "You are heretofore relieved of your command and ordered confined to quarters until you're summoned to appear at your court- martial at the Marine Disciplinary Board. I'm going to recommend that you be given thirty years of hard labor plus a dishonorable discharge. That will be all. Dismissed."

Second Lieutenant Steven Taylor had a rather hard childhood and was raised in a rather dysfunctional family. Taylor was born on December 5, 1946, to Perry and Aulene Taylor, followed by his brother Glen, born on February 13, 1949, and Alfred, on April 21, 1950. His mother was born Aulene Ophelia Holden on January 7, 1927, to Maurice and Doris Holden and raised in grinding poverty. She had two brothers, both younger than her. Her parents were both habitually drunk, and to make matters even worse, Aulene was sexually abused by her father and his drunken friends from time to time, usually for money, since he couldn't hold a job for long. Finally when she was sixteen, she ran away. That was during WWII, and jobs were rather easy to get. In 1945, she met Perry Taylor, twenty-six, who just returned from the war. She eventually told Perry everything about herself, but he accepted her anyway. They were married in

January 1946. Perry, on the other hand, had a very normal childhood. Unfortunately, the marriage was not to last. In 1948, Aulene met this policeman by the name of Lehigh Wilson, twenty-four, also a WWII veteran. Finally Perry found out and sued Aulene for a divorce for two-timing him. Neither could anyone be sure of who the father of either Glen or Alfred was since no paternity tests were ever performed. Aulene did remarry in 1954 to a hoodlum by the name of Vancel Purle, twenty-seven, who made a living by gambling, extortion, stealing, and selling liquor to minors. He was arrested time and again for the same offenses. They had a daughter born in July 1956 and named her Vanessa. She had brown hair and green eyes. By the time she was born, Steven was serving time in a juvenile detention facility commonly known as Mo Hills on the Missouri River, just north of St. Louis. He was almost constantly in trouble with the police. While he was in custody, a priest by the name of Father Hector Tarleton, thirty- two, came to see him one day and wanted to know what he could do to turn his life around. Finally, Taylor told him, "Is it possible that I could be sent to Boys Town of Missouri in St. James?"

Father Tarleton replied, "It won't be easy, but I believe it could be arranged."

Taylor replied, "If only I could just go there, since I can no longer go home to my dysfunctional family. I haven't seen my real father since I was three, and my mother consorts with the scum on the streets of St. Louis. Why she doesn't get together with a decent man, I don't know."

The deal went through, and Taylor was admitted to Boys Town in St. James on May 28, 1959, when he was twelve. There he thrived and did well in almost all his studies. However, he still missed his mother and his two brothers in St. Louis. One day totally out of the blue, his father, Perry, showed up at Boys Town to see him. Taylor was totally flabbergasted upon seeing his father for the first time since he was three. That took place in the summer of 1961. The two hit it off, and because his father served in the Marine Corps, Steve decided that was what he wanted to do.

In the summer of 1963, Taylor asked Father Harding, "Will it be possible for me to join the Marine Corps?"

Father Harding replied, "Yes, it will. When do you wish to join?"

Taylor replied, "As soon as possible, Father."

Then Father Harding said, "Okay, since you proved to be an excellent student here with an equivalent of a high school education, we'll arrange for you to enroll at the US Marine Academy at Quantico, Virginia. How does that sound, young man?"

Taylor simply replied, "Excellent, Father, and thanks a million."

In 1958, Aulene and Vancel Purle were divorced, and in 1960, Aulene met Greg Brieski, thirty-five, an electrician employed by the City of St. Louis to maintain and repair the city's streetlamps. The job paid very well. Aulene was working at that time as a waitress at McCartney's Restaurant. Even with this job, since the pay was not sufficient, Aulene still had to rely on Welfare to make ends meet. Steven was in Boys Town, and Glen was interned at State Hospital #1 in Fulton, Missouri, at that time.

At thirty-three, Aulene was very attractive with her shoulder-length black hair, rosy cheeks, glasses, and her full figure. In the fall of 1960, Aulene and Greg began seeing one another on a regular basis, and they finally married on June 9, 1961, when she was thirty-four and Greg, thirty-six and a lifelong bachelor. He lived with his parents, both immigrants from Poland along with his brother Jim and his wife, Annette, in Granite City, Illinois. By 1960, both his parents had died, and his brother Jim, suffering from a severe case of asthma, found himself compelled to move to New Mexico for his health. Between then and up to his marriage to Aulene, he lived alone in that house. Aulene found it strange since she never lived in a house in an upscale neighborhood with a low crime rate and, now married to Greg, no longer had to work or rely on Welfare. Now, she along with her son Alfred (Alfie) and her daughter Vanessa, almost five, were finally were able to lead decent lives.

In 1963, Aulene bore another son, Benjamin, and finally on August 21, 1969, a daughter by the name of Stephanie. Glen was last heard from in October 1968, when he and his hippie friends were living in Alamogordo, New Mexico, and experimenting with all kinds of drugs.

In July 1966, while on summer vacation from the Academy at Quantico, Greg drove down, picked up Steven, and drove him to his home in Granite City. Aulene as well as Alfie and Vanessa were elated to see Steven although Vanessa could hardly remember him. In the meantime, although Steven's father, Perry, was married and had four more children by his second wife, Wendy, and lived in Creve Coeur, Missouri, he remained in touch with him.

Because Steven had to endure so much as a child and was unexpectedly helped by two different priests, and now seeing his mother finally leading a happy life, he became quite compassionate and felt no sympathy for

Biway because of his callousness. This is why he felt that Biway must be held accountable for what he did to Private Lathrop.

In the meantime in August 1967, after Taylor relieved Biway of his command and ordered him confined to quarters, Biway spent most of his time getting drunk and cursing Taylor, calling him every filthy name under the sun. One day, Biway went to Taylor's superior, Lieutenant Howard Kingman, fifty, in order to appeal his court-martial, but to no avail. Finally, on Tuesday, August 15 at 10:00 a.m., the hearing at the Marine Disciplinary Board started, and both sides presented their arguments concerning the court-martial. Lieutenant Rex Patterson argued Taylor's case, while Lieutenant Bob Whitmore brought to the attention of the board Biway's impeccable thirty-two-year-long military record plus his exploits in Korea.

At the end of the hearing, Captain Henry Sutton, forty-eight, who presided at the court-martial, said, "Having heard both sides of this issue, you'll have our decision on Thursday, August 24 next at 0900 hours. Hearing adjourned."

At 9:00 a.m. on August 24, the sentencing phase of the courts martial began, and Captain Sutton said, "Having looked at both sides of this issue thoroughly, on one side, Second Lieutenant Taylor's recommendation that Sergeant Thomas Biway be given thirty years of hard labor plus a dishonorable discharge concerning what he did to Private Lathrop, leaving him permanently disabled, and the attention brought to us by Lieutenant Whitmore concerning Biway's impeccable military record, it is the decision of this board that Sergeant Thomas Biway be given a six-month suspension from the Marine Corps with pay and report for duty on February 24, next, here at Camp Lejeune. Court adjourned." Biway never felt so relieved, and in the days leading up to this sentencing, Biway had never felt such anxiety in his life. What frightened him was not so much the prospect of thirty years of hard labor but the idea of never getting the chance to serve in Vietnam. Taylor, who was present at this sentencing, was greatly disappointed at this outcome. Later that day, Sergeant Floyd Proctor, thirty-eight, a close friend of Biway's, said to him, "Don't let it get you down, Tom. Just think of it as a six-month vacation." Around 4:00 p.m., Biway collected all his belongings, packed them in his 1954

Ford, drove off, and headed cross country for Marysville, California, to see his ex-wife, Aggie, her husband, Bill, and his daughter, Kitty, twenty, before she returned to Berkeley University for her sophomore year. She majored in sociology.

On August 31, after a full week on the road, Biway arrived in Marysville, and his family was glad to see him once again. He noticed that her two sons, Bruce, six, and Robert, five, were both healthy and doing quite well. One night around 11:00 p.m., as Biway was nursing his fourth or fifth serving of vodka, the jukebox began to play a record by the name of "In the Wee Small Hours of the Morning" by Frank Sinatra, recorded around 1947, Biway's eyes began to fill with tears. He then turned to his ex-wife, Aggie, and said, "Today, I noticed Bruce and Bob playing outside, and that made me think, had we not divorced, those could have been my sons."

Aggie replied, "Yes, Tom, they could have been, but you had to get so damn devoted to the Marine Corps especially after our losing Paul that you never seemed to have time for Kitty and I anymore. Don't forget, Tom, Lenny and Paul were my sons too, and I too suffered over their deaths."

Then Biway said, "I'm sorry, Aggie, you are so right. Now that I see that you and Bill are doing so well these days, I'm happy."

Four days later, Biway decided to head for his hometown of Utica, New York, in order to see what became of his family since he hadn't seen any of them since 1935, not because he missed them, but out of sheer curiosity.

As he was driving through the Utah desert, he noticed a gang of Hell's Angels riding in the opposite direction and thought to himself, *If only I had those boys under my command, I'd have it made.*

He finally arrived in Utica on Tuesday, September 12. He then drove to the center of the city and registered in a hotel. The next day, he drove to 1830 Sturgis Street and found that the house he grew up in was now inhabited by blacks, as well as every other house in that neighborhood. That saddened him a little.

He then drove back to his hotel, picked up a phone book, and went into his room to see if anyone by the name of Biway still lived in Utica. He found two names, one a distant cousin by the name of Tad and the other, his brother, Rick, who lived at 447 Quinn Street. Early the next morning, Biway parked outside of Rick's apartment and spotted him going to his car before driving off to work. Biway followed him to Adkin's Heating and Air Conditioning Repairs and followed him in. Finally, Biway said to Rick, "Long time no see." Rick, totally stunned upon seeing his brother for the first time since 1935, could barely utter a word. Biway then said to him, "Don't you remember me, Punk?"

Rick, after recovering from the initial shock of suddenly seeing his brother, finally said, "Yes, Tom, I certainly do. Are you still in the Marine Corps, and did you ever marry?"

Biway replied, "Yes, I am, and yes, I did, did you?"

Rick replied, "No, I didn't." Rick then suggested, "Let's meet here after work around five o'clock and I'll fill you in about the rest of the family."

Biway said, "Yes, Punk, that's a deal."

Rick then asked Biway, "Why do you call me Punk?"

Biway replied, "I'll tell you that later when we meet at five o'clock." They attended their rendezvous at five o'clock, and Rick and he went to Walensa's Polish Restaurant in downtown Utica for supper. After supper, Biway said, "Now just out of sheer curiosity, what became of Mom and Pop and, of course, our grandma, Mary?"

Rick replied, "Grandma Mary died peacefully in her sleep on a Sunday morning, March 13, 1938, to be exact. She was not quite eighty-three. Since the Utica Police took you away that Sunday afternoon for raping Suzy, she became almost totally withdrawn and barely spoke to any of us thereafter. I guess it was because she could hardly believe what you did to Susanna and I. Before that, she really doted on you."

Biway then asked, "What about Mom and Pop?"

Rick replied, "Pop is now in the Meadowbrook Nursing Home in nearby Oriskany, and we no longer go there to visit him since he no longer recognizes any of us. You can go there to see him, but it'll do you no good. He is now eighty-five and has a severe case of Alzheimer's. Mom is now living with Terry, her second husband, and their three children on the west side of town. She now suffers from macular degeneration and is slowly going blind. I can give you their address if you like."

Biway said, "No, that won't be necessary, but thanks anyway, Punk. By the way, whatever became of Suzy?"

Rick replied, "Suzy married in 1948 and moved to Syracuse with her husband, Frank Crocker, two years later. They now have two children, a boy and a girl, and are quite happy." Finally Rick asked, "Tom, why do you call me Punk instead of Rick?"

Biway replied, "It's simply that you look like Pop. Did you ever know that he never served in WWI like other kids' dads did?"

Rick replied, "That's because he suffered from asthma, but did you really deem him a coward, Tom, and is that why you disliked him so? No one with asthma can ever get into the Army or the Navy. You ought to know that."

Biway said, "Thank you, Punk, or should I say Rick, for the enlightenment. Now with my curiosity satisfied, I will now head to New York City."

The next day, Biway paid his hotel bill, packed, and headed for New York City to wait out the rest of his suspension from the Corps.

When Biway arrived in New York City on September 16, and as he was driving through Staten Island, he decided to check in at the Regina Hotel on Hayes Avenue and Tyler Street. It was owned by the Gambino crime family as part of the Mafia and was being run by a Cuban couple, Fernando and Christina Dellanos. Biway soon noticed that there was gambling and escort services in that hotel. The next day, Biway went down Tyler Street and rented a flat where he intended to wait out the rest of his suspension from the Corps. That night, he returned to the hotel in order to pick out a Hispanic prostitute to consort with. He asked Christina which one of them was available that night, and she said, "Dulce, over at that table. I'll introduce you to her." Biway paid up, and they went up to one of the rooms upstairs. However, Biway noticed Christina and how attractive she was. Although she was thirty-nine at that time, she was still extremely sexy in her blue miniskirt. She had bleach-blond hair, five feet, six inches tall and weighed around 165 pounds. Although Biway spent a pleasant night with Dulce, he couldn't get over his desire for Christina.

Christina Dellanos was born Christina Serelegui on May 8, 1928, in an upscale neighborhood in Havana, Cuba, the only child of Hector and Gladys Serelegui. Hector Serelegui was a successful real estate businessman who also dealt with the Mafia, which was slowly moving into that country, especially since they were being persecuted by the Mussolini regime in Italy during the 1920s and '30s. In 1946 when she was eighteen, Christina entered the University of Havana, where she majored in journalism. She graduated in 1950, and a short time afterward, she married Fernando Dellanos. Both were twenty-two at that time. Fernando's parents, like Christina's, had strong ties to the mob. Fernando was a Cuban Air Force pilot who had a love of flying. They eventually had three daughters, Alejandra, born in 1951; Myrka, born in 1955; and Sofia, in 1958.

In 1959, Fidel Castro and his revolutionaries took over and expelled both the dictator Fulgencio Batista and the Mafia. With the aid of that organization, Christina and Fernando easily fled with their three daughters to Miami, Florida, in 1960 and, in 1961, to New York City, where both Fernando and Christina were given work, Fernando as the hotel manager and Christina as the head of the hotel escort service. They supported their three daughters quite well and resided in Elizabeth, New Jersey, across the Hudson River.

The next night, Biway went into the hotel and said, "I wish to talk to Christina. Is she here?"

The clerk replied, "Yes, she is, do you want me to send you to her office?"

Biway replied, "Of course I do."

Then Biway went into her office and she asked, "Is there anything wrong? Did Dulce do anything to offend you last night? I hope not."

Biway replied, "No, that's not it. The fact is, is that I wish to sleep with you if that's all right."

Christina replied, "No, I am just the madame here, and we have regular prostitutes for that. Besides, I'm married to a loving husband, and we have three lovely daughters."

Suddenly Biway walked up to Christina, threw his arms around her, put his lips to hers, and started kissing her with a passion as she tried her best to push him away. After three minutes, Biway let go, and she slapped him as hard as she could, yelling out, "Damn you! Damn you!" Then Biway again threw his arms around her, and her resistance broke down as she started kissing him back. Finally she said, "Okay, Biway, let's go to the room down the hall and order up a bottle of rum." Not since he consorted with Mrs. Ballard back in the late 1940s did Biway enjoy having sex as he did that night with Christina. The next morning, he took out $50 and offered to pay her. Christina replied, "No, Biway, that won't be necessary since I enjoyed last night as much as you did."

Then Biway asked, "Can we go on seeing one another?" Christina replied, "Of course we can."

For the first time in their marriage, Christina cheated on her husband, Fernando, which made her feel guilty, especially for the sake of their three daughters. As time went on, Christina started falling in love with Biway. Had Christina not been Hispanic, he may well have fallen in love with her too. As mentioned before, Biway considered only white women to be fit for him to marry.

When not consorting with Christina, Biway would spend his time playing poker or sitting in a local bar to meet and gab with his newly acquired friends. In the meantime, Christina forgot to take her monthly contraceptive pill, and as a result, she came up pregnant. Finally on Friday, November 10, Christina went to his flat, told him, and he flew into a wild rage over it. He slapped her as hard as he could and told her to get away from him before he did anything to really hurt her. He spent the next two nights in some local pub, getting drunk over the whole thing.

The following night after spending some seven or eight hours in O'Malley's Pub, drinking heavily and gabbing with any other patron who cared to converse with him, Biway left around 12:00 a.m., staggered to his car, and started driving recklessly through the streets. Finally as he was approaching Grant Avenue from Hilger Street, he didn't notice that the light in front of him changed, and as a result, he rammed another car going north on Grant Avenue with a family of five inside at a high rate of speed. All five people in the other car were severely injured, resulting in the death of a four-year-old girl and leaving her eight-year-old brother with a broken back. The police came, and all six involved in the accident were taken to Bellview Hospital for their injuries. Only Biway escaped with minor injuries, while the other three family members in the other car were to eventually recover fully. At around 6:00 a.m., the police arrested Biway for vehicular manslaughter since he was extremely intoxicated and a four-year-old girl died as a result. On Friday, November 17, Biway was arraigned in the Staten Island Magistrate Court before Judge Gerald Stevens. Judge Stevens was thirty-five and a negro. This made Biway feel rather apprehensive, not that he hated blacks, but had misgivings of how he would be sentenced. However, the judge said to Biway, "I am remanding you into custody on Rikers Island pending your sentencing on December

18, next at 1:00 p.m. for vehicular manslaughter. Next case, please." Later that day, Biway was transported to Rikers Island, taken to the JATC (James A. Thomas Center) and assigned to cell 8B. This was the toughest facility on Rikers Island to be in. For the second time in his life, Biway felt deeply frightened over having any chance he had of going to Vietnam crushed, but he managed never to show it to any his fellow inmates.

As for Christina, she went home and said to her husband, "I have to tell you something, dear."

Fernando, noticing the red mark on the side of her face, said, "What happened, and who slapped you?"

Christina replied, "It was Sergeant Biway, but it's far more complicated than that. As much as I hate to tell you, I'm pregnant, and it's his baby. I don't know how, but I fell in love with him although I tried so very hard not to. I guess I'd better get my things together and leave now. Oh, Fernando, I'm so very sorry."

Fernando could hardly believe what he just heard. After recovering from the initial shock of learning of this affair, he finally said, "I want you out of this house right away. Besides, do you plan to continue consorting with him?"

Christina replied, "No, Fernando, it's all over between the two of us." Christina called her very close friend Diana Rivera, forty, to have her come and take her to her house. Christina and Diana have been very close friends since they were children in Havana. Diana was married, and she stayed home to raise her four children. In the meantime, that Monday morning, Fernando went to one of the Mafia bosses and told him, "I want a hit put out on this Biway. He got my wife pregnant, thus torpedoing our marriage." Fernando gave the boss all the information about Biway he got out of Christina and said, "I want this—dead, dead, dead!" Later that day, Fernando decided to sue Christina for a divorce. Upon hearing about all this, their three daughters cried in disbelief.

However on the night of November 27, Christina came over to their house in order to discuss the details of their divorce, but suddenly Fernando said, "Christina, there is something I have to tell you too. Since we've been married, I did consort with three different women at different times, so I'm not so innocent either. Tell me, Christina, do you still want the divorce?"

Christina replied, "No, not really, but can you ever forgive me for what I did?"

Fernando replied, "Yes, I can, Christina. Let's just call off the divorce and reconcile. How does that sound to you?"

Christina said, "I couldn't be happier." And when the three girls heard it, they became elated.

They reconciled and the projected divorce was cancelled on November 30. Fernando then returned to the Mafia boss and said, "I want this hit on Biway cancelled since Christina and I have reconciled, but I still want you to find Biway's family and tell them what he did."

The boss replied, "Sure, if that's how you want it."

The mob sent two men to Marysville, California, to tell Biway's ex-wife and daughter about the affair and how Biway got Christina pregnant. After about two or three months, both Christina and Fernando changed their minds about putting the baby up for adoption and decided to keep it as one of their own. This made the girls even happier over the prospect of having a baby brother in the house.

The baby was born on Friday, July 5, 1968, and they named him Julio. Unbeknown to Biway, he did have a son after all, but since he was at Camp Pendleton at the time of Julio's birth, he had no way of knowing about it, nor did he care.

Biway's first cellmate was a homeless elderly man with hardly any income except for what he got from Welfare. He was sixty-seven and was forced to live on the streets of New York City. He had no surviving family members he could recall. Both his children were already dead as well as his wife. He was finally released on Sunday, November 26. The next day, Biway acquired a new cellmate by the name of C. T. Tennyson.

At first, he and Tennyson seemed to be hitting it off, but as Biway began to brag about his exploits in Korea and his yearning to go to Vietnam, Tennyson became disgusted and as Tennyson explained the reason he was there, that is, protesting the war in Vietnam. Biway became irate over it. In time, the two began to loathe one another, but as Tennyson witnessed the fight between Biway and Gary Johndro on Saturday morning, December 2, and watching Biway beat Johndro hands down, Tennyson made it a point never to provoke him.

Since his incarceration on November 12, Biway had not had sex, and as time went on, he became sexually starved, as most inmates were. In the total absence of women, Biway wouldn't hesitate to settle for another man. Since Tennyson, who was twenty-one at that time and never lost his baby fat, he reminded Biway of his sister Susanna with his light-brown kinky hair. Finally on the night of December 12, Biway made his move. Around 10:00 p.m. after the lights were put out, Biway picked up his blanket, tiptoed over to Tennyson's bunk, and leaped on top of him. He then threatened Tennyson not to make a sound or tell anyone else about what he was about to do. Tennyson was now in total disbelief over what was happening to him. Biway's first orgasm came in less than three minutes, so after another forty- five minutes or so, he raped Tennyson again.

The next day in the dayroom, Tennyson suddenly leaped out of his chair, ran to Captain Mike Orchard, fifty-four, and said, "That filthy creep raped me last night!" He pointed to Biway. "And please don't force me to share that same cell with him tonight."

Orchard irately replied, "If you don't shut up and get back to your chair, you'll be more afraid of me than you are of him."

Later, Captain Orchard asked Biway about it, but Biway simply said, "That's a lie! That punk will say or do anything to get me in trouble, and besides, can he prove it?"

Captain Orchard replied, "No, I guess not." He later told the second shift captain, Roy Downs, forty-six, about it, and Captain Downs later had Tennyson transferred to a different cell.

As his sentencing date of December 18 drew ever closer, Biway became increasingly apprehensive over his fate, not that he feared prison so much as not having the chance to go to Vietnam and do more of his exploits there. The Marine Corps was his life now, and that for him mattered above everything else.

On Monday, December 18, he was taken over to the Staten Island Magistrate Court to learn his sentence. At 1:00 p.m., he was brought before Judge Leon McCartney, fifty-seven, to learn what his future held. Surprisingly enough, that was Biway's lucky day. In the end, the judge said to Biway, "As you know, you face serious charges here resulting in a possible twenty- to thirty-year prison sentence. Had you not been so devoted to the defense of this country over the past thirty years or so, I'd send you there, but in light of your military record, I not only suspend your sentence but put your conviction aside so you can return to the Marine Corps and eventually go to Vietnam as you wish to. Goodbye and good luck, sir."

Michael Wentz, twenty-seven, one of Biway's arresting officers, listened to the judge in total disbelief as he let Biway off the hook, especially after the indifference Biway showed over the death of the four-year-old girl and the crippling of her eight-year-old brother. He found this totally ridiculous. After the cancellation of his sentence, he approached Biway and said, "Have you absolutely no sense of decency in you at all? Don't you even care about what you did to that family?" Biway just simply made an obscene gesture at Officer Wentz as he was being taken back to Rikers Island to collect his belongings. Thereafter Biway took a subway back to his flat on Staten Island to collect the rest of his gear, hopped on a bus, and returned to

Marysville, California, to wait out what was left of his suspension.

As for C. T. Tennyson, he was released on Wednesday, December 27, after serving out his thirty-day sentence for protesting the war in Vietnam. He would never be the same since his rape, and he slowly recognized it. Although he improved with the treatment he received in a mental hospital, other circumstances, such as the tragic deaths of both his younger brothers, one in an automobile accident and the other in Vietnam, plus two different disappointments with two different women, inexorably drove him to commit suicide in a Queens hotel on Friday morning, December 27, 1968, a year to the day of his release from Rikers Island.

During that fall, as Kitty was attending Berkeley, she dated a fellow student by the name of George Beaver one Saturday night. On that date, George said to Kitty, "I noticed that your last name is Biway. Ironically, my older brother, Dennis, was serving in the Marines in Japan in 1959 and had a sergeant by the name of Tom Biway. Nobody liked this sergeant, especially after what he did to Private First Class Mettler. Mettler was rather large and had a gentle look on him, and that's why the other men referred to him as the Gentle Giant.

"Mettler had always been a very capable Marine whose only fault was that he tended to drink excessively at times. He only had at that time a year and a half left to serve before his retirement. For some reason or other, Biway had it in for him and was determined to court- martial him, and he eventually succeeded. Mettler went home a broken man. About a week and a half later, my brother, Dennis, wrote Biway an anonymous letter and slipped it into his mailbox, telling him that one of the men was going to murder him one way or another. Biway called inspection in order to find out who wrote that letter. No one ever knew up till now except for my brother before he finally told me. They all went into a thirty-day lockdown, but Biway never found out who wrote that letter. About two weeks after they came out of lockdown, Biway was transferred back to California, and they were all tickled pink to see him go."

Kitty listened in disbelief as she realized that George was talking about her father but said, "Oh no, that's my uncle Tom. He has been in the Marines for over thirty years, and that's his life. Yes, he does tend to become overzealous at times."

For the first time in her life, Kitty began to have misgivings about her father. She also noticed that he never once discussed his family or whether they were alive or dead. Those misgivings were further exacerbated around Christmas, when two young men who appeared to be Italian and from New York City came to her home, introduced themselves, and told her about what he did to Christina Dellanos, getting her pregnant, slapping and threatening her. Kitty refused to believe it.

On December 26, the day after Christmas, Biway arrived in Marysville and was put up in Bill and Aggie's house. It was just by sheer luck that Biway missed the two Italian men who talked to his daughter about him. Kitty herself never mentioned the visit.

Finally one day, Kitty did ask Biway about his family, but he simply replied, "They're all dead now, so there is nothing left to tell."

Kitty asked her mother, Aggie, "Mom, why is Dad so secretive about his family, and why doesn't he talk about his childhood?"

Aggie replied, "There are some things that had better not be brought up. Someday I'll tell you, but not now." Thereafter Kitty dropped the subject.

In the meantime, Biway brought a white 1948 GMC Pickup and spent his days either fishing or hunting before returning to Camp Lejeune, North Carolina, on February 24, 1968, to report for duty.

The day after he returned to duty, he was called into Lieutenant Klingman's office, and Klingman said to him, "Look, Biway, I don't know what kind of strings you pulled in order to get back here, but it stinks to high heaven, and I don't like it. I'm only going to tell you this once, the very first time you screw up here, I'll personally have you booted out of the Corps once and for all. Am I understood, Biway?"

Biway replied, "Yes, sir."

Klingman said, "Right now, you'll report to Second Lieutenant Ed Howard. Dismissed."

PART II

BIWAY'S NEMESIS

CHAPTER 1

A Most Vicious Attack

It was a hot and balmy Friday night in Chicago, Illinois, April 22, 1955. Around 10:30 p.m., Mrs. Oleta Brassfield, sixty-six, was out walking her Pekingese terrier when she started to hear some terrible screams half a block away. It was a man attacking a girl with a razor as she was walking up to her house after her boyfriend dropped her off after they left the Lo Piccolo Bros Lounge and Grill on Michigan Street on the north side of Chicago. It was in an upscale neighborhood where violence rarely occurred, even at night when the streets were well lit and no one expected this. As the attack was unfolding, the neighbors started turning on their porch lights one by one to see what was happening. The attacker was a large white man, around six feet, two inches tall, appeared to weigh about 250 pounds, had gray hair, and wore a red baseball cap. Before anyone could get close enough to identify him, he got away in his red 1949 GMC pickup truck, and therefore no one could get his license number. The girl had four slashes across her face, a huge one on the left side plus three more on the right side. She had blood on both her face and hands and had to be rushed to the ER at St. Simon's Mercy Hospital for emergency treatment.

The girl's name was Thalia Gomez, nineteen, the youngest of four daughters born to Rogelio, seventy-two, and Carlotta Gomez, sixty-one. The other daughters were Rosamaria, then twenty-eight and living in Mexico along with her sister Guadalupe, twenty-six, while Odalys, twenty-five, was married and working in a Chicago beauty salon.

Rogelio Gomez and Carlotta Uribe were married in 1915 in Monterrey, Mexico, at a time when that country was undergoing several revolutions. In 1917, the same year Rosamaria was born, Rogelio decided to move to Chicago, where his cousin already had several businesses. Since Rogelio had several business interests in both Chicago and Monterrey and most of them lucrative, he had no trouble in putting all four of his daughters through college. Later on, both Rosamaria and Guadalupe decided to return to Mexico, but Odalys and Thalia remained with their parents in Chicago.

That Monday night four days earlier, Thalia, along with her friends, decided to go to the Lo Piccolo Bros Lounge and Grill to celebrate her nineteenth birthday. While she and her friends were drinking and talking, she was suddenly approached by a middle-aged man who appeared to be in his midfifties. Thalia told him that she and her friends were there to have a good time, nothing more. Then he offered to buy her a drink and did. Upon receiving the drink, Thalia suddenly became quite angry and threw the drink in the man's face. Then the man began cursing her with every filthy name in the books and making a scene. Finally, one of the Lo Piccolo brothers, Sal, forty- seven, reached under the counter, pulled out a billy club, and said to the man, "Unless you leave here and now, I will bury this in your miserable skull, and don't ever came back here again."

The man cursed Sal Lo Piccolo and told Thalia, "This isn't the end of this." Four nights later, the man made good on his threat.

Thalia was in her first year of college at Northeast University of Chicago with a major in dramatic arts, and since she was exceptionally pretty, she received several offers from different people who were looking for talent in the acting business after her graduating in 1958. Thalia was hoping to get into acting in local theatres and maybe even go to Hollywood itself. If not, she could always return to Mexico, where her older sisters were influential in the entertainment business, especially Rosamaria. But now that was all brought to a tragic end because some perverted fool couldn't take no for an answer.

Of all the people who were involved in the case, few were more outraged than Officer Odell Williams, twenty-one, and her parents, Rogelio and Carlotta. Williams joined the Chicago PD in August 1954 after graduating from Chicago Tech with an associate degree in criminal justice. Williams now wanted one thing only and that was to bring the person responsible for this heinous attack to justice.

Odell Williams was born Odell Daniel Williams on December 5, 1933, on the north side of Chicago, the youngest of two children born to Greg and Alberta Williams. The other was Margaret Williams, born on September 7, 1930. His father worked at the Ford plant in downtown Chicago, while his mother owned a soda grill on the northern outskirts of Chicago. As a child, Odell was neither very popular nor very mainstream. While other boys were out in the streets playing baseball or football, Odell would be working in the family garden in back of the soda grill. At other times, he would be studying insects, birds, or reptiles. In 1942, his father bought him a world globe and he became fascinated to learn how many different countries there were around the world. Even at Hattie M. Carsten Middle School, Odell made few friends, with most of the others either excluding him from whichever game they were playing or bullying him. He was even less popular with the girls. While he was in James D. Buchanan Senior High, a girl by the name of Margaret Childers went as far as telling him how disgustingly ugly he was. However, by that time, he became inured to all this. In 1949, he entered James D. Buchanan Senior High School, and while he was there, he witnessed a lot of bullying and even finding himself on the receiving end of some of it at times. It was here that Williams made up his mind once and for all what he wanted to do in the future. As far as he was concerned, the high school bullies were no different than the street criminals, and as a cop, he may be able to make a difference and help people. Moreover, he didn't want to join the military since that would mean going to some country where we really didn't belong and killing people who didn't deserve to die. In 1952, when he graduated from James D. Buchanan Senior High School, the Korean War was on, and he won a student deferment and later an occupational deferment since he joined the Chicago PD. He was always sensitive to the misery of others.

Catching the man who attacked Thalia in such a vicious manner became a near obsession with Williams. Even his immediate superior, Sergeant Kevin Hurley, thirty-four, told him to slow down and let the detectives handle the case.

The next night when he was not on duty, Williams went to the Lo Piccolo Bros Lounge and Grill in order to dig up whatever information about the perpetrator he could. Sal Lo Piccolo, forty-seven, said to Williams, "I already told the detectives who were here earlier all I know. However, there are two men here who may be able to help you." He pointed to them sitting in a booth.

Williams went over to them and asked, "Do you know who the man is who threatened a girl here the other night?"

One of them replied, "Not really, but I believe his first name is Will and works at McPherson Plastics on third shift and drives a red GMC pickup."

After he left the Lo Piccolo Bros Lounge and Grill, he drove to McPherson Plastics Inc. and spotted a red 1949 GMC pickup truck in the parking lot. He copied the license number and ran it through the Illinois DMV. It came back: Red 1949 GMC Pickup. The owner: William Strohlbein, age fifty-three. Address: 11337 McNair St., Chicago, Illinois. Williams then contacted the two detectives in order to pass the information on to them although they were rather irate at receiving this unwanted assistance. Finally on Thursday, May 5, 1955, the detectives Harold La Page, thirty-six, and Don Adkins, forty-one, showed up at Strohlbein's home with an arrest warrant and took him into custody. Everyone was greatly delighted that the Chicago PD had their man and that he was about to face justice, but it was not to be that simple.

CHAPTER 2

The Perpetrator

Will Strohlbein was born Peter William Strohlbein on Sunday, June 2, 1901, in Spring Valley, Illinois, the third of five children born to Emil and Bertha Strohbein. The others were Florence, born on November 18, 1894; Norman, on July 27, 1896; Will; Oleta, on March 3, 1906; and James, on May 15, 1908. Emil Strohlbein (1863–1918) owned a lucrative grocery store in downtown Spring Valley, and Bertha (1864- 1944) was a housewife.

Will Strohlbein had a very normal childhood, doing well in school and going either hunting or fishing on weekends. However as he progressed to middle school and since he was large for his age, he began bullying other students, sometimes extorting lunch money from them. When he entered high school, his teachers called him in and told him to stop that kind of activity. At first he did but resumed it later. Finally, they called his parents and told them. The father said, "Will has always been a strong-willed kid, so please excuse him." Strohlbein never liked his first name, Peter, so he started going by his middle one, Bill, but since there were six or seven other boys going by the same name in his class, he started calling himself Will. The name stuck.

In the spring of 1918, during his junior year in high school, Strohlbein's math teacher called him into his office and said, "Will, this bullying needs to stop here and now. Not only are the boys being harassed but also the girls. Making passes at them will get you in trouble, so when you go home, think it over." By this time, Strohlbein was getting sick and tired of both his school and his teachers. At the same time, his father, Emil, caught Spanish influenza and died from it. He was fifty-five.

However at that time, WWI was raging all across Europe, so in July 1918, Strohlbein decided to enlist in the US Army. He passed his physical quite handily. He was first stationed at Ft. Leonard Wood in Missouri and then at Ft. Riley, Kansas. Early in November, he and his unit shipped out for northern France, but before they could get there, the armistice was signed on Monday, November 11. Strohlbein and his unit were then diverted to England. While they were there, some British official said, "Instead of sending these boys home, let's send them to Murmansk, Russia, to assist in our cause in the Russian Civil War." (1918–1922.) The request was submitted to the US government, and President Woodrow Wilson (1856–1924), being once again bamboozled by the British who told him they were still "fighting the Germans," readily agreed. Of course, this was not true. Strohlbein was glad to hear this so that he may at last come home a war hero to the people of his hometown.

Strohlbein and his unit arrived in Murmansk on December 2 in order to join the 130,000-man American expeditionary force to help the Russian Fascists defeat and overthrow the Bolsheviks, whom the Americans referred to as Bolos. They almost succeeded. When Strohbein first arrived in northern Russia, there were hardly three hours daylight during the day, from around ten thirty in the morning to around one thirty in the afternoon, and it was extremely cold.

As the days wore on, they became increasingly shorter, but after Christmas, they began to get longer, and by the end of May, there were only four hours of night, from 10:00 p.m. to 2:00 a.m. There was relatively little military action there as the Fascist generals controlled that part of Russia. One day in the distance, there were five people passing on foot to a nearby store in order to barter for food. At that time, there was already widespread hunger, which was to get far worse later.

As Strohlbein was observing them, he hollered out, "I see five Bolos about a mile south of here, and I'm going to knock them off!"

Another man in his unit said, "Strohlbein, let's see who these people are first."

Strohbein replied, "I already know, and I'm going to knock off at least one or two of them. I've been here five months, and I haven't killed anyone yet. This is getting far too old." He loaded his rifle, ran to the top of a mound, and took aim at the passersby. Then he opened fire, not only taking out one or two but all five. Later it was ascertained that the people Strohlbein slaughtered were not Bolos at all. Instead they were civilians caught up in the civil war. Among them were three men, a woman, and a ten-year-old girl. However, for Strohlbein, this made little difference, if any at all. That was in May 1919. Now Strohlbein acquired a taste for killing, and he wanted more of it so he could tell the girls in his hometown of Spring Valley, Illinois, about it. As the unit moved farther south, they saw more and more action, but as always, the people Strohlbein managed to kill were all civilians.

By August 1919, a huge offensive was underway by the Fascists led by the British beginning in the Ural Mountains, aiming for Moscow, and it came very close to succeeding. In fact, the Bolshevik forces, called the Red Army, was fighting on its last leg. There was finally a huge battle less than one hundred miles east of Moscow. Surprisingly enough, the Red Army came out on top. No one expected this, least of all the British, since they came so close with nearly four million men under their command. The Red Army under Lev Trotskiy (1879–1940) followed up this victory culminating in the drive to the east heading for the Urals. About two months later, the Fascist general Yudinitch launched a drive south, heading for Petrograd, but it too failed, and finally, another drive north to Moscow from Ukraine eventually failed too. Finally by January 1920, the League of Nations held a meeting concerning Russia. All parties except for the Japanese knew it was a lost cause, and they voted overwhelmingly to pull out of Russia altogether. No one was more unhappy with that decision than the British politician Winston L. S. Churchill (1874–1965). In fact, it was said that he went home and cried like a baby and hardly spoke to anyone for the next three days. Whether that was true or not is not known.

Just as disappointed at this outcome was Strohlbein himself. Not only did he fail to become a war hero, all those he killed were unarmed civilians. Even some of the other men in his outfit would no longer have anything to do with him. Finally, he and his unit had to cross the whole of Russia to reach Vladivostok (still controlled by Japan), board a ship, and finally return to America.

When he finally reached his hometown of Spring Valley, there were no parades or any other kind of fanfare. The townspeople simply ignored him, and some of the girls cringed at the sight of him, and this made him feel bad. At that point, Strohlbein decided to leave Spring Valley and join his older brother, Norman, in Chicago.

After his most disappointing homecoming in Spring Valley, Strohlbein said, "They can take this town and shove it up their—!" That was in June 1920, three months after he returned from the Army. Since his brother Norman was already gainfully employed at McPherson Plastics Inc. in Chicago, he asked to get a job there. On Monday, June 28, Strohlbein was hired, and the job paid very well. Here he was happy to make a new start. Strohlbein, his brother Norman, and Norman's wife, Marcia, lived in an Italian American neighborhood. Since the 1890s, there have been a great number of Italians migrating to Chicago, and by 1920, they became quite numerous there. One man by the name of Vittorio Lo Piccolo migrated straight from Naples, Italy, in 1915 with his wife, Diana, and their five children, Gina, born in 1894; Fiorina, born in 1898; Giuseppe (Joe), born in 1900; Giacomo (Jim), born in 1906; and finally Salvatore (Sal), born in 1908. The three sons were later to become proprietors of the Lo Piccolo Bros Lounge and Grill in 1933 after their father decided to return to Naples with his wife, Diana. Also in that neighborhood, there was another Italian family by the name of Lo Bianco. Like Vittorio Lo Piccolo, Umberto Lo Bianco along with his wife, Chiara, migrated to America in 1915 and settled in Chicago a year later, where he worked as a baker. They had two daughters, Angela, born on January 17, 1902, and Constanzia, born on June 30, 1906, in Genoa, Italy.

On Friday and Saturday nights, Strohlbein began frequenting the Lo Piccolo Italian Restaurant (it later became the Lo Piccolo Bros Lounge and Grill in 1933). Here he met several people of different ethnic backgrounds, but about half the clients were Italian Americans. Among these were Angela Lo Bianco and her sister, Constanzia, who by this time most people called Connie. Strohlbein was attracted to both girls, but he found Connie especially attractive. Connie was seventeen and Strohlbein twenty-two, in March 1924, when they first met. Connie's sister, Angela, was married in July 1923 to Umberto Cocirella. Connie was five feet, four inches, rather heavyset, with pitch-black hair, and a kind and gentle-looking face. After Strohlbeln proposed to her for the third time, she finally said yes. They were married on June 22, 1924, three weeks after Connie graduated from John Adams High School.

Since Strohlbein was becoming rather wealthy, he brought a house in northwest Chicago in an upscale neighborhood in September 1924.

However, their marriage turned out not to be a happy one. Strohlbein became increasingly possessive of Connie, and after they had their first child, Vernon, on May 25, 1925, he began to isolate Connie more and more from both her family and friends, making it painfully clear to her that only his friends and family were welcome in their home. As the years progressed, it gradually grew worse. On February 2, 1929, they had their second son, Steven.

Life for the two boys became increasingly miserable as they got older as well as for their mother, Connie. The Strohlbein boys were never allowed to have the things the other boys in the neighborhood enjoyed. They never had a dog, a bicycle, a wagon, a baseball bat, a catcher's glove, a football, or anything else a boy would cherish. Their father simply told them to do without, and when one of them got out of line, he would tie him to a chair and lash him five or ten times with a barber strap, and he would slap Connie really hard whenever she said something he didn't like. Why Connie put up with this abuse throughout the years remains a mystery to this day. Did she love him that much, or was she too afraid to do anything about it, even come to the rescue of her sons when they were being beaten?

In time, both Vernon and his brother, Steven, hated their father with a burning passion, especially after seeing how he treated their mother, Connie. Time and again, one of them would say to their mother, "Mom, why do you put up with this? As children, we have no choice, but you do. I can't wait till I'm eighteen so I can go to Spring Valley and move in with my uncle Jim and his family." Connie never quite knew what to say to her sons. In 1943 upon turning eighteen, Vernon joined the US Army and was severely wounded fighting the Japanese in the South Pacific. He was returned to the United States and interned at the VA hospital in Dearborn, Michigan, where he eventually recovered. Steven left home in 1946 and went to Spring

Valley to live with his uncle Jim. Jim Strohlbein never quite put any credence in Steven's story over how he and his brother, Vernon, were raised. He simply couldn't believe his brother Will could be so cruel.

Shortly after Steven left, Connie came up pregnant for the third time. Upon finding out, Strohlbein became extremely furious and started slapping Connie, brutally yelling, "Who's the father, and don't lie to me!

Come on, Connie, tell me, who is he and how dare you start seeing another man behind my back?"

Connie simply replied, "There is no other man, Will. Ask anyone around here, and please don't slap me again."

Strohlbein said, "There is no way on earth we're going to raise another child in this house. I had it with children, especially with my two miserable sons. What we're going to do is to put that baby up for adoption."

Connie replied, "Why not let my sister, Angela, and her husband, Umberto, take it? After all, Angela is my sister."

Strohlbein said, "Okay, Connie, then that's what we'll do."

The baby was born a girl on August 31, 1946, at St. Simon's Mercy Hospital. Since the adoption was already arranged, Connie had to have her eyes bandaged shut so she couldn't see her baby. Connie went home brokenhearted but was able to take comfort in the fact that her older sister was the baby's foster mother.

Not only did Strohlbein make life miserable for his own family, but for others in the neighborhood as well. He would curse the neighborhood children for coming on his property, calling them every filthy name imaginable. At one time, he grabbed a neighbor's cat just for prowling in his yard, picked up a ball peen hammer, and bashed its head in. The cat's owner, who lived across the alley, saw what he did and protested, "I was coming to get that cat. Why did you have to do that? My daughter will be brokenhearted over this."

Strohlbein simply replied, "So what? And get the—off my property, you—!"

At another point, Strohlbein called the police because two boys were playing baseball in front of his house, and on another occasion, Strohlbein threatened his next-door neighbor not to play his radio after 9:00 p.m.

Throughout the years as his circle of friends began to shrink, he started to feel lonely. Even his wife, Connie, could no longer keep him satisfied sexually. By 1948, he was promoted to third shift manager at McPherson's Plastics Inc. After a year or so, he would leave around 1:00 or 1:30 a.m. and put his assistant, Greg Morgan, in charge. Although this was unfair, Greg, for some reason or other, chose not to complain about it. At the end of 1952 or the beginning of 1953, he would drop in at the Lo Piccolo Bros Lounge and Grill when he would take off from work in order to get a drink or two before going home for the night. It was here he first laid eyes on Thalia Gomez in early 1955.

After the incident with Thalia on the night of her nineteenth birthday, or better said, the early morning of April 19, 1955, Strohlbein told Thalia he would get even as he was being told to leave by Sal Lo Piccolo welding a billy club. Four nights later, Strohlbein made good on his threat. That was shortly before 10:30 p.m. that Friday night, April 22, after Thalia's boyfriend dropped her off at her parents' house, where she lived.

On May 6, 1955, the day after his arrest, Strohlbein was arraigned in the Cook County Magistrate Court. At the advice of his lawyer, Bill Becker, forty-nine, he pleaded not guilty in spite of the evidence against him. Bill Becker told Strohlbein, "Don't worry, Will, we have an ace in the hole." That "ace" he was talking about was none other than the Assistant DA Victor Dixon, forty-two.

ADA Victor Dixon always disliked minorities, and the ones he hated most were the Mexicans, who began migrating to Chicago in greater numbers. This resentment began to cloud his judgment, and Strohlbein's attorney knew it. Victor Dixon looked somewhat like the then VP Richard Nixon with his shifty eyes and kinky dark hair.

The trial opened on Tuesday, May 24, at 1:00 p.m. with the bailiff announcing, "Docket no. 352777: The State of Illinois versus William Strohlbein, fifty-three. The charge: aggravated Battery resulting in permanent bodily injury. Judge Daniel Bass presiding."

Then came the bombshell that no one expected. ADA Victor Dixon simply walked up to the judge and said, "Due to insufficient evidence, the people decline to prosecute Mr. Strohlbein, and the people ask that these charges be dropped." Both the judge and the jury were totally flabbergasted over this.

No one in the courtroom could believe what the ADA just said, especially Rogelio and Carlotta Gomez, Thalia's parents. Officer Odell Williams, who was present at the trial, did all he could do in order to contain himself. Even the newspeople who were sent to cover this trial were also appalled by what the ADA said. The judge bitterly told all those present, "Today we've all seen a gross miscarriage of justice here, and I feel totally ashamed to have to let this monster go."

Later, Rogelio Gomez remarked, "In this country, there is no justice for us. We might as well return to Monterrey, Mexico." They did so in 1958, taking Thalia with them with her face mutilated once and for all. Thalia ended up living with her sister Guadalupe and her husband in Queretaro, not far from Mexico City.

As for Strohlbein, he found himself in great danger, not only from Thalia's boyfriend, Julio Ruiz, but also from his neighbors, who were all aware of what he did to that young woman and how he got away with it. Finally upon learning that McPherson's Plastics Inc. was opening another plant in nearby Oak Park, he requested and got a transfer there. He and his wife, Connie, were never heard from by the people in that neighborhood again. However, Strohlbein acted the same way toward his new neighbors in Oak Park as he did toward those in Chicago.

CHAPTER 3

The Helen McMurray Case

'T'he Strohlbein case was not to be the only miscarriage of justice Williams was to witness. There had been grisly murders, forcible rapes, children being sexually abused (sometimes by their parents), and all kinds of cases of aggravated battery.

There was the case of a thirty-one-year-old woman who, out of her drunkenness, hit and killed a six-year-old boy and then simply drove off. That took place on Wednesday afternoon, October 3, 1956. She was five feet, eight inches tall, weighed around 165 pounds., had red hair, green eyes, and her face was covered with mascara, especially below her eyebrows. The car she was driving at the time was a white two-door 1953 Mercury. Officer Williams along with his partner, Sergeant Kevin Hurley, were called to investigate the case. While Sergeant Hurley was canvassing for witnesses, Officer Williams searched the scene of the accident thoroughly and did turn up some trace evidence. One of the witnesses questioned by Sergeant Hurley described the driver as a redheaded woman who appeared to be in her midthirties. Another witness described the car as either a 1952 Ford or Mercury. No one was close enough to get the license plate number: As Hurley and Williams were driving through a neighborhood not far from the accident, they noticed a white 1953 Mercury parked in an apartment parking lot. They stopped, went up to the car and saw the damage on the right side with traces of blood near the cracked right headlight. They ran the license plate number and it came back: White 1953 Mercury with two doors and a visor over the windshield. The owner: Ms. Helen McMurray, thirty-one, 11442 Ridgewood Avenue, apartment 4D, Chicago, Illinois. That was Ms. McMurray's address, and the two policemen went up to her apartment to interview her. They knocked, and she said, "What the—do you want?" Sgt. Hurley replied, "There has been an accident over on Hillyer Blvd forty- five minutes ago, and we would like to have a talk with you." The woman's belligerence slowly began to give way to apprehension.

At first, she strongly denied it but decided not to say anymore. They began to smell alcohol on her breath, and Hurley asked her, "Just how much did you have to drink today, ma'am?"

The woman replied, "That is none of your—business, Mr.! Now just get the—out of here."

The woman's name was Helen McMurray and she and her boyfriend had recently broken up since he was already planning to marry another woman. Helen was totally devastated when he told her about the upcoming wedding. That was a week and half earlier on Monday, September 24. Thereafter she turned to drinking heavily. She was born Helen Grace McMurray on February 9, 1925, the oldest of three children born to Mike and Dorothy McMurray. Her two brothers were Pete McMurray, born on March 11, 1928, and Kevin, on May 31, 1930. Mike McMurray was a ne'er-do-weller who spent most of his time drinking and hanging out with his ne'er-do-well friends rather than working. One night in 1937 when Helen was twelve, some elderly man who noticed how good-looking she was with her red hair and rather plump figure began stalking her. Later that night, he pulled her into his car, drove to an isolated hut on Lake Michigan, and dragged her inside, where he began to perform oral sex on her before brutally raping her. The ordeal went on for about four hours. After that, he drove her back to her neighborhood. Neither her father, Mike, nor her mother, Dorothy, ever notified the Chicago Police nor sought medical attention for her.

Helen would never be the same after this, and what made it even more painful to her was the fact that her parents didn't care enough to call the police or take her to a nearby hospital to see that her injuries were looked after. In the summer of 1941 when she was sixteen, she finally left home once and for all only to be heard from some nine years later. She settled in downtown Chicago, where pimps and prostitutes hung out, some of them working for the Chicago Mafia. She soon fell in with a brutal pimp by the name of Jesse Cook, forty- four, who readily noticed her red hair and full figure. To him, she was a gold mine as he made more money off her than all his other girls. Fortunately, he was not associated with the Chicago Mafia.

Helen was arrested time and again for prostitution but always went back to it, not because she liked it, but out of sheer necessity. In the summer of 1944, while she was serving another stretch in the Cook County jail, she fell in with a woman named Diane McMahon, forty- four, who was an avowed lesbian and a partner of Madame June Lortz, forty-six, who ran an escort service in downtown Chicago. For a while, Helen and Diane had a lesbian relationship, but that was to be short-lived. In February 1947, Diane developed a case of nephritis and succumbed to it ten days later. However, her partner, June Lortz, took Helen under her wing and employed her as a professional prostitute. Here Helen made quite a bit of money, but in the spring of 1949, her big break came. One night as two Chicago businessmen were patronizing June Lortz's lounge, they soon noticed Helen and what a perfect figure she had plus her red hair. It turned out that one of the men worked for a modeling agency. Finally one of the men asked Helen directly, "How would you like to work as a model?"

Helen replied, "Would I ever? Of course I'm interested." Then the man said to Helen, "Well then, it's settled."

This meant that Helen could really make a great deal of money, and she'd never have to work as a prostitute again. After signing the contract with the agency, Helen began to acquire more wealth than she knew what to do with, so she decided to pay her parents a visit. That was in March 1950.

When Helen reached her parents' rat-and-roach-infested apartment, she was rather appalled to see the miserable conditions her parents had to endure. Mike was compelled day after day to go out in the gutter to collect empty soda bottles and turn them in for cash. Her brother Pete was in the Navy at that time, sending them what money he could spare, and Kevin helped out the best he could.

When Helen knocked at the front door, her father, upon opening it, simply said, "What do you want? You can plainly see we have nothing to give you."

Her mother, Dorothy, said, "Please, Mike, don't be so rude. After all, she is the only daughter we have."

In a way, one cannot truly blame Mike. He was already seventy-five years old with his eyes going bad and had a lump on his right side. Dorothy, although she was nearly sixty-seven, was still in relatively good health.

Mike said, "Please, Helen, forgive me. I didn't mean to be so rude, but with this never-ending pain on my right side, I can barely sleep at night."

Helen replied, "That's all right, Father, I forgive you. Besides, can I take a look at your right side where the pain is?" Mike said, "Yes, Helen, you certainly can."

As Mike pulled up his shirt and exposed his right side, Helen noticed a huge lump there. She asked, "Father, how long have you had this lump, and did you tell your doctor about it?"

Mike replied, "Just who can see a doctor these days? They charge too much."

Helen replied, "That's no problem, Father. I'll pay the bill if you'll only go and see one. Now I'll set up an appointment with the nearest doctor."

Finally Mike said, "I cannot thank you enough, Helen, for what you're now doing for us. I only wish I'd been a better parent." After setting up the said appointment, Helen opened her purse and pulled out ten twenty-dollar bills and laid them on the table. Mike asked, "Why are you doing this, Helen?"

Helen replied, "It's a gift from me to you. I'll be back next week to see how you're doing. Goodbye, folks." She left the bills on the table.

Helen did return as promised and learned that her father was stricken with a form of cancer. The doctors told Mike that it would be rather expensive to have the lump removed, but upon hearing this, Helen said, "If you go and have that lump removed, I'll pay the medical bills." Neither Mike nor Dorothy quite knew what to say upon hearing Helen's offer. Helen simply told them. "I am now a professional model, and the work pays extremely well."

"In fact," Helen went on, "I'd love to buy you a house in an upscale neighborhood far away from this unholy rat-and-roach-infested dump. It's a wonder that neither of you have hepatitis by now. In fact, instead of trading in my 1941 Studebaker for a new Ford, I'll give it to you for a gift. Although you're almost blind, Father, Mom can see well enough to drive it."

True to her word, Helen did buy a house early in 1951 in an upscale neighborhood on Chicago's north side and helped her parents move in. After the operation, Mike did improve, although his eyesight continued to slowly deteriorate. For the first time since they were married, Mike and Dorothy found happiness. Even Helen's two brothers could hardly believe what she did for their parents.

Mike was always a ne'er-do-well person and lived in poverty with his mother until she died in 1922, when he was forty-seven and still unmarried. Not long after that, he met Mrs. Dorothy Stevens, who was thirty-nine at that time. Dorothy herself had a rather tragic life, first losing her husband Frank in WWI and her son Donald nine months later in 1919, when he succumbed to Spanish influenza. Finally in 1924, with Dorothy pregnant, they got married and had Helen six months later. Even at that time during the roaring twenties, they continued to live in grinding poverty.

Finally Helen turned to her brothers and asked how she could help them out. Kevin finally said, "I bought this 1947 Frazer Manhattan, but I don't know how I'm going to come up with enough money to make my next payment."

Helen said, "Relax, Kevin, I'll make the payment for you. After all, what are brothers and sisters for?" Helen not only made the monthly payment but paid off the balance altogether.

Throughout the years as Helen prospered in her career, she began to date men but had to tell them of her shady past. Most of them appreciated her honesty. One night in May 1955 as she and her friends were having a night out in a posh downtown lounge, she met a sailor by the name of Fred Brockton from a small town in Connecticut. As a child, he was always fascinated by the open seas, so he joined the Navy in 1947 after graduating from High School when he was eighteen. She caught his eye, and he asked her for a dance and offered to buy her a drink, and she accepted.

Ensign Fred Brockton was born on June 9, 1929, in the small community of Quinebaug in northeastern Connecticut, the only child born to Lloyd and Theresa Brockton. As he grew up, he was always fascinated with the open seas around the world, so after graduating from high school, he enlisted in the US Navy. In 1955, he was stationed at the Great Lakes naval base near Chicago when he met Helen. The night they first met in the lounge, Fred and Helen hit it off quite well. Later that night, Fred became rather intoxicated, so he was hardly able to drive, so Helen decided to take him to her place in order to sober him up since his forty-eight-hour liberty was due to expire the following Monday night at 6:00 p.m. That took place on Saturday night, May 28, 1955. As she didn't bring her own car, she asked her friends June and Virginia, whom she rode with, to help her with Fred. During that night, she and Fred engaged in sex although he was still extremely intoxicated. The next morning as Fred was sobering up, he asked Helen to forgive him, which she did. That afternoon, Helen took Fred out and drove around northern Chicago and even driving as far north as the small town of Glencoe. They had a huge dinner and later returned to her apartment.

The next day, Helen drove Fred back to the naval base, and upon arriving there, Helen asked him, "Will I see you again, Fred?"

Fred replied, "Of course you will, Helen."

Helen didn't quite believe him although she gave him her phone number. To her surprise, Fred called her the day after and said, "In a week from this coming Saturday, I am going on a twenty-four-hour liberty and would like to date you."

Helen simply replied, "That'll be splendid. I can hardly wait."

This "romance" went on for over a year. For Helen, 1955 was an excellent year careerwise and 1956 proved to be even more successful. She was always required to travel to cities across the United States, and in the summer of 1956, she was required to spend two months in Paris, Madrid, and Munich, Germany. She made a great deal of money modeling but sorely missed her boyfriend, Fred.

In the meantime, as Fred was on furlough visiting his parents in Connecticut, he noticed a young woman by the name of Barbara Jannich and couldn't quite get her out of his system. Barbara was born on September 8, 1934, the third child to Helmut and Gretchen Jannich. The others were Dieter, born in 1925; Stefan, in 1927; and Marlene, on August 3, 1937. Helmut and his wife immigrated to the United States shortly after WWI because the German economy gravely suffered as a direct result of the 1919 Treaty of Versailles, so Mr. Jannick could find no work, and the Deutschmark became practically worthless. First, they settled in Boston, but since he was an electrician by trade, he had no trouble in finding a high-paying job. In 1929, they moved to the small community of

Quinebaug next door to the Brocktons. Although Fred and Barbara were neighbors since she was born, Fred didn't really notice her since she was rather heavyset with mousy brown hair. Barbara never liked her first name, Ulrike, so she went by her middle name instead. In the late summer of 1956, that all changed big time. Barbara graduated from Yale University in New Haven that spring with a bachelor's degree in anthropology. She was hoping to go to the Middle East to learn more about the ancient Akkadians as well as the other ancient peoples of that part of the world. Upon seeing Barbara, Fred asked her out for a date. She agreed, and within two weeks, Fred realized just how beautiful she became and fell in love with her. He proposed to her on September 8, her twenty-second birthday, but she said, "I'll have to think it over, Fred." Finally on Sunday, September 23, after proposing to her for the third time, Barbara finally said yes, and the wedding date was set for Saturday, October 6.

Barbara asked Fred, "If you are stationed in some remote area such as the South Pacific, can I live there to be near you?"

Fred replied, "Of course you can, Barbara."

The next day, Fred took a plane back to Chicago, and when he arrived, he called Helen and said, "Helen, there is something I must tell you."

Helen asked, "What is it, Fred?"

Fred replied, "I can't tell you over the phone, so can I see you at your apartment this evening?"

Helen said, "Of course you can. You should know by now you're always welcome here. I'm looking forward to seeing you tonight around six o'clock if you can make it."

At 6:00 p.m., Fred did show up and said to Helen, "In a week and a half from now, I'm going to be married in my hometown to a very wonderful young lady. You'd love her too if you met her. We grew up together, as she was my next-door neighbor. Until this summer, I never truly knew just how beautiful she really is. Right now, I'm inviting you to our wedding if you can get away on Saturday, October 6. That's the day we're going to be married."

Upon hearing this, Helen's jaw dropped and could hardly believe what Fred just told her. First, she went for a drink and offered Fred one too. She sat on the sofa dumbfounded for about an hour and a half, but as she recovered from this initial bombshell, she became quite angry and threw her fourth or fifth drink in Fred's face. Then she started yelling obscenities at him and even spat in his face. Fred became frightened and hurriedly ran out of the apartment, fearing that Helen may injure him severely. Since that night, Helen was almost constantly intoxicated, which culminated in the October 3 hit-and-run accident, which left the six-year-old Leonard W. Corey dead.

After being taken into custody, Helen became totally indifferent to her fate. She was arraigned on the following day, October 4, and as she pleaded no contest, her sentencing date was set for Friday, October 19. She was also ordered to surrender her driver's license. The judge sentenced her to a prison term from two to ten years for vehicular manslaughter and driving while intoxicated. After paying the $10,000 bail required for her freedom, she went back to her apartment and gave her landlord notice, turned her Mercury over to her mother, Dorothy, and gave her other possessions to her brothers, Peter and Kevin.

A week later on Friday, October 26, she was put on a state bus to be transported to the Illinois Correctional Facility for Women in Dwight, Illinois. Here she was to spend the next two years of her life. She got along fairly well with the other inmates and even tried to set up some kind of lesbian relationship with an eighteen-year-old girl by the name of Sharon Decker from Quincy, Illinois. Sharon would have none of it and warned the staff. Later on, Helen caught her in a secluded place in the hallway and threatened her, saying, "That was a very stupid thing you did, Sharon. Whether you like it or not, you're going to be mine, and you will do whatever I tell you to. Even if you succeed in having me put in solitary confinement, I'll eventually get out and really hurt you. You see, I already killed a six-year-old boy, and that's why

I'm here." Helen then proceeded to stick her finger into Sharon's rectum and then into her vagina as she protested and begged, "Stop it, don't do this to me," but Helen persisted.

The next morning on March 9, 1957, Sharon suddenly climbed to the top tier of Building C and threw herself off, landing on her back. Sharon was immediately rushed to the prison dispensary, where she was told she would never walk again. Later on, Helen took this news with total indifference.

In June 1957, a guard by the name of Zachary "Zack" Gallagher was assigned to Building C, where Helen was housed. He was forty- two, had kinky brown hair with a bald spot on top, married but had no children because he and his wife, Elaine, both agreed never to have any. They were married for the last twenty years and lived in the nearby community of Odell, situated between Dwight and Pontiac. He was assigned the second shift when he met Helen. One night, she offered him sex in exchange for vodka and cigarettes. He gladly accepted and even brought her small amounts of marijuana. The affair lasted about four months, until the prison warden, Mrs. Dora Schroer, forty-seven, became suspicious of Gallagher's activities and promptly had him reassigned to another building. However, he was never truly able to get Helen out of his system.

Finally on Wednesday, January 28, 1959, Helen was released from prison, and her brother Pete drove down to Dwight to pick her up and take her home to his house. Although his wife, Frieda, had misgivings, she reluctantly accepted her company. Even Helen's parents were truly overjoyed upon hearing about her release. Helen wanted to go back to work again as a model but had no transportation. She did buy herself a black two-door 1950 Ford Tudor, but on Tuesday, March 24, when she went to the Illinois Department of Motor Vehicles in order get to her driver's license restored, the lady clerk told her, "I'm sorry, ma'am, but you've been blacklisted by the Illinois DMV, and therefore we cannot renew your driver's license. You'll probably have to go to court and sue for it."

Helen, upon hearing what the woman told her, got angry and yelled out, "—you, you—!" and stormed out of the building. She was from then on compelled to depend on others for transportation. She did find work at local department stores and advertised lingerie in the commercial section of the *Chicago Tribune*. She later rented a modest apartment on Chicago's near north side.

On Friday night, June 12, after she just returned home from work, there was a knock on her door. It turned out to be none other than Zack Gallagher himself. She asked, "How did you find me, you creep? You— men are all alike, you! Now tell me exactly what you want and then get the—out of here!"

Zack simply said, "Helen, I understand that some man has really hurt you in the past, so please don't judge all men by what he did to you."

Suddenly Helen broke down in tears and said to Zack, "Please forgive me, Zack. Since I was dropped by that sailor three years ago, my attitude toward men has become truly bitter. If you'd like to, since I have no special plans for tonight, go out with me to a local restaurant for a meal and a drink."

Zack replied, "Excellent, let's do it."

Suddenly Zack started to feel guilty since he was now, for the first time in their marriage, two-timing his wife, Elaine. Zack married Elaine in the summer of 1937 when he was twenty-two and she, twenty. They mutually agreed never to have any children and lived quite happily for the last twenty-two years in Odell. Since he met Helen, his feelings changed, and he moved to Chicago to be near her.

Finally on Wednesday, October 21, 1959, Zack proposed to Helen. Helen said, "You already know that I have a criminal record, and besides, I can't even drive a car."

Zack replied, "That's no problem since I own a 1956 Dodge, which is a good car."

Later that night, Helen said, "Yes, Zack, I'll marry you, but first you'll need to divorce your wife, Elaine."

Zack replied, "That, I plan to do that as soon as possible."

The next day, Zack told Elaine that he found someone else and that he fell deeply in love with her. Upon hearing this, Elaine became totally devastated since she still loved him deeply. At first, Elaine said she was not going to divorce him, and she would do all she could in order to hold their marriage together.

Two days later when he was half drunk, he came to Elaine and said, "Just what right do you have to rule my life? I'll give you anything you want, but let me go and marry the woman I love."

Elaine said, "It won't be that simple."

Then Zack became even more violent and turned over the kitchen table, dumped food out of the refrigerator, and turned over the bookcases in the living room before storming out of the house. He said to Elaine, "I'll get my divorce if that's the last thing I ever do, so please don't try to stop me."

In the end, Elaine saw the handwriting on the wall and told Zack, "I'll give you your freedom if it means that much to you."

Zack replied, "It does. I'm truly sorry, Elaine, but that's the way I feel."

The divorce became final on March 24, 1960, and Zack and Helen married on May 21, two months later. Both Zack and Helen were in a state of supreme euphoria, and Helen came up pregnant four months later with her first child. The child was born a girl on March 25, 1961, and they named her Mildred, after Zack's mother. She was rather chubby like her mother was, with very light-brown hair. Both Zack and Helen adored her. Unfortunately, this was not to last. In August 1961, Helen was diagnosed with a form of ovarian cancer.

Both ovaries had to be removed before the cancer could spread to her bladder and uterus. The operation took place at St. Leo's Mercy Hospital on Chicago's north side on November 21, and it was successful. The ovaries were removed, and there was no sign of cancer anywhere else. After several checkups, there was absolutely no sign of the cancer returning. However, since her ovaries provided her body with female hormones as well as testosterone, she began to sink into a severe depression for the lack of them. Finally in June, she told Zack, "I'm severely depressed now, and I never felt this way before. Right now I won't be any good for either you or Millie. I also told my gynecologist, and she recommended that I go to Chicago Lakeshore Hospital for treatment. I think that's best." Zack agreed.

Helen was admitted there on June 11, and she stayed for about four months. She was released October 26. At first, Helen seemed to be her old self and enjoyed the company of both Zack and Millie. By the end of January however, all that began to slowly change as her depression was once again returning. Finally Helen told Zack, "I want you to take Millie and yourself back to Odell and live with your parents. As you see, I can no longer function either as a model, a wife, or a mother. Please, Zack, do as I ask."

Zack sadly acquiesced to her wishes, took Millie, and moved back to Odell, where he was hired by the State of Illinois as a guard at the State Training School for Boys in neighboring Pontiac.

In the meantime, Helen had a delivery boy bring her groceries as she would no longer venture out of the house. Even her friends stopped coming around to see her. As the weeks went on, Helen's depression grew progressively worse, and she was almost always intoxicated in order to fight it. Finally on Friday, March 29, she did go out for a walk, and as she walked through different neighborhoods, she saw a blue-and-white 1955 Hudson parked along one of the streets. She noticed that the key was still in the ignition, so she slid into the car, started the motor, and drove off.

As she drove around, she suddenly stopped, dropped into Brendell's Liquor Store, and bought a quart-size bottle of vodka. Finally around 10:30 p.m. or so as she was driving along the shores of Lake Michigan, she found a secluded spot, parked the Hudson, and started drinking. This was the very same spot where she and her boyfriend, Ensign Fred Brockton, would spend hours on end making love while looking out over Lake Michigan back in the fifties, but now that was but a mere memory. As she sat in the car and continued her drinking, it was becoming crystal clear to her that the proverbial light at the end of the tunnel was not to be but only more tunnel at the end of the tunnel. Around 3:20 a.m. as she continued to drink, she watched the crescent moon rise up over Lake Michigan in the eastern sky. It was a pretty sight to behold, but it only added to her misery. By this time, she knew she would never be happy again as there was no longer a way out of her depression except suicide. Shortly after four thirty, Helen noticed a pier near where she parked, started the motor, and now driving at a high rate of speed, drove on to the pier and then straight into Lake Michigan. However, there was a witness to this suicide. He was Mr. Otto Taflinger, seventy-six, who was walking his

English bulldog along the shore when he saw the blue and white 1955 Hudson plunge into the lake from the pier. He went to the nearest phone booth and called the Chicago Police. The police then ordered the car to be pulled out of the lake. Inside it, Helen was found dead. The car was owned by Henry Holtmeyer, twenty-one, who reported it missing earlier that morning.

After the initial inquest, the police wrote out their findings, which said, "Date: March 30, 1963. The decedent: Mrs. Helen Grace McMurray Gallagher. Age: thirty-eight. Married, with one child. Race: white. Eyes: green. Hair: red. Height: 5'8". Weight: 172 lbs. Occupation: Model. Cause of death: A nervous breakdown and a severe depression culminating in her suicide by drowning. DOB: Feb. 9, 1925. DOD: March 30, 1963."

This was terrible news for her parents, who were by this time very old, and both her brothers. Even Officer Williams, who arrested her in 1956 for a deadly hit-and-run accident, felt sorry for her.

CHAPTER 4

The Feud with Willie Floyd

On a balmy Monday afternoon, April 13, 1959, as Officer Williams was beginning his shift, he suddenly saw a woman walking in his direction. She had black hair and appeared to be between forty-five to fifty years old. In fact, one could take her for the twin sister of Italian actress Ana Magnani (1908–1973), but she appeared to be slightly younger. Upon seeing Williams, she suddenly stopped, made the sign of the cross, and said to herself "II stesso diavolo!" and then she hurriedly crossed the street in order to avoid him. Women generally disliked Williams, but that was the first time one accused him of being the devil. On Saturday, April 18, he arrested a seventy-two-year-old man by the name of Herbert George for beating a five-year-old boy with a baseball bat. The boy was severely injured, and Williams wanted this old man prosecuted, but the old man's sleazy lawyer managed to get the case thrown out.

Finally on Wednesday, April 22, Williams's superior, Lieutenant Randall Rodgers, fifty-four, said in a gruff voice, "Williams, you're being transferred. Get your gear together and report to the seventeenth precinct right away."

This was more or less of a lower-class neighborhood, where crime was more rampant. Williams knew he was going to be quite busy as long as he was assigned there.

Two years later on Friday, September 8, 1961, Williams and his partner, Officer Ted Flannigan, forty-five, were called to Quincy H. Hadley Elementary School around 2:30 p.m. The incident involved an acid-throwing incident. The victim was Rodney Fairchild, nine, a negro pupil in the fourth grade, as well as his attacker, Willie Floyd, also nine and black. In fact, most of the teachers and students there were black.

Willy Floyd's full name was William Floyd Quarles, born to Nathan and his wife, Jennifer. The family was well off since Nathan was successful as a realtor. The three older children of Nathan Quarles turned out to be good people, but not Willie Floyd. Willie Floyd was born on January 29, 1952, the youngest of the four Quarles children.

Even at an early age, his parents noticed how he would love to torture insects and especially ants. As he grew up, he graduated to drowning kittens and killing birds for apparently no reason. In school, he showed the same cruelty toward other students in his class. Finally on Friday, September 8, after winning $1.25 from Rodney Fairchild in a game of dice, he told Rodney to pay up. Rodney reached into his pocket and pulled out two quarters, two dimes, and a penny and said, "Willie, this is all I have right now. I'll pay the rest next Monday."

Willie replied, "That's not good enough. I want all my money now, now, now!"

Later that afternoon, Willie snuck into the school chemical lab and pilfered out a beaker of sulfuric acid. He again said to Rodney, "You pay up now or else!"

Rodney again told Willie, "I can't," and Willie threw the whole beaker of acid into Rodney's face, causing him to lose his left eye and leaving his face disfigured for life.

After arresting Willie Floyd and taking him to the police station, Williams asked him, "How do you feel now about what you did to your friend Rodney today?"

Willie simply replied, "I feel nothing. Should I? I won $1.25 in a dice game from him, but he didn't want to pay up. I had to show him I meant business."

For Williams, this was truly shocking since many criminals showed some remorse over what they did, but Willie Floyd acted as though nothing happened. This was by no means to be his last run-in with the law.

After being taken to the Cook County Jail and placed in the juvenile section, the judge in his case decided to send Willie Floyd to the Illinois State Training School for Boys at Pontiac, Illinois. There he remained for the next nine months. He was sent there again in October 1963 for robbing a restaurant with a firearm in which he drew a year. This time while he was in Pontiac, on April 10, 1964, he raped another black boy, who was two years younger than he was. The

Warden then gave him a simple choice, spend the next four months in solitary confinement or spend another year in Pontiac. Willie Floyd opted for the latter.

In the meantime back in Chicago, a six-year-old girl was grabbed, taken into an isolated garage, and raped by a middle-aged white man on May 26, 1964. Her name was Margie Schoenwetter. Officer Williams was assigned to the case and was determined to catch the creep who did it. After she was taken to St. Simon's Mercy Hospital and treated for her injuries, she later confided in Officer Williams since she perceived how sincere he was and gave him a description of her attacker. He was in his middle fifties, rather heavyset, about five feet, nine inches tall, and had gray hair. After surveying that neighborhood, Williams noticed a man fitting the description of Margie's attacker and put him under surveillance. It wouldn't be long before Williams noticed him stalking another girl. Williams stopped the man and asked him, "What is your name, and where do you live?"

The man replied, "Melvin Morgan. if that's any of your—business, and I live at 3252 Oakdale Street. Aren't there enough real criminals out there for you to harass? I'm a poor man just trying to get by." Moreover, Melvin Morgan was not the man's true name, as Williams later found out. It was Douglas Gould.

Later on, Williams ran his rap sheet and discovered he had several convictions for child molesting, including a six-year-old girl by the name of Shelly Reeves, who managed to get away before he could do her any harm. For that he drew two years in Joliet Prison. Since the laws on child molesting were rather weak in those days, they could never keep this man incarcerated for more than two years at a time.

He was born Douglas Manfred Gould on March 11, 1908, in downtown Chicago, the youngest of three children born to Nicholas and Beatrice Gould. In 1932, he married Ms. Josephine McKenzie. She was two years younger than he. Even back in the 1930s he had a penchant for luring little girls into his truck, saying "I lost my kitten, will you help me find it?" or something like that. Most of the time it worked. Finally on Saturday night, April 25, 1936, Josephine finally went into the basement and caught Douglas performing oral sex on a seven- year-old girl. She called the Chicago Police to have him arrested and then sued him for a divorce.

Early in 1965, the ABC-affiliated local TV station allotted Reverend Charles McIntyre, forty-four, a half hour slot between 6:30 and 7:00 p.m. The program was called "The Pastor's Study." Reverend McIntyre was an Episcopalian bishop who always ranted against corruption either in Chicago's City Hall or on the Chicago police force. Beginning in May of that year, he came up with the conspiracy theory that the CIA used the Chicago Mafia to assassinate President John F. Kennedy (1917–1963). One night, he pointed out the fact that Vice President Lyndon Johnson (1908–1973) wanted the war in Vietnam, whereas Kennedy didn't. Later on, he pointed out that mob boss Sam Giancana (1908–1975) felt betrayed by President Kennedy, so he turned to the CIA since they were the masters of deceit and could either fabricate or destroy important evidence.

As the weeks went by in June and July, Sam Giancana became increasingly agitated by what this preacher was saying each night on TV. He finally had enough and decided to do something about it, but what? One of his lieutenants finally told him, "I have a very good idea, Sam. Let's just find someone to throw acid in his face. That'll shut him up once and for all." The man went on to say, "I have a very good candidate for the job. His name is John Ramboletti, and although he's only nineteen, he will get the job done. He has no compunctions about how much he may hurt anyone. To him, a job is a job."

Sam Giancana replied, "Excellent idea."

The next day, Ramboletti was called into the office of one of Giancana's lieutenants who told him, "We have a job for you. We want you to shut this Reverend McIntyre up once and for all. First, you case the place and then sneak on to the grounds of that TV station with the beaker of sulfuric acid, then make sure no one sees you and hide yourself until he comes out. There will be his chauffeur, but we can take care of him. He's an old man married with children. Now do you understand the instructions I handed you?"

Ramboletti replied, "Yes, I do."

The man said, "Here's $5,000 now and the other $5,000 when the job is done."

Ramboletti replied, "Thank you, sir."

On Tuesday night, August 3, 1965, the plan was set in motion. Shortly after as Reverend McIntyre came out of the building and started walking up to his car, Ramboletti suddenly ran up to him and threw the beaker of acid in his face. Then Ramboletti ran off, threw the empty beaker to the pavement, shattering it into over one thousand pieces, jumped into the car waiting for him, and drove off. Later that night, Ramboletti was paid in full.

As for Reverend McIntyre, he was rushed to the ER in St. Leo's Mercy Hospital with both his face and hands burned to almost a cinder and totally blind. Later when the detectives came, Dr. John Henderson told them, "He'll never see again," and added, "What kind of a monster would be callous enough to do such a dastardly thing such as this?"

One of the detectives replied, "Whoever it is, we'll all work overtime in order to catch him!"

Sam Giancana knew that he and his henchmen would have to lie low for a good while until this case blew over. Officer Williams, as to be expected, worked exceeding hard on cracking this case and eventually did.

Officer Williams observed that John Ramboletti fit the description of Reverend McIntyre's attacker, so he put Ramboletti under surveillance. By the end of August, it paid off. Williams thereupon arrested Ramboletti and brought him to police headquarters. However, this move outraged Sam Giancana and his lieutenants.

The next day, Ramboletti was arraigned in Cook County Court with Judge Robert Foss presiding. However, Reverend McIntyre's chauffer, Paul Goodings, fifty-two, who was the only witness for the prosecution suddenly changed his testimony after positively identifying Ramboletti in a lineup the day before. He told the judge that he only saw the back of Ramboletti's head and refused to testify against him. The night before, after Goodings left the police station and returned home, two men approached him in front of his house as he got out of his car and told him, "If you go ahead and testify in court tomorrow, something very bad will happen to one of your family members. You see, we know where your wife works and where your kids go to school, so you'd better change your testimony fast. You'll say, 'I can't positively identify the defendant.'"

The chauffer complied and did what he was told. As a result, the case against Ramboletti fell apart, and the Chicago Mafia no longer felt it was under pressure.

As for Reverend McIntyre, he was severely disabled, blind, and totally under the care of his devoted wife, Mary Ann. He took this in stride as he felt God had a purpose in this. He and his wife later returned to Boston, Massachusetts. Given enough time and with the cooperation of the FBI, the CIA may have been exposed for what it truly was but that was not to be at that time.

Due to the publicity generated by the news media over the acid-throwing incident with his picture in all the Chicago newspapers, Ramboletti felt deeply compelled to leave Chicago and did so by enlisting in the US Army Special Forces on Thursday, September 23. He was later sent to Vietnam, where he served and thrived.

One morning in early April 1966, a night watchman was found beaten up and badly injured as he was about to report for work the night before. His name was John Burris, fifty-six. Later that morning as he seemed to get better, he told Officers Williams and Tom Swanson all he knew. He never got a good look at his assailants. All he knew was that they were juveniles.

In a warehouse not far from there, another elderly man was found beaten unconscious less than two weeks later. His name was Edgar Rodemann, and he was fifty-one. Since he was unconscious, he could tell the police nothing.

As time went on, there were more and more incidents like this, so Williams questioned a witness who saw a pink-and-white 1956 Dodge with four juveniles inside drive off after another elderly man was attacked on Friday, June 24. Williams canvassed the local neighborhoods. The next night, he did locate a car fitting that description. It was a pink-and-white 1956 Dodge parked at 11232 Vernor Lane. Williams ran the license number, and the owner turned out to be Russell Heimler, fifty. Moreover, he did have a nineteen- year-old son by the name of Jerry.

The following Monday night, June 27, Williams along with his new partner, Officer Tom Swanson, twenty, parked on Vernor Lane and observed a juvenile (probably Jerry Heimler himself) take out a six- pack of Stroh's beer, drive off, stop about four blocks away, and pick up two of his friends. Williams followed them without being noticed. Then he noticed that they were stalking another elderly man. Williams and Swanson went into the empty building, where the man worked as a boiler room attendant. Sure enough, the teenagers showed up to beat the old man to a pulp. Suddenly Williams and Swanson leaped out and nailed the juveniles after calling for backup. All four of the juveniles were taken into custody. The parents of these juveniles became outraged upon finding out about their arrests.

Later on, a negro woman by the name of Mrs. Sarah Bradley, forty-seven, came to police headquarters to identify the same four boys as the ones who drugged and forced her daughter Sandra, fourteen, into performing oral sex on them. That happened on Friday, May 13, a month and a half earlier. The case was almost forgotten, until those four boys were arrested. They were Jerry Heimler, nineteen; Kevin Noonan, eighteen; Chris Wilson, seventeen; and Johnnie Brown, nineteen. However, a sleazy city counselor by the name of Thomas Courtney, forty-nine, showed up to bail these hoodlums out. He told the police that these were essentially good boys and had a great future ahead of them since two of them were awarded college scholarships and the others were planning to go to tech school. Williams became indignant as he listened to this crummy politician. Williams approached the man and said, "There is a colored woman here whose daughter was taken, drugged, and forced to perform oral sex on these 'good' boys last month. What about her rights? I don't hear anything about her rights!"

Williams's superior, Lieutenant Dan Crawford, fifty-two, said, "That'll be enough out of you, Williams, and stop showing your moral indignation. It's making you look too superior. I strongly suggest that you adjust yourself to the world we live in."

Later Officer Swanson told Williams, "Don't let it get you down, Odell. This is not nor will it ever be a perfect world."

Unfortunately, City Counselor Courtney and the team of lawyers as sleazy as those "good" boys were managed, probably for a bribe, to get the charges against list them thrown out and get them off the hook, much to the disgust of Officers Williams and Swanson.

Shortly thereafter on Saturday morning, July 16, almost everyone in Chicago became aware of the Richard Speck case, where he murdered eight student nurses the Thursday night before. Williams suddenly remarked,

"At least those girls were lucky since their sufferings are over. The reason I say it is because I cannot nor ever be able to forget what happened to Thalia Gomez over ten years ago, not to mention what happened to Reverend Charles McIntyre last year."

Swanson replied, "In that sense, I can agree with you."

As time went on, Williams grew increasingly disillusioned with the Chicago Police Department with all its graft and corruption, plus its shady deals with the Chicago Mafia. With the release of those four good boys, as Courtney called them, Williams confided to his partner, Tom Swanson, "Just what are we really doing for the people of Chicago? The creep who blinded that minister last year got off, and I strongly suspect the Chicago mob. Look at what happened to Thalia Gomez. The animal who cut her face up is still as free as a bird in a tree. None of this is right."

Finally in the fall of 1967, Willie Floyd was released from the reform school in Pontiac for the umpteenth time. However, he and his close friend Richard Thorpe, with whom he attended school since both were in the first grade, decided to hold up a liquor store on Chicago's south side. The heist went off smoothly, but Willie Floyd was once again caught. Thorpe was released the same night, but Willie had to appear before Juvenile Judge Henry G. Fleming, forty-nine, on Saturday, February 3, 1968 at 9:00 a.m. in Cook County Juvenile Court. Judge Fleming, who was known to be a so-called bleeding heart liberal, was expected to let Willie off the hook, which he in fact did. Willie's father, Nathan Quarles, showed up as usual to take him home. Later that day, Willie got together with his friend Thorpe, and the two planned to hold up the Chou Li-quang Chinese restaurant around 9:00 p.m. when business was in a slack period. Willie asked Thorpe, "Do you have an extra piece for me? The police took mine away." As expected, the owner, Chou Li-quang, was alone at that time cleaning up and closing down the restaurant before returning home at around 10:00 p.m.

Chou Li-quang was born in Shanghai, China, in May 1914. Like most Chinese in those days, he grew up in poverty and sometimes had to go out into the streets to beg for either money or food. In 1937, shortly after the Japanese invaded China, Chou married Ling Li, and the two eventually has three children, two of them born in China. About a year after their marriage, Chou decided to join the Chinese Army in order to fight the Japanese. In 1945, Japan surrendered, but peace in China was short-lived. During the Japanese occupation of northern China, Mao Tze-tung (1893–1976) and his men seized a large part of that territory and initiated successful military operations against the Japanese, and by the time the war ended, the Communists ruled much of northern China. However, Chinese president Chiang-kai-shek (1887–1975) found this unacceptable and ordered a drive to purge northern China of Mao and the Communists. In short, China was once again in the middle of a civil war. President Harry Truman sent General George Marshall to China in the fall on 1946 in order to get both sides to the negotiating table and finally bring peace to China. He succeeded but only for the next six months. In June 1947, Chiang-kai-shek decided to break the truce and launch a new offensive against the communists in the north. At first, it appeared that this offensive would be successful, but soon the tables turned. After the initial attacks by the Nationalists, the Communists seized the initiative, and even some of the Nationalists themselves joined the Communists on their drive south. By this time, Chou had had enough with China being constantly at war while the rate of inflation became so severe it would sometimes cost over $1,000 just for a single meal. Chou decided to apply for a visa to immigrate to the United States. His visa was granted in August 1948, a year before the civil war finally ended in a Communist victory.

Chou, his wife, Ling Li, and their two children, a boy and a girl, arrived in San Francisco, California. There they lived for the next three years. In 1949, they had their third child, another boy. In 1951, Chou decided for some reason to move to Chicago. He settled in Chicago's Chinatown in 1952, where he eventually bought a restaurant. The business there was quite lucrative.

On the night of Saturday, February 3, 1968, Willie and Thorpe made their move. Except for Cho Li-quang himself, the restaurant was empty. Willie and Thorpe pulled out their revolvers and demanded that Chou turn over all the cash he had on hand. Chou complied with the demand, but for Willie, that was not enough. He suddenly developed the urge to hurt the Chinaman as he noticed a pot of boiling grease on the stove.

Willie suddenly grabbed the Chinaman, putting his arms underneath his, and started pushing his face into the boiling grease. As the Chinaman begged him to stop, to no avail, and screamed out of sheer pain, Thorpe said, "Willie, let's get out of here before someone comes."

Willie replied, "Okay."

Later as they headed north for their next heist, Thorpe said to Willie, "That man gave us all the money he had, but why did you have to burn him like that? He never did anything to us."

Willie simply replied, "I just felt like doing it."

About twenty minutes later, Officers Williams and Swanson showed up to investigate the robbery and the vicious burning of Chou Li- quang. Almost immediately Williams knew that it was done by none other than Willie Floyd, who just got out of jail that morning. By this time, Williams was totally outraged over this and became determined to stop Willie Floyd once and for all. After the ambulance took Chou to the St. Luke's Hospital Burn Unit, Williams and Swanson were again called into action. This time it was a holdup at a Kroger Supermarket on Chicago's near north side. When they arrived, the heist was still in progress. As they looked through the window, they recognized Willie and Thorpe right away with their guns drawn. When they rushed in, Thorpe threw his hands up and surrendered his firearm. Willie Floyd managed to slip out the back door, and Williams said to Swanson, "You stay here and take care of business, while I run out back and catch this cursed Willie Floyd."

Then Swanson asked him, "Shouldn't we wait for backup first?" Williams replied, "They'll be here soon enough but remember, the—is mine!"

Williams ran out in back of the Kroger Supermarket in pursuit of Willie Floyd. He was not going to let Willie Floyd get away with what he did to that Chinaman earlier. Willie stopped several times and fired his revolver at Williams until he ran out of bullets. Thereafter Willie Floyd tried to get away from Williams but was boxed in by a chain-link fence. Williams grabbed Willie Floyd by the arm and said, "Do you remember that Chinaman you burned earlier tonight? He was your huge mistake."

Willie replied, "I don't know what the—you're talking about." Williams said, "That's the wrong answer, Willie. Try again."

Willie already knew that Williams was on to him, so he simply started to grin. Williams began to slug Willie several times in the face until he broke his lower jaw on both sides, and then he proceeded to put one of his arms in the Dumpster and slam the lid shut before he did the other. By the time backup did arrive, Willie Floyd had a broken jaw along with both his arms and legs. Williams just simply lost it that night.

When Williams returned to headquarters later, he knew he had it. Thereafter he finished making out his report for the night. Before he went home, he was told to report to his superior, Lieutenant Dan Crawford, the following Monday.

That Monday, Williams went into the office and reported to Lieutenant Crawford as ordered. Crawford said, "Ever since you joined us thirteen years ago, you've been a regular boil on the butt of the Chicago Police Department. There are dirty cops and lazy cops, but your kind is the worst of all. You have no respect for the rights of criminals, and you were time and again overzealous in your duties. Last Saturday night you went too far. You not only apprehended Willie Floyd but broke his jaw plus both his arms and legs. I understand you know what he did to that Chinaman, but that's no excuse. I assure you, I didn't like it any better than you did when I found out about it later."

Lieutenant Crawford went on, "As you know, we not only can bust you from the police force once and for all, we can also have the State of Illinois prosecute you and eventually have you sent to Stateville prison in Joliet. There are at least six or seven guys there who would like nothing better than to tear you from limb to limb. However, for you, Williams, there is a way out of this. I have a twin brother in the Marines whose name is Stan Crawford and is currently a recruiting officer here in Chicago, and I most strongly recommend that you go to him as soon as possible in order to enlist in the Corps. Just tell him his brother, Dan, sent you." Crawford then pulled out a slip of paper, wrote on it, and said, "Here is his address on Clark Avenue. In a week from now, if you pass the physical and enlist, I'll expect to see your resignation on my desk saying you left for the good of the department. That'll be all for now, Williams. You are heretofore suspended from the Chicago Police Department."

Williams did as instructed, knowing that otherwise he would face prosecution from the state and a possible stretch in Joliet. He reported to Lieutenant Stan Crawford the next day and said he wanted to become a Marine, although he didn't mean it. He was scheduled for a physical on Monday, February 12, and he passed. Then he wrote out his resignation and handed it over to his former superior, Lieutenant Crawford. Crawford said, "Good luck in the Marine Corps, and good riddance." For Officer Williams, joining the Marine Corps presented him with a new dilemma. Officer Odell Williams had always prided himself on the fact that during his thirteen-year tenure on the Chicago police force, he never had to kill anyone. The idea of killing people, especially those who didn't deserve to die, always repulsed him. Since he was coerced to join, he was constantly trying to figure out a way of not killing anyone since he knew he would sooner or later be sent to Vietnam against his will.

On Monday, March 4, 1968, Williams along with fourteen other recruits were put on a military bus and taken to Camp Lejeune in North Carolina for basic training before shipping out to Camp Pendleton in Oceanside, California.

PART III

THE CONFRONTATION

CHAPTER 1

The War in Vietnam: A Hindsight

The War in Vietnam was one of the greatest tragedies of the twentieth century. As in Korea, the question arises, "Could the war in Vietnam have been averted?" Like Korea, the answer is "Yes, it well could have."

Now let's place the blame squarely where it belongs, and that is on those idiot politicians in Paris who wanted complete control of French Indochina as they had before WWII along with the politicians and war profiteers here in America.

In 1941, France was a defeated and occupied country, and as a result, the Japanese moved into Indochina effortlessly. However in 1942, a group of Vietnamese led by Ho Chi Minh (1890–1969) and General Vo Nguyen Giap (1911–2013) got together and formed a formidable guerilla organization under the name of Viet Minh. They were so successful that the French returned to Indochina in 1945 almost without a shot being fired. Out of sheer gratitude, the French allowed the Vietnamese to set up a semiautonomous state in Tonkin and northern Annam later that year.

Unfortunately, motivated by sheer greed, the politicians back in Paris wanted complete control of Indochina and, on November 21, 1946, initiated the French-Indochina War (1946–1954) by bombing and seizing the port city of Haiphong.

The idea of granting the Vietnamese a right to become a French Commonwealth State never occurred to those idiots in Paris. It should have, and the war would have been settled peacefully if the Vietnamese agreed.

At first, it appeared that the French were going to be successful, but early in the 1950s, that began to change. The French were losing more and more territories to the Vietnamese, and by late 1953, the Vietnamese controlled much of northern Vietnam, especially the area surrounding Dien Bien Phu along the Laotian border. In the meantime, after spending over three billion dollars and thus exhausting their treasury, the French were compelled to turn to the United States in order to borrow two billion dollars more to prosecute the war further.

At this point, both the then vice president Richard Nixon (1913–1994) and the then secretary of state John Foster Dulles (1888–1959) strongly urged then president Dwight D. Eisenhower (1890–1969) to send in American troops in order to bail the French out. On February 10, 1954, Eisenhower put his foot down, saying, "At this point, it would be quite tragic to send in our troops, so we need to stay out of it."

In the meantime, back in Indochina beginning in November 1953, the French seized the stronghold of Dien Bien Phu in the heart of Vietnamese-ruled Vietnam, the strategy being to set up a perimeter and expand it in all directions until the area was cleared of all Vietnamese fighters.

Unfortunately for the French, this strategy backfired. The Vietnamese managed to surround Dien Bien Phu and began to slowly close in on them. Finally in the early morning of May 7, 1954, the Vietnamese overran the French base, thus compelling the politicians in Paris to sue for peace. Shortly after, both the French and the Vietnamese attended the Geneva Conference, chaired jointly by the British and the Russians. All parties to that conflict attended. First, the host countries of Great Britain and Russia, then the warring parties, France and Vietnam, and finally the third party countries, such as the United States and China.

The talks went on for the next two months. Finally in July, Russian Foreign Minister Vyacheslav Molotov (1890–1986) successfully persuaded the Vietnamese to accept a temporary partition of their country at the 17th parallel to be settled by a plebiscite on July 19, 1956, two years to the date of the signing of the peace accords. All sides agreed, and when Chinese foreign minister Chou-En-Lai (1898–1976) reached out his hand to US secretary of state John Foster Dulles to celebrate with him the signing of that treaty, John Foster Dulles blatantly refused, thus showing that he harbored nothing but utter hatred and contempt for both Chou-En-Lai and the Chinese people. Chou-En-Lai felt hurt at that gesture. For this country, that gesture was truly a national disgrace. Two years later in July 1956 at the behest of the United States, South Vietnamese president Ngo

Dinh Diem (1901–1963) decided to abrogate the plebiscite since it was common knowledge that the north Vietnamese would easily win. This was the step that was to lead to the tragic war in the 1960s and 1970s with the rise of the Viet Cong.

In the meantime, the United States was gradually sending in more men and materiel to South Vietnam. At first, it appeared to be successful, but in 1963, that all changed. It was discovered that the government of Ngo Dinh Diem was secretly negotiating with the Viet Cong. The CIA then felt compelled to do something about it and probably did. On May 8, 1963, in the city of Hue, a group of Buddhist monks were flying both South Vietnamese and Buddhist flags. The Hue Police told the monks that they could only fly the government flags. The monks refused to put down their religious flags, and some of the policemen opened fire, killing eight of the monks. This turned the war in Vietnam into a three-way conflict, finally culminating in the capture and subsequent murders of both Ngo Dinh Diem and his brother, Ngo Dinh Nhu (1911–1963) on November 1, 1963.

Later on when President John F. Kennedy (1917–1963) found out about this, he began to have misgivings and was most probably contemplating getting out of Vietnam, and that was probably a factor in his assassination on November 22, 1963, but we'll never know for sure. At any rate, since his successor, Vice President Lyndon B. Johnson (1908–1973) wanted the war, we were well on our way in. To further assure this, the CIA, on Saturday, August 1, 1964, staged the so-called Gulf of Tonkin incident, under which Johnson retaliated by bombing cities in north Vietnam. On Tuesday, August 4, a repeat performance was carried out. Next, Johnson turned to the US Senate and had the Gulf of Tonkin Resolution passed by a vote of eighty-eight in favor, three against, with nine abstentions.

Since 1964 was an election year, with Johnson running as the "peace" candidate against Senator Barry Goldwater, a known warmonger, Johnson had to lie low regarding Vietnam.

On Tuesday night, December 1, 1964, NBC News aired a documentary revealing that the Viet Cong were slowly winning the war in Vietnam. That was four weeks after the landslide election of President Johnson over Senator Barry Goldwater.

On February 8, 1965, after the attack on the Army base at Pleiku, South Vietnam, killing eight American soldiers, Johnson finally found an excuse to turn Vietnam into an American war. In fact, some people here in America were hoping that this would eventually lead to an all- out war with China to the north, just as General McArthur wanted in Korea. On the other hand, several college students along with their professors and other intellectual groups took to the streets in protest. In fact, an eighty-two-year-old woman from Germany set herself on fire on the streets of the Capitol in Washington to protest the war. However, most people supported President Johnson since they knew no better. As far as they were concerned, the government was always right.

Aside from the antiwar protests, another deep disappointment for President Johnson was the lack of support he got from Europe since not one European country offered to send in any of their troops. On top of that, French president Charles de Gaulle (1890–1970) stated that if the US bombings of north Vietnam were to lead to war with China, the United States would not have French support.

As the months went by, Johnson kept on sending in more and more American troops while bombing more and more cities in north Vietnam. By the summer of 1968, the United States had a total of 549,000 troops in south Vietnam.

Although the Viet Cong were talking about a winter spring offensive in the fall of 1967, General William Westmoreland (1914–2005) bragged that the Viet Cong were already too weak to do much damage, and the United States was on the winning side. Suddenly on January 30, 1968, the Viet Cong launched the Tet Offensive, and it turned out to be more spectacular than anyone in either the US military or in Washington imagined. Although it was a military disaster for the Viet Cong, it did have both the desired psychological and political effect for them. It made it painfully clear to the American people that a military victory was not just "around the corner," as many of them believed. Thereafter, the earlier huzzah the people felt about Vietnam began to fade and fast.

Finally at the New Hampshire primary on Tuesday, March 12, President Johnson beat his antiwar opponent Senator Eugene McCarthy by only 7 percent of the Democratic votes. On March 31, President Johnson realized what a mistake Vietnam had been and announced over the air that he was no longer seeking a second term as president and stopped the bombing of north Vietnam north of the 19th parallel, eventually leading to the Paris peace talks in May.

For Johnson, this war ruined his political career, just as the Korean War did Truman's, but for opposite reasons. In 1951, the American public wanted a military victory, but by firing General McArthur, Truman denied them that. In 1968 in contrast, most Americans were disillusioned with Vietnam and wanted out, victory or no victory. Even CBS Anchorman Walter Cronkite finally denounced the Vietnam War.

This country may have gotten out of Vietnam either by late spring or early fall of 1969 had Richard Nixon not been elected on November 5, 1968. Unfortunately, Senator Robert Kennedy (1925–1968), the brother of the late JFK was shot down by a certain Sirhan B. Sirhan (1944–) on June 4, 1968, and thus paving the way for another four years in Vietnam by assuring the election of Richard M. Nixon that fall. In fact, the Vietnam War would indirectly end the Nixon presidency too since without Vietnam, there would most probably never have been a Watergate scandal.

It was not to be until April 1975 that the conflict would truly end. Even the Vietnamese were not celebrating since far too many people were either maimed or killed along with the massive destruction. The countryside remained laden with all kinds of land mines, and many cities in north Vietnam were bombed into rubble. It took the Vietnamese decades to dig out of the mess created by the war.

Enough of Vietnam.

CHAPTER 2

Sergeant Biway Meets His Nemesis

s was pointed out earlier, Sergeant Biway reported for duty on Saturday, February 24, 1968, at Camp Lejeune in North Carolina to Lieutenant Howard Klingman. However on Monday, March 25, barely a month after Biway reported for duty, Lieutenant Klingman called Biway into his office, telling him that he was to be transferred to Camp Pendleton in Oceanside, California. Klingman said to Biway, "As of Monday, April 1, at 0900 hours California time, a week from today, you will report to Lieutenant Stanley Gould, commander of Company 4. Right now I'm giving you this week off so you can collect your gear and make the grueling drive to California. Have you any questions, Biway?"

Biway replied, "No, sir, I have none."

Then Klingman said, "Dismissed and good riddance!"

Biway collected his gear, put it in his white 1948 GMC pickup, and started the long drive to California. He arrived in Oceanside, California, that Sunday, spent the night in a local motel, went to Camp Pendleton the next morning, and reported to Lieutenant Gould for duty. On his way to Lieutenant Gould's office, he ran into both Sergeants Floyd Proctor and Tom Posey. Floyd said, "How was your six-month vacation? And don't tell us how dull it was."

Biway replied, "Floyd, if you knew how it really was, you'd never believe me. However, sometime when we have the time and get together, I'll tell you all about it."

At 9:00 a.m., as ordered, Biway reported to Lieutenant Gould. Once in the office, Lieutenant Gould said to Biway, "I don't know which strings you pulled in order to get here, but I assure you I don't like it. My friend Lieutenant Steven Taylor told me all about you and how you wound up breaking Private Andrew Lathrop's back. Today he is in a wheelchair thanks to you. Then again, I guess you couldn't care less any more than you did for that four-year-old girl in New York who perished in an automobile accident that you caused in your drunken state. Now I want to warn you, on no uncertain terms, if you harm one hair on any man under your command here, I personally guarantee that I will personally have you court-martialed and have you busted from the Marine Corps once and for all with a dishonorable discharge. Yes, I studied your school records and police records from Utica, New York, and the fact you raped your own sister shows what a lowlife you truly are. You even abused your kid brother. Enough said. Have you any questions, Biway?" Gould asked.

Biway replied, "No, sir, I do not." Gould said, "Dismissed."

Biway then reported to his assigned unit and began inspections at 4:00 p.m. On Saturday, May 25, 1968, when Biway was given a thirty- six-hour liberty pass, he drove up to Marysville to visit his ex-wife, Aggie, and her husband, Bill. His daughter, Kitty, was there too. Aggie and Bill's boys were already five and seven and growing like weeds. Otherwise when on liberty, Biway found another brothel teaming with Hispanic prostitutes near Oceanside. Soon he found his favorite, a thirty-six-year-old woman who went by the name of Pepper. She was five feet, nine inches, weighed around 175 pounds, had pitch-black hair she usually wore in a ponytail, and wore glasses. With her voluptuous figure, she had no trouble in attracting men and especially Biway. Her real name was Isabella Quevedo from Juarez, Mexico. She was born Isabella Cisneros on July 27, 1931, the only child of Enrique and Alejandra Cisneros. In 1948, she married Emilio Quevedo, twenty-one, and had two boys, Andres, born on July 3, 1949, and Julio, on February 4, 1951.

However on Friday night, November 16, 1956, in Oceanside, California, Emilio came home early and found Isabella with another man in bed with her. The man was a US Marine second lieutenant from Camp Pendleton. His name was Lee Wilson, twenty-two. He was from Raleigh, North Carolina, born to a Native American father and a white mother. In fact, both parents were part white, part Indian. In other words, both were mestizos. Lee, like Isabella, had pitch-black hair and was rather handsome. He finally got around Isabella, and she finally gave in. It was he who first started calling her Pepper, and she liked it.

After they were caught, Isabella tried to explain to Emilio what happened, but he went ahead and filed for divorce. Since he was the injured party in that case, he managed to gain full custody of the boys and took them back to Mexico. He remarried two years later.

That following February, Lee Wilson was transferred to a Marine base in Okinawa, Japan, never to be heard from again. However, only a month before, Pepper's mother suffered a debilitating stroke at the age of fifty-six, and her father needed someone to assist him in taking care of her. At this time and all alone, Pepper went into the prostitution business, and since it was so lucrative, she soon had enough money to buy a house and have her parents move in. Thereafter, both she and her father no longer had any trouble in taking care of her mother. By 1968, she built up an impressive list of clients, including three Oceanside policemen. Whenever Biway couldn't get together with her, he became quite agitated.

On Monday, July 29, 1968, a group of twenty-one new recruits arrived from Camp Lejeune, North Carolina. Among these were Privates Odell D. Williams, thirty-four; Alfie Miller, twenty-four; James W. Smith, twenty-five; John Drennon, twenty-six; Ralf Bullen, twenty- two; Richard "Dickey" Davis, twenty-three; Howard Quatham, twenty- five; Gerald "Jerry" Williams, twenty-two; and Fred Tuttle, forty-one, just to name a few.

When Biway first saw Williams, he instinctively took a dislike to him, and ironically, Williams felt the same way about Biway. Upon seeing Williams, Biway yelled out, "Hey, punk. What's your name?"

Williams replied, "Williams, sir, Private Odell Williams, sir."

Suddenly Biway hit Williams with a karate chop and asked Williams, "Did that hurt?"

Williams replied, "Yes, sir, it did, sir." Biway said, "I certainly hope so!"

To make matters worse, on Friday, July 26, Williams went on twenty-four-hour liberty and went to the same brothel frequented by Biway. There he noticed Pepper and how sharp she looked. Williams asked another prostitute if she was available. The prostitute said yes, but she would be rather expensive. He then went directly to Pepper and asked her outright, "How much do I need to have sex with you?"

Pepper replied, "Usually $50, but for you, $30." Williams said, "It's a deal."

For Williams, this was the first time he had sex with a woman. Pepper, surmising that, said, "I can tell this is your first time, but don't worry, I've done this over fifty thousand times already." For Williams, this was a very pleasant experience.

Later on when Biway learned that Williams was consorting with his favorite prostitute, his hatred of him grew even stronger. Finally one night, Biway called Williams into his office and said, "I heard that you were tough cop in Chicago. You took some poor black bastard and not only busted his jaws but both his arms and legs as well, and that's the reason you wound up here. Isn't that right, Copper?"

Williams replied, "Yes, it is, sir, but remember, that 'poor black' bastard burned a Chinese restaurant owner's face earlier that night and had to be punished. If you saw the face of that man after it was burned, you'd fully agree with me, sir."

Then Biway said, "How dare you consort with my favorite prostitute, Pepper? She's the best in the business, and since I'm a sergeant and you're nothing but a—private, I think that gives me dibs on her."

However, Williams replied, "Don't you think that Pepper has a right to decide who she prefers to do business with, sir?"

Biway simply said, "I'm going to make your—life as miserable as I can if you keep on consorting with that woman, and besides, there are plenty of other Hispanic prostitutes around, and some are quite pretty too."

For Biway, the relationship with Pepper was purely physical and nothing more. Since he was severely snubbed back in 1964 by the niece of Austrian Consul Erich Meyer, he never truly fell in love with another woman. He did, however, love his ex-wife, Aggie, and was glad to know how happy she was with her husband, Bill, and their two sons.

With Odell Williams, on the other hand, Pepper felt quite differently. At first, their relationship was on a business level, but as time went by, their relationship grew into something more. Williams, although a former cop, began to understand Pepper and the pain she felt over never seeing her two sons who lived with their father and stepmother in Juarez, Mexico, and the need she had to support her parents, who by 1968 were both very old. Her father was seventy-two and her mother, sixty-eight, and partially impaired by the stroke she suffered back in 1956. Moreover, Pepper realized that Williams was a good judge of character and that made her feel comfortable with him. Williams, on the other hand, felt that Pepper was the only woman who ever took the time to listen to him and take an interest in his problems. Williams did try to persuade Pepper to go into a more respectable line of work, which she eventually planned to do.

Unfortunately, before the relationship could grow into something more serious, Williams was notified that his platoon was to ship out on Monday, September 9, for duty in Vietnam. That was exactly what Williams dreaded most.

After he arrived in Vietnam, Williams did write to Pepper twice, but for some reason or other, she never answered him. In the meantime, she decided to go on with her business.

However, two and a half years later, Pepper finally married. His name was Lieutenant Oliver O'Donnell and was stationed at Camp Pendleton. The wedding took place on March 27, 1971, in Paoli, Indiana.

CHAPTER 3

Lieutenant Oliver "Ollie" L. O'Donnell, USMC

It was on a Friday night, October 16, 1970, when Lieutenant O'Donnell, along with Lieutenant Mark Slagle and Lieutenant Marvin Massey went to Rogelio's Hotel and Lounge, where Pepper worked. Suddenly as O'Donnell was ordering a second round of drinks for his friends and himself, he noticed a woman in a green tight skirt with matching high-heeled shoes. She wore medium rimmed glasses and had her black hair done up in a bun. She was serving drinks to the other patrons at the time. She was extremely attractive and caught O'Donnell's eye. For O'Donnell, this was truly a miracle since he had been plagued by his homosexual proclivities since he was thirteen back in 1957, when he lived with his parents in Paoli, Indiana.

Lieutenant O'Donnell was born Oliver Lawrence O'Donnell in Paoli, Indiana, on December 19, 1943, the second of Paul and Mary O'Donnell's three children. His parents always called him Ollie, and the name stuck. The first was John Patrick O'Donnell, born on July 13, 1941, and Phoebe Grace, born on February 2, 1950. Paoli is located in southern Indiana surrounded by very pretty farming country, and Ollie had a very normal childhood until he had a strange experience in 1957, when he noticed that he had a crush on another boy by the name of David Schultz. A year earlier, Ollie did have a crush on a girl by the name of Marianne Brogan, but as juvenile crushes go, it quickly died out.

On October 7, 1957, he wanted to get alone with David, who was almost a year younger than he was, but he knew this was definitely wrong, so he made every effort to avoid him afterward. One night in May 1959, he finally broke down and told his mother, Mary, what was going on with him. He said, "Mom, I know this is wrong, but I have these horrific homosexual tendencies, and I want to get rid of them."

Mary replied, "I'll take you to see a priest at St. Nicholas Church so you can talk to him and see if he can help you."

Ollie said, "Mom, please don't tell Dad."

Mary replied, "I won't, Ollie, if that's what you wish."

Father John Schoener at St. Nicholas Church simply told Ollie later, "Just pray until those proclivities of yours go away. God willing, they will eventually disappear."

Mary never told her husband Paul what Ollie said.

In 1959 after graduating Paoli High School, Ollie's brother, John, decided to join the Marines in order to fulfill his military obligations. He was honorably discharged from the Corps in 1963 and went on to Indiana University in Indianapolis to study electrical engineering. Ollie's sister, Phoebe, married in 1968 after her graduation from Paoli High School and moved with her newlywed husband, William Bledsoe, shortly thereafter to nearby French Lick, and they eventually had four children.

In 1962 after he graduated from Paoli High School, Ollie decided to join the Marine Corps in order to prove he was truly a man. It seemed to work for a while, and he managed to suppress his homosexual feelings. He went directly to the Marine Academy in Quantico, Virginia, and graduated with flying colors in 1966.

In the meantime, at Johns Hopkins University in Baltimore, Maryland, a young girl by the name of Sharon Hegeler graduated that same year. She was also twenty-two. The two first met on a blind date set up by Johns Hopkins in collusion with the Marine Corps on Friday, June 24, 1966.

Sharon Hegeler was five feet, six inches tall, weighed around 153 pounds, had light-brown hair, green eyes, and still at the age of twenty-two, never lost her baby fat, which made her very attractive. Many boys tried to go steady with her.

Sharon was born on December 31, 1943, in Tacoma, Washington, where her father, Dan Hegeler, was stationed in the US Army at nearby Ft. Lewis. Her mother was Mrs. Bernadette Hegeler, who was eighteen at the time of her birth, and her father, Dan, was twenty-nine.

In fact, Bernadette only married Dan in March 1943 in order to get away from her home in Quakertown, Pennsylvania. At that time, she had four siblings, with a fifth one on the way. In 1945, Bernadette sued Dan for divorce so she could marry her high school sweetheart, Tom Clevenger. Their marriage lasted nine years until he succumbed to liver cancer in 1954. The following year, she married Frank Braddock, twenty-six, and they had a son named John born on February 3, 1956. Unfortunately, Bernadette died of a urinary tract infection on October 13, 1962, when Sharon was eighteen and her brother John, six. Although the parents of Frank Braddock, who lived in Jefferson City, Missouri, took their grandson John in, they made it painfully clear to Sharon that they liked neither her nor her mother. This made Sharon feel hurt in addition to being forcefully separated from her kid brother, who unfortunately died on May 3, 1963, from the same disease that claimed his mother's life. Thereafter Sharon went to Baltimore, Maryland, to live with her maternal aunt Chrissy, thirty-one, her husband, Vernon, forty-five, and their two small sons. Here she attended Johns Hopkins University with a major in medicine so she could one day become a registered nurse. Ollie, on the other hand, was six feet, three inches tall, weighed around 204 pounds, had short black hair with hazel eyes.

When he first saw Sharon, he thought, *This girl is a living doll if there ever was one. She must either have a boyfriend or even a husband. If not, I'll do all I can to get with her. Hopefully in that case, she'll help me to rid myself of this demon called homosexuality. It's been plaguing me since I was thirteen and I'm sick and tired of it.*

At the end of that date, when Ollie took Sharon home, he asked, "Will we see one another again? It has been a real pleasure being with you tonight. In a week, I'm due to go to Camp Lejeune in North Carolina to assume my first command. I'll need your address so I will be able to write you."

Sharon replied, "Yes, Ollie, for me this date has also been a true pleasure. Hopefully I'll see you one more time before you ship out."

Ollie replied, "That'll be great."

For the first time in nine years, Ollie felt truly happy as he was sure he was either rid of his demon or would be once he and Sharon got together.

On Thursday, June 30, just the day before Ollie was to ship out, he and Sharon went out on their second date. It was just as pleasurable as their first one. The next day, Ollie shipped out to Camp Lejeune in North Carolina.

Thereafter the two corresponded on a regular basis. Finally for Christmas, Ollie was granted a two-week furlough, and he told Sharon he wanted to take her to Paoli, Indiana, to meet his family. She agreed, and the two met at the John Foster Dulles airport to fly to Indianapolis, where Ollie's father, Paul, picked them up and drove them south to Paoli. It was a very pleasant Christmas for both of them.

The following Easter, Sharon and Ollie decided to visit Sharon's aunt Chrissy and her husband in Baltimore. He was a church deacon as well as a reserve naval officer. He recently flew several missions over north Vietnam, and this worried Chrissy as she was afraid of hearing one day that he'd been shot down. Unfortunately, Chrissy's youngest child, Larry, who was not quite two at that time, was quite ill with intestinal influenza, which never went away. He finally succumbed on April 22, 1967.

One night when Sharon and Ollie were on vacation while resting in a motel room in Castle Rock, Colorado, she asked Ollie, "How come you never asked me for sex? We've been going steady for over a year now, and you never made a pass at me. Is there something wrong?"

Ollie simply replied, "No, it's that I'm a strong Roman Catholic, and we were brought up to believe that any sex outside of marriage is wrong. I hope you forgive me. In fact, I do want to marry you, Sharon." Sharon replied, "On April 25, 1969, I will receive my license as a registered nurse, something I always wanted to do, but I will marry you the day after if you like."

Ollie said, "That will be great. Now that we're engaged, I can hardly wait to tell my parents in Paoli."

The wedding was set for 1:00 p.m. on Saturday, April 26, 1969, at St. Nicholas Church in Paoli, and the honeymoon was to be spent in Louisville, Kentucky. The wedding was a gala affair, with all of Ollie's family, including his sister, Phoebe, and her husband, as well as his brother John and his family, Sharon's aunt Chrissy, her husband, Vernon, their son Albert and their six-week-old baby boy John were there as well. When the wedding concluded around 5:00 p.m., Ollie and Sharon got into Ollie's jeep and began their drive to a motel just east of Louisville, where they had weeklong reservations.

Unfortunately in the meantime, one of the second lieutenants, Sabastian Schroeder, twenty-five, under Ollie's command, fell sick with

ALS and needed to be replaced. That replacement arrived at Camp Lejeune on Sunday, March 31. His name was Eugene Stuart, twenty-two. He was quite handsome with his light-brown hair and blue eyes and caught Ollie's eye. *Oh my god,* Ollie though, *my old demon has come back to haunt me. Why did they have to send this man here?* At first Ollie came down on him hard during inspections, and the other men took note of it too. Fearing that this could be a giveaway, Ollie later made it a point to avoid Eugene as much as possible. During the night, Ollie tried hard to push the image of Eugene Stuart out of his mind as much as possible, but sometimes to no avail. He began to despise Eugene for somehow pushing his life out of balance, but he still looked forward to his wedding day, which for him was not to be a moment too soon.

Ollie now felt that once he and Sharon began having sex together, that would at last cure him of this demon which had bedeviled him for half his life. He even began praying that this was to be his final salvation from the "curse" of homosexuality.

Around 10:30 p.m. Ollie and Sharon arrived at their motel in Louisville to spend the night. However, the two didn't engage in sex that night, Ollie telling Sharon that he was simply too tired and so he needed the rest. She agreed, and both soon went to sleep.

The next morning, Ollie slept late, but Sharon got up rather early. As she was fixing him breakfast, she asked Ollie, "How did you sleep last night?"

Ollie replied "Quite well."

As the day wore on, Ollie was becoming more and more depressed over the return of his demon. He realized now that the wall between him and Sharon never truly disappeared, as the image of Eugene Stuart kept coming back into his head. After breakfast, the two went out for a drive around town and in the surrounding countryside. During this time, Ollie succeeded in hiding his depression from Sharon. They stopped at a restaurant around 5:00 p.m. and had supper before returning to their motel for the night.

After they returned, Sharon put on her light-blue see-through nightgown and sat by Ollie as they were watching TV. Sharon finally said, "Ollie, are you ready for sex yet?"

Ollie replied, "I'm so sorry, Sharon, I have this splitting headache, and right now I don't feel like doing anything."

Sharon replied, "That's all right, Ollie. There's always tomorrow." Then they went to bed for the night, but Ollie was at this point so depressed he could hardly sleep.

As he lay in bed wide awake, his depression was slowly giving way to anger, and the angrier he became, the more he hated Eugene Stuart for bringing this feeling back to him. He finally managed to doze off around 4:30 a.m.

The next day proved to be more of the same for Ollie. His mood began to swing from a severe depression to outright anger and back again. However, he did manage to hide these feelings from Sharon, who was becoming increasingly perplexed by his behavior. They went out and again had supper around 5:00 p.m. before returning to the motel. Before they returned, they stopped, and Ollie bought himself a quart-sized bottle of Jack Daniels bourbon and told Sharon, "Tonight we celebrate."

Sharon, still perplexed, asked Ollie, "What?"

Ollie now felt that if he drank enough bourbon, the wall between him and Sharon would somehow disappear, and the two would finally engage in sex later that night. Unfortunately, he was wrong. He poured Sharon a small glass but drank most of it himself. As he continued to drink, his depression gave way to anger, and at first, that anger was directed at Eugene Stuart, but later on, his anger began to focus on Sharon and her failure to cure him of his homosexuality, and as he drank, his anger grew.

Sharon, as she did for the last three nights, put on her see-through bathrobe and sat next to Ollie. As she threw her arm around him, Ollie suddenly flew into a wild rage, jumped up, and slapped Sharon as hard as he could. Then he threw her against the coffee table, slammed her head into the wall, kicked her in the stomach, and almost put out her left eye while yelling obscenities at her. Sharon could hardly grasp what just happened. Her husband, Ollie, suddenly turned into some kind of beast, and she could not understand what provoked him. Shortly thereafter, she lost consciousness and had to be taken to St. Francis of Assisi Mercy Hospital in Louisville.

Ollie suddenly stopped and thought, *Oh my god, what have I done?* He summoned room service for them to call both an ambulance and the police. After the ambulance took Sharon to the hospital, the Louisville Police questioned Ollie in order to find out what happened. Ollie simply told them, "I guess I just lost it. Take me in," and they did since he was obviously intoxicated.

Ollie spent the rest of that night in the jail drunk tank before being integrated into the general jail population. The next morning as Ollie was sobering up, he asked the guard if he was entitled to make a phone call. The guard said yes and allowed him to use the office phone. He called his mother, Mary, in Paoli, Indiana, and told her what happened the night before and that he was now in jail. She could hardly believe what she heard and summoned her husband, Paul. Paul took the phone and asked, "Ollie, I understand you and Sharon had a fight last night. Just exactly what caused it?"

Ollie replied, "Please, Dad, I must speak to Mom now."

He explained to her carefully what happened, and she understood. Mary turned to Paul and said, "We need to go to Louisville right away. Both Ollie and Sharon need us. Ollie's in jail, and Sharon's in the hospital, badly beaten. She may end up losing her left eye. Thank God they didn't decide to go all the way to New Orleans." They packed and started out for Louisville around 10:30 a.m.

They reached the city jail around 4:30 p.m. to see Ollie, but he was released only an hour earlier. On their way down to Louisville, Mary broke down and told Paul that Ollie had homosexual proclivities. Paul asked Mary, "How long did you know about this, Mary?"

Mary replied, "Since 1959, when Ollie was fifteen." "Why didn't you tell me?" Paul asked.

Mary said, "Ollie thought that you would disown him if you ever found out. Ollie always wanted to prove that he was true man."

Paul simply said, "As the saying goes, 'Nobody's perfect.' I'll accept Ollie whether he is a homosexual or not."

Mary replied, "That's the best news I heard in a long time."

After Paul and Mary left the city jail, they drove over to St. Francis of Assisi Mercy Hospital to see Sharon. That morning, the eye surgeon succeeded in saving Sharon's left eye. Later that morning when the Louisville police came to interview her, Sharon simply told them that under no circumstance was she going to press charges against her husband,

Ollie, so they had to release him, but Ollie's parents had yet to find out about it.

When they arrived at the hospital, Mary said, "Hello, Sharon. Paul and I are devastated to find out about the fight last night between you and Ollie. Can you tell me what caused it? This just isn't like Ollie to fly into a rage like that."

Sharon replied, "For the last three nights, I did notice a change coming over him, but even now I can't put my finger on it."

Mary finally asked outright, "Did Ollie ever reveal to you that he harbored homosexual tendencies?"

Sharon, now dazed, said, "No, he never did. Is that what caused it?"

Mary said, "Maybe I should have told you long ago, Sharon, but I was hoping he'd beat me to it." Then Mary said, "Sharon, Paul and I are fully willing to pay you $10,000 if you agree not to reveal Ollie's homosexual tendencies to anyone."

Sharon thought for a moment and said, "Yes, Mary, I will accept the money as a down payment for the horrific pain Ollie put me through. I will never be the same as I was before and maybe never be able to have any children. After this payoff, I never want to see or hear from you slimy people again!"

After Paul and Mary left the hospital, they went to the motel where Ollie was staying and found him watching TV and drinking more bourbon. They knocked, and Ollie opened the door and said, "Hello, Mom, and hello, Dad. I guess you heard about the ruckus we had last night. For some reason, Sharon refused to press charges against me this morning, and I don't understand why she did it."

The next day, Ollie, accompanied by his parents, went to the hospital to visit Sharon. Ollie said, "Sharon, can you ever forgive me for what I did to you Tuesday night? I am so sorry that I never told you about my homosexual tendencies and how I felt. I've been fighting this thing for the past twelve years.

"Please, Sharon, I will go to any top flight psychiatrist in the country in order to get professional help. That, I swear to God. All I want now is for you to take me back so we can face this thing together."

Sharon replied, "Just how were you planning to break it to me? Can't you see, Ollie, men your age almost never come out of it, no matter how hard they may try. There is no longer an 'us.' The only solution now is the annulment of our marriage."

Ollie said, "Please, Sharon, don't say that."

At that point, Mary, Ollie's mother, said, "Ollie, it is now as clear as day that she hates all of us. Let's all go back home now."

Ollie replied, "Yes, but I won't give up on Sharon so easily."

That Sunday, both Sharon's maternal aunt Chrissy and her father, Dan Hegeler, showed up at the hospital to see her. Chrissy said, "Sharon, I want you to come and stay with me and Vernon. I'll make sure that neither of my boys bother you."

Later on, Dan said, "Sharon, if you prefer, Patsy and I would love to have you come to Guttenberg and stay with us."

Sharon replied, "Does that mean I can have all the privacy I want? Right now I just want to stay in my room only to come out to either eat or take a shower."

Dan replied, "Yes, Sharon, if that's the way you want it, but please come to Guttenberg. Besides, you're the only child I ever had."

Sharon replied, "Yes, Dad, I will come and stay with you, but remember, right now I'm not very good company."

Chrissy, having left her seven-week-old son, John, with her sister Barbara in Quakertown, Pennsylvania, accompanied Sharon, Dan, and his wife, Patsy, to Guttenberg, Iowa. She drove Sharon's beige two-door 1960 Ford, while Dan and Patsy drove their 1957 blue-and- white Pontiac.

They arrived in Guttenberg after two days of driving. Chrissy returned to Baltimore when Vernon came and picked her up three days later.

For the first month and a half, Sharon rarely came out of her room, which was upstairs. She spent most of her time smoking, drinking, and listening to the radio. Gradually, however, she began to spend more time outdoors and made trips to downtown Guttenberg to tend to her own business, such as depositing the "hush money" Mary O'Donnell paid her to keep quiet about Ollie's "problem," which was quite unnecessary since Sharon never had any intentions of revealing Ollie's secret to anyone. She also acquired her Iowa driver's license and her license to practice nursing in Iowa.

Finally on Wednesday, August 20, Ollie made a special trip to Guttenberg in order to try to persuade Sharon to change her mind but to no avail. Sharon simply said, "Please, Ollie, just give me the damn divorce. How many times do I have to tell you, there is no 'us.'" Thereafter Ollie decided to give up. After all, since he was married, he could dispel any notions anyone had about his homosexuality.

In the meantime, Dan's health was slowly deteriorating. Finally they discovered that Dan was suffering from renal cancer, and he eventually died on June 11, 1970. Sharon, being a registered nurse, did all she could for him.

Sharon was eventually hired at the Riverbend Nursing Home in Dubuque, south of Guttenberg. One day, Sharon said to Patsy, "Since Dad died last June, there is really no reason for me to stay here in Guttenberg, and since I now work in Dubuque, I was thinking about purchasing a house there where both of us can live."

Patsy replied, "Although I'll miss this house, I agree with you. Let's do it."

In October 1970, Sharon bought a house near the Mississippi River with a nice view. Three years later, Patsy remarried, but Sharon never did, and the three shared the same house.

In the meantime, after Ollie finally gave up on Sharon, he volunteered for another tour of duty in Vietnam. He left Camp Pendleton on November 30, 1969, and returned there on September 30, 1970.

Finally on October 16 after being granted a forty-eight-hour liberty pass, he and his friends went to a nearby bar and brothel, where he saw Pepper for the first time. When he first laid eyes on her, he noticed something quite strange. There was no invisible wall between him and her. He asked another prostitute about her and was told that she was rather expensive. He said he didn't care how much she would charge him. Finally Pepper came to his table and said, "I hear you want to do business with me. Is that true?"

Ollie replied, "That's right. When can we get together?" Pepper replied, "In another forty-five minutes or so."

Finally Pepper invited Ollie upstairs to her "office." When they got in bed, Ollie experienced a true miracle. Unlike the other women he had been with in the past, there was no wall between him and her. He could barely believe this. In fact, he experienced three orgasms with her before the night was over.

The next day, he still had a difficult time believing what happened between him and Pepper. Later on it dawned on him that he was never attracted to any other man since he last saw Second Lieutenant Eugene Stuart. Was this the miracle that he and his mother prayed for after all these years? It appeared that way.

Two weeks later when on twenty-four-hour liberty, Ollie returned to the same brothel, but Pepper was not available that night. Instead Ollie settled for another Hispanic prostitute by the name of Odalys, who was twenty-two. She had pitch-black hair with a rather stocky build and quite nice looking. Even with her, there was no invisible wall, nor with another Hispanic prostitute by the name of Fatima, whom he did business with some three weeks later. She was thirty and also nice looking, but it was Pepper that he was truly in love with. Finally on the night of December 19, his twenty-seventh birthday, he proposed to Pepper. Pepper said, "Please, Ollie, I am thirty-nine years old and have in invalid mother and a very old father who need me. Besides, I was married before, but I had an affair with a twenty-two-year-old Marine fourteen years ago. My husband left me and took away my two boys. Besides, you're only twenty-seven and deserve someone more your age."

Ollie replied, "No, Pepper, I love you and won't give up that easily." In fact, Ollie did propose marriage to Pepper twice again, and she finally said yes. In the meantime, Ollie wrote home and told his parents what happened and the change he experienced. Upon hearing this, both parents were tickled pink as well as his brother, John, and his sister, Phoebe.

The wedding took place in Paoli, Indiana, on Saturday, March 27, 1971, and it turned out to be fantastic. Later, Pepper asked Ollie's parents, "What about my parents? Since Ollie may be reassigned to a post overseas and I will want to be with him, my father will have a very difficult time taking care of my mother back in California." In order to solve that problem, as Ollie's mother advised her, Pepper went to the Schaeffer Bros. Real Estate Agency in Paoli in order to buy a house for her parents instead of leaving them alone in California. Jerry Schaeffer, the Realtor said, "Right now there are no such houses available here in Paoli but I have one in neighboring Orleans which I'll be glad to show you." Pepper agreed and went with him to Orleans just north of Paoli. Pepper liked the house and decided to buy it. A week later, Pepper's parents moved in, and she sold their old house in California.

That June, Ollie learned that he was being promoted to the rank of captain and was told that he was to ship out to Camp Umayoshi in Japan. In spite of the fact that she was already pregnant, Pepper wanted to go with him. Ollie agreed, and Pepper settled with other Marine officers' wives and children just outside the base. They eventually had three children, Larry, born on March 9, 1972; Mark, born on December 12, 1973; and a daughter, Julie, born on June 5, 1975. A year later, Ollie told Pepper, "Honey, I don't want the kids to be brought up here in Japan." Pepper promptly agreed and took the kids back to Paoli and decided to raise them there. It was a most successful marriage, and Ollie's old demons never came back to haunt him again.

In 1984, Ollie was finally promoted to the rank of colonial at the age of forty.

CHAPTER 4

Corporal Alfonse "Alfie" J. Miller, USMC

While on a search-and-destroy mission near Khe Sahn, Biway's lance corporal, Michael Ford, twenty-five, was shot by a Vietnamese sniper and rushed to a Marine field hospital, where he died later that day. Michael was a negro from Baltimore who had always been a very capable Marine.

Now Biway needed to replace him, and he chose Private First Class Alfie Miller for the job. At first, Miller said he'd have to think it over but did agree to the promotion the next day. Miller, who never liked Biway in the first place, began to hate him with a burning passion a month and a half later. What caused it was when his squad went out on a search-and-destroy mission on Tuesday, November 19, 1968, they came upon the village of Quang Minh. In the middle of that village sat a Roman Catholic Jesuit mission compound called La St. Francois Xavier Mission de Misericorde. There were four priests; one was Monseigneur Gerard Flanague, fifty-two, who died of cardiac failure a month and a half earlier. Another priest was Pere Joseph, thirty-nine. His full name was Joseph-Pierre Lebrecque, and he served at that mission since 1963. He was born in 1929 in Orleans, France. He was five feet, eight inches tall, rather slender, and wore glasses. In addition, there were several nuns headed by La Mere Superieure known as Mere Therese. She was fifty-four and still quite attractive even in her nun's habit. She had gray hair, was of medium height, and rather stocky.

When the squad reached the mission, Biway asked Pere Joseph if there were any Viet Cong around. The priest, not knowing any English, couldn't understand what he was asking, and Biway knew no French. Private Williams offered to act as an interpreter since he was the only one in the squad who knew any French. Upon receiving the offer, Biway snapped, "Shut your—mouth, Copper!" Copper was the name Biway called Williams since he was a former policeman. "That—will understand me one way or another." Then Biway began slapping Pere Joseph.

As Miller witnessed this brutal treatment of Pere Joseph, he became quite angry. Thereafter Biway barged into the convent where the nuns were, and after looking the nuns over, he began staring at Mere Therese and becoming glassy-eyed. She was the first white woman he saw outside the base. Then he looked around and saw half his squad standing around him, including Corporal Miller. Thereafter he went outside again. Biway then shot a thirteen-year-old Vietnamese boy in the head, whereupon Private First Class Jerome Alcantor, twenty-five, said to him, "Why did you have to shoot that boy, sir? He wasn't doing us any harm."

Biway replied, "As far as I'm concerned, he was part of the Viet Cong, and that's the way I'm going to report it."

Later on, the men returned to base. Around 6:30 p.m., Biway said to Miller, "Right now you're in charge. I have some business to do elsewhere," and Biway hopped in a jeep and drove off. It wasn't hard to surmise what Biway's "business" was. He drove straight back to the village of Quang Minh.

Before Biway left for the village of Quang Minh, he went to the base PX and bought a fifth of Smirnoff's vodka to take with him. On the way, he opened the bottle and drank a few snorts but was careful not to get intoxicated too fast. When he first arrived at the Mission, he called for Pere Joseph, and when the priest appeared, he started beating him up, and when he was on the ground, began kicking him in the ribs. After Biway got through working Pere Joseph over, he barged into the convent, searching for Mere Therese. When he found her he said, "I want you to come with me." Mere Therese knew almost immediately what Biway wanted with her. For Mere Therese, this was old hat since she had been raped on two different occasions in France during WWII. The first time was in May 1941, when a German SS Officer snuck into the convent where she was staying and raped her. That happened in the city of Orleans. The second time was in October 1944, when two American soldiers who were on leave became quite intoxicated and decided to force their way into the convent in Soissons where she was and raped by both men. One was middle-aged and the other was in his twenties. For Mere Therese, this was to be her third time around. The Vietnamese nuns who were witnessing this started to become frantic. Mere Therese simply told them, "Ne vous vous affolez pas, c'est moi qu'il veut" and Biway raped her twice after performing oral sex on her.

Mere Therese was born Therese-Julie Frejus on April 25, 1914, in Grenoble, France, the third of four children born to Georges and Claudette Frejus. The others were Charles, born on October 3, 1909; Danielle, born on January 5, 1913; and Gaston, born on May 7, 1916. She was born just before the outbreak of WWI and never knew her father since he was killed in the Battle for Verdun in northern France in 1916. After the war, Claudette remarried, but the family still lived in poverty, as most French people did due to the wrecked economy caused by four years of war.

In 1929 when Therese was fifteen, she decided to become a nun since she wanted to help others. In 1932 after graduating from high school, she entered St. Catherine's Jesuit Convent in Toulouse. In 1939, she graduated with a bachelor's degree in medicine, thus becoming a nurse, took her final vows, and became a Jesuit nun. The Jesuit Order was established by Brother Ignacio de Loyola in Spain in 1534 for the purpose of converting Muslims in the Middle East to Christianity.

However, it wasn't until 1946 that Soeur Therese left France for a foreign country. The first country she was assigned to was French Equatorial Africa. Two years later, she was reassigned to French Indochina at the Jesuit mission of St. Francois Xavier. She not only taught the Vietnamese children but assisted in giving people medical attention when needed. In time, she became highly esteemed by not only the villagers but the Viet Minh as well since she treated many of them for their wounds during the French Indochina War.

As Biway was raping Mere Therese, he not only was satisfying his carnal desires but his emotional ones as well. At one point, he took another snort of vodka and forced Mere Therese to take one too. She obliged him. Biway never got over the 1929 incident when Sister Mary Arnold slapped him in front of Diane De Wolfe, which left him totally humiliated. In his mind, he felt that somehow he was punishing Sister Mary Arnold. Moreover, he never got over the whipping he got from Brother Joseph about an hour later, which could explain why he beat up Pere Joseph.

By the time Biway was finished, he was so drunk he could hardly make his way to the jeep out front but managed to drive it back to the base. He parked the jeep in front of his quarters, staggered his way in, and fell on top of his bed. Before he left, Mere Therese said to him, "Je vais prier pour vous."

The next morning around 9:00 a.m., still drunk and disheveled, he went out and showed up for inspection, but then he realized that he was still quite drunk, turned to Miller, and said, "You're still in charge, Miller," and retired to his quarters.

On Saturday morning, November 23, Williams asked Biway for a twenty-four-hour liberty pass. Biway said, "Just what makes you think you deserve a pass, Copper?"

Williams simply replied, "I believe I earned it, sir," and he was granted a pass. Thereafter Williams went to the base motor pool and rented out a two-door green 1949 Ford and drove it to Quang Minh, taking both a camera and a tape recorder with him. When he first arrived at the mission, Pere Joseph had misgivings about him since he was a Marine. Williams said to him in French, "Je suis ici pour apprendre ce que vous a passe avec Le Sgt. Biway mardi soir lorsqu'il arriva ici tout seul." Thereafter Williams and Pere Joseph began conversing in French. Williams who noticed the marks and the bloody nose Pere Joseph had, asked him if he could photograph them. Pere Joseph said yes, and Williams showed Pere Joseph a tape recorder and asked if he could tape their conversation, and again Pere Joseph said yes. Thereafter Williams went on to interview Mere Therese and some of the Vietnamese nuns. After he finished, Williams thanked them and explained that he and the other men under Biway's command wanted to have Biway court-martialed for his brutal tactics, and thereafter he returned to base.

When Williams returned to the base, he handed both the camera and the tape recorder back to Private First Class Alcantor, as requested. Later, Alcantor promptly turned the evidence over to Second Lieutenant Wilkinson to be taken to Colonel Hughes in order to be used as evidence against Biway.

Corporal Alfie Miller was born Alfonso Giacomo Graziano on January 15, 1944, to Ugo and Giovanna Graziano in the village of Vecchio Umbarletti, not far from Naples in southern Italy. In June 1943, Ugo was killed as he and his comrades were being staffed by an American plane in North Africa. Shortly thereafter, Giovanna, already pregnant with Alfonso, returned to live with her parents in the city of Gaeta in central Italy.

In April 1944, some Moroccan soldiers who were passing through Gaeta broke into the house of Giovanna's parents to rob them and rape Giovanna. Fortunately, an American squad headed by Sergeant Ralph Miller just happened to be passing by and noticed the commotion in that house. Ralph and his men barged in just in time to keep Giovanna from being raped and her parents robbed. The whole family couldn't tell Ralph how grateful they were since none of them could speak English. On June 5, 1944, a day after the taking of Rome by the allies, Miller went on a three-day furlough and drove south to Gaeta in order to once again see Giovanna. He found her and told her that he wanted to teach her to speak English since he could speak no Italian. They began to communicate by sign language at first, and as Giovanna got better at speaking English, she said she wanted to go steady with him. Sergeant Miller, who was divorced at that time, decided to marry Giovanna.

The wedding between Ralph and Giovanna took place on Saturday, August 12, 1944, at La Chiesa di Santo Giuseppe in the heart of Gaeta. Both Ralph and Giovanna were twenty-five. However, it would be almost another year before Ralph would be discharged from the Army. In the meantime, Giovanna remained in Gaeta with her parents and her baby boy, Alfonso. Finally on May 22, 1945, Ralph got his discharge and planned to take both Giovanna and Alfonso to his hometown of Effingham in Central Illinois, where he was born and raised. Ralph was born there on February 22, 1919, to Hubert and Pamela Miller.

Upon returning to the United States, he persuaded Giovanna to Anglicize her name to Joan and change Alfonso's to Alfonse James from Alfonso Giacomo. As he grew up, Alfonse was called Alfie for short. At first, the marriage appeared to be a happy one, but as time went by, Ralph became interested in his high school sweetheart, Lila Ferrell, and as Joan went out to work in a local restaurant to make ends meet, she met a truck driver by the name of Arthur Tuttle. He was thirty-five with a stocky build, salt-and-pepper kinky hair, and was never married. He lived in St. Louis, Missouri. On the night of November 23, 1948, Ralph and Joan began confessing to one another about their extramarital relationships and mutually agreed to a divorce. The divorce took place six months later, and both were remarried within the next six months.

Unfortunately, Arthur lived in the near south side of St. Louis, which was a rather high-crime neighborhood. In 1950 at the tender age of six, Alfie began to engage in criminal activity such as shoplifting and car burglary. He felt neglected at home by his mother and stepfather. In 1951, Joan and Arthur had a baby daughter, Lisa, followed by a son, Charles, two years later. In school, Alfie began to engage in bullying other pupils. For this, he was disciplined several times. As he grew older, he engaged in more serious crimes and was placed in the St. Louis City Juvenile Detention Center several times and was sent on three different occasions to Mo Hills on the Missouri River for "reeducation."

In the meantime, on June 4, 1956, Arthur suffered a massive heart attack on US Highway 40 as he was hauling glass bottles from Kansas City to a Pepsi Cola plant in Greeley, Colorado. He died later the same day. Joan was devastated, and Alfie was serving time in Mo Hills for the second time. A year later after she was hired at the law firm of Billings and Thigpen, Attorneys at Law, she and Walter Thigpen began a new relationship. Like Joan, he too lost his spouse a year earlier. Unlike Arthur, Walter lived in the St. Louis suburb of Crestwood to the southwest. Here everything was new, and the surrounding landscape was beautiful, a far cry from the inner city of St. Louis. On September 8, 1957, Joan and Walter were married at St. Paul's Church in Crestwood since they were both Catholics. The next day, Joan along with Lisa, six, and Charlie, four, moved into Walter's Crestwood home.

Just a month and a half before their marriage, Alfie along with two of his buddies decided to go out joyriding. They soon found a four- door green 1947 Frazer Manhattan with the keys still in the ignition. All three jumped in with Alfie at the wheel. They drove over fifty miles before they were finally caught by a St. Louis County Deputy in nearby Valley Park. That took place on Friday, July 26, 1957. The next day, Alfie and his friends were arraigned in the St. Louis County Juvenile Court in Clayton. Miller was given a year in Mo Hills although the DA wanted to have him sent to the State Training School for Boys in Boonville, but Joan pleaded Alfie's case to the judge, and he listened and agreed.

While he was in Mo Hills for the third time, Alfie started taking an interest in electronics. He wanted to learn all there was to know about radios and television sets and was slowly losing interest in his criminal activities at the same time.

At first when he met Walter, Alfie didn't like him, but as the months he spent in Mo Hills went on, Alfie began to change his mind. He was released on May 5, 1958, and went to Crestwood to live with his mother, Joan, his sister, Lisa, his brother, Charlie, and Walter. When he first moved in, he was stunned at the difference between Crestwood and the near south side of St. Louis. Since it was so late in the school year, Alfie had to wait until fall before enrolling in high school.

On Tuesday, August 26, 1958, Alfie's mother took him to St. Anthony's Catholic High School to be enrolled. Two days later, Brother George explained to Alfie and his mother, "Due to Alfie's rather extensive juvenile delinquency record, we cannot accept him here at this school." Both Alfie and his mother were deeply disappointed over this. However at St. Paul's Catholic Church, there was a Monseigneur by the name of Joseph Gruenwald. He was already seventy-two years old but was still quite compassionate. Walter knew him quite well and told Joan to go and see him. The day after Alfie was rejected by Brother George at St. Anthony's, Joan and her husband along with Alfie went to see Monseigneur Gruenwald. He said he would do everything in his power to help Alfie get into St. Anthony's. On Tuesday, September 2, Brother George called Alfie into his office and said, "The other day Monseigneur Grunewald came to see me to intercede for you. Since he has faith in you, we decided to give you a chance here. But remember, this is your one and only chance so make good." Upon hearing this, Alfie was so glad he broke down in tears. He tried at least two dozen times to find a way to thank Monseigneur Grunewald but didn't know how. This was what made Alfie Miller intensively loyal to the Catholic Church and why he was to hate Sergeant Biway some ten years later.

About this time, Alfie Miller had a total change of attitude. He no longer felt that he had to have his way all the time and took a deep interest in his studies at school. Joan and Walter were extremely delighted with him. The following summer, Joan, Walter, Alfie, along with Lisa and Charlie took a trip to Gaeta, Italy, to see Joan's parents. Her father was already seventy years old and her mother was sixty- six, but they were quite glad to see Joan and Alfie again.

By the time Alfie Miller graduated from St. Anthony's in 1962, he decided he wanted to become an electronics engineer. That fall, he enrolled in Washington University in St. Louis with a major in Electrical Engineering and a minor in Geometry. He graduated on Thursday, June 2, 1966. Three weeks later, Miller was notified that he was being drafted by the Army but decided to join the Marines instead.

After passing both his physical and mental exams, he was sworn in on June 27. Miller knew he'd never really like being in the Marine Corps, but it was here he decided to fulfill his military obligations. He left his girlfriend, Barbara Abbott, also twenty-two, at the bus station, got on the bus and headed for Camp Lejeune in North Carolina to begin his basic training.

The Murder of Private Williams and Biway's Second Court-Martial

On Wednesday, September 25, 1968, around 9:00 a.m. as Biway was in the middle of inspection, his superior, Second Lieutenant Fred Wilkinson, thirty-seven, came to him and said, "After inspection, you are to report to Colonel Henry Hughes."

Biway replied, "Aye, aye, sir."

After he went into Colonel Hughes's office, Hughes said, "Biway, I've been studying your military record, and in particular about your court-martial last year. What gets me here is the fact is that you never showed any remorse whatsoever over what you did to Private Lathrop. He is now in a wheelchair and will never walk again. Second Lieutenant Steven Taylor wanted to have you sentenced to thirty years of hard labor plus a dishonorable discharge. Instead, Captain Henry Sutton, considering your thirty-two-year-long impeccable military record, decided to give you a six-month suspension with full pay.

"Even while on suspension, you got drunk and ran into another car in New York City, killing a four-year-old girl and crippling her eight-year-old brother for life. Still you failed to show any remorse and spent about a month on Rikers Island before some crackpot judge released you. I even spoke to Master Sergeant Kenneth Frisner, who was with you in Korea. He said that you enjoyed the war and killing gooks in particular. Remember him?"

Biway replied, "Yes, I do, sir. In fact, I saw him in Japan nine years ago and exchanged greetings."

Then Colonel Hughes said, "The Marine Corps is a great outfit. In fact, my sons, Frank and Sid, are serving here in Vietnam this very minute.

In short, I take great pride in commanding this regiment, and I will not tolerate anyone like you to soil its reputation. In other words, there will be no unnecessary killing of POWs or civilians nor any abuse of any man under your command. Do I make myself clear, Biway?"

Biway replied, "Yes, sir, you do. I fully understand, sir." Hughes said, "Our business here is concluded. Dismissed."

Biway got up, saluted Colonel Hughes, and left. Once outside, Biway lit up a Swisher cigar, turned to Hughes's office, and made an obscene gesture.

Colonel Henry Hughes was born Henry Graham Hughes on January 17, 1925, in Coffeyville, Kansas, the second of two sons born to Charles and Bertha Hughes. The other son was Willard, born on March 3, 1921. Charles was a newspaper editor for the Coffeyville Times. However due to the depressed economy back in 1931, the paper had to close down. Fortunately for Charles, his uncle who ran a paper in McAlester, Oklahoma, told him they needed a new editor. This was a lucky break for the Hughes family.

Also in McAlester lived Hughes's future wife, Madeleine Phelps. She was born on March 30, 1925, the third child to Norman and Edith Phelps. The others were their son, Theodore (Ted), born on August 12, 1921; daughter Christine, born on May 25, 1923; and daughter Phyllis, born on August 24, 1929. Norman Phelps worked as a prison guard at the Oklahoma State Prison for Men in McAlester. In school, Henry and Madeleine met and eventually fell in love. On Saturday, June 12, 1943, they married shortly after their graduation from McAlester High School. When Henry was notified that he was being drafted into the Army, he decided to enlist the Marine Corps instead. He fought quite bravely during WWII especially in the South Pacific and the Philippines and was awarded several medals for his bravery.

In 1945 when the war ended, Henry decided he wanted to go to the Marine Academy in Quantico, Virginia, in order to become a Marine officer. His superior, Lieutenant Fred Holbrooke, forty-five, handed him an application and a test paper. Henry took the exam and passed. Thereafter he was accepted at Quantico. His wife, Madeleine, moved there in order to be near him. Here he studied for the next four years. In the meantime, Madeleine gave birth on November 7, 1946, to Frank, their first child, followed by Sidney on December 15, 1947, and finally Harold on July 5, 1949, shortly before Henry's graduation. Thereafter Henry was sent to Camp Lejeune in North Carolina to assume his first command. Madeleine followed him there with their three sons.

In June 1950, the Korean War broke out, and Henry was notified that he was to be transferred to Camp Umayoshi in Japan. Madeleine wanted to follow him there too, but Henry objected. Besides, Madeleine's maternal aunt, Mrs. Sadie Bradshaw, sixty-four, who was widowed a year earlier, wanted Madeleine and her three sons to move in with her in the small town of Atoka, Oklahoma, south of McAlester, and Madeleine agreed. In November 1952, Henry was granted a two- week furlough, and when Madeleine was told, she took herself and her three sons to Japan to meet their father for the first time in two years. They had a fabulous time, but it was short-lived. Henry had to return to Korea and Madeleine to Atoka.

In the meantime in 1954, Harold, who was only five at that time, was involved in an automobile accident. The church group, which was taking Harold and fellow kindergarten pupils on a fall outing south to Durant, was hit head-on by a drunken twenty-year-old girl who lost her boyfriend the day before. She came out of it rather unscathed, but two of Harold's fellow pupils died, and Harold had to be taken to a local hospital. He survived his injuries but came out of it mentally challenged later on due to them.

By 1960, Henry became a major, and by 1965, a lieutenant colonel and was transferred to Camp Pendleton, California. For Henry, 1965 turned out to be a bittersweet year. First, he learned that his wife, Madeleine, was pregnant for the fourth time, and both were hoping for a girl. In mid-October, however, Henry noticed he had a pain in his stomach. He thought at first that it was simple indigestion, but the pain never went away. In fact, it seemed to have grown worse day after day. Finally on November 2, he went to the Marine Medical Center to have his stomach examined. Three weeks later on Tuesday, November 23, Henry was given the grim diagnosis. It turned out to be cancer of the esophagus, and he was required to have an operation as soon as possible. Harold agreed, and the operation took place on

December 17. Not wishing to worry Madeleine, Henry never mentioned any of this to her.

In the meantime, Henry also noticed that he was losing a lot of weight. At the beginning of 1965, Henry was five feet, eleven inches tall and weighed 242 pounds. He was quite handsome with his curly black hair. In fact, his wife, Madeleine, was quite good-looking herself with her black hair and green eyes although she had to wear glasses. In fact, Henry's second son, Sidney, strongly resembled him as he grew up. By April 1966, as he was granted a two-month furlough so he could be with Madeleine in May, when she was due to have her baby, Henry could no longer conceal from her the fact that his health was deteriorating. By the time he came home, he weighed only 145 pounds. Madeleine became quite upset and demanded Henry to tell her everything, and he finally did. For her, this was a severe blow.

On Saturday night, May 7, just before 11:00 p.m., Madeleine gave birth to a baby girl just as she and Henry had hoped. They named her Catherine Josephine, and she weighed 6 pounds and 8 ounces. She looked very much like her mother. A month later in June, both Frank and Sidney enlisted in the Marines since they wanted to be like their father. However, in Vietnam, they didn't serve under him since they were assigned to a different regiment, and Henry returned to Vietnam that same month.

On September 11, 1967, Lieutenant Colonel Hughes was notified by Brigadier General Gary Caldwell, fifty-three, that he was being promoted to the rank of colonel. However, his cancer had gotten worse, but he was still quite capable of his command. For a year, Colonel Hughes was happy with this assignment, but then Sergeant Biway and his platoon arrived and were placed under his command as part of his regiment. Before Biway arrived, Lieutenant Stanley Gould notified Colonel Hughes of Biway's past record by mail. When Biway arrived, Colonel Hughes wanted to know all there was to know about him.

On Sunday, November 24, just a day after Private Williams handed Private First Class Alcantor the camera and tape recorder, Sergeant Biway assembled his squad and went out on a search-and-destroy mission. They captured six Vietnamese POWs. Just before they returned to base, Biway ordered the POWs to be locked up in a makeshift cage just off the base. Private Williams was already aware of Biway's sinister plans for those men and decided to do something about it.

Around 4:00 a.m., Williams got up, got dressed, hopped into a jeep, and drove out to where the POWs were. When he got there, he picked up a shovel, busted the lock, opened the cage, and asked the POWs, "Y-a-t' il quelqu'un parmi vous qui connait francais?"

One of them replied, "Oui, J'en parle."

Williams then said, "Allez-en vite, on vient ici pour vous tuer a l'aube. II faut que vous partiez le plus tot possible et n'oubliez pas vos armes."

The POWs didn't know what to say next so they collected their rifles and melted into the elephant grass.

An hour later, Biway with three of his men arrived and were shocked that Williams had released the POWs. At this point, Biway became so angry he almost turned purple. He turned to Williams and hollered, "Your—is Mudd! I'm going to have you court-martialed, you—."

Williams retorted, "I bet Colonel Hughes will be quite glad to find out what you've been up to lately." Then Biway ordered the three men to return to base but told Williams to remain. Biway had suspected all along that Colonel Hughes had something up his sleeve but couldn't quite figure it out up to that morning. Biway, now red in the face with anger, hollered, "So you're the mole Hughes planted in my squad to spy on me and my activities, but now you'll never tell him anything more,—."

Williams replied, "I don't quite understand."

Biway picked up a shovel, and looking Williams square in the eye, he noticed that Williams harbored no fear, which made him even angrier, raised the shovel, and hit Williams upside the head and hit Williams in the head until he fell to the ground. By this time, Williams's skull was bashed in with blood coming out of his eyes, nose, and ears. After Williams fell to the ground, Byway stepped on his neck in order to make sure he was dead.

Thereafter, Biway dragged Williams's body into the elephant grass, dug a hole, buried him, and threw the blood-soaked shovel farther into the elephant grass. He then hopped into his jeep, drove back to base, got rid of his bloody uniform, and took a shower just in time for the 9:00 a.m. inspection.

Ironically, Private Williams was not the mole Biway suspected him to be. That was Private First Class Jerome Alcantor.

On Friday, September 27, two days after Colonel Hughes interviewed Biway, he called Major Henry Sutton into his office and said, "I understand that you presided over Sergeant Biway's court- martial last year at Camp Lejeune, North Carolina."

Sutton replied, "Yes, I did, sir. Sergeant Biway broke the back of a newly recruited private by the name of Andrew Lathrop in a fit of temper. His immediate superior, Second Lieutenant Steven Taylor, wanted to have him sentenced to thirty years of hard labor followed by a dishonorable discharge. However, in light of his past thirty-two-year record of impeccable service to the Corps, we decided to be lenient and give him a six-month suspension from the Corps with pay. Evidently we made a mistake, sir."

Colonel Hughes replied, "Think nothing of it. We all make mistakes." Hughes went on to say, "What I need right now is to plant a mole into Biway's outfit to keep me and my men abreast of what he is up to. If there are any brutal tactics with the local civilians or any unnecessary or undeserved punishments meted out to any man under his command, I want to know about it. Could you locate any such man willing to take on this assignment?"

Major Sutton replied, "Yes, I believe I can, sir." He had Private First Class Alcantor in mind, and on Monday September 30, he called Alcantor into his office and said, "I have a special assignment for you if you care to take it."

Alcantor asked, "What is it, sir?"

Sutton replied, "We need to plant a mole into Sergeant Biway's outfit to keep us informed of every move he makes. This includes the mistreatment of both the POWs and the men under his command. Moreover, we'll need evidence of Biway's misconduct to be handed over to either Lieutenant Walter Stevenson or Second Lieutenant Fred Wilkinson. I'll give you the next three days to decide whether or not you wish to take this assignment. Remember, you don't have to take it if you rather not."

Alcantor waited twenty minutes and said, "Sir, I don't need three days to decide. I'll accept this assignment now."

Private First Class Alcantor was twenty-five, five feet, ten inches tall, and very slender with black hair. When he first enlisted in the Marines, he wanted to marry his fiancée, Barbara Price, but both decided to put it off until he returned. After he graduated from Harry Truman High School in 1961, he went on to the University of Missouri in Kansas City to study criminal justice, and that was why Major Sutton picked him.

Private First Class Jerome Alcantor was born Jerome Gabriel Alcantor on July 31, 1943, in Kansas City, Missouri, to Alfred and Madeleine Alcantor. He was an only child. His great-grandfather, Emilio Alcantor, along with his brother Doroteo fled Mexico in 1862 because the French took over that country, and they were afraid of having all their wealth confiscated, so they fled north to Texas. Both men later joined the Confederate Army, but when the war ended, Emilio moved north to Kansas City.

On Saturday, October 5, while on a search-and-destroy mission, Private Howard Quatham, twenty-five, stepped into a bear trap laid by the Viet Cong. Quatham was rescued but had to be taken right away to the nearest field hospital where he got the grim diagnosis. His left leg had to be amputated as soon as possible.

On Monday, October 7, around 10:00 a.m., Private First Class Alcantor reported to Sergeant Biway and announced, "I am Quatham's replacement, sir."

Biway replied, "Make yourself at home."

The day after Alcantor joined Biway's squad, the squad went out on another search-and-destroy mission, capturing one POW. While the men were searching the village, Biway and the POW disappeared into the surrounding elephant grass. About forty-five minutes later, Biway reappeared alone, and this aroused Alcantor's suspicion. During the whole week, Alcantor became increasingly disgusted with Biway's behavior and his unnecessary use of profanity, especially while addressing Private Williams. On another search-and-destroy mission on October 12, Williams along with the rest of the squad were ordered to hide in the elephant grass, seeking out either Viet Cong or North Vietnamese regulars. Williams did spot three North Vietnamese soldiers from his position in the elephant grass but refused to open fire, and the North Vietnamese went on their way without anyone else in the squad knowing about it.

As the weeks went by, Private First Class Alcantor was increasingly anxious to turn Biway in for his brutal tactics, but he still needed proof. One night, he approached Private Williams and said, "I noticed that you've become favorite whipping boy for Sergeant Biway. How do you manage to put up with it?"

Williams replied, "Biway and I have a mutual loathing for one another. He hates everything I stand for since I was a cop on the Chicago police force, and I hate him because he apparently loves to kill, especially for self-amusement.

"He apparently puts no value on human life, so anything he says to me has become rather banal. He even told Private Jerry Williams, a negro himself, what I did to a negro boy in Chicago while I was still on the force. I explained to Jerry what that kid did to a Chinese restaurant owner and how he pushed his face into a pot of boiling grease. Thereafter, Jerry and I became good friends."

Finally on Wednesday, November 20, Alcantor said to Williams, "I understand that you're the only man in this outfit who can speak French as I noticed yesterday when you offered to translate what Biway was saying to Father Joseph. I understand that next Saturday you're due for a twenty-four-hour liberty pass. The reason I'm asking is that I want to have both Mother Therese and Father Joseph interviewed on tape and pictures of any injuries Father Joseph may have sustained. I now have both a camera and a tape recorder for that purpose. Will you do it, Williams?"

Williams replied, "That I will gladly do, Jerry." So the plan was set for that Saturday.

On Monday morning, November 25, about ten minutes past 9:00 a.m. or ten minutes into the inspection being conducted by Sergeant Biway, as he was shouting profanities at his men, both Lieutenant Walter Stevenson and Second Lieutenant Fred Wilkinson appeared.

First, Wilkinson said to Biway, "You are heretofore relieved of your command. You're being court-martialed as of now. The charges being murder, rape, assault and battery, and conduct unbecoming a Marine officer. You are ordered confined to quarters except to go to the PX or chow, accompanied by two MPs. Lance Corporal Alfie Miller is now Sergeant Alfie Miller."

Biway angrily replied, "Just who the—are you to take away my command, and aren't you man enough to tell me that in private instead of out here in front of all these men?"

Wilkinson then ordered two Marine MPs to take Biway away, but before they did, Lieutenant Stevenson called out Private First Class

Alcantor in order to pin a silver star medal on him, saying, "A job well done, Alcantor. Thank you."

As Biway saw this, he was in total disbelief. His mole was not Williams at all but Alcantor instead. He trusted Alcantor and thought that they had become good friends, but apparently he was wrong.

As Biway was being led away by two Marine MPs, his replacement, Sergeant Alfie Miller, continuing the inspection, said, "At 1300 hours, we'll reassemble here and conduct a search for both Private Williams and the POWs he turned loose, beginning where we left Biway alone with him this morning. Dismissed."

In the meantime, Private First Class Jerome Alcantor's eyes became swollen with tears over what he did to Sergeant Biway but no one seemed to notice. Alcantor felt quite bad about it as a cowardly thing to do.

The search for Williams began at 1:00 p.m. as planned, starting with where Biway and Williams were last seen together, and after some two and a half hours of searching through the elephant grass, they found a newly created mound of dirt, dug through it, and discovered the body of Private Williams with his head bashed in and covered with blood and mud. After looking further through the elephant grass, they found the shovel Sergeant Biway used to bludgeon Private Williams. Thereafter having collected these items, they returned to base around 5:00 p.m. Both Williams's body and the shovel used to slaughter him were turned over to the naval forensics unit to be examined at the main base in Da Nang for evidence.

Before being led to his quarters, Biway requested to be allowed to go to the PX and purchase two quarts of vodka and a box of Swisher cigars. Permission was granted, and after Biway purchased the said items, was led to his quarters. Soon after he lit up one of his cigars, poured himself a glass of vodka, and started drinking in order to get the courage up for his planned suicide later.

He skipped chow and continued to drink and think. Finally around 10:00 p.m. or so, he passed out. This time he knew that as a Marine, he was all washed up, and everything he fought for was a total loss, thus destroying his very reason for being. The only way out for him now was nothing less than suicide.

Shortly after 1:00 a.m., he came to, and again the grim reality for him set in. After taking two more shots of vodka, he reached into his desk drawer and pulled out his pistol, loaded it, and pointed it to the right side of his head, but for some reason, he couldn't pull the trigger. Then he wondered, *What's wrong with me? Am I just as much of a coward as my father was? Maybe he's inside of me, laughing at me this minute. Then again, was my father truly the coward I deemed him to be? Maybe he did tell me the truth after all. I was only nine at the time. I also had an infant sister who died from asthma when she was only two months old. Just who do I blame for this ignoble mess I now find myself in?*

He took another shot of vodka and thought, *No matter how much of this stuff I pour into me, it won't change the grim reality.* He put down his last drink, looked out the window which faced west, and noticed the half-moon beginning to set. He ceased to drink and began to think, *Who do I blame? Private Williams? No, he didn't even want to be here except that he was coerced to enlist. My parents? Maybe.*

As he was slowly sobering up, he began thinking about his interviews with Second Lieutenant Taylor, Lieutenant Klingman, Lieutenant Gould at Camp Pendleton, and finally with Colonel Hughes here in Vietnam, who all said pretty much the same thing. To him, it was like looking into a mirror, and the more he looked, the less he liked. He began to wonder what made him like that, a sociopath. Was it his parents? Yes, in part. He remembered his father, Joseph, who never at any time laid a hand on him and his mother, Margaret, who never yelled at or scolded him even after Dolores Farber came over one day in 1929 to plead with her to somehow get him and his gang to stop harassing and cursing at her father, Paul, at his house. Margaret did admonish Biway to quit it, but that lasted but a week and half, and then the harassment started all over again and didn't stop until August 12, 1930, when Mr. Farber had a stroke and died later that same day at the age of seventy-two. Even after he was suspended from St. Paul of Tarsus Elementary School for "attacking" Diane De Wolfe in October 1929, neither his mother nor his father punished him. In short, his parents may have been too lenient with him.

Even as he grew up during the Great Depression of the 1930s, he had everything a boy could wish for. When he was three, his father bought him a tricycle, at seven, a bicycle, at eight, a football and a catcher's mitt, and at twelve, his parents bought him a dog, which he named Bozo. At the same time, many other boys were compelled to do without these things, and some were never to have the chances he did. Even after he and his friends beat up and injured a seventy-nine- year-old man with brass knuckles, his parents didn't ask him whether or not he had anything to do with it.

Finally on Sunday, July 14, 1935, when he raped his sister, Susanna, his father finally called the Utica Police to have him arrested. Even as he was being led away by the police, the last thing he said to his father was, "Pop, at least I'm not yellow like you are." That remark deeply hurt Joseph in addition to the rape of Susanna and learning about the abuse perpetrated on his younger brother, Rick.

As he was being led away, he noticed the hurt look on the faces of both his parents and the hurt he inflicted on his maternal grandmother, Mary McDougall, who always doted on him. She was eighty years old at that time. As Rick was to tell him many years later, "Since you were apprehended by the Utica Police, she hardly spoke a word to any of us." She finally died on March 13, 1938, just before her eighty-third birthday. This further added to Biway's remorse since as good as both his parents and his grandmother were to him, this was how he repaid them. No wonder they never answered the letters he wrote them after he joined the Marine Corps.

For the very first time in his life, Biway started to feel remorse. That feeling was totally alien to him. All his life he thought mostly about himself and obtaining gratification either sexually or physically, no matter who got hurt or even killed in the process.

Later on, he began to think about Mere Therese and the way he raped her twice. He not only obtained sexual gratification, but in his mind he was punishing both Sister Mary Arnold, who slapped him four or five times in front of Diane De Wolfe thus humiliating him and Brother Joseph for beating him with a barber strap. Then he remembered what Mere Therese said to him after he raped her, "Je vais prier pour vous," and several other things she said to him. Although Biway couldn't understand French, he knew pretty much what she said to him. Could this new sensation he was now experiencing be the answer to her prayers? It was beginning to appear that way.

Then he became even more remorseful as he continued thinking about Mere Therese, a woman who came so far and helped so many people and the fact that he had to rape her. And then there was Pere Joseph, whom he beat up for apparently no reason except in his mind he was punishing

Brother Joseph. After all, the two did share a common name. At this time, if he could apologize to them, he would and tearfully so.

As dawn approached, he remembered Private First Class Hermann Mettler and his undeserved court-martial back in 1959. Was that fair? No. Now Biway himself was being court-martialed for far worse. As all these thoughts were spinning through his head, he decided to take another shot of vodka in order to clear his head, so to speak.

Around 8:00 a.m., two MPs escorted Biway to the mess hall where he had breakfast and then escorted him back to his quarters. Again he began to think, and for him it was becoming pure torture so he took another shot of vodka. At 10:00 a.m., a certain lieutenant by the name of Ron Maplethorpe announced himself to the MPs and said he was there to represent Biway at his court-martial, which was to take place on Thursday, December 5, in Da Nang.

After Maplethorpe introduced himself, he told Biway that he needed to plead guilty to the charges against him since he consulted with Lieutenant James Walters earlier that morning, who was to prosecute him. The evidence Walters had against him was overwhelming. He told Biway, "In light of all the evidence Walters has against you, you will need to plead guilty and throw yourself to the mercy of the Marine Tribunal so you won't have to face the firing squad. You've been charged with the murder of Private Williams plus the rape of Mere Therese and the battery on Pere Joseph in Quang Minh."

Biway replied, "Maybe I should face the firing squad since my life as a US Marine is over with anyway. I have very little left to live for, and the men who were under my command hate my guts."

Maplethorpe said, "All I want to do here is to save you from your death, and Lieutenant Walters will do all he can to have you executed since he considers you a disgrace to your uniform and the Marine Corps. You still have your family in California, and I'm quite sure they will want you to live even if you are dishonorably discharged from the Corps. I know things look grim for you now, but given time, your attitude will change. Right now I'm going to prepare for your defense and use your thirty-two-year impeccable military record on your behalf and, maybe if you're not executed, win you a reduced prison sentence." Then Lieutenant Maplethorpe said goodbye and went on his way.

As morning gave way to afternoon, Biway was once again thinking. This time it was what he was to tell his ex-wife, Aggie, and his daughter, Kitty, when they found out the truth about him. He didn't know what to say to them. As the afternoon dragged on, he further agonized over what he did to people in the past, such as Mrs. Nancy Ballard, who loved him while he got her pregnant and ditched her back in 1948, and then there was Christine Dellanos, whom he got pregnant and slapped her for just being Hispanic. Furthermore, he thought of the student by the name of C. T. Tennyson, whom he raped in his cell one night on Rikers Island. The more he thought, the more tormented he became. Since he couldn't kill himself the night before, the Marine Corps would do it for him, or so he hoped. He now knew he had every right to be executed, especially for the brutal murder of Private Williams.

When he first thought about Williams, he said to himself, *The— bastard had it coming for turning those—scumbag Vietcong POW's loose and spying on me.* But then again he remembered that the mole Colonel Hughes sent to spy on him was not Williams at all but Private First Class Alcantor.

All Private Williams wanted to do was to be a good policeman, but in light of all the atrocities perpetrated by so many criminals on ordinary people, he sometimes found it quite difficult to control himself. Finally Williams was compelled to resign and join the Marine Corps. He did all he could do to avoid killing anyone while in Vietnam. At one point, Biway took an unarmed captured north Vietnamese regular and ordered Williams to shoot him. Williams fired but deliberately missed, not once, but three times. Then Biway said, "If you don't kill that scumbag, Copper, I'll kill you instead, you—!"

Williams looked Biway square in the eye and said, "So be it."

After this incident, Biway hated Williams to no end and abused him especially whenever he got drunk, and Alcantor noticing it became totally disgusted as well as the other men in the squad.

In fact, all the men under Biway's command were afraid of him except for Williams and Alcantor. Williams even asked Biway, "Why do you have so much hate in you, and why are you so anxious to kill or have your men do it for you? This war shouldn't be happening, and we have no right to be here."

Biway replied, yelling, "Shut your—mouth, Copper, you—! Not another sound out of you or I'll literally beat you into the ground. Got it,—?"

On another occasion on Wednesday, October 16, after completing a search-and-destroy mission and after leaving the hamlet of Huang Li, Biway ordered Private First Class Ralph Bullen, the squad's radio operator, to call in an air strike on the hamlet. Bullen protested, "We just came out of there, and there were no Viet Cong to be found."

Biway quickly slapped Bullen in the face and said, "If you don't call in an air strike, I will kick your—guts out,—! Got it—?"

Bullen reluctantly complied and called the air strike in, and while witnessing the napalming of that hamlet, Biway turned to Private First Class Alcantor and said, "This is one time I regret not having joined the Marine Air Corps. Those guys get to slaughter a lot gook—.

Then again, from the air, you can't really see how much damage you're doing or how many gooks you kill. At least down here you can pretty much see what you're doing."

Private First Class Alcantor became thoroughly disgusted at Biway's remark, as did the rest of the squad. Because the other men feared Biway, they kept their mouths shut.

Finally on Friday, November 29, two MPs came to Biway's quarters to take him to a helicopter to be flown to Da Nang, where his court- martial was to take place. He was placed in the main brig to await his day at the tribunal. He was allowed, however, to purchase all the vodka plus all the Swisher cigars he wanted. As thinking tortured him so, he spent most of the next six days either drinking vodka, playing solitaire, or smoking a cigar.

In the meantime, Colonel Hughes asked his superior, Brigadier General Gary Caldwell, fifty-five, for permission to attend Biway's court-martial, and it was granted. At the same time, Brigadier General Caldwell told Hughes, "Since your cancer has spread, and in light of your deteriorating health, I plan to have you sent to the VA hospital in Ft. Smith, Arkansas, so you can be near your wife and little girl as of December 31. How do you feel about it, Colonel?"

Hughes replied, "Sir, you're right. Yes, my cancer has gotten worse, and I wish to spend the little time I have left to live with my wife, Madeleine, my son, Harold, and my little girl, Cathy Jo, who will turn three in May. I can't show my gratitude enough for what you're doing for me, sir."

On December 31, Colonel Hughes was first flown to Camp Pendleton in California and then to the VA hospital in Ft. Smith, Arkansas, in order to undergo further treatment.

On Thursday morning, December 5 (ironically Private Williams's birthday), two MPs came to Biway's cell and first led him to the mess hall for his breakfast and to the tribunal where his court-martial was to be held. At 9:00 a.m. after Biway was led into the courtroom, Corporal Delmar Fraley announced, "The court-martial of Sergeant Joseph Thomas Biway. The charges are as follows: The murder of Private Odell Williams, the rape of Mere Therese, the assault and battery on

Pere Joseph, and the unnecessary murder of a thirteen-year-old Vietnamese boy. Major Leonard Briggs presiding."

Major Briggs asked Lieutenant Maplethorpe, "How does the defendant wish to plea to the charges against him?"

Maplethorpe replied, "Guilty as charged, sir."

Then Lieutenant James Walters made his opening statement asking that Biway be placed before the firing squad and executed. The only question here was, will Biway be put to death or spend the rest of his life in some federal prison somewhere?

In the meantime, in order to keep this court-martial out of the press, Brigadier General Gary Caldwell ordered six sentries to stand in front of the tribunal and tell members of the press, whether from the AP, the UPI, CBS, ABC, NBC, or any other news organization, that this tribunal was not open to the public and were escorted elsewhere and given other stories to cover on the war. The reason for this action was to keep this story away from the American public whose enthusiasm for the war was already on the decline, not to mention what this story would do to the men and women in the Marine Corps by lowering their morale. The courts martial was successfully kept out of the Press and thus sparing the American public this scandal.

First, Lieutenant Walters called the now Sergeant Alfie Miller to the stand. He proceeded to ask Miller how he felt about his former commander, Biway. Miller replied, "I hate his—guts, sir. That savage"—pointing to Biway—"needs to be put out of his misery, the filthy animal! Anyone who would beat up on a priest or rape a nun should be put to death with no questions asked. We all know he did it, not to mention the thirteen-year-old boy he shot down in cold blood." Thereafter all the men who were under Biway's command were ordered to testify at the court-martial. They all said pretty much the same thing about Biway, as did Miller. Later, Lieutenant Walters told the tribunal that he had the tapes that Lieutenant Stevenson obtained from Private First Class Alcantor, but since no one at the tribunal understood French, he decided to summon Sergeant Danielle Vache, twenty-five, to the tribunal in order for the tapes to be translated into English by her since she understood French fluently. Both her parents were born and raised in France, but after WWI, which ruined the national economy, they decided to immigrate to America, where jobs were more plentiful. Danielle was the youngest of three children born to Henri and Louise Vache. She had two brothers who were older and successful in their careers, but she decided to become a Marine. At 10:00 a.m. the next day, she showed up, and Lieutenant Walters called on her to listen and tell the tribunal what the tapes said. He also had the photos of Pere Joseph, showing the injuries he received from Biway.

As Sergeant Vache listened, she told the tribunal word for word what was on those tapes. There were three voices to be heard, that of Private Williams, Pere Joseph, and Mere Therese. First, Williams interviewed Pere Joseph, who explained how Biway attacked him without provocation, and he even kicked his pet, Gigi, a French bulldog, for no reason except that he was both angry and drunk.

Then Williams entered the convent to interview Mere Therese. She began to tell the graphic details of her rape. She said, "At first, Biway grabbed me, led me into the dorm where we sleep, then he tore off my habit, stripping me naked before throwing me on my bed. He began by sucking my breasts, then he licked my belly before he performed oral sex on me. At the same time, he forced me to share his vodka, to which I complied. Thereafter he proceeded to enter me, not once but twice. When he finished for the second time, I told him that I will pray for him and then said, 'Odell, please to do the same and ask the other men in your outfit to do likewise.' That man needs divine help."

As the members of the tribunal were listening, they became thoroughly disgusted, while Biway's eyes started to become filled and swollen with tears. For the first time in his life, he realized what a savage he truly was.

Then Lieutenant Walters called Private First Class Bullen to the stand. He asked Bullen about the way he was forced to call in an air strike on the hamlet of Huang Li on October 16. Bullen proceeded to tell the tribunal what transpired that day.

Around 3:00 p.m. after all the testimony was heard along with the tape recording Williams had with both Pere Joseph and Mere Therese and the photos taken of Private Williams's mutilated head from the bludgeoning Biway gave him, Major Briggs announced, "This hearing is now adjourned and will reconvene tomorrow at 0900 hours."

Lieutenant Walters objected, saying, "I have one more witness to present, and his name is Sergeant Kenneth Frisner. He's now stationed in Japan and won't be here before Sunday at the earliest. I hereby request that the hearing be rescheduled for Monday at 0900 hours, sir."

Major Briggs replied, "Request granted. We're adjourned."

As Biway was being led back his cell, he asked the MPs who were escorting him for permission to go to the PX in order to purchase two more quarts of vodka plus another box of Swisher cigars. They replied, "Permission granted," and Biway was then led back to his cell, where he was to spend the weekend.

Again he began to think, especially about what Mere Therese said to Private Williams on the tapes he heard. The more he thought, the more he knew he had every right to be executed, and then he remembered his brother, Rick, and his sister Susanna and how he hurt them. Then he wondered, *How did Rick, Theresa, and Susanna turn out to be such ordinary people, while I ended up being such an animal? They had the same parents I did.* Thereafter he started to drink heavily in order to stop thinking. He passed out around 6:00 p.m. but came to around 2:00 a.m. He looked out his window, which faced west, and watched the full moon as it began to set in the western sky. Then he thought, *I guess this is the last full moon I'll ever see since I expect to be placed before the firing squad and put to death soon.* Then for the first time in his life, he thought of God. Biway was never religious, although his hatred for the nuns, monks, and priests were quite strong. He wondered, *In light of all I did here on earth, how will God judge me?* And that thought terrified him. Since he stopped praying after he was expelled from St. Paul of Tarsus Elementary School in 1931, he simply forgot how to. Then he thought of both his ex-wife, Aggie, and his daughter, Kitty, and asked himself, "How did a monster like me become a husband to such a good woman as that, and how did I become a father to a girl such as Kitty?" He finally said to himself, "These people do not deserve me, and since I expect to be executed soon, it will no longer matter." In fact, he refused to answer the recent letter Aggie sent him. As he continued to think about them, a sense of self-loathing set in.

At 9:00 a.m. on Monday, December 9, the trial reconvened. Lieutenant Walters called Sergeant Frisner, forty-three, to the stand and said, "State your name, rank, and serial number to this tribunal."

Frisner replied, "I am Master Sergeant Kenneth Frisner, and I now belong to the Second Marines and currently stationed in Japan. My serial number is 189558, sir."

Walters asked Frisner, "Do you know the defendant, Sergeant Biway?"

Frisner replied, "Yes, I do, sir."

Then Walters asked, "How long have you known him?"

Frisner replied, "For the last sixteen years. We met in Korea in 1952 in the midst of the Korean War, when I was in the First Marines, and we were assigned to the same platoon."

Waters then asked, "How did you two get along?"

Frisner replied, "At first, we got along quite well, but then there was this incident at Heartbreak Ridge. Biway succeeded in capturing three North Korean soldiers, whereupon he shot them at point blank range, threw their bodies back in the foxhole they came out of and rearmed their corpses. That happened in November of 1952. The longer we fought side by side, the more I got to dislike him. He seemed to enjoy killing, and he said as much. Finally on April 13, 1953, I watched him murder a Chinese soldier as he was surrendering himself by breaking his neck. He simply said, 'The only good gook is a dead one,' whereupon I felt disgusted."

"Have you anything to add, Sergeant?" asked Walters, and Frisner replied, "No, I don't, sir."

After Frisner finished testifying, Major Briggs asked Lieutenant Maplethorpe if he wished to cross-examine. Maplethorpe replied, "No, sir, I do not."

Then Briggs announced, "Let the closing arguments begin." Walters went first, arguing how Biway disgraced the uniform he wore and for the firing squad, and then Maplethorpe reiterated Biway's thirty-two- year-long impeccable military record.

Major Briggs turned to Biway, ordered him to stand up, and asked him, "Have you anything you wish to say to this tribunal before sentence is imposed?"

Biway replied, "Yes, I do, sir. First of all, all the charges which have been brought against me here are quite true. Yes, I did murder Private Williams by bludgeoning him with a shovel, and yes, I did rape Mere Therese, and I did beat up on Pere Joseph simply because as a ten- year-old boy, a monk by the same name beat me with a barber strap, and I murdered that thirteen-year-old Vietnamese boy and reported him as a Viet Cong guerilla, and finally, I forced Private First Class Ralph Bullen to call in an air strike on the hamlet of Huang Li although there were neither any Viet Cong nor North Vietnamese present.

"Now I want to admit to other charges here that were never brought up of which I'm guilty. On two different occasions after capturing either Viet Cong or those suspected of being Viet Cong operatives, instead of bringing them back to base where they were to be handed over to South Vietnamese government troops to be executed later, I would put them in a makeshift cage and return the next day with four or five men under my command. Then we turned the POWs loose to hunt them down one by one, and I did it simply for my self-amusement. I told the men to keep their mouths shut, and they complied. The first time was on Wednesday, October 30, and the second was on Tuesday, November 12.

"The morning I murdered Private Williams on November 25, would have been the third time. I murdered Williams simply because he turned them loose. Yes, I have done all these despicable things I mentioned here, and I am now prepared to take whatever punishment you care to mete out to me, sirs."

Major Briggs replied, "Thank you, Biway. We deeply appreciate your coming forward and admitting to what you did."

"At 0900 hours on Monday, December 16, a week from today, you will have our decision regarding your sentence, Sergeant Biway. This trial is concluded."

Then Biway protested, "If I am to be placed before the firing squad, why not sentence me today and get it over with? You heard all the testimony presented against me here, sirs."

Briggs replied, "Captain Fred Callan, Captain Larry Brockmeyer, and I will need a week to discuss this evidence in order to decide which is the appropriate punishment for you," and he said again to the rest of those present, "Hearing adjourned."

For Biway, this was to be a week of pure unadulterated torture. He had to languish in his cell, not knowing whether or not he was going to be put to death or sent to some federal prison for life. Then he remembered Rikers Island in New York and the criminals he met there. Later on, he remembered God and wondered how he was to be judged after his death, and that made him fear being put to death anytime soon. The only thing that made those days bearable for him was the vodka he was allowed to consume. Otherwise, he felt if he had to continue thinking, he'd lose his mind. Each minute seemed more like an hour to him, and for him, the time went extremely slow.

Then at 9:00 a.m. on Monday, December 16, Biway walked into the courtroom, wondering what his future held, if he had one at all. Major Briggs announced, "Sergeant Biway, or more appropriately, former Sergeant Biway, you are hereby dishonorably discharged from the First Marine Infantry and will be declared unfit for military service either in the Marine Corps or any other branch of the U.S. military.

"Furthermore, since you not only admitted to the charges brought against you at this tribunal but freely admitted to others you committed here in Vietnam, we hereby sentence you to a term of ten years in the US Federal Penitentiary in Leavenworth, Kansas. You will be placed on the next ship to Camp Pendleton, California, and then remanded to US Federal Marshals to be transported to the said penitentiary. In the meantime, you are ordered to surrender your sword to Corporal Delmar Fraley."

Biway complied and handed Corporal Fraley his sword. Fraley took the sword, put up his right knee, and broke the sword in half while Biway watched him, and as he did, his eyes filled with tears. Then Biway was ordered to surrender any or all the medals he received throughout the years he earned while fighting in Korea. Then Biway was taken back to his cell, and he handed all his medals over to the MPs who were guarding him, and in turn, they handed them to the members of the tribunal.

Two days later accompanied by four MPs, Biway was put on a Navy ship bound for Camp Pendleton. There, he was put in a brig, and on Sunday, December 29, four US Marshals came and took Biway, and they got into the 1968 Lincoln Townhouse allotted to them by the US Justice Department. They reached Leavenworth, Kansas, on the morning of January 3, 1969. Here Biway was processed in and he began his ten-year sentence. Biway was at this time relieved that he hadn't been put to death. The admission sheet read, "Prisoner No. 183856. Name: Joseph Thomas Biway. Age: 50. Height: 6'1". Weight: 189 lbs. Hair: gray. Eyes: green. DOB: 12/25/1918. Reason for Incarceration: homicide. Term to be served: ten years. Dated: Jan. 3, 1969."

Ironically on the same day Biway entered Leavenworth Prison, Colonel Henry Hughes entered the VA hospital in Ft. Smith, Arkansas, for further treatment for his cancer, which had spread to other parts of his body. However, his wife, Madeleine, and his son, Bubba, were glad to come and visit him. Finally, Henry asked the doctors to quit treating him, saying, "This will only postpone the inevitable. Right now I just want to go home and spend my last days with my wife, my son, my dog, and of course, my two-year-old daughter." The doctors agreed, and on Friday, January 17, Henry's forty-fourth birthday, Madeleine Hughes drove up in her 1968 Buick La Sabre in order to take her husband home. However, one of the doctors said that Henry needed further treatment and that he was in bad shape. Madeleine snapped, "I don't care how sick my husband is, I just want to take him home now, now, now!" The doctor finally agreed but told Madeleine to give Henry just enough morphine to keep his pain in check and only when he needed it, and Madeleine agreed. Then they wheeled Henry out to Madeleine's car. Thereafter Madeleine drove Henry to their home in Atoka. After he got home, he was glad to see his little girl, Cathy Jo, once again. Since he was in the military most of the time, she barely knew him. He wanted very much to bond with her and eventually did.

As long as Henry was on his morphine and took only as needed, his biggest problem was the dizziness he felt upon standing and loss of appetite. Otherwise, his stay at home was extremely pleasant. As winter was slowly giving way to spring, he noticed the crocuses outside in full bloom followed later by the daffodils, hyacinths, narcissuses, and tulips. At night, he and Madeleine would make love. In short, the last few weeks of Henry's life were extremely pleasant, but he knew his days were numbered.

Henry finally succumbed at 4:30 a.m. on Friday, April 25, only twelve days before Cathy Jo's third birthday. The whole family was devastated, including Frank, Sidney, Harold (Bubba), as well as Madeleine's aunt Sadie.

Three years later, Madeleine remarried, this time to a successful Atoka businessman by the name of David Baldwin. He was fifty-two at the time and a lifelong bachelor who owned four different businesses. On Cathy Jo's seventh birthday, David gave her a Boston terrier pup, whom she named Henry in honor of her late father. In addition to Cathy Jo's pup, the family had two other dogs. There was Henry's pet German shepherd, old Rinty, who by that time was almost fourteen years old, and Madeleine's pet, a Boxer by the name of Checkers. Both David and Madeleine were quite happy although Madeleine still missed Henry.

As for Private Williams, the Navy forensics lab took pictures of his bashed-in head and samples of his blood and subsequently turned them over to the Marine tribunal in Da Nang for evidence. After they finished doing that, they put his corpse in a body bag and put a tag on it, which read, "Pvt. Odell Daniel Williams. Age: 34. Height: 5"7" tall. Weight: 143 lbs. Eyes: brown. Hair: brown. Cause of Death: homicide."

Thereafter they had his body shipped to Chicago, where his mother, Alberta, now sixty-eight, had a private mass said over him at St. Stephen's Catholic Church on Clark Avenue and later had his body sent to the Mills Bros. Crematorium to be cremated. That done, they took his ashes out to the middle of Lake Michigan and promptly poured them into the water.

By then, sadly enough, no one on the Chicago police force even remembered his name. Such was the legacy of a man who wanted to help so many others in his lifetime but received little or no recognition for it.

CHAPTER 6

Biway's Final Years

After Biway was processed into Leavenworth, he found the conditions harsh, but he soon adjusted to them. Biway was assigned a cell on the top tier. A week later, one such inmate by the name of Tom Calvert, thirty-five, did pick a fight with him. As on Rikers Island, Biway, using his skills in martial arts he learned while in the Marine Corps, quickly beat Calvert. The fight took place on the top tier of the prison. After Biway finished with Calvert, he twisted his arm, pushed his head over the railing, and said, "The next time you—with me, I'll throw your worthless —— over this rail, and by the time you hit the floor below, you'll make one hell of a splash!" Thereafter, the prisoners who witnessed this fight decided to stay away from Biway whenever possible.

The construction of the Leavenworth Federal Penitentiary began in 1897 as ordered by an act of Congress. The first prisoners were admitted in 1903. Today it houses around 1,900 inmates. It is surrounded by a wall forty feet high and forty feet deep. It has three tiers. Here, Biway was to spend the next ten years of his life. About a week after his incarceration, Biway received a second letter from his ex-wife, Aggie, forwarded to him by the Marine Corps. In the letter, Aggie said she was quite worried since she didn't hear from him over the last two months. At night in his cell, Biway began to think about Aggie and what she said in her letter. Finally on Thursday, January 16, Biway decided to answer her since he felt it was unfair not to. He asked the guard for a pen, a sheet of paper, and an envelope. Once he obtained the said items, Biway began to write Aggie. The letter said as follows:

Dear Aggie,

I am now incarcerated at the US Federal Penitentiary in Leavenworth, Kansas. Last month, I have been dishonorably discharged from the Marine Corps for murdering one of the men under my command and subsequently sent here. In addition to that, I beat up on a French priest and raped a French nun.

Now I know that those two people never had it coming. It was me. In fact, Aggie, there are still some things about me I never told you. For instance, I lied to you about my childhood. I was not brought up in an orphanage like I told you back in 1946 before you married me, and St. Paul of Tarsus was not an orphanage but a Catholic elementary school, nor were my parents and my two sisters killed in an automobile accident. I simply made it up in order to hide the truth from you. Moreover, when I was sixteen, I raped my sister Susanna, who was fourteen at the time, whereupon my father called the Utica Police and had me arrested over it. The judge later gave me a three-way choice, and I opted to join the Marine Corps. When I was ten, I tried to make love to my ten-year-old classmate, whose name was Diane De Wolfe. I was punished with a two-week suspension. I was finally expelled from that school in 1931 when I was twelve. That's not all I did either. I also abused my brother, Rick, by forcing him to perform oral sex on me as well as my buddy, Buddy Androszech. I also had sex with four different girls beginning when I was thirteen. Yes, Aggie, you deserve to know the ugly truth about me and the ugly things I did in the past, and so does Kitty. Whenever you decide to break all this to her, please do it as gently as possible. Finally, if you decide not to answer this letter or ever see me again, I'll understand, but remember, I still love both you and Kitty, and give your husband, Bill, your sons, Bruce and Robert, my regards.

Yours truly,
Tom

Thereafter Biway folded the letter and handed it to the guard, who read it before placing it an envelope and mailing it.

In the meantime, Biway began to witness the homosexual rapes, stabbings, extortions, and even murders taking place there. It was even worse than on Rikers Island. Even prison guards were attacked time and again. In fact, Author Pete Early wrote about it in his book *The Hot House: Life Inside Leavenworth Prison*. It clearly described the day-to-day life in that prison.

As long as Biway could instill fear in other inmates, he remained relatively safe, but that was not always the case. In March, two months after he began his sentence, there was this inmate by the name of Virgil De Wolfe, forty-five, who ironically had the same last name the girl Biway tried to make love to at St. Paul of Tarsus Elementary School so many years ago. De Wolfe was six feet, four inches tall and weighed around 252 pounds. His face was heavily pockmarked, making him rather ugly. He was in for the kidnapping and rape of a fifteen-year-old girl in Arkansas. He received a twenty- year sentence for it. De Wolfe began to notice Biway in the prison mess hall, where they ate. One day while taking their showers, De Wolfe approached Biway and decided to ask him for a sexual favor. Biway promptly said no, and De Wolfe became angry over it.

Later that day, De Wolfe tried to rape Biway, but Biway fought back. When De Wolfe attacked, Biway simply put his two hands together, raised them, and brought them down rapidly, breaking De Wolfe's nose and causing him great pain. When the guards broke up this fight, both De Wolfe and Biway were sent to solitary confinement. Biway was there for a week, but De Wolfe was confined longer. De Wolfe told Biway whenever he got out, he was going to kill him. However, De Wolfe, for some reason, never carried out his threat.

On January 31, 1969, two weeks after Biway wrote Aggie, the guard handing out mail to the inmates said, "Biway, this is for you." Biway took the letter and read the return address, which said, Aggie Decker, 411 Quincy St, Marysville, CA 95901. Biway opened the letter, which said as follows:

Dear Tom,

I got your letter last week, and I'm glad as hell you haven't been killed in Vietnam. As for being in Leavenworth, I hope it won't be for the rest of your life since you didn't tell me how long you'll be there.

Regardless of what you did or how many crimes you committed or even who you killed, Kitty and I still love you, as does Bill, Bruce, and Robert. I am glad you decided to come forward and tell it all.

Yes, I told Kitty all about you as you asked me to. At first, she took it rather hard as it took her three days to grasp it. Finally she said to me, "No matter what he did in the past, he is still my father and always will be. I hope to heaven he'll be getting out of that horrific prison one day and come here to California to live for good."

I'll close for now.

Love,
Your ex-wife,
Aggie

After Biway read the letter, his eyes became filled with tears, realizing that both Aggie and Kitty forgave him for the many crimes he committed in the past but he knew he had to spend the next ten years in that hellhole. In a follow-up letter, he told Aggie he was due to be released on January 3, 1979, and was hoping to return to California thereafter.

About a week and a half later, Biway received another letter, this time from Kitty. It read as follows:

Dear Dad,

Mom told me all about you three weeks ago, and like her, I too forgive you for every wrong or shameful thing you ever did in the past. You are still my father, no matter what.

I will graduate from Berkeley in another year and a half and hope to become a social worker one day. I now have a steady boyfriend, and his name is David Harris. He's from a small town in Oregon by the name of Cave Junction. It's just over the state line and not too far from Marysville.

Mom also said that you'll be getting out of that prison in 1979, ten years from now. If for some reason you are unable to live with Mom and Bill, you'll always be welcome to live with me. By that time I expect I'll be married to Dave and living in Oregon, or at least I hope so, but one can't really tell what the future holds. One day next summer, I hope to make the trip to Kansas and visit you. Hopefully Dave, Bill, Aggie, and the boys (Bruce and Robert Decker) and I will all come together to see you.

I'll close for now.

Love,
Your daughter,
Kitty

Biway felt quite good after reading this letter, knowing he had a loving family outside after his old family rejected him back in the 1930s. As he remembered, he wrote them on four or five different occasions, but they never answered him. Then again after what he did to Rick and Suzanna, he could hardly blame them, which in turn saddened him, knowing how his parents loved him and especially his grandmother, Mary, who doted on him.

In the meantime in the mass hall, he met a young inmate by the name of Markie Marshall, twenty-five. Markie was sentenced to fifteen years for manslaughter. He was from Pine Bluff, Arkansas, where he worked in a US post office. One of his coworkers, by the name of Joe Cox, forty-nine, would poke fun at him because he had a highly strung nervous temperament which caused him to act rather irately. One day, Markie decided he had enough and punched Cox in the mouth. Cox fell backward and hit his head on a hard, blunt object. Cox later died in a local hospital, and Markie was charged with manslaughter. Since it happened in a U.S. post office, Markie was tried in a federal court and subsequently sent to Leavenworth to serve out his fifteen-year term.

Like many other inmates, Markie was afraid of Biway. One day, he offered Biway one of his cigarettes which was laced with marijuana. Biway lit it up and began to feel rather euphoric. Then Biway asked Markie, "Where did you get these cigarettes?"

Markie replied, "From a guard by the name of William Strolheim, one of the few genuinely homosexual guards working here. He brings us these cigarettes in exchange for homosexual favors."

Then Biway asked Markie, "Will he also bring vodka if asked?" Markie replied, "Yes, he will. In fact, he already does for other inmates."

In fact, William Strolheim, fifty-two, was one of the few homosexual guards to be employed at Leavenworth. He hired on in the summer of 1946 after WWII and held that position ever since.

William Strolheim was six feet, two inches tall and weighed around 250 pounds. He had gray hair and a round face. Since he was heavyset, Biway would later become physically attracted to him. Strolheim liked performing oral sex on the prisoners. William Strolheim was born on December 8, 1916, in the small town of Cold Springs, Minnesota, the youngest of five children born to Everett and Emma Strolheim. The others were Linda, born on March 31, 1900; Wanda, born on January 31, 1904; Fred, born on July 5, 1906; and James, born on February 7, 1911.

By the time Strolheim reached the age of twelve, it became clear to him that he was different as he became attracted to other boys rather than girls. One day in high school in 1932, when he was fifteen, he got to be alone with one of his fellow classmates by the name of Keith Zerkel, also fifteen, and made a pass at him. Since Strolheim was rather big for his age, Zerkel became frightened of him and told his parents what happened after he got home. The next day, Mrs. Edith Zerkel came to Strolheim's house and confronted Strolheim's mother about it. Emma in turn told her husband, Everett, and Everett asked Strolheim if what Mrs. Zerkel told his mother was true or not. Strolheim admitted that it was, whereupon Everett said, "When you reach your eighteenth birthday, I want you out of this house. We didn't raise you to be that way. Besides, have you read the book of Genesis, where God destroyed the cities of Sodom and Gomorrah? I strongly suggest that you do that!" That was the attitude most people had concerning homosexuality in those days all across the country.

When Strolheim reached his eighteenth birthday, he left home and settled in the city of Minneapolis to find work, which was difficult in those days. Because most people were homophobic, he did all he could do in order to hide his inner feelings. About a year after he settled in Minneapolis, he met a girl by the name of Joanne Morgan, twenty-two, and started dating her. In June 1938, after two years of going steady, they married. When Joanne found out about his homosexuality, she promptly took everything he owned and left him in May 1939. Strolheim threatened to sue her, but she told him that if he did, she'd tell everyone she knew about his sexual orientation. Thereafter, Strolheim simply let her go and quietly divorced her.

In 1940, Strolheim joined the US Army and served with distinction in the US Army Air Force during WWII. After his discharge in 1946, he moved to Leavenworth, Kansas, where he heard they were hiring new guards. He was finally hired in July 1946.

In the meantime, he fell in with a farmer by the name of Jesse Thornton, who had a farm nearby. On it Jesse grew marijuana, which he planted throughout the farm, making it look as though it grew wild. He began to sell some of it to Strolheim, who in turn laced cigarettes with it and took them to work with him to exchange them with some of the inmates for sexual favors. This arrangement worked out rather well.

In August 1968 shortly after Markie Marshall began his fifteen-year sentence, Strolheim began doing business with him, who in turn introduced him to Biway several months later. As well as bringing in marijuana-laced cigarettes, Strolheim also brought in vodka for Biway. With this arrangement, Biway, Marshall, and Strolheim generally avoided conflicts with other inmates as they kept to themselves when they engaged in sexual activities.

However in August 1977, an inmate by the name of Joseph Druce began his five-year sentence for extortion and racketeering as he was convicted under the RICO Act. He was thirty-one, had long shoulder-length black hair, five feet, nine inches tall, and weighed 169 pounds. He looked somewhat like Hollywood actor Sylvester Stallone. In fact, he was born on the same day Stallone was, on July 6, 1946. He was from Chicago, born into an Italian American family and was a distant cousin to John Ramboletti, who threw acid in the face of Reverend McIntyre, thus blinding him and disfiguring his face back in 1965.

In 1955, when Druce was nine years old, a parish priest by the name of Father Norman Zwychi, forty-one, began to molest him by sodomizing him. He did this on many different occasions. Father Zwychi threatened him never to tell anyone, and Druce complied. He would be haunted by this for many years to come, and his hatred for homosexuals slowly grew into an obsession. So when he started to serve in Leavenworth, he soon learned that William Strolheim was a homosexual, and he began planning to either injure him severely or kill him.

After formulating his plan, Druce managed to pilfer a screwdriver out of the prison workshop and pilfered a second one some three months later and hid both of them in his cell under his mattress.

Finally around 2:30 a.m. on June 12, 1978, Druce made his move by inviting Strolheim into his cell in order to exchange sex for vodka and marijuana. As Strolheim was getting ready to perform oral sex on Druce, Druce reached under his mattress and slowly pulled out the two screwdrivers and suddenly jabbed out both of Strolheim's eyes, whereupon Strolheim threw his hands over his face, which was suddenly covered with blood, and started screaming, "My eyes, my eyes!" and hurriedly ran out of Druce's cell and down the tier corridor, bumping into several objects along the way. Other guards intercepted and led Stolheim to the tier office, where the guards realized that Strolheim had both his eyes punched out. They rushed him to the prison dispensary, where Strolheim was told he would never see again. Strolheim was totally devastated and wanted to die. While in the dispensary, Strolheim called his sister, Wanda, who lived in the town of St. Joseph, not far from Cold Springs, and told her what happened to him. Wanda said she would drive down to Leavenworth to pick him up and take him to her house whenever he was discharged and up to making the trip. Strolheim agreed, and when Wanda brought him to her house on June 23, her husband, ET Wilson angrily said to her, "I do not want to have this queer of a brother of yours under my roof. As soon as he is fit, I want him out of here. Am I understood, Wanda?"

"Yes, ET, you made yourself quite clear," replied Wanda. Wanda then called her brother Jim to ask him if Strolheim could live with him since ET hated homosexuals. Jim said he could, and arrangements were made for Strolheim to move in with him, his wife, Matilda, and their two dogs, Pat and Mindy. Jim's two sons were already grown up and married. Later Jim told Strolheim, "Homosexual or not, we're still brothers. I hate the way Mom, Dad, and ET treated you over something you couldn't help. Maybe now people are becoming more enlightened, or at least I hope so."

Strolheim said, "I can't show my gratitude enough, Jim." Jim replied, "What are brothers for anyway?"

Strolheim finally died in a nursing home in St. Joseph after both his brothers, along with Wanda and Linda, had all died, leaving him all alone and in total blindness on October 20, 1989, at the age of seventy-two.

In the meantime in the summer of 1974, the warden announced to the inmates in the prison auditorium, "We have decided to start up computer training classes for all of you who are interested. These classes will begin two weeks from now, and if you're interested, sign up here with this man you see here before you return to the dayroom." Biway said, "Since I've already served half my sentence already, I think I will sign up for it. I'll need to have a new skill when I get out of here."

However when Biway signed up for the new class, the professor asked him, "Did you finish high school?"

Biway replied, "No, I didn't. When I was sixteen, I joined the Marine Corps, only getting as far as the tenth grade in school. Is that a problem, mister?"

The man replied, "I'm afraid it is. However, you can start this course as soon as you get your GED. You can get that here as soon as you sign up for it."

Biway agreed and decided to get his GED. He got his GED on February 6, 1976, and thereafter began his courses in computer science. In the summer of 1978, he finished them and thus graduated.

Finally on Wednesday, December 27, 1978, one of the guards told Biway, "On January 3, a week from today, you'll be released. Do you want to call someone to make arrangements for you when you get out?" Biway replied, "I guess I'd better," and Biway called Aggie, who promptly sent him money for the long train trip to California.

Biway was released on January 3, 1979, whereupon he took a bus to Kansas City and then took a train from there to Sacramento, California, where he was met by Aggie and Bill Decker, who drove him to Marysville.

For Biway, this was all so new to him. He was like a night owl who was suddenly blinded by the early light of dawn. After some eight years of being incarcerated, he almost forgot what it was like to be with a woman, let alone see one. How so very beautiful some of them appeared to him. It was not only the women but the whole countryside was unbelievably beautiful to him too. He could hardly get enough of this newfound freedom. He began feeling like a bird suddenly let out of his cage, and it felt wonderful.

Bill and Aggie took Biway to their house on Quincy Street once they reached Marysville, gave him the guest room, and told him he could have it as long as he wanted it. He was greeted by both Bruce and Robert Decker, who began calling him Uncle Tom. Even their two dogs, Prissy and Target, seemed to like him.

Two days after he settled in, Biway decided to look for a job in the computer field and went to IBM to seek employment. However after he submitted his application, he was interviewed by Mr. Gary Atkins, thirty-seven, who told him that while his time in Leavenworth wouldn't bar him from hiring on at IBM, his dishonorable discharge from the Marine Corps would. Atkins told Biway, "I'm afraid your dishonorable discharge from the Marine Corps will prevent us from hiring you here. All I can say is that I'm terribly sorry."

Thereafter Biway went to Bill and Aggie's Bar and Grill (the name was changed from Bill and Aggie's Place in 1975) deeply disappointed. Bill told him, "Tom, you can always work here as a bouncer and a bartender. If you do, we'll pay you a third of the profits this place turns over. How's that for a deal?"

Biway replied, "That'll be great. When do I start?"

"Next week if you like," replied Bill. In the meantime, Bill had one of his bartenders show Biway the ropes. Biway started on Monday, January 15, and worked the noon-to-eight shift.

While Biway was languishing in Leavenworth, his daughter, Kitty, graduated from Berkeley in June 1970, got a job as a cashier at a local supermarket, waiting for a position as a social worker. Later on September 19, she married her boyfriend, David Harris, and they moved to Cave

Junction, Oregon, soon after. David got a job as a quality control supervisor at the Mott's Food Processing plant in nearby Fruitdale and Kitty hired on as a social worker for the Josephine County Welfare Department in Grant's Pass. Later that year, Kitty came up pregnant and bore a son on Friday, September 3, 1971. They named him Mark. On March 16, 1975, they had a second child, a daughter whom they named Beverly. Both grew into healthy, happy children. On Saturday, January 27, 1979, Kitty, Dave, and the two children drove down to Marysville, and Biway was thrilled to meet his grandchildren for the first time. In fact, he hadn't seen either David or Kitty since 1976. Kitty looked much like her mother, Aggie, except that she was taller and slightly slimmer. Aggie was always rather short and slightly heavyset, and Biway liked her that way. The visit lasted for about a week, and thereafter Dave, Kitty, and the children returned to their home in Cave Junction.

In the meantime, Biway went to the California License Bureau and got his driver's license. As he walked by McIlwain Ford in downtown Marysville, he saw a green 1972 Ford Mustang with a price tag of $1,850, and he wanted to buy it but had no credit since he had to spend the last ten years in Leavenworth. Later he told Aggie about it, and she replied, "That's no problem, Tom. Bill and I will loan you the money, and you can pay us back as soon as you can."

Biway replied, "Thanks a million."

So Aggie went to the bank in order to withdraw the money to loan to him. The next day, Biway bought the car, and he was thrilled to drive it around town.

During the following month, Biway decided that he wanted a place of his own. He told Bill and Aggie first, and then Bill found an apartment for him at 612 Raleigh Street. It was a one-bedroom apartment, and Biway was pleased, so he took it.

At this time, Biway was becoming extremely happy as everything seemed to be going smoothly for him, but he still didn't have a woman to call his own. Even at sixty, he still had strong sexual desires and was strongly attracted to women. Since he had to languish for the last ten years in Leavenworth, women now appeared more appealing to him than ever.

On Saturday night, March 3 around 8:00 p.m., as he was bartending and serving customers, he noticed four women coming in and sitting at a table whereupon he served them. One of them caught his eye. Biway asked the bartender who was working with him who those women were. He told Biway that they were high school teachers who came in frequently on Saturday nights.

The one woman who caught Biway's eye was around five feet, eight inches tall and weighed about 165 pounds. She had pitch-black hair, which was cut short, and wore a green miniskirt, and she was quite shapely. Even with glasses, she looked rather sharp. Biway couldn't quite get her out of his system. Around 11:30 p.m. as the women were leaving, Biway asked the other bartender, "Who is that woman with black hair and glasses in the green miniskirt, and do you know her?"

The bartender replied, "No, not personally, but I know that her name is Edith Connelly and that she teaches math at Marysville High School."

For the next three weeks, the women did not return, but they did on Saturday night, March 31, around the same time.

When they sat down at a table, Biway asked for the rest of the night off. The bartender said, "No problem. We can handle it." Biway changed his clothes and sat at the bar and ordered a Coors beer.

As Biway was nursing his beer, the jukebox started playing some golden oldies music. Then Biway got up, went over to the table where the teachers were sitting, and asked Edith, "May I have this dance?" At first Edith didn't quite know how to reply, but one of the other teachers said, "Go on, Edith, dance with him," and the two started to dance.

When they finished dancing, Biway asked Edith, "May I buy you a drink?"

Edith replied, "Yes, of course you may."

Then they sat down at a separate table and began to converse. Edith Connelly was born Ursula Edith Connelly on August 31, 1937, in nearby Yuba City, the youngest of three daughters born to Eugene and Hazel Connelly. The other two were Florence, born on May 24, 1930, and Linda, born on February 26, 1932, during the height of the Great Depression.

Eugene Connelly was born in nearby Wheatland on May 3, 1887.

He became a stockbroker and was quite good at it. He first married Mabel McGuinness, also twenty-six. A year later, they had a son by the name of Edward. In 1917, Eugene was drafted and served in France. While he was there, Ed contracted Spanish influenza and died shortly thereafter.

In 1919, Mabel contracted the same disease and also died, leaving Eugene devastated. Hazel Connelly had a similar tragedy with her first husband, Tom Jones, having been killed in France fighting the Germans in 1918. Both Hazel and Tom were twenty-two at that time. Eugene and Hazel first met in 1927, and in June 1929, they married, some four months before the big crash on Black Tuesday, October 29. The two managed to muddle through the Great Depression of the 1930s, so the girls didn't have to do without the things other girls did at the time.

As Edith hated her first name, Ursula, she asked to be called by her middle name, and thereafter everyone called her Edith. In the fall of 1949, Edith, like her two older sisters, had to be fitted with eyeglasses. Even with her eyeglasses, Edith was still quite attractive, and many boys swooned over her. In 1948 upon graduation from high school, Florence married, and a year later, Linda did too, dropping out of high school. In 1956, Edith graduated, and since she did so well in math and science, she won a scholarship to attend the University of Sacramento.

Since she hated her mousy brown hair, she decided to have it dyed red, thus making her even more attractive. She had two neighbors living next to the apartment she shared with two of her fellow students. They were Harold and Donna Ginsley. Harold was a lab technician and Donna, a registered nurse. They had a son named Donald, born on December 3, 1940. He grew up to be quite handsome. Don and Edith met for the first time in September 1959, when he was eighteen and she, twenty-two. They were quite attracted to one another, and so they began to date. That grew into a rather serious relationship. Upon graduating from John Adams High School in June 1960, Don decided to join the Marines in order to fulfill his military obligations. Before he left, Edith told Don that she was in love with him, and Don replied that he felt the same way about her, and so the two became engaged.

Don's parents approved of her although she was three and a half years older than he was.

In July 1962, Edith joined Don's parents on a trip to Japan, where Don was stationed. They remained there for a week and then returned. It was a pleasant trip. Don returned to Camp Pendleton that fall.

However, on Sunday morning, March 10, 1963, after completing maneuvers the night before, five of the Marines, including Don, decided to warm up, the temperature in the highlands where they were being around forty degrees Fahrenheit. As they were huddling around a fire, they used empty grenade boxes to keep the fire going. Unfortunately, one of the boxes contained a live grenade, which exploded in the fire.

In the explosion, two of the men were killed outright, a third blinded, and a fourth crippled. Don had his face blown off and was rushed to the Marine dispensary at the base but died three hours later. Two days later, Don's parents were informed, and they passed the news on to Edith. All three were devastated over this.

Edith took a job as a substitute teacher in Sacramento upon her graduation from Sacramento University in 1961 with a master's degree in math and science in order to be near Don's parents. In 1963, Edith decided to move to Marysville and went to work for Aggie and Bill as a cashier. She held that job for a year until a science teacher's job opened up for her at Marysville High School in September 1964. During the time she worked for Bill and Aggie, she and Aggie became very good friends.

At first, Edith enjoyed teaching at Marysville High, but as time went on, some male students began making passes at her and talked about her shapely body. However in the fall of 1966, when miniskirts were becoming fashionable, and at the same time, a student by the name of Gary Wiggins attended her algebra class. He was fifteen and she, twenty-nine, almost twice his age. In spite of this, the two became strongly attracted to one another, so she started wearing her yellow miniskirt to class in order to further impress him. However on Friday, September 16, Vice Principal Hope Langley, forty-four, called Edith into her office after school and scolded her, saying, "We have a dress code here forbidding you to dress so provocatively. If you want to keep on teaching here, you'll need to wear a full-length skirt from now on." Thereafter Edith complied. Even in a full-length skirt, she was still attractive with her crimson-red hair. In the meantime, she and Gary couldn't quite get over the attraction they had for one another. Sometimes she would invite him to her apartment to talk about his grades. She even gave him passing grades when he really failed his tests and upgraded some of his results to a B when he should have gotten a D.

In the fall of 1973, one of her male students, a certain David Jennings, sixteen, who was the son of Harold Jennings, forty-four, who taught art classes at that school, began to say things like, "Ma'am, you do have very pretty legs and a shapely body. You need to start coming here wearing a miniskirt to show your legs off more" and "How many men do you have hanging around your apartment at night when you're not here?" His parents would let him do whatever he wanted and say anything he felt like. He also drank like a fish whenever he was with his buddies. Where they got the alcohol from wasn't known. And then there was this female student by the name of Ethel Cook. She had light-brown hair, was obviously a lesbian, and was as big and full figured as Edith was. But unlike Edith, she had rather masculine facial features, making her rather homely. She would follow Edith to her house after school and park out front, sometimes for hours on end. This unnerved Edith quite a bit. Finally on Tuesday, April 2, 1974, Ethel followed Edith into the girls' bathroom at school and made a pass at her. Thereafter Edith snapped and said, "Young lady, if you want to graduate next month, I strongly suggest that you stop harassing me. Just leave me alone and stop coming to my house, and furthermore, don't ever come anywhere near me again!"

Ethel replied "Go to hell, you—!" and stormed out of there. Ethel was eighteen at that time.

Except for the friends she made with her fellow teachers, Edith hated her job, but she had to make a living. On September 12, 1967, around 10:30 a.m., Edith was called into the principal's office and was told, "Something terrible has happened to your father, Edith. He had a severe stroke about an hour ago. You are excused from your classes so you can leave as soon as possible."

Edith's father, Eugene, eighty, suffered severe stroke, leaving him paralyzed on his right side. She drove home, picked up her mother, Hazel, seventy-one, and drove to St. Joseph's Mercy Hospital in Yuba City, where Eugene was taken. The prognosis was grim as the doctors told both Edith and her mother that Eugene would only recover slightly at best.

Finally on Friday, October 13, the doctors at St. Joseph's told Hazel, Edith, and her two sisters, "We did all we could do for this man here. He needs to be placed in a nursing home as soon as possible."

Florence replied, "I'll contact the Oscar Greeley Rehab Center to have my father admitted there. It's only seven miles east of Marysville, on State Road 20 near the Yuba River."

Edith objected, saying, "No, I won't let my father be put into the hands of strangers. You don't know what those people there are like. Instead I'll vacate my apartment and move in with Mom so we can both take care of Dad. Mom during the daytime and me at night."

All agreed, and Eugene was taken home later that day. Thereafter Edith lived at home but sorely missed her social life as she was no longer free to join her friends on Friday and Saturday nights or date as frequently as before.

In the meantime, Gary Wiggins graduated from Marysville High School in 1969 and enlisted in the Marine Corps to avoid being drafted. He was born on December 4, 1950, to Bernard and Ferona Wiggins, the youngest of their two sons. The other was Thomas, born on September 8, 1947. Both his parents were part Indian, but mostly his mother was. He had pitch-black hair, was five feet, five inches tall and weighed around 150 pounds. He had rather tawny skin like a Native American and was proud of his heritage. He finally left the Marine Corps in 1977 after eight years of service. He decided he wanted to join the Yuba County Sheriff's Department. In December 1977, he was accepted and became a deputy sheriff. One Saturday night after he got off duty, he and his friends went to Bill and Aggie's for a beer. At the same time, Edith along with her friends stopped in for a rare Saturday night get-together. Gary suddenly recognized Edith and went over to talk to her. He said, "Hello, Edith, long time no see. Do you remember me from high school?"

Edith replied, "Of course I do, Gary. How are you these days?"

Gary replied, "Great. I just joined the Yuba County Sheriffs Department. By the way, did you ever get married, Edith? I bet you did, as attractive as you are."

Thereupon Edith said, "No, Gary, I didn't. My father had a debilitating stroke ten years ago, and he never recovered and never will. Mom and I look after him. He is already ninety years old and won't live much longer. We just want to make him as comfortable as we possibly can," and then she asked, "Gary, are you married now?"

Gary replied, "No, but I do have a girlfriend." Edith said, "That's good."

Then Gary said, "She doesn't hold a candle to you, Edith. In fact, if I had my way, you'd be my girlfriend instead.

"When I was in your class, I had a strong crush on you, and I still have rather strong feelings for you even today."

Edith said, "I had the same feelings for you but couldn't reveal them because of my position as a teacher. Maybe one day after my father dies, we may get together. How serious is the relationship between you and your girlfriend now?"

Gary replied, "Not so serious that we can't break it up. In fact, I'd like nothing better right now than to start seeing you."

Then Edith said, "I feel the same way."

A few months later on Thursday, May 25, 1978, Eugene succumbed at the age of ninety-one. A few days later, his will was read, giving Florence, Edith's oldest sister, the house. Since his medical bills were so high, the family was left with few resources, and Florence promptly told Edith to collect her belongings and leave as soon as possible. Edith eventually found an apartment at 783 N. Clark Street and moved in.

When Gary learned about it, he broke up with his girlfriend and started coming to Edith's apartment to see her. The two were deeply in love although she was already forty years old and he, only twenty- seven.

Their relationship went rather strongly until the night of January 17, 1979, when Gary's paternal uncle Russell Wiggins, fifty-six, accompanied him to Edith's apartment. Russell was a habitual drunk who said whatever he felt like when or wherever he happened to be. In Gary's presence, Russell sat down by Edith, pulled out his wallet, pulled out a $20 bill, and said, "Honey, this is yours if you let me go to bed with you tonight."

Edith blushed at the proposition and said, "No, I don't do things like that. Besides, I'm Gary's girlfriend." Then Russell doubled the offer to $40, and again Edith said no. Then he put his left arm around her and, with his right hand, reached into her blouse to feel her breast, while Gary sat next to them and said nothing. Then Russell offered Edith $100 for sex. Finally Edith snapped and said, "Get out of my apartment, both of you! I will not be treated like a common prostitute." Then Edith snapped at Gary, saying, "Why didn't you say anything? You heard what your uncle said to me and saw him reaching into my blouse. Just get the hell out of here!" They left, and thereafter Edith started to cry.

In 1975, Edith had her hair cut short and had it dyed pitch-black. Even with her short black hair and glasses, she was still quite attractive.

That Friday two days later, Edith had two of her friends come over, and she told them what transpired between her and Gary two nights earlier. One of them, Virginia Blakely, forty-five, told her, "Forget him, Edith. There are many other men out there, and you're bound to find one who'll truly respect you."

Edith said, "Thanks, Virginia."

As it turned out, Virginia was right. Later on that Wednesday night after he and his uncle left Edith's apartment, Gary began to cry over the loss of Edith, as he truly loved her. Such was Edith Connelly's background.

During their conversation, Biway asked Edith if she had a boyfriend somewhere. Edith replied, "I did, but we broke up last January. His name is Gary Wiggins. and he's with the Yuba County Sheriffs Department." Around 11:30 p.m. as Edith's friends were getting ready to leave Bill and Aggie's to turn in for the night, Biway asked Edith if he could drive her home. After a slight hesitation, Edith said yes and said goodbye to her friends as they were leaving. When they reached 783 N. Clark Street, where she lived, Biway asked her for a good-night kiss. Edith said she had a better idea and invited him into her apartment for a nightcap. Biway told Edith, "I had a great time tonight with you. I want to do this again if you agree."

Edith replied, "Of course I do. You can come over tomorrow if you wish to."

Biway said, "That I will. How about twelve noon?"

"That'll be fine," replied Edith, and Biway left after he finished his nightcap.

Later on after he got home, Biway wondered, *Does Edith know about my background, my ten years in Leavenworth, and my dishonorable discharge from the Marine Corps for bludgeoning one of my men? Judging by the way she acts, it doesn't appear that way.*

He came over the next day, and they had a pleasant time. Finally on the following Saturday night, April 7, Biway came over to Edith's apartment and resolutely told her everything about his past, his ten years in Leavenworth, his dishonorable discharge, his murdering a man under his command, and finally said to Edith, "If you never want to see me again after all I told you tonight about me, I'll understand. I'm so sorry, but you have every right to know, Edith."

Edith replied, "Don't be sorry. We all made mistakes in the past, and we learn from them. Besides, your ex-wife, Aggie, told me all about what you just said to me tonight. Yes, I will continue seeing you as long as you want me to."

Biway suddenly felt as if he had a 150-pound millstone lifted off his back, and he was relieved. Two weeks later, Edith and Biway drove north to Lake Oroville to do some fishing. They stopped at a local motel and rented two rooms, one for her and the other for him. That Saturday they went to the lake, rented a boat, caught five different trout, and brought them to Edith's motel room, and she cooked them. They had an excellent supper. The next day, they returned to Marysville. That night, Biway finally asked Edith if they could have sex. Edith said yes but asked why he didn't ask her sooner. He said, "I just didn't want to spoil our relationship since I love you." It had become crystal clear to Biway that he was deeply in love with her. She was the fourth woman in his life he fell in love with.

At this time, Biway was reaching the zenith of his euphoria. He could hardly believe the way things were going for him. He was free, had a job, a car, but most of all, a woman. In fact, he was so happy it almost frightened him. There was this adage, "What goes up must come down," but Biway tried to ignore it. He was too happy.

In the meantime after he was thrown out of Edith's apartment, Gary was never able to get over Edith and slowly realized that he was still deeply in love with her although he dated two other women since. On May 20, he broke up with his second girlfriend as he realized he still loved Edith. He began to follow Edith and often parked his 1974 green Fiat in front of her apartment, and she noticed it and realized that although she was going steady with Biway, her feelings for Gary never faded away as she hoped they would. Since Tuesdays and Wednesdays were Gary's days off, he finally showed up at Edith's apartment around 5:00 p.m. on Tuesday, May 22, and knocked.

Edith answered and said, "Gary, what are you doing here?"

Gary replied, "Edith, no matter how many times I tried to deny it, I still love you and always will. I even found two other women since we broke up, but since I still loved you, I never had any feelings for either one of them. God, Edith, I need you and need you badly. The last four months have been pure torture for me."

Edith, with tears in her eyes, replied, "Gary, I feel exactly the same way about you, but I couldn't stand the way your uncle Russell treated me that night, which made me feel cheap."

Gary said, "Edith, there is no way on God's green earth I will let that pig of an uncle of mine get anywhere near you again. I swear it."

Edith replied, "Gary, as long as we get back together, I really don't care what comes next. I'd be happy with you anywhere."

Then Gary took out an engagement ring and asked, "Edith, will you marry me?"

Edith replied, "Of course, Gary, I'd like nothing better!" And the two became engaged. Then Edith wondered, *Oh my god, what am I going to tell Tom when I see him? Since this Friday is my last day of teaching class, I'll tell him when my friends and I arrive at Bill and Aggie's around six o'clock.*

Around 6:00 p.m. on Friday, May 25, Edith along with two of her friends showed up at Bill and Aggie's, where Biway was on duty, tending bar. Edith ordered a Coors beer and said to Biway, "Tom, there is something I must tell you. Last Tuesday night, my former boyfriend, Gary, and I became engaged, and we plan to marry two weeks from now. It happened so fast. Please, Tom, inasmuch as I tried, I tried to get rid of my feelings for him, but to no avail, and he had the same feelings for me. Tom, I didn't mean for this to happen, but I deceived myself as well as you. I'm so dreadfully sorry to tell you this. Please try to forgive me if you possibly can."

After hearing her out, Biway's heart sank like a rock in a well. He could hardly believe what Edith just said. He finally replied with tears in his eyes, "I guess you couldn't tell me this in private instead of out here in front of all these people. Now get the—out of my sight. I never want to see nor hear from you again, you—!"

Dan Graybow, the bartender who was on duty along with Biway, said, "Tom, I'll call Aggie and we'll take over since you're no longer in the mood to work."

Biway replied, "Thanks, Dan."

Aggie came over fifteen minutes later. Later Biway left, stopped at a local liquor store, bought two quarts of Old Crow bourbon, and went home. As he sat in his living room, nursing his first drink. He thought, *How could she have done this to me? I thought she loved me as much as I loved her. Now she managed to turn my life upside down.* Biway now felt as if he were on a ship at the bottom of the Pacific Ocean after all the water was drained out. For him, she was the only thing that counted, but he lost her. This was the worst feeling he had since his court-martial in Vietnam. By 11:00 p.m. after drinking so much, he got up, staggered his way to his bed, got in, and passed out soon thereafter. Around noon the next day, he came to and slowly realized just how much Edith had hurt him. He felt sick at first, but later on as he started feeling better, he started drinking again.

Around 2:00 p.m., Aggie called and said, "Tom, I called you around ten o'clock this morning, but you didn't answer the phone. We've all been terribly worried about you since last night after Edith told you about her impending marriage to Gary. Just before I called you this morning, Edith called me to explain just how horrifically sorry she was over hurting you. Tom, she has just as much of a right to be happy as any of the rest of us. You'll need to let her go and get her out of your system. In other words, time is what you need right now. Tom, I know just how upset you are, but please don't do anything foolish, and remember, you still have me, Bill, and the boys, not to mention Kitty. I'll call you again tomorrow or maybe come over to see you if you wish. I'll let you go now. Also remember, Edith and I are still close friends. Goodbye, Tom."

Biway replied, "Thank you, Aggie, for calling me. I'll talk to you tomorrow. Goodbye."

Around 3:30 p.m., Biway resumed his drinking after he made himself a beef sandwich for lunch. Around 8:30 p.m., after so much drinking, he passed out again but came to just before 12:30 a.m., finished off his first quart of Old Crow, open his second bottle and resumed his drinking. As he continued his drinking, his hurt was slowly giving way to anger. The more he drank, the angrier he became. This time he started drinking to dowse his anger rather than nursing his deep hurt. Finally around 4:45 a.m., he suddenly sprang up, grabbed his keys, ran out the front door, and hopped into his car. He was so intoxicated at the time he forgot to put on his clothes, so he drove over to Edith's apartment in his underwear and barefoot. On the way there, he was so drunk he sideswiped two other cars, damaging both of them as well as his own. When he arrived at her apartment upstairs, he began banging on her door and calling her every filthy name in the books. As he was yelling profanities at Edith from outside her door, one of the other tenants from downstairs stepped out and said, "Hey, you with the vulgar mouth up there, you'd better shut that cussing up or I'll call the Sheriffs Department."

Biway yelled back, "—you and mind your own—business!"

As Edith heard Biway yelling obscenities at her from outside her door, she became frightened and decided to call the sheriff's office. Before she got to her phone, she heard the sirens outside getting louder and then a thud outside her door and the yelling of profanities suddenly stopped. She tiptoed to the door and opened it narrowly, just enough to find out why Biway suddenly stopped hollering. He was lying on the floor, trying to say something to her but couldn't. He was also urinating in his underpants. Two minutes later, two of the deputies showed up. One went upstairs to talk to Edith, while the other one stayed downstairs to question the man who called them. The one talking to Edith decided to examine Biway, and when he did, he learned that Biway had a stroke. His left side was totally paralyzed, and he lost control of his bladder. The deputy then told Edith, "Ma'am, this man will never bother you again. He just had a debilitating stroke, and I'm going to call an ambulance. If you like, I can stay here till some of your people come over to comfort you."

Edith simply replied, "Thank you."

The deputy then said, "By the way, aren't you Gary's fiancée? By the way he talks about you, one would think you were a queen, and now I know why he feels that way. He'll be here after eight o'clock, when he gets off duty."

In the meantime, the paramedics came, went upstairs, put Biway on the stretcher they brought with them, placed him in the ambulance, and drove to St. Joseph's Mercy Hospital in neighboring Yuba City. After he had his stroke and due to the huge amount of bourbon he consumed, Biway passed out again but came to in the hospital emergency room around 11:30 a.m. As he opened his eyes, he noticed he couldn't see out of his left one, and then he noticed that the whole left side of his body was paralyzed, and due to the amount of alcohol he consumed, he felt sick.

About ten minutes after Biway came to, Dr. Dan Foley, fifty-eight, walked into the emergency room, leaned over Biway and said, "Tom, can you hear me? If so, then try to blink yes or no. Can you? Blink once for yes and twice for no." Biway blinked once, meaning yes. Then Dr. Foley explained, "This morning you suffered a debilitating stroke, and that's why you're here now." Since Biway showed up at Edith's apartment in his underwear and couldn't tell the deputies anything, Edith had to tell them who Biway was. As he was slowly sobering up, Biway was beginning to realize the gravity of his condition and sank into a severe depression. He wanted just to simply die. Around 2:00 p.m., Aggie along with Bill showed up to see him, but he couldn't utter a single word to them. He thought, *Oh my god, why did they have to bring me here in this—condition. Now I'm as good as dead.*

Biway still felt sick that day but felt better the next, and he was transferred to the ICU unit. A week later, he was moved to a regular room for rehabilitation. There, one of the nurses, Ms. Thelma Freeman, twenty-four, came into the room and said to him, "I'm your nurse, and I'm going to try to help you as much as I can." Biway tried to thank her but still couldn't articulate a single word. Ms. Freeman had dark-brown hair, full figured like Edith and Aggie, and very attractive. She asked Biway, "Can you write, since you still have the use of your right arm?"

Biway blinked "Yes" and Ms. Freeman brought him a clipboard, a pen, and some paper and said, "I'll hold this for you so you can write whatever comes to mind."

Biway wrote, "Is there any way you can bring me two cyanide pills? I so want to die." Then he wrote, "Why are these—bastards keeping me alive and for what? Tell me please, Nurse."

Ms. Freeman replied, "I know you're severely depressed right now, but in time you'll be able to accept your condition. Countless others already have."

On Thursday, May 31, Edith came to see him. When Edith walked into the room, Biway was stunned to see her. Edith said, "You must really hate me right now, and I can hardly blame you for doing so. Like I told you before, I never meant to hurt you nor for any of this to happen, and I still feel terrible about it. If you permit, I'd love to take you to our new house in Olivehurst after Gary and I get married and nurse you myself. I did the same thing for my father, as you already know, and I'll gladly do it for you. Don't answer me right now, but think about it. I'll leave you now, but remember what I said."

Later that day when she told Gary about her offer to Biway, Gary snapped, "Forget it, Edith. I will in no way, shape, or form have that man under the same roof as you and I. Besides, the next time you plan something, let me know first."

Edith replied, "I'm sorry, Gary. I had no notion you felt that way about it. I won't let it happen again."

Thereafter Edith never came to see Biway again.

That same day, Kitty and Dave came down to see Biway and how serious of a condition he was in. Around 6:00 p.m., Kitty walked into Biway's room and was shocked at what she saw and became very upset over it.

Two days later around 8:00 p.m. that Saturday, as Dave and Kitty were at Bill and Aggie's, nursing their drinks, Edith along with two of her friends walked in, sat down at a table, and ordered three margaritas as usual. Then Kitty noticed Edith as she was savoring her drink and turned to Dave, saying, "Guess who just walked in," and Dave replied, "Please, Kitty, don't make a scene. I already know how you feel about her. Just ignore her." At first Kitty complied but then got up, walked over to the table where Edith was sitting, and poured her drink on Edith's lap. Then she started hollering at her, "Do you realize what you did to my father and have you seen him lately? How could you do that to him after all he went through? Are you truly that heartless? What the hell kind of a person are you anyway?"

Edith got up and said nothing to Kitty but turned to her two friends and said, "I guess we shouldn't have come here, knowing how this young lady feels about me." And the three left. Thereafter Kitty returned to her table and started to cry.

On June 9, as planned, Edith and Gary had their wedding, which was rather festive, and Gary's maternal aunt gave them a pet English bulldog as a wedding present. Since Edith had already seen Japan, they decided to spend their honeymoon in New Zealand for the next two weeks. Edith didn't renew her teaching contact for fall classes as Gary, who didn't want her to work, was now making enough money to support them both. Edith became a housewife and came up pregnant later that year. Gary Jr. was born on May 27, 1980, followed by a daughter, Phyllis, born January 15, 1982, and finally their second son, Andrew, born on March 1, 1985. Their marriage was quite successful.

In the meantime, as the hospital staff tried to rehabilitate Biway, Dr. Jerome Fitzpatrick told Bill and Aggie, "We did all we could for Tom here. Now he needs to be placed in a nursing home for further rehabilitation. I know of just such a place. It is called the Oscar Greeley Rehabilitation Center and is located some seven miles east of Marysville on the Yuba River."

Aggie replied, "Yes, Doctor, if you think that's best for him."

Dr. Fitzpatrick replied, "I do, and then I'll set up the arrangements for his transfer there as soon as possible."

On Friday, July 13, Biway was transferred to the Oscar Greeley Rehabilitation Center. Unfortunately for Biway, the conditions at that nursing home were very deplorable. It was grossly underfunded and understaffed, and the staff members were underpaid and poorly trained. On top of that, the staff members were quite lazy and never did any more than they had to. The food was both bad and unappealing and patients went unsupervised. One night, a seventy- nine-year-old man sneaked into the room of a seventy-seven-year-old woman and raped her, but upon hearing about it, the staff did nothing. The food was not only bad but prepared under unsanitary conditions in the rat-and-roach-infested kitchen. The kitchen itself had not been sprayed in ages. After he was admitted, Biway was assigned to a dorm in the B section. The A section had the least disabled patients, while section C had those who were totally without any hope of getting better. In all three sections, the patients were treated rather badly.

Was this place always in these deplorable conditions? The answer is no. The nursing home and rehabilitation center was built in 1937 and was well financed. The staff members were quite professional and treated the patients well. It had five different physicians to take care of the patients, and the food was generally good. The place was sanitary and inspected on a regular basis.

Then in 1969, all that began to change thanks to the then California governor Ronald Reagan (1911–2004). Like all of California's spending programs, the nursing home underwent budget cuts. First, the number of doctors was reduced from five to just one, and number of nurses underwent a similar reduction, laying off many, while the ones left behind became overworked as they were forced to pick up where the others left off. Even the number of those inspecting the nursing home was reduced so the place was no longer inspected on a regular basis, and conditions there became unsanitary, and the food wasn't always safe to eat. This process is better known as Morganization. Although the place was called a rehabilitation center, no one has been rehabilitated there since 1974.

In 1975, Jerry Brown replaced Ronald Reagan as governor of California. He tried to reverse Reagan's budget cutting programs, but the Republicans in either the State Senate or the State House of Representatives managed to block many of his proposals, and then came Proposition 13, voted on by California voters on June 13, 1978, in order to cut property taxes so conditions in that nursing home continued to deteriorate further, under which Biway was to suffer.

On July 13, 1979, the day Biway arrived at the nursing home, he was assigned to Room 17, which he had to share with a certain Lou George. Mr. George was eighty-six years old and suffering from an advanced stage of Alzheimer's disease. He was only five feet, four inches tall and weighed around 130 pounds. He had thinning gray hair on the top of his head and looked very much like the character film actor Percy Helton (1894–1971). Only his daughter Alice would show up and visit him, but he no longer knew her. Sometimes Mr. George would get up in the middle of the night, walk over to Biway's bed, and urinate in his face. One such night was on July 19, 1979, six days after Biway was admitted. As Mr. George was urinating in Biway's face, Biway sprang up and tried to hit him but fell to the floor. Then Biway reached for the buzzer in order to summon a nurse, got it, and buzzed. The nurse who answered it rushed into the room and snapped, "Who the hell rang that—buzzer?" and Biway raised his hand, indicating it was him since he couldn't speak. The nurse turned to Biway and slapped his face, saying, "Get your—back to sleep, you. I don't want to have to come back here again." She walked out of the room without examining Biway's face.

The registered nurse (RN) was Ms. Abigail "Abbie" Perkins, thirty-four. She was five feet, eight inches tall, weighed around 165 pounds, giving her a rather buxom figure, had red hair and green eyes. Her eyes were usually covered with blue mascara, giving her added sex appeal. She worked the twelve midnight to eight in the morning shift.

Although she was still unmarried, she did have a married boyfriend by the name of Robert Courtney, forty-one, a truck driver who lived in Sacramento, which wasn't far from Marysville. Ms. Perkins wasn't necessarily a bad woman, but she suffered greatly from PMS every month. The reason she cursed and slapped Biway isn't exactly known.

Was it because she was having that time of the month, or was she just simply overworked? However in the meantime, Mr. Courtney eventually divorced his wife and married Abbie on Saturday, September 25, 1982, in Sacramento. She quit her job as a nurse shortly thereafter. A year later on October 29, 1983, they had a daughter and named her Phoebe. The third-shift RN who replaced her was hardly any better, and Biway continued to suffer. He often wondered, *What on God's green earth did I do to deserve this ignominy?* Then he thought of Edith, but his resentment of her faded away as he realized that she meant what she said about deceiving herself as well as him. He just simply wanted to end it all then and there.

The other nurses and orderlies hardly treated Biway any better. In fact, all the patients were generally treated badly or ignored and neglected.

Shortly after being admitted, Biway thought he had figured a way out of this cauchemar he found himself in. He just simply stopped eating one day and tried to starve himself to death but, unfortunately for Biway, it didn't work. One afternoon around 5:00 p.m. after Biway was served his supper, the second-shift RN walked into the room and noticed that he didn't eat for the second day in a row. She yelled at him, "Are you going to eat your supper, or do I have to cram it down your—throat? Eat! Otherwise we'll have to feed you intravenously." Then Biway reluctantly started to eat his supper. Otherwise he was generally ignored by the staff. The second-shift RN's name was Mrs. Ruth Phillips, forty-four. She was black, married, with three children, five feet, seven inches tall, weighed around 140 pounds, and had a hateful demeanor.

In the morning, Biway would be awakened at 6:00 a.m., assisted out of bed, handed a crutch since he still had the use of both his right arm and right leg, had his breakfast brought to him, and later limp his way to the day room, where he just sat and stared at the TV or just simply thought to himself. He hardly had anything else to do. He'd limp to the dining room around noon, return a half hour later, and finally limp his way back to his room around four thirty in the afternoon. Such had become the daily routine of Biway's life. He had nothing in common with any of the other patients except that they were incapacitated like he was, and he never cared to be in their company. If there were any therapists working there, he never saw one since no one made any effort to rehabilitate him. Soon Biway noticed he had bedsores because no one came to turn him over or clean up after him.

One day as he was sitting in the day room, he noticed Mr. George blowing snot on Mr. Hector James, a seventy-year-old black patient who was suffering from a brain tumor. Mr. James suddenly became angry and slapped Mr. George. Then Mr. James started to chew him out for blowing boogers on him. The orderlies who saw this take place just simply stood by and watched and did nothing but watch Mr. George cry. Later, one of them walked up to Mr. George, saying, "You have company," and led Mr. George to the visitor's room, where his daughter Alice was waiting to see him. Finally on September 23, 1982, Mr. George died from a massive stroke. Only his daughter Alice attended his funeral in the town of Wheatland, south of Marysville.

In the meantime, on April 26, 1983, Bill Decker suffered a massive coronary and had to be taken to St. Joseph's Mercy Hospital in Yuba City. He was then seventy-seven. On May 3, a week later, he returned home but had to quit working so Aggie had to curtail her working schedule in order to spend as much time with him as possible. As Bruce was due to graduate in June, Bill handed his real estate business over to him, and at the same time, Aggie put their Bar and Grill up for sale. It was finally sold to Glen and Thelma Baker for a sum of $12,000 total. In other words, Bill and Aggie retired. Robert graduated from UCLA in June 1986 with a bachelor's degree in civil engineering. He later moved to Saskatchewan, Canada, in 1989 with his Canadian wife, Maggie, and their two children because she became homesick for that place.

One Monday, August 18, 1986, which was to be Kitty's thirty-ninth birthday, Aggie came to see Biway with tears in her eyes. She could barely speak as she sobbed but finally managed to say, "Something terrible has happened to Dave and Kitty. They were in an automobile accident Saturday night, and now both are dead. I am so sorry to have to tell you this, Tom." Biway was stunned upon hearing this and later wanted to die more than ever as he sank further into another depression over this terrible loss.

On Saturday night, August 16, 1986, in order to celebrate Kitty's thirty-ninth birthday, the couple drove the kids over to Dave's parents' house, dropped them off, and drove north to Roseburg to have supper, take in a movie, and drive around the town. Around ten thirty, they decided to go back to Dave's parents' house, pick up the kids, and head back home. As they were driving south on I-5, there was another driver heading north at the same time in a white 1979 Dodge pickup truck. He was quite intoxicated and suddenly lost control, crossed the median, and hit Dave's red 1980 Toyota Corolla head on. Both Dave and Kitty were severely injured, while the driver of the Dodge pickup was only slightly hurt. All three were taken to Ellsworth Toomey Memorial Hospital in Roseburg. Kitty succumbed to her injuries shortly after 2:00 a.m., and Dave died twelve hours later around 2:00 p.m., just one day short of Kitty's birthday.

The driver of the white Dodge pickup truck was Joseph N. Dowd, fifty, of Eugene, Oregon. There he lived with his then girlfriend, Ms. Eleanor Bergman, forty-six, a school teacher. He was five feet, five inches tall, weighed around 150 pounds, and had kinky graying black hair. He was married, with two children, but since his wife could no longer put up with his constant drinking, she finally divorced him in 1975. After the accident, Mr. Dowd was arrested by two Douglas County Sheriff's deputies upon his release from the hospital the following morning and charged with one count of vehicular manslaughter, but after Dave died, it was raised to two counts. When the deputies came to arrest him, he cussed them out as hard as he could. He never had any compunctions against using foul language. Later at his trial, he pleaded no contest, and the judge sentenced him to a fine of $5,000 and three years' probation plus had his driver's license suspended.

When Aggie learned about it, she became furious that such leniency was accorded to Mr. Dowd by the Douglas County Magistrate Court judge since she lost her daughter and son-in-law.

Now at sixty-seven, Biway outlived all three of his legitimate children but never knew of what became of his illegitimate ones, such as the one by Mrs. Nancy Ballard or the one by Mrs. Christina Dellanos. For all he knew, there could have been even more since he consorted with prostitutes in Japan, Korea, and Vietnam.

After Aggie left, he sank into a severe depression over this loss and never fully recovered from it. Not long after that, he began to lose his cognitive powers. At first, he thought that it was Alzheimer's disease since his father died from it sometime since 1967, when his brother, Rick, told him about it.

In the meantime, the care given to the patients by the staff deteriorated further. Not only did the staff either ignore or abuse the patients, they began to engage in sexual activity while on duty. It was no longer unusual to see nurses and orderlies engaged in sex late at night in one of the many side rooms there but even brought a Hi-fi into the cafeteria to play loud music often while they drank or did drugs.

One of the nurses, by the name of Wendy Hobart, thirty-two, would be heard hollering, "Yes, yes, ohhh more, more, more," and so on while engaging in sex with an orderly by the name of Nick Wilson, thirty-nine. This started early in 1987, after she was promoted the position of third shift head nurse in section B. Wendy was married with two children at home in Yuba City, and so was Nick Wilson, with a son in Wheatland. Not only did the nurses and orderlies do it, there were two orderlies, by the names Walter Fleming, thirty-seven, and Victor Pate, thirty-two, who would engage in homosexual activities throughout the night. On top of that, during their breaks and sometimes even on duty, the staff would go into the cafeteria, drink, do drugs, and play heavy metal music on the Hi-fi at full blast, thus depriving many of the patients their sleep.

There was even an orderly, by the name of Chuck Lampe, twenty-nine, who was hired in May 1987, who would occasionally sneak into the dormitories of female patients and sexually assault them. One in particular by the name of Rosa Jimenez, seventy-eight, was raped on four different occasions, but when she complained, no one did anything about it, so it just went on.

However, there was one conscientious nurse by the name Mrs. Christine Donohue, fifty-six, who was constantly sickened by the things that went on there. She was married, with three children. They were Bert, twenty-five, living in Orlando, Florida; John, eighteen, living in Maryland; and Judy, eleven, still living at home in Olivehurst. Her husband, Vernon, seventy, suffered a debilitating stroke that same year. The plight of her husband helped to make her more conscientious, and she did all she could do to help Biway.

On July 20, 1987, Mrs. Donohue was appointed the third shift head RN for section B, replacing Wendy Hobart, who suddenly failed to show up for her shift, giving no prior notice. The reason for that is the fact that her husband, Ron, also thirty-two, who learned that she was engaging in sex while on duty, could no longer control himself, finally murdered her on Tuesday morning, the fourteenth. He had suspected such for a long time, but when he learned about it for sure, he picked up a tire iron and started to bludgeon her.

Thereafter he called for an ambulance, and she was taken to St. Joseph's Mercy Hospital, where she succumbed to her injuries two hours later. She was five feet, seven inches tall, well built, and quite attractive with her shoulder-length black hair. She left behind two boys, Ron Jr., six, and Denny, two. Her lover, Nick Wilson, was thirty- nine years old, six feet tall, weighed around 190 pounds, and bald. Wendy Hobart was born Wendy Schulz on January 3, 1955, in Walkerton, Indiana, the youngest of two daughters born to Ronald and Eliza Schulz. Ronald was a deputy for the St. Joseph County Sheriff's Department. In 1959, he and the family moved to Sacramento, California, since he had a cousin on that city's police force, which had an opening for him. He took it. Wendy grew up there and graduated from the University of Sacramento with a bachelor's degree in medicine and subsequently hired on as a nurse at the Oscar Greely Rehabilitation Center since St. Joseph's Mercy Hospital was fully staffed in 1978. She held that position for the next nine years until she was murdered by her husband, Ron. Ron was later convicted and given a term of fifteen years to life in San Quentin.

As was said before, Mrs. Donohue was very conscientious and truly cared for the patients. One night as the other staff members were in the cafeteria, drinking booze, smoking marijuana, sniffing cocaine, and playing what one would call heavy metal music, she went in there and promptly told them to turn the Hi-fi down. They told her to—and called her filthy names. However, Mrs. Donohue eventually did manage to get Chuck Lampe fired for sexually assaulting some of the female patients. She was not only sickened by the activities of other staff members but had to put up with the abuse she received from them as well.

In the meantime, she would come into Biway's room, change his bedpan, and brought him his breakfast whenever she could. She would also communicate with him and thus help relieve him of his loneliness during the night.

Unfortunately, it was during this time that Biway began to lose his cognitive powers. He would forget to go to the cafeteria and even wandered outside one day only to be brought back by one of the orderlies. He eventually forgot that he even had a daughter by the name of Kitty, or better said, Catherine, since that was her true name, so he was no longer in pain over her loss. He eventually forgot almost everything else such as having served in the First Marines or his time in Leavenworth.

On Thursday, August 27, Aggie showed up with tears in her eyes and announced to Biway that her husband, Bill, had died the night before. Biway replied writing on a sheet of paper, "Who's Bill, and should I know him?" Aggie was shocked upon reading this. It was now clear to her that Biway was becoming senile. A month later on Saturday, September 26, Biway didn't even recognize Aggie when she paid him a final visit. She never returned to see him again.

What Biway was suffering from was not Alzheimer's disease at all but something far worse, known as Lewy body disease. Here Biway was not only losing his cognitive powers but the control over the rest of his body as well. He was finally transferred to Section C, where the most seriously impaired patients were being warehoused. Here the third- shift RN was not nearly as conscientious as Mrs. Donohue was but totally indifferent as her only concern was the amount of money she was being paid. Her name was Evelyn Ortega, thirty-three, with reddish brown hair and wore a mini uniform, which showed her shapely legs, giving her much sex appeal. Unlike Mrs. Hobart, she was never married up to that point nor had any children. Like the rest of the staff, she too engaged in sexual activity and eventually married one of the orderlies on staff known as Jerry Green, twenty-four, on June 13, 1988. They eventually had three children, two girls and a boy. A year later, she quit the nursing home to go to work at St. Joseph's Mercy Hospital since the pay there was much better and to get away from all the debauchery going on at that nursing home.

Unfortunately in this day and age, it is becoming increasingly normal for this kind of activity to take place in nursing homes all across the country, and it doesn't appear that this kind of abuse will abate anytime in the near future since the politicians in Washington couldn't care less as long as their own family members get the best care money could buy, such as private care in the comfort of their own homes.

Such was the way Biway spent his final years, languishing in a nursing home, which turned out to be ten times worse than Leavenworth, and no longer knowing anyone or anything. He finally passed away on Wednesday, October 5, 1994, from his illness and was buried behind Bill Decker's grave just north of Marysville as Aggie directed the funeral chaplain to put him. Only Aggie and Bruce attended his funeral since Robert was in far off Saskatchewan in Central Canada. On his tombstone was simply engraved,

"J. T. Biway, 1918–1994." While on Bill's it read, "Decker" (on top) and below it read, "William Howard, 1905–1987" to the left and to the right, "Christine Agnes, 1921–2010" after her demise. Aggie died on October 17, 2010, from pneumonia at the age of eighty-nine. Kitty and Dave were buried just outside of Grants Pass, Oregon, and on their tombstones it read, "David Austin Harris, 1948–1986" and "Catherine Matilda Harris, 1947–1986."

ABOUT THE AUTHOR

⋇ 231 ⋇

D. J. Cotton is seventy-three years old and holds an associate degree in criminal justice. He is also interested in psychology narcissism in particular. The following is dedicated to that subject and sometimes people can be redeemed, but not always.

9 798893 897616